HIVE MIND

Trinity of the Hive (Book Three)

by

Grayson Sinclair

License Notes

This is a work of fiction. Names, characters, businesses, places, events, and incidents are either the products of the author's imagination or used in a fictitious manner. Any resemblance to actual persons, living or dead, or actual events is purely coincidental.

This ebook is licensed for your personal enjoyment only. This ebook may not be re-sold or given away to other people. If you would like to share this ebook with another person, please purchase an additional copy for each recipient. If you're reading this book and did not purchase it, or it was not purchased for your use only, then please return to your favorite book retailer and purchase your own copy. Thank you for respecting the hard work of this author.

Contents

"The thing about happiness is that you only know you had it when it's gone. I mean, you may think to yourself that you're happy. But you don't really believe it. It's only looking back, by comparison to what comes after, that you really understand; that's what happiness felt like."

\- *Conrad Kellogg*

Chapter 1 - A Favor For The Gods

Sampson

"You've got to be kidding me."

I sighed into my palm as I stared at the redheaded goddess in front of me.

The Morrigan wore her black dress well; it hugged her slender frame and toed the line between elegant and immodest. Her jewelry was adorned with emeralds that matched her eyes, but one item stood out of place, a large ruby and gold amulet clasped around her throat.

She was pristine, her eyes alight with deviousness as she stared me down.

Now the gods themselves are coming to me.

I need a drink. As I glanced back at the shattered and ruined shelves that still poured amber down the wood and to the cobblestone floor from where Miguel had thrown his glass, the sharp, medicinal scent of alcohol filled the air and watered my mouth.

Shattered glass and expensive liquor littered the stone behind the bar. The subtle drip was constant as my nose burned and I breathed in deep.

Want a drink but can't have a drink. Withdrawal fucking sucks.

It was all the proof I needed that I had been deluding myself for years, a fact that Magnus had so easily seen about me.

I was an alcoholic.

But in times like these, that doesn't seem like a bad thing.

It wasn't exactly easy, but I composed myself and took Eris's and Raven's hands, squeezing tight. The mere presence of them was sufficient to get me out of my head enough to deal with Morgan.

"All right, why do the gods need a thug for hire?"

Morgan smiled at me, and a flash of predatory delight filled her eyes. Her shadow stretched behind her as it fell across the many tables and chairs of the Gray Cask and danced in the firelight.

"It's quite simple. I need you to stop a war that's brewing."

"A war?" I scratched my chin. "Between whom?"

Morgan walked over to the bar, where Miguel sat nursing one of the few remaining unbroken bottles of whiskey and plucked it from his slack fingers.

He barely noticed.

She sat down on the stool and leaned back against the bar top facing me. Morgan took a swig and set the bottle down with a sigh of contentment.

"The rabbitmen and wolfmen."

I scoffed, "Whatever the hell for?"

Morgan chuckled and took another sip from the bottle. "The Aminah clan leader's daughter has been kidnapped and they have reason to believe that it was the Holste clan's doing.

"The two races have always been enemies, but this goes beyond petty squabbles. The entire balance of power for the Pale Everlands hangs by a frayed thread, and this couldn't come at a worse time."

Her words gave me pause as a small spark of recognition jolted through my brain. *Lyahgos and the other rabbitmen back at Gloom-Harbor mentioned something about the Aminah Clan when we rescued them from the slavers. They said something precious had been taken, but they didn't know what.*

I guess I know now.

Personally I didn't really see the point of helping. The rabbitmen and wolfmen were far removed from the rest of society. I'd only encountered their two races a few times in my thirty years on Nexus. Because of the slavery laws of the Compass Kingdom, they rarely left the Everlands.

"As the goddess of demi-humans, I get that you want to resolve the conflict. But I really don't see the need to drop everything and run off to play mediator to try and stop a war. Not when I have so many other problems to deal with right now.

"A much bigger threat is coming. I don't have time to deal with this."

She nodded. "Yes. We are all aware of Magnus and his intentions. But that doesn't mean we can ignore everything else to focus on one single threat." She paused and looked to Eris for a second before glancing back at me. "If the clans go to war, the wolfmen will undoubtedly win. If that happens, they will exhaust their food supply and will begin hunting for new prey."

"Shit," I cursed as I caught her meaning. "If that happens, then the wolfmen would come down from the mountain and start hunting. The closest town to the Northern Mountains is Wyston, but beyond that, it's just the Compass Kingdom."

Morgan nodded. "They would descend on the North Kingdom like a plague, and though the humans outnumber the wolves ten to one, many lives would be lost, and the loss of life would inevitably shift the power in the region."

Damn it. Why is this happening now? I started pacing from the bar to the tables and back again, trying to work through my thoughts. Eris and Raven went and sat down next to Morgan, and Eris began speaking to her goddess in a hushed, reverent tone.

The problem was actually much, much bigger than a simple clan war. Wolfmen were by far the strongest race on Nexus, barring the Hive. They were only kept in check by the rabbitmen, who, while strong themselves, couldn't measure up to the wolfmen in strength, but made up for it in numbers.

I tugged at my ponytail and pulled it loose, letting my long copper hair fall around my shoulders. My hair was soft as I ran my fingers through it to dislodge any tangles. *If the war goes as Morgan says—which, let's be honest, is incredibly likely—the wolfmen would attack the Compass Kingdom and would eventually be wiped out, but the kingdom would take heavy losses and probably lose the North Kingdom entirely before it was over.*

And when it was over, the Compass Kingdom would be significantly weaker. And Aldrust and Yllsaria might be emboldened to attack. The balance of power between the nations is fragile, and there is no love lost between the humans and other races.

"It's a domino effect. The whole of Nexus would be dragged into the war."

"Precisely," Morgan said. "It's not just about the two clans, but the fate of the isle as well. Something we can't afford right now with the threat Magnus poses. It couldn't come at a worse time, and right now we need to make sure the peace between kingdoms doesn't fall."

I turned to Raven and Eris. "What do you think?"

"We should help them, Sam. It's the right thing to do," Eris said.

"I agree," Raven said. "Helping is the right thing to do, but also having the gods owe you a favor isn't something you can lightly pass up."

I flashed both of them a grin, and they returned it in spades. "What would I ever do without you two?" I went and sat by them. I pulled the wooden stool out, wincing as it scraped loudly against the stone and sat, turning my body to face Morgan. "Despite everything, I'm still a mercenary at heart, and if you want me for a job, then I expect to be compensated."

"Of course." She nodded. "The rewards will be numerous and well worth the trouble, I assure you."

"Care to elaborate, goddess?"

Morgan nodded and held up a finger. "One. As your shapeshifter friend said, the gods and I will owe you a favor. Something like that, doesn't come along very often." She held up a second finger. "But as I've come to understand about you humans, words—even ones spoken by a goddess—mean little to you. So, I would like to offer you a more tangible reward."

"And that would be?" I asked, motioning her to continue.

"Power," she said simply. "Power that may give you and your bondmate an edge in the battles to come."

It was a tempting reward, but she knew that. She was a goddess, after all.

Though I had only interacted with her once before, she seemed on the level, and I thought I could trust her to play it straight with me. Though stopping a war was a hefty task; one I didn't know that I could handle.

I've never been good at dealing with delicate or complex issues. Anything more complicated than swinging a sword was most of the time out of my wheelhouse, but I had to give it a shot. Too much was coming to a head all at once, and it would quickly spiral into oblivion if someone didn't get a handle on things.

But why am I the one who has to deal with this shit? She couldn't have picked a more unqualified individual.

I sighed, knowing that I'd already decided on helping and stalling wasn't going to get me anywhere. "Fine, I'll help. But you better hold up your end of the bargain, Morgan."

She smiled widely and inclined her head. "Absolutely. A bargain struck with a god is a sacred thing, young guardian."

I froze. "You know about that?"

"Of course. The death and birth of a guardian are very important moments. Though you are not a full guardian yet, the sentiment is there, and you've earned the title. The gods and I have high hopes for you." She waved her hand. "Here you go, Sam."

A quest notification appeared in front of me.

Quest: Mediation

Prevent a war between the wolfmen and rabbitmen clans

Type: Unique

Difficulty: A

Reward: 35000 Exp!

I accepted it without a thought.

"All right, but it will take a few days to get started. I'll have to fly back to the castle, prepare, and then fly to Wyston, not to mention the hike just to get to the Everlands."

"Speaking of." Morgan pulled a roll of parchment from seemingly out of nowhere and held it out to me. "This is a map to the Pale Everlands. It will guide you to exactly where you need to go."

She paused for a long moment and reached behind her neck. She undid the clasp to the ruby amulet around her neck and handed it to me. "Though I'm loath to part with it after all I did to acquire it, your need of it might be even greater than mine at the moment."

I took the necklace from her and marveled at the weight as it settled in my palm. The precious metal was warm from Morgan's body heat, and my face reflected in the many facets of the gemstone. It was a gorgeous amulet, but far, far too gaudy for my tastes.

"What is this?" I asked.

"It's an artifact of the gods, something that was lost for many years until I found it again recently. Touch the stone."

I did as she said and placed a finger on the cold ruby.

Artifact: Amulet of Teleportation

Rarity: S

Allows wearer to designate up to four party members—these party members can travel with you when teleporting.

I gaped. "Wait, does this include NPCs?"

She inclined her head. "You can see how valuable the artifact is. And I do expect it back when this is all over."

As amazing as it is, I really wish it were less ostentatious.

I chuckled at the thought. *An artifact that cuts down a day or two of travel to a few minutes and I'm complaining because it's a bit flashy.*

"Thank you, Morgan. This will help tremendously."

"I'm sure it will." She stood from the bar and walked towards the door. "Miguel knows how to get in touch with me once you have completed your task."

"You mean if?"

Morgan shook her head. "I said what I said. Have a little more faith in yourself. Your bonded is confident in you, and so am I."

I turned and looked at Eris; her large, compounded eyes filled with warmth and love. "I love you."

"As I you."

Her faith in me was staggering, and even if we technically were no longer bonded, I didn't need our previous connection to know what emotions were running through her; she wore them on her face plain as day.

When I turned back to Morgan, she had already disappeared. The wooden door to the cask shut with a soft click behind her.

Silence stretched as I stared at Miguel, Eris, and Raven in turn. The weight of what I'd just agreed to settled around me.

"Holy fuck, how in the hell am I supposed to stop a war?" I asked.

Raven sat up from the bar, grabbed the unattended bottle of whiskey sitting between her and Miguel, and chugged a good portion of it. She wiped her mouth and sauntered over to me, her pale cheeks tinged with roses as she pulled me down for a kiss.

It was warm and tasted of liquor, which I loved. My addiction flared as I greedily ran my tongue through her mouth.

Raven pulled back a few seconds later, a knowing glint in her eye. She knew I had a problem and was trying to wean me off in her own unique way.

I've got to say, if AA had her as a method, I think quitting could be a lot easier. Even the barest kiss of whiskey had settled me, and I calmed down.

She kissed me once more and leaned over to whisper in my ear. "You don't stop it alone, darling."

I wrapped my arms around her waist and held her close. I hadn't known her for long, but she had changed so much for both me and Eris in the short time we'd been together.

There were only three words that could describe my feelings for her.

"I love you," I whispered back.

She purred in my ear. "Of course, you don't get any other choice."

I laughed, and it broke the unease in the air. *She's right. I can't do this alone. And that's my problem. The lone wolf act has gotten old. It's time to stop shouldering everything myself.*

"All right. Seems like we have a lot to do. We should get going." I looked over to Miguel, who hadn't really moved since we'd arrived.

He'd just been staring at the wall after Morgan had arrived. He wasn't exactly a friend, but he was an ally and that mattered to me. "You going to be okay, Miguel?"

He nodded and waved me off, running a hand through his jet-black hair. "I'll be fine, sport. Always am. But the Cask is done for. With Kincaid on the hunt for us, I'm going to have to go to ground."

"You want to come back to Gloom-Harbor?" I offered.

He shook his head violently. "I appreciate the offer, but that's the last place I should be, the last place you should be either. Everyone knows that's where the Gloom Knights live. It's not going to be safe for you there anymore."

Unfortunately, he's right. With Kincaid out for blood, we're sitting ducks. We'll have to have a meeting when we get back and decide on what we need to do. I sighed at the headache already forming. *This whole situation just keeps getting worse.*

"Alright, Miguel, but don't hesitate to reach out if you need us."

He nodded and stood. "Obliged, Sam. I don't know where things are going to go from here, but it's been one hell of a run so far."

Miguel pulled a cigar from his inventory and a match. He lit the cigar, spinning it around slowly and taking short puffs to evenly light the tobacco.

Miguel sighed as he took a long drag of the cigar. "This is a Gurkha. It's infused with cognac, and it's divine. Hard as hell to replicate exactly in this world, but damned worth the effort. I paid more gold than you'd believe for a box of twenty of them downstairs." He paused. "I've got rare spirits and liquors from the elves, moonshine from the dwarves, dozens of cigars in a specially crafted humidor, and blackmail files on hundreds of nobles and influential figures all across Nexus."

"I spent fifteen godsdamned years building my empire."

He took another puff of his cigar and glanced around the room; his eyes filled with melancholy. For a long moment he just stared at the room, taking it in.

The Gray Cask had never been homey, but it had been home to Miguel, and to me. I'd been there when the doors first opened, back before I was a Gloom Knight and had just been a bandit. I had a lot of fond memories in this bar; but Miguel undoubtedly had many, many more.

"I loved this fuckin' bar." He turned to the bar top and flicked his burning cigar onto the mess of dripping liquor.

At first nothing happened and I figured the flash point on any of the liquors wasn't high enough to ignite, but a second later, there was a puff of fire and small orange flames began licking at the wood.

It didn't take long for more of the alcohol to heat up as the flames rose the temperature and more of the whiskies and vodkas ignited. Soon the wood blackened and cracked as the entire bar was consumed in flames.

"We should go," Miguel said, his voice lifeless and flat.

He turned and without looking back, left the Gray Cask to burn.

***

The three of us teleported back to the entrance to Gloom-Harbor, and I wasted no time calling a meeting to explain everything.

I sat back in my chair in the guild hall and waited for everyone to join us. I'd added two more chairs next to me for Raven and Eris. Even though they weren't members of the Gloom Knights, they were a part of our dysfunctional family and deserved to be here next to me.

I laid my head on the table and sighed, trying to figure out what we were going to do next.

"It'll be okay, love," Eris said, placing her hand on top of mine.

"I don't know if that's true. It just seems like everything is getting stacked against us all at once and I don't know how to stop it."

"We take it one problem at a time," Raven said. "And we don't stop until all of the problems have been dealt with."

Reminds me of an old saying. How do you eat an elephant? One bite at a time.

One problem at a time.

I can do that.

Though I was in an odd headspace, I couldn't let the others see me like that, so I sat back, glanced at Eris and Raven with a small smile of gratitude, and waited for the others to join me.

While I waited, I pulled up my character page. I wanted to check to see if the bounty had been posted yet.

Character Name: Durandahl

Level: 69

Exp: 3800/6900

Race: Demigod

Class: Hive Knight (Errant)

Reputation: Wanted Criminal

Bounty: 251300 Gold

Stats (-)

Strength: 100 (Max)

Sub-Stats (-)

Attack Damage: 50

Constitution: 100 (Max)

Sub-Stats (-)

Health: 25

Health Regen: 25

Durability: 85

Endurance: 100 (Max)

Sub-Stats (-)

Battle Fatigue: 50

Battle Fatigue Regen: 10

Agility: 50 (95)

Sub-Stats (-)

Attack Speed: 25

Movement Speed: 20

Wisdom: 25 (40)

Sub-Stats (-)

Mana: 20

Luck: 0 (35)

Charisma: 0 (15)

Errant Knight: +10 to all Main Stats (+15 within 20 meters of Hive Monarch)

Arachne's Blessing: +15 to Strength and Agility

Scorpius's Blessing: +15 to Constitution and Agility

And there it is. Two hundred and fifty thousand reasons to want me dead. Fantastic. I sighed and closed my screen as I waited on the others.

They were improving; it only took them most of half an hour to join me, and by the time everyone was seated, I really wanted a drink.

Amber brought in a round of ale for everyone but me. I was stuck with water, which should've been a crime punishable by death.

"All right, everyone. There is a lot we have to go over, and absolutely none of it is good, so I need your full attention."

I revealed what Miguel had told me about the bounty and about Kincaid. I laid out the facts in a concise, mechanical fashion and told everyone to hold their questions until after I was finished speaking.

After I finished one story, I immediately launched into the second half. I told them about Morgan being *the* Morrigan and that gods themselves had asked a favor of me.

By the time I was done, I'd spoken for nearly fifteen minutes, and I greedily guzzled the mug of water sitting on the wooden table in front of me. It was cool, refreshing and—above all else—not an ale.

When I finished speaking, I sat down heavily, the wood creaking in protest.

"All right, so there you have it. I left nothing out, so what's our best course of action?"

No one said anything for a good long moment, just absorbing the information. Loud breathing and a few coughs were the only sound for all of a minute before someone spoke.

"Fuck," Wilson said.

"Couldn't have said it better myself," Yumiko replied, her crimson eyes downcast.

Mika cleared his throat and shot his hand up. "I know I'm new here, but does this sort of thing happen often?"

I chuckled dryly and shook my head. "World's ending, or coming close to it, so it stands to reason that things are going to be flying off the handle. But I don't know what we can do that others can't. This just seems to be too much at once."

Wilson tugged at the hair on his silver beard and drummed his fingers on the table. He'd forgone his usual formal attire for a much more relaxed white cotton tunic that left a good portion of his chest exposed, showing his myriad tattoos.

"We do what we always do. Survive. Kincaid is a dangerous foe, and his magic is something feared by all. But he's just one man, and even he can't take us all by himself. If our bounties just went up, it will take time to organize a force large enough to take this castle.

"Magnus tried with hundreds of troops and a full guild just a few months ago. And look how that turned out. No, we have time to plan and prepare for that eventuality."

"So we divide and conquer," I said. "Wilson, can you shore up the homefront and make sure we have several exit strategies in place in case we need to bolt in a hurry?"

He nodded. "Still have a few safehouses that I had set up when we first started selling the gloom shrooms—I'll make the necessary preparations to ensure that we have adequate protection if we need it." Wilson turned to me and scratched his cheek. "That just leaves you to handle the war negotiations."

"Yep, but I can't do it alone. Any volunteers to help me stop a war?"

"If we leave it up to you, you'll probably end up making things worse," Gil said with a heavy chuckle.

I looked over at the dark-skinned giant and laughed. "Yeah, you're probably right. So how about you come with me, keep me out of trouble?"

Gil smiled wide, his green eyes sparkling as he bared his bright white teeth. "Haven't been on a quest with you in ages. Definitely haven't tried to stop a war before. Should be fun."

I nodded. "That's one down; any other volunteers?"

"Well, I might as well earn my keep around here," Mika said. "Besides, Aldrust was hell of a lot of fun, so let's see what trouble we can stir up with the wolfmen."

"We're going there to defuse trouble, not start it, but I know what you mean," I said and glanced around the room. "That's two; got one more spot to fill for a party."

I looked around the room at everyone. Levi and Behemoth were out on a quest, killing a few monster nests that had popped up around the Rolling Hills and Lake Gloom, so they weren't here. My gaze swept across Alistair and Evelyn's chairs, and I couldn't stop the pit of grief that welled in my chest.

The world's gotten a lot more complicated. We can't be so frivolous with our lives anymore, and what we're about to do is absolutely risky. I don't blame them for hesitating.

"Harper, you want to go?" I asked.

He shook his head; his bright orange fauxhawk shook slightly as he leaned back in his chair. "Hell no. It's cold as balls in the Northern Mountains, not to mention the wolfmen. I've never fought them before, so I have no idea how useful my bow skills will be."

"I'd go," Makenna said, looking up from her interface. "But I think I'd be better off here working with Markos and Wilson to help prepare for the Merchants Guild."

Well, all that leaves is Adam and Y—

Yumiko slammed her mug of ale on the table hard enough to crack the glass. "Fuckin' hell. I'll do it. No one else wants to."

Her pale face was flushed with booze, and it tinged her cheeks and neck red. Her red eyes shifted my way, and she nodded, a hint of a grin teasing her cherry blossom lips.

"Thanks, Yu. Well, that makes four members. Thank the gods NPCs don't count toward party members."

"Yeah, whatever would you do without your two lovely ladies beside you? They're the best thing to happen to this guild since it was founded. In fact, we really only keep you around to spend time with them," she replied, laughing a little too loudly.

I laughed along with her and stood. "All right everyone, we leave in the morning. I expect these coming days are going to be trying for all of us, and I just want you to know that I'm proud and grateful to each and every one of you.

"The Gloom Knights are one of the strongest guilds on Nexus because of you. And no matter what this godsforsaken world throws at us, we'll kick its fucking ass!"

A round of cheers went up at my lame speech, and glasses thumped on the table, sending droplets of ale everywhere.

I dismissed the meeting and everyone dispersed, but despite the heavy atmosphere that crept in and settled around us, I didn't let it affect me. We could do nothing about the coming storm. We couldn't stop what was coming for us, but I was confident we could weather the storm at least.

Everyone left but Adam. He remained in his chair, staring at his untouched drink.

I turned to Raven and Eris. "Would you mind giving me a moment?"

"Of course not, love. I actually need to go train some more." Eris turned to Raven. "Care to spar with me? You're much better at close quarters than I am."

"Yeah, but I can't shoot a bow for shit. Let's go practice."

Both of them gave me a parting smile and left the room.

Adam hadn't said anything during the entire meeting; he'd kept his eyes down, and his pale face was set, his jaw clenched and his mouth a hard line.

It's only been a week since Evelyn's death. I'm still struggling to deal with the fact that she's not here anymore. It's going to take a lot of time for Adam to get over it. If he ever can at all. I was the world's worst at dealing with my emotions. It was only because of Eris that I could confront my losses and deal with them.

There wasn't a person alive on Nexus who hadn't lost someone dear to them, but people dealt or didn't deal with their grief in their own ways. There was never a one-size-fits-all approach to dealing with the death of someone you loved.

I'd lost so many. My parents, Micah and Sofia. And now Jasmine and Evelyn joined them. Each one tore at me in different ways.

"How are you holding up?" I asked.

Adam looked up at me, his face haggard, deep purple bags under his golden eyes. "I'm not. To be honest."

"I know that there is nothing I can say that will make you feel better, but I'm here if you need me."

He nodded and I got up to leave. As I reached the door, he spoke again.

"I'm tired, Sam."

"I know. Get some rest, bud. As much as you need."

Adam picked up his glass and drained it in one long pull. He dropped it on the table and walked past me out into the hall. "Think I'll do that."

He left, and I watched him go, a slew of emotions roiling in my gut. And I didn't know how to calm any of them.

I walked slowly up to my room; combat practice with Eris and Raven didn't seem as fun as it did a few moments ago. Too many thoughts ran through my head and none of them good, so I took my time walking up to my room and slipped inside without talking to anyone else.

My room had changed very little since Raven and Eris entered my life. The only new additions were a separate wardrobe for each of them, and I had made another nightstand for the other side of the bed so they could store whatever they wanted in it.

Other than that, my room was still my sanctuary, the one place where I could relax and leave my worries behind. I could lower my guard here.

Which is why fury boiled in my chest and threatened to spill over into uncontrollable rage.

I gnashed my teeth and clenched my fists tight as I looked past my bed to my balcony where a figure leaned on the railing with my bottle of whiskey next to him—the last person I ever wanted to see again.

I marched across the room, and he turned at my footsteps.

He was handsome, with noble features and a hint of roguish charm in his brilliant green eyes. The mess of sandy blond hair swept across his forehead and into his eyes as the corners of his mouth lifted in greeting.

"Sampson," he said, his warm voice jovial.

Fire burned in my throat and I fought the nearly overwhelming urge to scream and rush the man in front of me. I held in my hatred as I spoke, putting as much fury into my voice as I could.

"Magnus."

Chapter 2 - Time Yet to Come

Sampson

"What the hell are you doing here?" I demanded, getting in his face.

"I came to talk," he said.

What? Why? Those were the questions that ran through my head, but my emotions didn't care about logical questions at that moment. Black, unending hatred rose up in my gut and I couldn't contain it.

I grabbed Magnus by his expensive black silk shirt and lifted him up. He could've broken free, could've ended my life with a snap of his fingers, but he stood there and let me pick him up and shove him against the stone wall of Castle Gloom-Harbor.

The only thing running through my mind then was that he had killed Evelyn and wanted to kill Eris. It was worth risking my life for me to try to kill him.

He sighed but made no move to try to break free. "I understand your anger, I truly do. Which is the only reason you're alive right now. But we won't get anywhere if you continue to let your rage control you."

"Give me one reason why I shouldn't try to kill you right now?"

"I'll give you three. One: you'd die before you could even raise your hand against me. Two: even if I did let you, I've timed out your abilities. You can't use any of them right now. And three—"

Magnus disappeared from in front of me.

I whirled around, and he was behind me, his emerald eyes sparkling ever so slightly.

"You can't kill what you can't hit."

He turned and walked back to the railing and picked up his drink. "Come, join me for a drink."

I smacked the glass from his hand, it tipped over the railing and tumbled to the ground far below us, shattering. "Fuck you."

Magnus chuckled. "That was rude." He snapped his fingers, and the crystal tumbler reappeared with the whiskey still in it, like I hadn't just watched it smash to a million pieces. "Come now, let's have a drink."

I shook my head and sighed. "I quit."

"Good for you!" Magnus grinned and inclined his head as he picked the glass up from the gray stone railing.

He took another sip and sighed with contentment.

"This is actually quite delicious. I've grown too used to my expensive wines and liquors that I've forgotten what good cheap whiskey tastes like. It's been too long." He took another sip and leaned against the railing, staring out at the great swathes of green hills in the distance and chuckled. "In fact, James, Jessica and I used to sneak into their parents' liquor cabinet and sneak a couple drinks when we were like twelve. James had the bright idea to replace the whiskey with sweet tea, and not realizing the error of such a plan, we went along with it.

"We didn't fool anyone, and man, did our parents wear our hides out for that when they found out." He paused and closed his eyes, a small, wistful smile on his lips. "I can't believe I'd forgotten that."

Magnus tugged at the collar of his cloak, staring down at the amber in his glass.

"I'd give anything in this life to go back to those days before the Night-Fall. Just for a day, an hour, a minute. I'd trade everything I have for just a glimpse again."

I knew the feeling; it was one I had nearly every day of my life here, but I hadn't felt that tug in my heart, the longing for my old life, in a while. It was all thanks to Eris. I knew that. I was a lot like Magnus—I knew that too. But unlike him, I'd finally found a reason to live in this world rather than pine for a life that I was never getting back.

It had taken too many years for me to realize that, and practically no time at all for my mindset to change.

"I know how you feel," I said, sidling up to him. "Before I met Eris, I couldn't stand this world, always thinking about what I'd lost rather than what I'd gained in this life. It's not the same—it's not the home we lost, but it is home." I laughed. "Such a simple concept, and it took me more years than I care to admit to understand that. But I'm just a dumb thug, so I shouldn't be surprised."

"From the mouths of babes," he replied with a smile and finished his drink.

Neither of us said anything for a time, both of us too wrapped up in thoughts of the past. But finally, I had to ask, "So, what did you want to talk about?"

He sighed and set the glass down, turning to me. "The future. As I told you last we spoke, this world is withering away, and fast. I don't know how much time is left. It could be centuries, or just a couple of years, but the world is falling apart."

"I'm going to stop it."

"On that, we agree. But you won't be using Eris to do it."

Magnus looked away from me, his lips pinching to form a hard line. He gripped the empty glass in both hands, and it looked like he was trying very hard not to break it. When he looked back up, his eyes were pained, filled with sorrow.

"I don't want to do this, Sam. Believe me, I don't. If there was any other way, I would take it. But Edna refuses to budge. I'm left with no choice here."

"I'll die first before I let you lay a single finger on her."

He nodded. "If that is how you wish to spend your final life here. I know what she means to you, and I know what I have to do is unforgivable, but there is no other option. You don't have to die along with her, Sam. You have Raven now, too. Are you just going to leave her all alone?"

Magnus paused letting the full weight of that last sentence settle around me.

I loved Eris more than my own life. I would die for her in a heartbeat. But if I went against Magnus and failed, he would take her anyway, and that would leave Raven on her own. I loved her too—not in the exact way I loved Eris—but I couldn't imagine my life without either of them in it anymore.

But that went both ways, I imagined. *What would they do without me in it?*

I didn't have an answer, but it didn't matter right now.

"We don't need to be enemies. I'd rather us be allies," he said. "It won't make up for what I have to take from you, but you and Raven can live a happy life together after this is over. I will make sure you never want for anything the rest of your existence."

"There's no chance of that happening," I said through clenched teeth. "You can't have her. I won't give her to you."

"I know." He nodded and looked down at his glass. With another snap, it refilled itself and he took a long drink. He set the glass down and leaned back against the railing. "Which is why I will have to take her from you."

I had to stop myself from taking a step toward him. I'd have lashed out at him on principle, and it would have ended badly for me. I knew he could kill me and take what he wanted with barely any effort. Without access to *Aura of the Antimage,* I couldn't even touch him.

Which begs the question why he isn't just taking her? I can't stop him. He said he wants to be allies, but is that the extent of it?

"You had no problem killing Evelyn, so why not do just that and take her? Why are you not killing me right now and taking what you want?"

Magnus blew out a breath and tugged at his beard. "Because it's not how I like doing things. I don't want to kill you, Sam. I didn't want to kill Jessica, either."

"Bullshit, you didn't hesitate."

"Oh, I assure you I did." His eyes flicked to mine and there was steel behind them. "Jessica stood in my way, and I gave her ample opportunity to move."

I shook my head and jabbed a finger at him. "I don't buy that for a second. With the power you wield, you could have easily immobilized her rather than taking her life. You killed her because you wanted to. Don't even try and pretend otherwise."

He grimaced and bit his lip, laying his palms back on the railing. "Not because I wanted to, Sam. Because I had to. Jessica was the only person on Nexus capable of countering my abilities. She stood against me, and if I had let her live, she would have stood against me in the future. I wouldn't have gotten the chance again, so I took it."

"Wasn't right. Wasn't noble or even justifiable. But it was necessary."

Magnus pushed off the stone and stood. He turned to me with a somber look.

"I am currently preparing to counter the system crash, but it's going to take some time to get everything ready and in place. Two months, Sam. You have two months to spend with Eris. Make them count. If you don't bring her to me in two months' time, I will come hunting for her, and you won't like the outcome."

Before I could say anything, I blinked, and he was gone.

Damn it!

I slammed my fist against the wall and bit down a scream of pain as my skin tore and a dull ache resonated up my arm. *What do I do?*

Blood dripped down my mangled hand as I turned to face the Rolling Hills, and a stiff breeze rolled through.

The howling wind gave no answers.

***

My night was filled with little sleep and far too many bad dreams. I normally slept in the middle of the bed, and though I didn't tell either Eris or Raven that Magnus had visited, they could tell something was wrong with me.

So Eris slept in the middle, and I held her close all night.

It did nothing for my nightmares, but I still liked having her in my arms.

In the morning, groggy and with aching eyes, I got up and started getting ready to head to Wyston.

Morgan's quest to the Pale Everlands was so far down on my list of priorities compared to everything else, but her promise of power made it essential. *I have no idea what kind of power she's offering, but it's coming from a god, so it must be something substantial. And right now, I need every advantage I can get.*

I didn't give a damn what Magnus said. I didn't give a damn about his power or wealth. I wouldn't let anyone take anything from me ever again, especially the person I loved more than anything else in this life.

I'll beg, bargain or steal whatever power I have to in order to win. I'll even make a deal with the Alice if I have to.

Magnus would not touch Eris. Ever.

She lay curled on her side, her hand wrapped around Raven's waist and her face pressed into her back.

Eris's petite frame was adorable. The softness of her pale skin. Her thick golden hair lay strewn in a tangled mess across her neck and cheeks. Her long ears were so sensitive to touch. The slight curve of her hips and the pronounced ridges of her spine and shoulder blades were hypnotizing as she breathed in and out, each breath ruffling Raven's midnight hair.

She was the most beautiful girl in the world, and my heart swelled to bursting as I stared down at her.

I can't lose her.

I leaned over the bed and placed my hand on her hip, running my fingers across her skin.

She shifted on the bed, and her breath quickened. She turned over and blinked the sleep from her large stygian eyes.

Eris smiled when she found me staring at her. "Good morning, love," she whispered, casting her eyes over at Raven.

"Good morning," I whispered back.

I crawled over the bed, my shadow falling across her chest and neck as I leaned down and took her cheek in my hand.

She responded by sitting up and scooting closer to me. "What's wrong?" she asked, leaning into me. "You've been acting strange since last night. Even without our bond anymore, I can tell something is bothering you, Sam."

My voice caught in my throat, and I looked away. "Nothing's wrong. I promise."

But she knew I was lying. Eris took hold of my chin and tilted my head towards her. She knelt between my legs on the bed and pressed her forehead against mine, our noses nuzzling against each other.

"Something is, but you don't have to tell me if you don't want to, beloved. Just know that I'm here for you no matter what."

I pulled her close and kissed her cheek. She leaned back and brought her lips to mine. It was such a simple and chaste kiss, but it said everything that my words couldn't.

When we broke apart, I kissed her quickly once more. "I love you, so very much."

"As I love you, for now, until eternity," she said.

I leaned over and glanced at Raven who was still asleep. "Let's wake her up and get ready. We have a lot of ground to cover today."

She shook her head and kissed me again. "Let's stay like this just a little bit longer, okay? I love Raven, and I'm so incredibly thankful to have her with us, but we haven't had any alone time in a few days. Let me enjoy this for just a bit longer."

I nodded and pressed my lips to her cheek and then her collarbone. The scent of oakwood and pine needles clung to her skin and swam through my lungs with each breath as I inhaled. Eris always smelled of the forest, and it had quickly grown to be one of my favorite scents.

"Okay, just a few more minutes."

By the time we got up, dressed and got everyone ready, a few hours had passed. It would have been a problem if we were going to take horses, or fly on Raven, but since we had the amulet that the Morrigan had given me, a few hours meant nothing when we could teleport.

It had been months since I'd regularly used the teleporters, but it would save us days on our trip.

Raven, Eris, and I met Gil, Mika, and Yumiko at the outer bailey.

They had outfitted themselves well. Gil wore his signature mix of leather and chainmail, although he wore a newer set than the one I'd last seen him in. It was a dark oxblood leather over startling bright Aldrustian steel chainmail.

Mika wore his shadowsteel armor forged in the style of the samurai of old. Yumiko had a light breastplate, vambraces and greaves under a forest green cloak on the outside, but the inside was lined with thick white fabric.

Smart plan for the Everlands. Our dark armor will stand out in the snow-capped mountains. I sighed. *Nothing I can do about it on short notice. If I'd thought about it, I could have had some made.*

"Smart move, Yu. Good thinking."

She shrugged. "Well, one of us has to." Her blood-red eyes lit up with humor. "I went ahead and made some for all of us. Nothing fancy, but they'll suffice."

I laughed and smiled wide at her. "Thanks for watching my ass, Yu."

"Oh, I just didn't want my apprentice's lover to get an arrow lodged in his foolish head because he failed to think about the little things."

Yumiko pulled an almost identical cloak from her inventory and tossed it to me. She did the same for all of us.

I donned the shadowsteel armor Magnus had given me and equipped my sword. I glanced down at the silver and emerald hilt and smiled. *I'll use the armor and weapon you gave me to end you Magnus—count on it.*

When my armor settled on me, I threw the cloak around me, and it fit nearly perfectly.

I glanced over at Yumiko and inclined my head. "Thank you, again. I'm glad one of us is thinking ahead."

"I just wish you'd thought a little more ahead, Yu," Gil said, exasperated.

We all turned and looked at him. He wore the cloak Yumiko had made for him, but she had neglected to account for his stature.

The cloak stopped at his waist, rather than his knees. It made him look comically large. Gil was tall, bordering on seven feet, and I often used the term giant to describe him, but the short cloak made him look like an actual giant.

"Gil, you look handsome," Eris said with a completely straight face.

"You look…tall," Raven said, her pale cheeks flushed as she bit her lip, barely hiding her laughter.

I, on the other hand, doubled over, barking with laughter and clutching my sides as I tried to stop and utterly failed.

"You look like a tool!" I fell over on the sparse grass and kept laughing.

He took it in stride and laughed along with me. "Better to look like a tool than be one, Dura—Sam." Gil offered me a hand and I took it.

As he hauled my ass up, he clapped me on the back, harder than he should have, but I deserved it.

"You're lucky I like you, or I'd take my axe to your hide."

"You couldn't hit me, and you know it. You'd tire your mammoth arms out before you could land a scratch on me."

"Shut up," he growled.

We both looked at each other and grinned. All was forgiven.

"All right, let's get moving. We've got a long way to cover, and taking the teleporter is the easy part of the day."

The six of us left the castle and stepped through the gate.

A bright, swirling mass of blue light enveloped me, and a subtle warmth tugged at my skin and my hair, worming over me and pulling me forward. It lasted only a second, and then I was through the portal, stepping out onto the snowy, sleepy streets of Wyston.

Cold, clear mountain air kissed my face when I walked down the white marble steps that led to the portal. Frost settled in my lungs, but each breath was sweet; the sharp, clean scent of winter clung with every breath.

Wyston was a calm little town. A few dozen cobblestone and wooden houses comprised the majority of the town with a few shops, taverns and restaurants thrown in for good measure.

I turned around and waited for Eris to come through. Though I had the amulet and Morgan told me it was safe, terror gripped me as I waited for her to appear. I knew all too well what normally happened to NPCs if they tried to teleport, and to even imagine that happening to Eris made me want to vomit.

But she stepped through a second later without a mark on her.

She held a hand to her head, shaking it slightly.

"By the void, that was strange." When she looked up, she marveled at the snow drifting around her and a bright smile lit up her face. "It has been so long since I've seen snow."

I walked over to her and wrapped my arms around her neck before kissing the top of her head. "I was worried about you. I'm glad you're safe."

The others quickly filed out of the portal. Yumiko, followed by Raven, Gil, and then Mika. Each of them stopped as the cold air slapped them in the face. They all clutched at their cloaks and brought them closer to their skin.

"Balls, I forgot how cold it was up here," Mika said.

Standing here with Mika brought up a few old memories.

I smiled, despite the bitterness that still lurked in my heart. "Yeah, it has been a long time since I was here. Think it was that nest of changelings that had infested the mana crystal mines in the mountains."

Mika let out a quick laugh. "I'd almost forgotten that little adventure. That was a crazy quest. I mostly remember Lonny bragging about his hero-tier sword for most of the trip."

"Yeah, he was proud of that sword," I laughed, "though I liked it a lot more before he used it to cut my head off."

His smile dropped. "Yeah. I'd rather think of the good days, before Sophia…you know."

"Yeah."

It'd been a while since I'd thought about her. Or Micah, for that matter. Their deaths still weighed on me, but it wasn't even close to what it had been. I'd come to accept their loss, and I was working on moving on. They were dead, and they deserved to rest.

Eris gripped my hand tightly, and the heat of her skin brought me back to the moment.

I shook my head, trying to clear it and focus. "All right, enough standing around in the cold." I pulled out the map Morgan had given me and put it on the ground between us.

We crowded the portal, but Wyston wasn't a destination most players visited often, and I figured we could get away with hogging the space for a few minutes.

The map was hand drawn, but the person who created it was obviously talented, and it showed in detail the path we needed to take from Wyston to the Northern Mountains and from there where to go to reach the Pale Everlands.

It would take us more than a day to reach our destination, so we would have to stop and make camp somewhere along the way. The cartographer who had drawn the map had thought about that as well and marked several locations that would serve as ideal campsites.

Though it's going to be quite cold once we get closer to the top. Eris and I might be fine, but the others are going to be miserable. Might need to buy some low-heat fire stones and use them as warmers.

I turned to Mika to ask, "Wasn't there an alchemist shop around here somewhere?"

"Yeah." He nodded. "If I remember right, we bought quicksilver there. Why? Whatcha thinking?"

"That we might freeze before we reach the top. Should buy some fire stones to keep us warm."

Gill nodded. "Not a bad plan. I doubt the cloaks will be enough when we get closer to the peak."

The others agreed, so we went in search of the alchemy shop.

From what the portly old man running the shop told me, they were in high demand, so he had plenty to spare. I paid a few gold for about ten low-heat stones and passed them around. I even broke one apart and dropped slivers in our waterskins.

While I normally didn't like drinking warm water, it would help keep our temperatures balanced, and it was worth the annoyance. Despite my acclimation to colder temperatures, I still didn't want to risk hypothermia if I didn't have to.

With our preparations complete, I pointed up the mountain. "All right, everyone. Let's get to hiking."

I set a moderate pace for all of us, and we made decent time while we trudged through the snowy, barely tamed paths up the mountain. I was used to hiking. During my hunt for the elder dragon, we'd spent plenty of time trekking through the forgotten places of Nexus, but the others weren't used to such strenuous exercise.

Eris was fine; in fact, she was holding up better than I was, but Raven was having trouble.

I glanced over at her, and though we'd only been walking for an hour or so, her breathing was labored and coming out in sporadic gasps.

She's having difficulty adjusting to the air. She's more bird-like than I think she wants to admit, and it's having a negative effect on her right now. Her bones were thin and hollow, which were perfect for her shapeshifting, but it meant she couldn't perform strenuous exercises for long periods. I'd noticed it when we sparred, and we were at the base of the mountain. It would only get worse as we went higher.

She won't say anything, but we should pick up the pace now that everyone's had a chance to warm up. She'll likely fall behind if that happens though. I sighed in frustration, but quickly cut it off when an idea came over me.

I broke away from the group and walked over to Raven and smiled. "Hey."

"Hey," she replied, a little breathless.

Her long black hair was tied back, but a few missed strands whipped up around her temples as she fought to keep from shivering. Her cheeks were red from the windchill, and she had her arms wrapped around her chest.

I pulled her close to me and let her rest against my chest. "Gil, take point. I'll catch up in a minute."

He turned back and nodded. The others followed his lead, but Eris looked back, a concerned expression on her face.

I gave her a smile and waved her to go on.

When they were suitably out of earshot, I leaned down and kissed Raven's cheek. "You can't keep up, can you?" I asked.

"I'll be fine," she said, forcing fire into her words.

"No, you're freezing." I tugged off my gloves and placed my warm fingers against her cheeks and neck. "It's only going to get colder, and you're already struggling."

Raven opened her mouth to respond, but I moved my finger to her lips. "I'm not saying that to hurt your feelings or to piss you off, love. It's just what is, and it's nothing to be ashamed about. But we have to push ourselves and you can't keep up."

Hurt flashed in her eyes, but she nodded, leaning into me. "I'm not meant for cold weather. It's suffocating, and my entire body hurts. I can barely move."

I held her close for a moment. "Why didn't you say anything?"

"I didn't want to be a burden on anyone."

"You should have said something," I replied, rubbing her cheek. "You can tell me these things. I'll never fault you for something like that and you know it."

Raven nodded, her whole body shivering.

"All right. Shift and change into your small raven form and climb under my cloak, I'll keep you warm."

"Okay, that sounds nice—wait, I've never shown you my small form. How did you know I had one?"

I chuckled. "It wasn't hard to figure out since you were the one who kidnapped me from my balcony and brought me to Magnus in the first place."

Her smile fell as she turned away from me. "I'm sorry, Sam. I should have told you a lot sooner. But it never seemed the right time. When we first met, I thought it would only make you hate me more, and then when we started getting close, I didn't want anything to ruin that. But I should've been the one to tell you."

Snow drifted to her hair, and I brushed it back, the heat from my skin melting the snowflakes around her. "It's okay. I understand, and I don't fault you for it. But the others are probably waiting for us, so let's get you out of the cold so you can save your strength for when we get to the top of the mountain."

She nodded and quickly shifted. With a ruffle of black feathers that sprouted from her back, she changed, and inky black down obscured her form.

When she changed, a small black raven stood next to my calf and looked up at me with blood-red eyes.

I bent down and picked her up; she jumped onto my wrist as I brought her to my chest and under my cloak. Raven hopped onto my shoulder and worked her way to my neck. I threw up my hood, and she poked her head out, laying it in the crook of my throat.

"You're so warm, Sam. Thank you for doing this for me."

"Of course. Now let's catch up to the others."

I adjusted my cloak, made sure Raven wouldn't fall off or get hurt while I moved, and set off at a quick pace to catch up with the others.

It didn't take long, and ten minutes later, I caught up with the others.

"Where's Raven?" Eris asked when she spotted me.

"I'm right here," she said, peeking her head out and glancing at Eris.

The sight of Raven in her small form caused Eris's compound eyes to light up and widen as she took in the little bird.

"By the void, you're so cute! Can I pet you?"

I couldn't help the smile that grew on my face seeing Eris suddenly so enamored. She had lived a hard life, and the moments where she got to experience true innocent joy were few and far between. I wanted that look of wonder to stay on her face for as long as possible.

"Well, Raven. How do you feel about it?"

Raven chuckled. "Being treated as a pet? Seems like it could be fun," she said, a sultry undertone to her words.

I shook my head and nudged her with my chin. "Well, go let Eris spoil you rotten."

She turned her head and winked at me. "Only if you promise to spoil me later."

After I promised her that I would, she took off and flew to Eris's arms. Eris immediately held her gently against her chest and ran her fingers over Raven's feathers.

"Oh, that's actually lovely. It's like a full body massage. Please continue," Raven said.

We all laughed, and I took over for Gil as lead. We shared a fist bump as we passed, and I picked up our pace.

It took several more hours, but we finally reached the first spot where the map indicated a good place to camp. So we all stopped, made camp, and got a roaring fire going.

I was designated chef and started getting everything set up to cook.

Footsteps interrupted my work. "Need a hand?"

Raven stood over me and knelt by my rolls of canvas as I pulled out ingredients and utensils.

"Are you offering to be my sous chef?"

She smiled, her blooded eyes lighting up in mischievous humor. "If you'll have me."

"Always," I said and we started getting everything ready.

Raven was just as much of a hand in the kitchen as I was, and even if our kitchen was currently a few miles above sea level, it didn't seem to matter as we quickly prepared a hearty stew for everyone.

Stew was one of my staple foods to cook when on the road, even if it wasn't my absolute favorite. It would do its job nicely and fill us up.

We diced and seasoned the meat and then tossed it in the world's largest cooking pot and let it and a slew of other vegetables simmer over the fire. When it was done, I went to grab my ladle to taste it, but it was gone.

"Say ahh," Raven said, holding the missing ladle.

"Seriously," I said with a raised eyebrow.

Raven huffed. "Just play along and do it."

I grumbled, but immediately relented. "Fine."

She held the ladle to my lips, and I took a bite. The stew was nearly perfect, the meat tender and the broth only a hair saltier than I would have preferred. A dash or two of pepper, garlic, and onion would balance it out though, and I quickly added them.

"You have a little something there," she said, pointing at my face.

"Where?" I asked.

"Right," Raven began and moved closer to me. She threw her arms around me and kissed me. Her lips were soft and welcoming as she leaned heavily on me. "There," she said when she pulled back.

I smiled as I caught my breath. "Thanks for getting it for me."

"Hey, lovebirds. When's dinner? I'm wasting away over here," Gil shouted.

Chapter 3 - The Holste Clan

In the morning I woke early, but the cold chill in the air immediately made me want to roll back over and fall back asleep. I shivered, despite my innate body heat and curled up between Sam and Raven. I pressed my body into Raven's back while my feet slid over Sam's.

He immediately jumped as we touched.

"By the nine kings of hell, Eris. Your feet are like icicles!"

"Warm them up for me," I replied and wrapped my hands around Raven.

She chuckled at my response and leaned back into me, her backside nestled into my waist. "You're warming me up just fine. What time is it?"

"Just after seven," Sam said with a groan. "We should get moving. We have a lot of ground to cover today, and I'd like for us to reach the Pale Everlands before it starts getting dark."

I knew just from his tone that we had to get up. I wanted to sleep in a little bit more, but Sam was using his guild leader voice, and he would just smirk and admonish me slightly if I tried to argue with him.

"Okay, we're up, we're up," Raven said with regret in her voice and slowly unstuck herself from me.

She'd kept out a lot of the chill, and a cold rush swept over my skin and goosebumps dotted my arms. *Guess I have to get up and put some clothes on.* I even had to wear shoes now. It was far too cold for me to run around barefoot. I didn't exactly like them, but I had to admit they kept me warm, and I was at least thankful, if not grateful for them.

The three of us dressed quickly, and when finished, I padded over to kiss Sam good morning.

"Morning, love," he said.

I rubbed his smooth cheeks. "I miss your beard."

"I don't," he grumbled, "but I may grow it out a bit while we're here."

After I kissed Sam good morning, I did the same with Raven, and the three of us exited the tent after Sam had packed away all of our supplies.

Gil, Mika, and Yumiko were already awake and sitting by the fire eating what remained of last night's stew.

"Look who finally decided to join us," Gil said.

"It's cold, Gil. Can you blame us for not wanting to get up?" I asked.

He shook his head. "So it's okay for you to stay nice and cozy all snuggled up together, but we have to freeze our asses off out here." His voice dripped false indignation as he tried not to crack a smile. "I see how it is, Eris. I thought we were friends."

"The very best of friends, and as friends, surely you'd want your friend to stay nice and toasty, right?" I teased.

Yumiko laughed and handed me a bowl as I sat down beside her. The stew had been good last night, but it had aged well and was even better in the morning.

We all ate, talking between bites about our plan for the day, and when we were done, camp was packed up and we set off.

Most of the day was spent hiking, which would have been fun if not for the cold. I'd spent much of my youth alone, walking the woods of the Nymirian Forest to my heart's content. Though I had friends now, a family, it still brought back those few fond memories.

But as always, my thoughts quickly turned sour. Because I thought of my mother. Aliria.

Though I can't remember, something tells me that wasn't her original name. Her real name was erased, just like mine. Though whatever it was, I much prefer Eris now. It just feels right, and it was the name my bonded chose for me.

That thought made my breath catch in my chest. Sam wasn't my bonded anymore. Not technically. Though he would always be my mate, we were no longer bound to one another. A fact that made me both happy and incredibly depressed at the same time. I was free, free to be my own person and not beholden to Sam, nor he to me.

He was an errant knight now. One free of the monarchy of the Hive. But in some dark part of my heart, I wished for him to still be mine. I wanted him to be my knight.

I laughed quietly at the thought. *Sam will always be my knight. Even if it's not official, I know that he will always be by my side.*

After everything I had done, I don't deserve him, but I'm so happy I have him. And Raven, too.

Even without our connection, I could tell that Sam was still struggling to truly forgive me for what I had done. Sleeping with Reina had been the worst thing that I could have done to him, and I did it anyway.

I regretted the pain I'd caused him, if not the action itself. It was something I had to do, but that didn't make it okay in the slightest.

It would take time for him to forgive me. I knew that. As I also knew that having Raven in his life was our saving grace.

If he hadn't fallen for her, I don't think he could have moved past what I'd done. It would have torn him apart; I know that now. She saved him; saved us.

I would be forever in her debt for helping to heal the rift I'd caused, and I loved her for that fact alone, if not for the numerous other reasons that made me fall in love with her.

I turned and looked at her. She was in her bird form, nestled in Sam's cloak with her head barely peeking out. She was utterly adorable, and even as a bird, the love she had for Sam was clear in her eyes.

With a smile no one else would see, I caught up with them.

The landscape blended into subtle shades of white and gray as we climbed, and the higher we got, the less we talked. The air was thinner here, and it made it difficult to breathe.

We pushed on for hours and hours, only stopping once for a brief lunch and once more when it was time to stop for the night. Our pace had slowed considerably, and it had taken us longer than we originally thought, so darkness came as we slowed to a stop and set camp.

The meal that night was lacking, because all of us were too tired to put much effort into anything, and the three of us set up our tent and were asleep before we could even tell each other goodnight.

In the morning, after a light breakfast we set off again.

It took most of the day, but we all acclimated to the change in atmosphere enough that it wasn't so hard to breathe.

I thought we were heading to the top of the mountain, but Sam pulled out the map and surprised me by taking a different route, and we started going down again.

The path was a steep one, and we all had to watch our steps as we traversed the narrow and rocky path littered with ice and snow. One wrong slip and we would fall who knows how many hundreds of feet to our death.

Eventually, the path began to even and widen, and the air became much easier to breathe. I assumed we were close when we started finding tracks and sparse signs of life as we hiked. There weren't many tracks but enough to know we were heading in the right direction.

My ears began picking up sounds other than the howling wind which had accompanied us the last few days. The rustling of trees and the subtle scent of pine wafted past as it was brought by the wind. My ears twitched as I strained to catch the slight echo of bird song in the distance.

The air grew warmer and heavier as we made our way over the trails. It wasn't much of a difference at first but compared to what was behind us, it was heavenly.

I cast my gaze at the white-capped mountains around us and smiled at the simplistic beauty of the alien landscape. Snow and the cold were never part of my childhood. It hardly ever snowed in the Nymirian Forest, so I was getting to see it in all its glory for the first time, and after two days, that novelty had yet to wear off.

As it became easier to breathe, Raven shifted back into her human form, and I walked side by side with her and Sam.

We finally entered a section of the mountains where trees could grow. Tall pines enveloped us and shrouded us from the bright sun, though the temperature dropped in the shade, and I already missed the sun's rays.

It was far too cold for much insect life to thrive, but there were a few of my little ones around, nestled into burrows or in the hollow spaces of the trees. I let them be and just watched the branches overhead sway in the breeze.

Though there was something off, but I couldn't immediately place it. The further we walked, the more noticeable it became. There was something wrong, but I didn't know what.

I had to speak up about it.

"Sam," I began.

"Yeah, I know," he said and turned back around. "You guys notice it too?"

Mika nodded. "Birds stopped chirping a while ago."

That's it! He was right, that was what I'd been missing, and if the birds had gone quiet, that meant only one thing.

"There's a predator nearby," Yumiko said as she pulled her bow and a quiver from her inventory.

Sam crouched low and motioned for us to do the same as he drew his sword. "Everyone be careful and keep on the lookout."

The rest of them drew arms, and I pulled at the Hive magic inside and summoned my bow and arrows.

We walked along, the crunch of our boots loud in the silent forest. Whatever was out there wouldn't have much trouble pinpointing us.

It didn't take long for us to find trouble.

My ears twitched as rapid breathing came from the right and left, and a thick musky scent filled my nose. The scents and sounds went undetected by the others, but I knew exactly where our assailants were hiding.

"Ambush! Right and left sides!" I shouted and nocked an arrow.

At my shout, the others immediately flowed into an organized formation and prepared to engage the enemy.

I turned as a figure rose from the underbrush and I fired on reflex.

The arrow took the rugged man in the chest, sliding through his leather armor and piercing his heart.

Others soon jumped out of their hiding places and surrounded us. Fifteen men and women, but they weren't human.

Each had various skin tones, but they were all pale from lack of sunlight. They were all lean; hard muscles covered their bodies. Their hair was long and thick, some reached down their backs. Each of them was different, but they all had two distinct features that marked them as demi-humans.

Two triangular ears that matched the color of their hair stood out on top of their heads and a matching fluffy tail at the base of their spines.

Our attackers were wolfmen.

Sam and the others didn't give them the chance to attack; they rushed the wolfmen as soon as they appeared.

I froze for a split second as the reality of the situation dawned on me and quickly shook myself and got my head in the fight. I was an archer; it was where my skills lay, so I had to get higher.

"Yu, on me!" I shouted to the vampire and ran for the nearest tree.

Yumiko turned at my call and raced over.

"Hold on to me."

Once more, I pulled at my magic and willed it to form at my back. Four long arachne limbs appeared as I grabbed hold of Yumiko. I jumped as high as I could and used the limbs to help me scale the thick tree.

I set Yumiko down, and the two of us took aim at the rugged wolfmen.

It wasn't easy to get clear shots when everyone was moving so fast.

Gil swung his massive black axe at a large wolfman with thick chestnut hair and a rugged beard. The axe nearly cut him in half.

He got it stuck on the wolfman's spine though, and two more demi-humans ran up behind Gil.

Yumiko and I reacted. She took one, I took the other.

She didn't have to tell me which one to take, because we'd practiced it dozens of times while shooting. Her voice echoed in my head. *Always take the target closest to you if shooting in pairs.*

Our arrows loosed at almost the same time and buried into our targets.

Hers impaled itself in the nape of the wolfman's neck, while mine tore through the leather of the wolfman's back and took out his heart.

All of that happened in a handful of seconds.

The rest of the Gloom Knights were equally as impressive as Gil. Mika and Sam teamed up to take on five of the thickest, roughest looking men, with Raven hovering in the air supporting them with her dagger like feathers.

Sam ran forward and charged the men as they attacked with crude axes and swords. Even to my inexperienced eyes, they lacked the form and grace Sam demonstrated every time he held a blade. Two of the men attacked in unison, ear-splitting howls rising from their throats.

Sam sidestepped the first attack and then stepped again, putting the wolfmen between each other. His sword arced upward, taking the first wolfman across the chest, neck, and then hewing a thick groove across the man's chin.

As the wolfman stumbled back and dropped his weapon to try to staunch the rush of blood spilling from his throat, Sam stepped forward and kicked the dying man into his comrade.

He backpedaled, his arms flying out and rotating in circles as he tried to find his balance and failed. The man careened back into his partner and they both went sprawling into the snowbank.

Blood turned the pure white snow a grisly pink, and Sam only added to the macabre display as he stepped forward and pinned the two men together as he thrust his sword downward, piercing the flesh of both men and twisting. Killing both.

A man who'd been waiting for that very moment lunged from behind a tree, twin daggers in hand as he rushed Sam.

Sam's sword was stuck, and he couldn't pull it free in time. He let go of his blade and raised his hands, preparing to engage in hand-to-hand combat.

My arrow took the wolfman in the forehead as Raven's feathers pierced his back. The man crumpled to a heap and lay still.

Sam looked up at Raven and then to me, his eyes alight with fierce pride as he gave us both a small smile and then retrieved his sword.

The twang of bowstring from beside me drew my gaze to Yumiko, who fired an arrow at a wolfman who had been about to run Mika through with a blade.

Mika, was fighting three more wolfmen. His katana was alight with sparks. Electricity arced from the black blade as he ran toward them.

He cut one down in a single fluid motion. His blade then swept back up and slid across the throat of another as the rancid tang of burning meat mixed with the sharp scent of ozone.

Yumiko provided Mika and Gil cover with her arrows, firing at any exposed flesh she could and scoring hits nine times out of ten. She was as good a shot as Evelyn had been, but she wasn't as good as Harper, supposedly—though I much preferred her company to Harper's abrasive personality.

I secretly wished it was Evelyn beside me, still teaching me. It wasn't that I disliked Yumiko; I just missed Evelyn far more than I could have ever realized. She'd been a big sister to me, even if she probably hadn't seen it that way. And there was a new ache in my heart left by her presence.

A nudge from Yumiko snapped me back to the fight. "You spaced out, Eris. Get your head in the game."

"Right!" I shouted and focused on the battlefield.

Though there really wasn't much for me to do. The Gloom Knights were more than capable of dealing out methodical death, and the skills of one nascent archer wouldn't affect the outcome of the battle by any meaningful degree.

Still, I did my best. I did have some skill, as Yumiko was always quick to point out when I got in my head about my usefulness. So I fired a few arrows when it was clear I wouldn't hit any of my friends.

When it was obvious that the Gloom Knights would be victorious and most of the wolfmen had been dispatched, Raven swooped down and landed on the tree next to me.

"Hey, love," I said while keeping my eyes on the battlefield to make sure there were no more surprises in store.

"Sunflower," she replied, scooting closer to me. Her hand brushed my own, and I fought the urge to shiver. Her hand was cold.

I pulled her closer to me, and she responded by nuzzling against me. It was rather lovely. Though I had a question that had been in the back of my head for a little while now—I just hadn't brought it up.

"You keep calling me sunflower, any reason why?"

She smiled over at me. "I thought it was an appropriate nickname since you're so warm and bright. When I met you, you immediately reminded me of a field of sunflowers. Like springtime just before summer creeps in."

My heart caught in my chest and I tried very hard not to cry at her words. They were probably the sweetest thing anyone had ever said to me.

I wound my hand around Raven's waist while we watched Sam, Mika, and Gil clean up the remaining few wolfmen.

When the fighting was over, I leaned over and kissed Raven on the cheek. "C'mon, love, let's go greet our other love."

Without waiting for her to agree, I scooped her in my arms and leapt off the tree. Before I could blink, I hit the ground and slammed into a foot of snow. My chitin exoskeleton absorbed most of the impact, but my knees still rattled and twinged a bit when I landed.

"Ow, okay. Maybe that was a bad idea."

"You think!" Yumiko shouted down at me. "How the fuck do you expect me to get down? And don't for one second think I'm jumping down into your arms like a fairytale fuckin' princess. Get your tree-climbing ass up here and get me down!"

Raven and I looked at each other and immediately burst out laughing.

"The mouth on her," Raven said quietly.

"I heard that, Birdbrain. You want to fly your ass up here? Be my guest. If not, shut it."

Neither of us could hold in our laughter at Yumiko, which only made her angrier.

After we both calmed, I climbed back up the tree and got her down. As soon as Yumiko was back on solid ground, her hostile attitude shifted, and she was back to her normal self.

"Next time you pull a stunt like that, I'll whack you upside the head." She jabbed a finger into my chest. "Got it?"

"Yes, ma'am." I nodded.

"Good." She smiled. "Also, good work today. You didn't take any needlessly dangerous shots, which puts you a step ahead of most novice archers."

Yumiko walked off and joined the others after her compliment. Raven and I followed her.

Sam came over and hugged both of us at once. "Good job, both of you," he said holding us tight. Both of us blushed furiously under his affection.

When he let go of us, we all walked over to where Gil and Mika were kneeling, going through the loot from the bodies.

"Odd place to stage an ambush, dontcha think?" Gil asked, picking up a small coin pouch and stowing it in his inventory.

"Kinda," Sam responded. "According to the map, we're still about ten miles from the Everlands. While this was a good spot for an ambush, it also means a good four hours hiking to reach their home. I'd set up much closer, but that's just me."

"You're not going to hear me complain regardless. Not after the experience I just gained."

"You said it." Sam looked off into space and whistled. "Twenty-three hundred per kill, that's impressive. I gained sixteen thousand experience for that little fight."

Mika's eyes nearly bulged out of their sockets, and he spluttered, nearly tripping on the cooling corpse of one of the wolfmen in the bloody snow. "What?" he shouted. "How the hell did you get so much? I killed nearly as many as you did, and I only got seven thousand!"

Sam smiled sheepishly and rubbed his chin, where the beginnings of copper stubble formed. "Ah, I may have access to a leveling booster of sorts, but it's not exactly something I can share, or I would. I promise."

"You've got to be kidding me," Mika said, falling back and using a dead body as a stool. He turned back and nodded at the dead guy. "Sorry for using your body like this, but you did try to kill us, so you fucking deserve it."

The body squelched as blood bubbled from the numerous lacerations across its neck and arms. Warm red blood spilled down its neck and I tried not to hurl at the sight.

"Um, Mika. Could you not. Thanks," Gil said, looking as green as I felt.

"What? He ain't using it anymore. Too bad the gear sucks. The profit on this trip is going to be abysmal."

The rest of the Gloom Knights checked over the dozen corpses and looted anything of value. I left them to it, since they had access to an easy version, and I didn't feel like pawing over dead bodies for a few measly coins.

I still don't see the need for the amount of money they have. Sam gave me a small fortune, and it didn't even put a dent in his coffers. I could buy a house and live comfortably for a good five years with the gold in my purse, and it's nothing but pocket change to them.

The thought wasn't worth dwelling on; money was a foreign concept to me, and I imagined it always would be.

When they were done looting, we set off again toward the Pale Everlands.

It was a modest hike, but after our brief fight, my adrenaline wore off and left me incredibly tired. I wanted nothing more than to lie down and take a nap, but I couldn't. I had to stay strong and keep walking.

If the others can handle it, so can I.

Though I did walk a little fast and catch up to Sam, winding my hand through his as we walked. It was nice and was something I'd missed during Sam's trip to Aldrust. I'd missed being close to him, and I was the luckiest girl in the world. Having Sam and Raven was proof of that.

As we pressed on, the trees thinned and a large path formed, which told us that we were on the right path.

We hiked for another couple hours in silence, broken only by our footfalls and the occasional birdsong. Each step we took brought us closer to the Everlands but also the unknown. None of us had ever been to this place before, and that put each of us on edge.

My nerves were tingling as we got closer. There was an aura in the air that prickled the back of my neck and made me want to cast my eyes around.

I knew the feeling. And I was sure the others knew it too.

We were being watched. By numerous eyes.

Sam's jaw was set; his teeth clenched as he unconsciously pulled me closer to him.

"Sam?" I asked.

"Don't worry," he said, keeping his eyes straight ahead. "They wouldn't let us know they were there if they meant us any harm. It's a warning and a threat rolled into one. If we step out of line, we're dead. But as long as we don't do that. We're fine."

I nodded, putting my faith in Sam for the hundredth time. He had never led me wrong, so I wouldn't start doubting him now.

The trees finally cleared, and we exited the forest to find a mountain range looming overhead. White, snowcapped gray monoliths rose to towering heights in front of us and stretched for as far as the eye could see. Fog rolled from the top of them and drifted down toward us.

They were unbelievably beautiful and also terrifying. It had been hard to breathe on this part of the Northern Mountains. I feared that none of us would survive a climb to the top of even one of them.

"Look there," Sam said, pointing at the base of the mountain.

Everyone followed his finger and looked to where he pointed. I didn't see anything at first. Long shadows stretched toward us, bathing us in frost and darkness, but after a second of squinting, I found what he'd seen.

Nestled in a nearly pitch-black shadow of the mountain was a large opening in the rock. It led deeper into the mountain and into unfamiliar territory.

"Is that where we have to go?" I asked.

"Looks like it," he said, pulling out the map and glancing at it. "So we're in the right place."

He pulled a torch from his inventory and lit it. The others did the same and together we approached the unknown darkness.

Chapter 4 - The Pale Everlands

As we reached the end of the dark tunnel, the rocky and frigid caverns around us opened into a clearing.

Nestled in between two gigantic mountains was the Pale Everlands. Clear blue sky shone far above us; white clouds drifted by as snow fell on what could only be described as a town.

It was a rather spacious village. The houses were mostly comprised of pine wood, with stone chimneys, but each house was crafted with loving detail, and I could tell at once that the builders had put their time and effort into the construction.

The village was quaint but calling it a village was almost an insult. It was huge, spanning several miles wide and back. Hundreds upon hundreds of rabbitmen were out and about or working.

The markings of several different clans were present. The white-eared Usaka clan and the gray eared Aminah clan were the most prevalent, but there were a few black eared Domia clan as well.

Strange, I thought the Aminah clan banished the Domia long before I was born. Though that was a thousand years ago, and with everyone's memories getting distorted, maybe they aren't rivals anymore.

Sam whistled, long and slow. "This place is something else," he said, staring around as he rubbed the back of his neck.

Though he shouldn't have whistled, because a number of the nearby rabbitmen turned at the sound, and their faces grew dark and hostile.

In a handful of seconds, we were surrounded by rabbitmen armed with small knives, rakes, and hoes being aimed in our faces as makeshift weapons.

"Peace, the Morrigan sent us," I said, holding up my hands as I slowly stepped in front of Sam. "We are not here to cause trouble. I swear. Can you escort us to see the clan leader?"

The rabbitmen turned to one another, and an invisible conversation went on back and forth between two of them for a moment before a black-haired male with sun-kissed skin and light green eyes and black ears spoke up.

"My name is Hahlys. I will take two of you. No more. The rest will remain here under guard. If you are telling the truth and the clan leader gives you her blessing, then the others will be free to do as they please."

"What if she doesn't?" Sam asked.

Hahlys shrugged. "Then you all die."

He looked over to Sam and back to me.

"I do not recognize your race, but it is clear you're a demi-human. You may see our leader." Hahlys glanced at Sam's sword. "If this one is to accompany you, he will need to disarm."

"Like hell I will," Sam said.

The rabbitmen tensed, clutching their weapons even tighter as they inched them closer to Sam.

He didn't look bothered by them in the slightest. Sam turned to Hahlys and spoke.

"You just threatened not only myself, but the lives of those I hold dear. I harbor no ill intentions to you or your clan leader, but I will be keeping my sword. You'll have to kill me before I hand it over."

Sam stood impassive, but his right hand rested across his stomach, ready to draw his blade if they so much as twitched the wrong way.

Hahlys stared him down for a long moment before blinking. He nodded and relented. "I think we can handle one lone swordsman." He motioned for us to follow him and led us through the town.

I couldn't keep my eyes on one single thing as we walked. Despite the threat and heavy tension in the air, the Pale Everlands was a beautiful place, being secluded and far removed from the rest of the world.

The mountains that surrounded the town acted as natural buffers for the wind, which meant the temperature was rather warm compared to what we had just come from. It was only by a few degrees, but it went from freezing to just shy of freezing, which was an improvement in my book.

Little rabbitmen children ran around under the watchful eyes of their parents, but they were soon shuffled behind them as we passed, the parents eyeing us with outright mistrust.

I wish they wouldn't look at us like that, but I understand. We're the outsiders here. We don't belong. Especially Sam as a human. I just hope the clan leader is amiable to us.

Hahlys led us deeper and deeper into the city, and we passed all manner of businesses. A blacksmith, bakery, and seamstress were all close to each other. I didn't know what the rabbitmen used as money or if they operated on a bartering system.

It seems they behaved more like the Arachne or the Hive than the humans, but I wasn't sure.

"Pardon, but I was wondering. I've noticed many shops, but I haven't seen any coin purses. Do you barter?"

He glanced back and nodded. "For the most part. We do have some small amount of coin that we use for trading with the outside world on the very rare occasions a traveler reaches us, or we risk heading down the mountain, but most of what we need we barter for. Everyone has something someone else needs and, if they don't, we use intermediaries."

"What do you mean? Intermediaries?" Sam asked.

Hahlys's face turned to a scowl as he looked to Sam, but he still answered the question.

"In the case of someone needing something from someone, but that person not having need of what the other is offering, another rabbitman may step in on the buyer's behalf and offer what the seller needs in exchange for the seller and the intermediary working out a deal."

Sam hummed and scratched his cheek. "So everyone gets what they want in the end. It's actually a very efficient method of business, but it wouldn't work in the Compass Kingdom or anywhere with a vast population. I imagine it would break down the larger the populace."

Hahlys grunted, neither agreeing or disagreeing, just acknowledging Sam's comment. "Perhaps you're right, but it works for us, and that's all that matters."

After that, we didn't really speak, though Sam took my hand as we walked the snowy streets until we reached a large hill.

Rough steps had been carved up the hill, leading to what I could only describe as a compound. It was built of wood and stone, as all the buildings in the town had been, but it was of finer construction, elegant where most of the other buildings were on the crude side. A large wooden fence separated the compound from the town.

Hahlys whistled, two long, a quick whistle, and then one long whistle.

The gate opened as we approached and a number of fully armored and armed rabbitmen approached. They all bore simple weapons and leather armor, but the quality was unmistakable.

A large rabbitman approached. He was older and his short, cropped hair was graying at the temple and his rabbit ears were speckled with silver.

However, he still bore lean muscles and a grace about him that I'd seen on every member of the Gloom Knights. The grace of a warrior.

He inclined his head to us. "My name is Rovarius and I am the Aminah clan's commander. You will follow me, and if you step so much as a toe out of line, you won't have time to regret your misstep."

Once inside the compound, we found numerous buildings, most simple one-stories, but the main building was a three-story structure that spoke of wealth, despite the simple construction. It was built with elegance, and was a little ostentatious.

Rovarius led us to the main house through a set of hand-carved wooden doors and into a room that seemed to double as a throne room and dining hall.

It was all dark wood and open windows with wooden shutters on either side. Torch sconces jutted from large pillars that lined the hall and there were half a dozen large fireplaces with roaring flames that heated the room quite nicely.

Long banquet tables were lined up; the heads of the tables pointed toward the far side of the room where a large chair sat pressed against the wall.

Sitting on the chair was a young woman.

She had fine golden hair that stopped just before her chin and a full face with wide, sparkling blue eyes. Her rabbit ears were gray, denoting her as a member of the Aminah clan and the clan leader.

Her lips lifted into a smile as we approached. "Welcome, strangers, to Aminah Hall. It has been many years since a human has stepped foot here." She then tilted her head to me. "And a demi-human the like I've never seen before. Tell me, child. What are you?"

I let go of Sam's hand and approached her. I stopped a respectable distance and bowed my head, keeping my eyes on her.

"My name is Eris. I am an entomancer, one of the last of my kind. Though your people would have no history of this. My kind and the other races of my kingdom and yours were allies many centuries ago. I am the queen of the Hive Kingdom—what few remains of it, at any rate."

The woman paused, smiling at me. "It's true that I have never heard of your race, but your words strike an ineffable resonance in my heart. Since your very existence defies what I've come to understand about this world, I am inclined to believe you. My name is Rhoa and I am the leader of the Aminah clan and the chosen representative for the entire rabbitman race. Now tell me, what brings you to my hall?"

At this Sam moved forward, coming to stand by my side. His hand brushed my lower back, and I instinctively moved closer to him.

"I was tasked by the Morrigan to come here and help broker peace between the rabbitmen and wolfmen clans."

Rhoa gasped, a small intake of breath, as Sam's words carried throughout the room. Whispers broke out as what he said registered. She sat up straight in her chair and looked down at Sam with renewed interest.

"The Morrigan has never deigned to offer her aid in the past. Why here, why now? She delights in the chaos of mortals. She wouldn't intervene. That is just fact."

She didn't so much as move, but the air became changed. Tension built as her guards gripped their weapons just a hair tighter, and they shifted on the balls of their feet. Just waiting for a command from Rhoa.

"I'm telling the truth, but it's not my concern if you choose to believe it or not. I was hired for a job, and I intend to do it. Your belief isn't required for me to complete my task."

Rhoa chuckled as she leaned back in her chair and crossed her legs. "Is it confidence or arrogance that drives you, human? Either way, you are bold to speak to me in such a manner. I could have you killed in a second."

Sam presented, a knowing smile that quickly turned ferocious. "You could try, but I'd slaughter everyone in here before you could lift a finger against me."

His fingers inched closer to his blade.

"Sam, enough," I snapped, reaching out to grab his hands. "We are guests here and emissaries of my goddess. I will not tolerate any violence upon those we were sent to help."

I then turned my gaze to Rhoa.

"That goes for you as well. We are not here to harm any of your people, and I expect you to be beholden to the same rules. There will be no violence. Am I clear?"

It was quiet in the hall for a second before Sam turned to me, his eyes wide and eyebrows raised. A shocked expression shone on his face before it faded to incredulity and then pride. He grinned and leaned over and kissed the top of my head.

"Put me right in my place, didn't you?" he said and laughed. Sam turned to Rhoa and inclined his head. "What my bonded says is true. We are here to help, and as the leader of my men, I swear that we do not wish for conflict." He paused once more. "We will not instigate any violence, but we will not hesitate to return it if attacked. Is that fair?"

"Sam," I hissed.

He shrugged and turned his gaze back to Rhoa.

She remained silent for a long moment, a bemused expression on her face. The silence stretched for a long time before she huffed and nodded.

"Very well. Though I still somewhat doubt that you were sent by our goddess. I shall not turn away help, not when we could so desperately use it."

Rhoa stood from her chair and motioned for us to follow her.

She and several of her guards led us to a large study. There were no books; instead, rows and rows of parchment sat on the wooden shelves, and despite the large size of the room, it held a cozy, homey atmosphere that immediately set me at ease.

There were several wooden chairs in a circle in the center of the room, and Rhoa bade us to sit as she took a chair herself.

"Would you like some tea? It's made from the bark of the loa tree, and it's quite delicious. It also helps warm the body nicely."

"We would love some," I said and nudged Sam. "Isn't that right, love?"

He chuckled and leaned back in his seat, casting his eyes around the room. He crossed his legs and turned to me. "Whatever you say. Seems you speak for me in this matter, but it's your wheelhouse, so I don't exactly mind."

I cocked my head to the side and smiled. "You're giving me permission to handle this?"

"Give?" He shook his head. "No, you took permission all on your own. But you are my chosen queen, and the rabbitmen are demi-humans, I think it's only right you take over…besides assertive suits you."

He winked at me, and I tried not to blush as I turned back to Rhoa.

She looked from Sam to me, laughing at us with her eyes, but it was a cute laughter that lit up the blue in her eyes. She spoke to one of her guards about the tea, and he quickly went to fetch it for us.

When he returned, he brought a large platter filled with expertly shaped wooden dishes and a wooden teapot. He poured the tea for us and then went to stand by his mistresses's side once more.

Rhoa motioned for us to drink, and we did. I picked my cup and sipped it with no hesitation, but Sam paused over his and sniffed. He took a sip and swirled it around his mouth.

"It's not poisoned. I wouldn't waste good tea like that."

Oh, I really should've considered that, but it's not like poisons have any effect on me, and they wouldn't harm Sam anymore...though I wouldn't necessarily mind the side effects.

I fingered the raised scar at the base of my throat where Sam's tooth marks lingered and blushed, remembering that night of deranged passion.

As much as Sam loathed what he'd done, I'd happily take another scar for a night like that again. It had been simple, where we didn't have to think about our actions and the consequences; we could just be with each other.

It had been lovely, and I wasn't sure it was something we could ever have again.

I sipped my tea and marveled at the taste. It was earthy, slightly bitter at first, but then a subtle sweetness like honey rolled over my tongue and spread warmth through my mouth. It was wonderful.

Before I knew it, my cup was empty, and I quickly refilled it.

"I'm glad you like the tea. The loa tree grows in a cave to the north of here, and we harvest its bark to make the tea. It's a rare drink that I'm sure outsiders such as yourselves wouldn't have tasted, so I'm pleased you got the opportunity to try it."

"It is good," Sam said, setting his cup down. "But we came here to work, not to drink tea."

She paused before smiling and set her cup down. "Very well. My daughter, Rosha, is missing. She's been gone for many months now, and I'm certain the wolfmen are to blame. One of mine saw her with a black-eared wolfman before she disappeared."

"And you think she's still alive?" Sam asked.

Rhoa shook her head. "I don't know. But I've spoken with the Holste clan's leader, and he swears he had nothing to do with her disappearance, but of course he would say that.

"Tensions have been building between our two races for hundreds of years. They are far stronger than us, be we outnumber them five to one. It would be a bloody battle on both sides if we were to go to war."

Bloody is right. We fought a couple dozen just a few hours ago, and they put up a good fight. but Sam and the others are hardened warriors. Most of the rabbitmen are simple farmers or laborers. Numbers may help them, but it would still be a slaughter, and the wolfmen would win.

"Okay. Well, that's one side of the story. We'll need to talk to the Holste clan tomorrow and get their side."

Rhoa nodded. "I understand, though please, if you can find my daughter, please do. I will reward you handsomely for finding her."

Sam's eyes lit up as he stared off into space. He whistled. "An A-ranked quest, and just look at that experience," he muttered under his breath. Though both Rhoa and I heard him. "We'll find her or find out what happened to her. I promise."

"Thank you. You and your compatriots may stay in my compound during your time here. Though I won't stop you from wandering through the village, I recommend doing so accompanied by one of my guards. They will deter any of the rabbitmen from causing trouble."

After our talk, Rhoa wished us well and retired. One of her guards came and retrieved us and brought us to the others waiting at the dining hall.

Gil and the others sat around a table and were talking among themselves when we came in.

"Hey, guys, this place is pretty amazing, right?" he said in a too-loud voice. "And you've got to try this tea. It's amazing."

I couldn't help but laugh at Gil's antics. Whether it was working in his shop, talking with the Arachne queen, or in a land far from home, he never changed, and that made me incredibly happy.

"We have, though I think the guard is going to show us to our rooms," I said. "We should get an early night. We have a big day in the morning."

They set down their cups, and we all followed the guard out of the main house to the back of the compound where a large wooden longhouse sat.

It was plain but quaint and looked cozy.

"You should find ample space inside, and there are several hot springs around back that you can use for bathing. There is also a bell next to the door, if you require food or assistance, just ring it," the nameless guard said and left without another word.

"Okay, so who's up for a little exploration?" Mika said and rushed off ahead of us.

Sam laughed as he watched Mika take off toward the building. "He never changes."

We all followed him into the longhouse. It was spacious and sectioned off into six different rooms. They were all identical in appearance with spartan furnishings limited to a couple beds, wash basins and dressers.

They were mostly comprised of wood. The beds were the same shade of wood as the walls and the basins to wash our faces which made sense, considering the limited number of building supplies the rabbitmen had at their disposal. Though plain, it was clean and warm thanks to a small fireplace in the corner, the only stone piece of construction in the room, and had plenty of room for all of us.

"Nice place," Raven said as she shifted out from under Sam's cloak and threw herself on one of the beds.

"Yeah. It's nicer than most of the inns I've stayed at in the Compass Kingdom, and it has a fireplace. Good, because I'm freezing," Sam said. He then grabbed one of the beds and scooted it closer to the fire, keeping only a couple feet between the bed and the open flames.

"That should be enough room for us to sleep comfortably and also not set the bed on fire."

"Well, since we're fucking up the layout anyway, might as well go all the way," Raven said, pointing at one of the beds. "You mind giving me a hand with this, darling?"

Sam helped push a second bed next to the first to that we could all sleep next to one another. The beds were small and only meant for one person, but two of them pushed together should be more than plenty of room.

"Yo, Sam!" Gill called from somewhere outside, his voice muffled and weak. "Check this shit out!"

On the far corner of the room was a sliding wooden door that led outside. I slid it open and stepped outside.

Gil was right. It was incredible.

Right outside our room was a walled-off hot spring. Wooden walls segregated each of the rooms into small, even sections with slits in the wood to allow water to pass by.

Steam curled off the small pond in front of me. It filled most of the space, flowing to the other sections on either side of us.

The water was clouded by the heat but looked decently deep and oh-so-inviting.

Not waiting to see what Sam or Raven was going to do, I hastily stripped out of my clothes and stepped into the hot water.

The first thing I noticed was that it wasn't as hot as I was hoping. It was several degrees cooler than the bath at Castle Gloom-Harbor, but after days spent in the snow and climbing a mountain, it was heavenly.

"You're right, Gil, this is wonderful," I called out.

"Figured you'd like it, Eris." There was a large splash and a thousand droplets of hot water sailed over the wooden wall that separated Gil's room from ours. "Water fight!"

He chuckled madly at his joke, though I didn't quite understand it. But hearing the delight and humor in Gil's voice, I decided that context didn't really matter if he was having a good time.

I shoved my hands under the water and sent back as big of a splash as I could manage. "Water fight!" I parroted.

He laughed, and our little pretend war went back and forth before Sam stepped into the bath.

"All right, enough of the splashing. We have a long day tomorrow, so we should all get some rest."

"You're no fun," Gil said, a smile in his voice. "But you're also right. This hot spring is too nice to horse around in. I could use a nice soak."

"Can you even fit?" Mika asked, shouting loud from beside Gil.

"Shut up!"

After our little dispute was settled, we all relaxed in the water for a long while. Raven stripped and came in to join us. She snuggled in between Sam and me and wrapped her hands around the both of us. Sighing with contentment as she settled in.

"Holy crow, this is phenomenal. I've never been to a place like this before."

"Yeah, they're nice. They were common back in my world. Though there wasn't any nearby my city, so I never had the pleasure of going to one in that life. Though Aldrust has a nice hot spring over a volcanic vent. Water gets so hot it boils some days, so you can't go every day, but there are some days it's just a little hotter than this."

"That sounds fantastic," I said.

"Oh, you'd love it." He leaned over and kissed my shoulder. "When this is all over with, I'll take you one day. Assuming Balthazar lets me keep my head."

Raven chuckled and quickly covered her mouth. "Yeah, we didn't really leave on friendly terms."

"Well, I did steal their most prized artifact. That tends to make people a little unfriendly towards each other." He laughed then his face grew somber. "I probably won't ever be able to go back. So, I guess I won't be able to take you after all."

"That's okay." I leaned my head on Ravens shoulder. "This is nice enough for me."

It was nice, just sitting there with my two favorite people in the world, and though Sam was right about having a long day tomorrow, I didn't want to get up. I wanted to stay and soak in the water.

Raven leaned over and pressed her lips to mine in a quick kiss. When she pulled back there was mischief in her ruby-red gaze.

"I think it's about time, don't you?"

"Time for—" My cheeks burned scarlet as I caught her meaning. "Oh." I smiled despite myself.

It was the one thing we had been putting off for numerous reasons, but I didn't think either of us could find a reason to hold back any longer.

I nodded and we both stood and moved to either side of Sam.

"What are you two doing?" he asked.

Raven kissed his lips while I kissed his chest to his jawline.

"Something we should have done weeks ago."

CHAPTER 5 – A FAILURE TO COMMUNICATE

Sampson

After an incredible night, I begrudgingly got up. I wanted nothing more than to stay in bed with Raven and Eris and continue what we'd begun last night, but I had a job to do, and nothing—not even the temptation of the two of them—could stand in the way of that.

"Come on, loves. Time to get up. We have much to do today."

Eris groaned and rolled over on the bed, snuggling closer to me, while Raven snored softly on her side next to the fire.

The others are probably up by now, and I need to get clean and dressed. We have a long way to go to reach the wolfmen clan's home and I'd rather not spend all day hiking in the snow again.

While I waited for the girls to get up, I checked my notifications.

Character Name: Durandahl

Level: 71

Exp: 6000/7100

20 Stat Points Available!

1 Ability Point Available!

The fight with the wolfmen had given me a good bit of experience, enough to level up, so I distributed my stats.

I added fifteen to *Durability*, bringing it up to one hundred. The remaining five points I added to *Attack Damage* so I could keep hitting hard. I also wanted to start getting my *Battle Fatigue* and *Attack Speed* up, but those were things I could focus on slowly. They would help, but not as much as getting extra sword damage up.

After I sorted my stats, came the big decision.

What to choose as my next ability?

First Tier List
~~*Aura of the Arachnid*~~
Poison Blade
~~*Exoskeleton*~~
~~*Chitin Shield*~~
Hive Guard

Second Tier List
Chitin Armor
Chitin Sword
Arachne's Blessing
Scorpius's Blessing
Mantearia's Blessing (Locked)
Apocrita's Blessing (Locked)
~~*Hive Mind (Passive)*~~

Besides the Hive Abilities, I had *Will of the Immortal,* and *Aura of the Antimage.*

I frowned as I deliberated on my new ability.

I wanted *Chitin Armor* to reduce the fatigue I acquire when I fight, but it's not a must-pick right now. I needed *Hive Guard*, because it's an instant recovery, and that's invaluable.

Return to Zero, which had been a final gift from Evelyn, was also an option. But I discounted it, despite its usefulness. It was a weapon to use against Magnus, but if he kept his word, I had two months to level up enough to acquire it. I could wait on that one.

My decision made, and I chose *Hive Guard*.

With that done, I closed my interface.

I had two quests tangentially related to each other, and I wanted to get moving on solving both of them and gaining the experience for them.

Despite what he'd said, and despite my decision to forgo *Return to Zero*, Magnus wasn't going to sit around forever, and when he eventually came for Eris, I needed all of the power I could possibly have at my disposal.

Though it took more convincing than usual, I managed to wake both Eris and Raven, and we took a quick bath. I waded to the far side away from them to keep my mind focused, but they couldn't help but laugh at me for my antics.

I let them get it out of their systems, and we then joined the others for breakfast. There was a small antechamber in the longhouse with a single banquet table that had been piled high with fruits and bread. There was no meat, which was a disappointment, but I could probably stand to have a little more balance in my diet.

"So how was your night?" Gil asked, barely holding in his laughter as he plopped a seedless strawberry in his mouth whole.

"You heard?" I asked, my face growing hot.

"Whole fuckin' rabbitmen city could've heard the three of you going at it like actual rabbits. Fuck, I know the whole 'when in Rome' saying, but you didn't have to take it so literally." Yumiko snorted and dunked her bread in a brown sauce that steamed delectably.

"I'll just go hang myself now. You guys have a nice life."

The others laughed entirely at my expense, and I busied myself with food while Raven and Eris joined us.

After breakfast we donned out gear and quickly spoke once more with Rhoa, who gave us a map with rough directions to the wolfmen city of Jole.

From the scrawlings, we determined it was about a half day's slow hike, but I was betting we could get there in about ten hours. However, it did mean we would have to find some sort of accommodations for the night regardless.

I sighed and tucked the map into my inventory. *Looks like another night of camping is on the menu.*

Rhoa wished us well and a guard accompanied out of the city nodding silently to the track we should take up the mountains once more. We hiked for a few hours at a steady pace, although it took me longer than I cared to admit to work the exhaustion from last night's proclivities out of my legs.

It had been beyond fun, but it probably wasn't a smart idea the night before we had to face the wolfmen.

I need to be on top of my game here.

Still, it was well worth a little bit of discomfort.

As we passed the four-hour mark, we stopped for a brief rest and grabbed a bite to eat. It was nothing more than trail rations and a bit of dried meat we'd brought along, but after my rather lackluster breakfast, I was happy for some protein.

Gil, Yumiko, and Mika chatted with each other while Raven and Eris whispered between themselves. They cast a few glances my way, so I could guess the topic of conversation.

It didn't matter to me; I let them get it out of their system, and I was glad they both had someone to talk to because I wasn't exactly up for a long conversation at the moment. In fact, I wanted nothing more than to go back to bed and sleep for another few hours. But that wasn't going to happen, so I stopped complaining to myself and stood.

"All right, let's get a move on, guys."

We kept going without incident until it grew too dark to continue, and we made camp for the night.

In the morning, we continued our trek once more.

The mountain grew colder with each step as we ascended, but we soon crested a large hill and came upon a small city.

It was built much in the same way as the rabbitmen city that I'd never bothered to learn the name of. They used the same construction materials and style of architecture.

"So that's Jole." I turned to the others. "I don't really expect that we'll have a warm reception there, so keep on your toes, okay?"

"You don't need to tell us twice," Mika said and placed his hands on his katana. "Long as the wolves keep the peace, so will we, but they're nothing but savages, so I expect we'll all have quite a few new levels by the end of the day."

I sighed and pinched the bridge of my nose. "Yeah, that's what I'm afraid of."

With nothing further to be said, we headed for the city.

Reaching the gates of Jole, we were stopped by a pair of heavily guarded wolfmen. They wore rich leather armor under thick gray fur cloaks.

They drew spears when we approached.

"Look what we have here. Humans. Should make for a fine stew tonight, what say you, Berrick?" one guard said to the other.

Berrick eyed us with a hungry gleam in his eye. "I'll say. Lotsa lean meat on these morsels. Should make for good eatin'"

I narrowed my gaze and grimaced. *They'll eat any kind of meat. Save for their own, but they're the closest this world has to cannibals.*

"We were sent by the Morrigan. You want to piss her off by eating her emissaries?" I asked, my hand going for my weapon. "How about you let us in to see the Holste clan leader and we won't be forced to murder you disgusting beasts and leave your rotten corpses for the crows."

The two men reached for their arms, but their eyes widened.

Two quick twangs pierced the air followed by thunks as dual arrows buried themselves next to the wolfmen's heads in the large wooden wall behind them.

Eris and Yumiko stook with their bows out, already having nocked another arrow. They stood ready to loose them. I glanced at Eris, at the determination in her eyes that hadn't been there when we'd first met.

She's grown. And I'm liking who she's becoming.

So much of her life she had been put down and told what to do by others. I imagined I was the first person who let her truly be who she wanted to be, and it may have taken some time, but that person was slowly breaking through the shell her family had placed her in.

"We really don't want to kill you, but if we must, we will. We were sent by the Morrigan. Do you really want to be the two people we make an example out of?" she asked, steeling her obsidian eyes.

"You can't take all of us," Berrick said, his voice shaky.

"No, but we can certainly kill you." I drew my blade and rested the tip against his neck. "All we want is a meeting with your clan leader. This is above your station, so why don't you run off like a good little puppy and go fetch him for us. Let him decide what he wants to do about it."

Berrick scowled at my insults, but he nodded and opened the gate to slip inside, leaving us with the nameless one as company.

It wasn't exactly pleasant, but the wolfmen were the opposite of the rabbitmen. They responded to strength and power. We had to stand our ground and prove we were the strongest or they'd eat us alive.

Literally.

Berrick was gone for nearly half an hour. And when he returned, he was out of breath, panting.

"The master will see you. I will escort you."

The large wooden gate opened, and we marched into the city.

Jole was cramped compared to the expanse of the rabbitmen city. The wall stretched and surrounded the city, and the small population of wolfmen built their houses close together. The construction was much worse as we walked past the houses.

They were built shoddily, almost as an afterthought rather than a place to live in. Nearly every single one of the buildings were ramshackle, worn down and neglected.

Wolfmen gathered to glare and snarl at us as we passed. Each of them making it clear they would happily murder us and devour our bones.

I ignored the looks and held my head high. We couldn't show fear, or they would gang up on us and we wouldn't survive.

We could deal a number of wounds to them, and we could kill a lot of them, but they would drown us in bodies, and I'd rather that eventuality not come to pass.

It took us about fifteen minutes to work our way through the chaotic street until we came to a single-story, cabin-style home. It was larger than most of the other buildings and only slightly better kept, so that alone told me that we were at the clan leader's house.

Before we could go inside, Berrick put his hand out and stopped us. "You will show respect when addressing our master. To disrespect him is to face death. Do you understand?"

"I understand that if you don't take your hand off me, you'll lose it." I shoved past him and entered the house.

It was quaint—or quaint in comparison to the city we just walked through. There were no decorations on the walls nor anything purely aesthetic. Everything served a function, a purpose. The house was very spartan, and I approved of the practice, even if I hadn't adhered to it nearly so well as I'd have liked.

Berrick led us to a small room that was meant to resemble a sitting room. Where Rhoa and the rabbitman had a respectful distance between their leader, the wolfmen had the opposite.

The man that must have been the wolfmen clan leader sat on an unadorned wooden chair next to a fireplace.

Rather than the lean hardass I was expecting to find, the man was rather grandfatherly. He had bright silver hair that ended at his shoulders. The silver crept to his black wolf ears but only accented his features. He bore a rugged face with many lines and a few scars. His blue eyes had dulled slightly but still held a sheen that time would never take away.

The man wore a simple black tunic with a fur cloak to shield him against the cold.

He inclined his head to us as we approached. "Guests, and human guests at that. Now I've seen everything." He peered at each of us before they landed on Eris. "And an unfamiliar demi-human. This just gets more interesting. You can call me Morn."

He reached over his shoulder and grabbed for a long-stemmed pipe, and he took his time lighting it. When he was finished, he took a few puffs and blew the smoke away from us.

"So, Berrick here says you're emissaries for the Morrigan. At first I was going to laugh in your faces and have my men disembowel you for lying." Morn pointed at Eris and sighed. "But I've never seen the likes of your kind before, and I'm inclined to believe that you aren't just adventurers looking to get yourselves killed. So tell me: what brings you here?"

Eris spoke up, repeating the same conversation, we'd had with Rhoa just the day before. She told Morn about the quest the Morrigan had sent us on and that she'd tasked us with stopping the brewing war between the clans.

"Huh." Morn scratched at his stubbled face. "Story just keeps getting interesting. I'm afraid I don't know anything about the rabbit's missing kid. Been too focused on my own missing son to even think about taking the Aminah clan's daughter."

I held up my hand. "Wait, your son is missing?"

"For about two months now." Morn nodded. "He's been gone for so long, I don't hold much hope he's still alive."

Two missing kids…

"And how old is your son?"

"Just reached adulthood last winter."

I turned and nudged Eris. "How old was Rhoa's daughter again?"

She paused and cocked her head before looking up at me. "About that age. I think that's what Rhoa said."

"Damn it." I sighed and rubbed the side of my jaw, trying to fight the headache I knew was coming. *So, two kids about the same age go missing at roughly the same time give or take a month or so. Either they're both dead...or this quest is looking a lot more like Romeo and Juliet than I care to deal with.*

"Is there anywhere your son likes to go? Maybe in town or nearby?"

Morn nodded. "There's a string of hunting cabins to the northeast. But my men already searched there. We didn't find anything. You think Jacoby could still be alive?" Morn asked, a sliver of hope in his voice.

"Maybe. I'm thinking it's too big of a coincidence that both the children of the clans go missing at the same time."

He shot up from his chair. "Wait, you think they're together?"

I shrugged.

"It's possible," Eris said. "I mean, back in the time of my people, the two clans intermingled quite often. Though the children born of such unions were always either rabbitman or wolfman, never a combination of the two."

Morn sighed and sat back in his chair. "If he's alive, find him and bring him back. You and yours have permission to travel through our lands for this task."

He dismissed us with a wave of his hand and motioned for Berrick to come to him. Another nearby guard showed us out. Once outside, we stopped as the guard gave us directions to the cabins.

"All right. So is everyone on the same page?" I asked.

"Yeah. Two lovebirds try to get away from their parents and end up nearly starting a war. Now why does this situation sound familiar to me?" Gil asked, dripping sarcasm.

I chuckled and drew my cloak closer to myself as my breath came in great puffs of fog. "Well, best bet is to check the cabins and see if the wolfmen missed anything, and if we find nothing, we camp there for the night and continue searching in the morning," I said.

"Sounds good," Mika replied, brushing some light snowfall from his hair. "It's going to be a cold one tonight, so I'd rather not get caught out in that if we can help it."

With nothing further to say, we set off in the direction the guard indicated.

It was supposed to be only an hour trek, so I was confident that we would make it and could have a good look around before nightfall came.

The cold air bashed against us as soon as we stepped outside the walls, a bracing, biting wind that chilled me to my core.

Even with the power of the Hive coursing through my veins, I can't fight this cold.

The hike was only made worse by the chill. It sapped our strength and made every step harder than the last. I fought down my fatigue and kept going.

Like hell I'm going to let a snowstorm get the best of me.

As we hiked, I paused. There was an uneasy atmosphere around us and a tickle on the back of my neck. I knew the feeling well, and it could only be one thing.

"We're being followed," I said softly.

"Yeah, caught wind of it myself just a moment ago too," Mika said. "My guess is wolfmen."

I nodded. "Either they're keeping an eye on us for Morn, or they're planning to cause some trouble."

Gil shrugged. "Probably, but not like either option is a good one. Think we should wait for them?"

"Hell, no. Let's set a trap for them. If they're playing it straight, we cut 'em loose. If not, we skin them alive," Yumiko said, with casual nonchalance.

I grinned at the plan. "Turnabout is fair play."

***

It took almost twenty minutes to find a good position to set our little ambush. We hid behind a brace of large boulders that had broken off of the mountain many years ago. They offered ample hiding space and gave us a good vantage point for the path.

Gil and Yumiko had gone with Raven to keep making tracks up the hill and then she'd shifted and flown them back to us.

Raven, Eris, and I were behind one boulder, while Gil, Mika, and Yumiko were behind the other. It gave us a good balance for team members and meant Eris and Yu could rain down death from both sides of the path at once. All in all, it was probably the best ambush we could've hoped for under the circumstances.

So, when we were in position, all we had to do was wait.

And we didn't have to wait long.

They came over the hill less than fifteen minutes later. Seven of them in total. All members of the Holste clan, but I recognized one of them. It was the nameless gate guard that had been with Berrick. He seemed to be the leader of the group, though the rest of the wolfmen were as unremarkable looking as their leader.

None of them seemed all that threatening, and I dismissed them as nothing but peons. They all wielded a mixture of weapons. All of them rusted and savage in their design. Effective tools for scaring weaker prey, but we were not weak prey.

"Hurry up, we're going to lose them at this rate," Nameless shouted.

"What's the rush? We know where they're going thanks to Berrick. We'll let them poke around the cabins and then ambush them when they come out. Cocky human scum. They don't belong here. Why Morn let them parade through our lands like they own the place is beyond me."

Interesting. They weren't sent by Morn, then. So that means they are going against him. Means we can kill them with impunity.

I smiled at the thought. *The amount of experience I'm going to get is insane.*

That thought gave me pause. And a sliver of cold that had nothing to do with the chill in the air crawled up my spine.

I'm not even concerned about killing them. I'm looking forward to it. That's not like me. It's like the Aspect is back influencing my thoughts again.

But that's impossible. The corrupted Aspect is gone. Which just leaves me.

I was excited by the prospect of killing because I'd grown used to the brutality of the Aspect and had even fed into it on multiple occasions.

I gritted my teeth and dug my fingernails into my palms. *Even after you're gone, you're still influencing me.*

Well, I won't let you.

I'm not a monster. Not anymore.

If only wishing made it so.

I was interrupted from my thoughts by a low whistle. The wolfmen were in position, and we were ready to go. If we were springing this ambush, it had to me now.

One quick whistle back later and we all sprang from our hiding places and surrounded them.

They froze at the suddenness, their animalistic instincts kicking in as they lowered to the ground and bared their weapons.

I didn't let them get into any kind of formation. I lunged forward, leaning into my thrust as I came at a young wolfman with rugged features and sharp blue eyes. My thrust took him in the chest. I pierced through his weak leather armor with ease, sliding through his heart and killing him.

A single kick and he went stumbling back. He slid himself off of my blade, and his dying body backpaddled into his friends.

They tried to dodge out of the way, but Gil and Mika were there to intercept them.

Mika drew his katana, and a crackling white light arced off the steel as he activated *Galvanic Slash*. He raised his blade overhead and brought it down on the nearest wolfman, who locked up as the electricity surged through his body. The electricity mattered little as Mika hewed a gash from the collar of the wolf to nearly his spine. Mika yanked his blade free with a heavy tug. It had likely gotten stuck on the dead man's spine. A rush of blood shot out as he pulled his blade out, but Mika sidestepped it, already preparing to engage another.

I joined the fray as Gil kept the others entertained with his gigantic axe. Not one of the wolves wished to get close to him as he swung wide, making them dance while he laughed.

One of them stepped back as Gil swung, and I intercepted him. I rushed forward, but the crunch of snow under my heel alerted him, his ears twitched, and he brought his hammer to block my sword.

My shadowsteel cut through the wood of his hammer with ease. The massive iron head dropped to the ground, landing on the clueless wolf's foot in the process.

He howled in pain as bones crunched. His eyes squinted as he fought back his pain and failed.

An arrow tore past and lodged itself in his throat before he could even shout.

I turned and found Eris glowing as she smiled at me. I smiled and turned back to the wolf with the vocal problem. I solved it by bringing my sword up and burying it halfway through his neck.

The wolfman fell and dripped crimson life over the disturbed snow.

The others quickly took care of the remaining wolfmen.

Raven and Gil teamed up to take out two of the wolves. Gil kept them at bay while Raven dropped down from above and slashed their throats with her vicious claws. They dropped to their knees, clutching at their ruined necks. Gill stepped forward and relieved them of their heads with two quick slices from his axe.

Yumiko picked off the straggler, the nameless guard from the gate, and just like our first fight against the wolfmen, we overwhelmed them.

As the fight was over, I pulled up my interface and checked my notifications.

Combat Results!
2 Killed (Wolfmen): 4600
Total Exp Gain: 4600
Level: 71
Exp: 7100/7100
Level Up!
10 Stat Points Available!

Level: 72
Exp: 3500/7200

I added all ten points to *Attack Damage*, bringing it up to sixty-five.

When I was done, all of us moved away from the corpses littering the ground and I leaned back against the boulder.

"I don't get it. That felt way too easy. The same with our first fight. These are supposed to be ruthless hunters, yet we're slaughtering them without any trouble." I shrugged. "What gives?"

Gil laughed and slapped me on the back. "We're a bunch of badasses. What do you expect?"

We all laughed, But Raven chimed in. "It was a funny joke, but I don't think he's off the mark. Not really." She held a hand up as she came to rest beside me.

Raven jumped up on top of the boulder and let her legs dangle on my shoulder. She pressed her ankle against me, and her red lips lifted in a half smile as she glanced at the others.

"For one, you are all strong. Near if not at max level. So that explains most of it." She grinned down at me. "You've also grown used to fighting alone, darling. Even before we met, it was just you and Eris against superior odds. When was the last time you fought in a well-coordinated party?"

"Huh?" I rubbed my chin, picking at a single thick beard hair that was bugging the hell out of me. "That's true, actually. And I'm betting it doesn't hurt that the wolfmen are cocky bastards. We ambushed them and they weren't prepared for it, but the first time they were overconfident, and we took them apart."

How long has it been since I fought with the others? It had to have been the elder dragon fight. I was on my own for most of the invasion. I've forgotten what teamwork feels like.

I'd missed working with the others. The Blade Master quest had been one of the hardest quests of my life until that point, but it had also been a blast; traveling with Gil, Levi, and Alistair as we tracked that storm dragon all across Nexus had been nothing but fun.

It's been a long time since I've had fun like this with my friends. We should enjoy it while it lasts. I have a feeling that with what's coming, we're going to be in for a lot of hard times in the near future.

I glanced at each of them. My friends, my family, and I smiled.

Should enjoy this while we have it.

Chapter 6 - Secrets Long Buried

The rest of the journey to the cabins Morn directed us to was, thankfully, free of any surprises. When we crested the hill, an amazing sight came into view.

Nestled in a small clearing, lay half a dozen small uniform cabins, all of them built the same and with the same materials. They were only slightly better constructed than most of the buildings back at Jole.

But the cabins weren't what stunned me.

Beyond them lay a drop-off, the sharp edge of a cliff.

I marched to the edge, ignoring the cabins for a singular moment while I stared at a view that rendered me speechless.

Miles below us lay the frigid, sparkling clear waters of the ocean, stretching as far as the eye could see and beyond. Sunlight turned the surface of the water to an ocean alight with flames, and I just basked in the pure, simple beauty for a long while.

It's breathtaking, but false. As real as this world is, I know what lies beyond that ocean blue.

Nothing. The end. A pitch-black void that will swallow this world whole.

There was nothing I could do to stop the incoming wave of disaster that threatened this world, but as Raven so often reminded me, I wasn't alone.

Edna or the gods would have some way to fix this. Magnus wasn't the only one with power in this world, and his method wasn't the only solution. I had to believe that, or I didn't think I could bear moving from that spot.

He wasn't taking Eris. There was no reality that would allow for that to happen.

I sighed and ran my hands through my hair, staring at the sight while Eris and Raven walked up beside me.

"It's beautiful, isn't it?" Eris asked.

"One of the most beautiful sights I've ever seen in this world or the one that came before." I turned to her and took her hand in mine. "But it pales next to your beauty." I grabbed Raven's hand and squeezed. "Or yours."

Both of them blushed at my compliment, and we stayed there for another few minutes before it was time to check the cabins with the others.

Gil, Mika, and Yumiko had started without us, taking one look at the sight and going back. I snorted as they left. *Guess I'm more of a sentimentalist than I thought.*

Five of the cabins were empty, holding nothing but a thick layer of dust. It was clear from the footprints that the wolfmen had been here recently, but they hadn't given the place more than a cursory search before giving up and going home.

We checked more thoroughly. The five cabins held no clues, but as we examined the sixth cabin, the largest of them, it was immediately clear that someone had been there recently, not just the wolfmen. The place was clean and the wooden walls and furniture were free of dust, like someone had been cleaning.

Though there were no other signs, and no belongings or clothing, I knew someone had been there.

"This is the place. Check everything," I said. "Someone was here recently. The bed's not even made."

From there, it didn't take us long to discover the trapdoor hidden under the dining room table.

I stood to the side, sword drawn as I opened it, just in case someone was waiting with a blade. I pulled it open and when nothing came flying out, I peered down into the dark.

A rough stone stairwell led deeper underground. I shook my head and looked at the others.

"Villains!" I shrieked. "Dissemble no more! I admit the deed! Tear up the planks! Here, here! It is the beating of his hideous heart!"

The others looked at me as if I was insane.

"Dude, did you really have to quote Poe right now?" Gil asked, shaking his head.

"What?" I shrugged. "It felt appropriate."

"If there's a bloody, beating heart down there, I will stab you," he replied and pulled out a torch and stared down the steps.

We followed Gil down, pulling out our own torches as we stepped deeper and deeper into the earth. The stairs curved, moving away from the edge of the cliff and heading deeper in.

The stairs went down for about a hundred feet. And I was guessing that whatever had been down here, had been buried for a long damn time.

As we got to the end there was a door made of stone. Carvings ran along the rock, detailing something. The words were written in Script, and I couldn't read it.

"What the hell is this place?" I muttered as we stepped closer.

"Not a fuckin' clue," Yumiko said as she walked up to me. "But this place is old, centuries old by the looks of it. I don't think this has anything to do with the two missing kids. This door is opened by blood magic."

I turned to her and raised an eyebrow. "Seriously?"

She scoffed and pointed to a word on the wall. "You think I fuckin' wouldn't recognize the word for blood? Of course, I'm fuckin' sure, you jackass."

I held up my hands, trying not to laugh at the vampire's outburst. Though she was quite touchy about the whole entire subject.

"So, what do we do about it? Think the kids are behind it?"

She shook her head. "Oh, hell no. As I said, this door has been here for a long time. And I have no idea how to open it, except that it requires blood. No way a bunch of kids are hiding out here."

Shit. This is complicated. What do we do?

There was a reason we were here; no way this just a coincidence, but we were hired to find two missing kids, not investigate strange ruins.

"I think this could be a dungeon," Yumiko said, staring at the wall intently. She tapped another word. "This is the word for cage, or prison. Which could also be translated to dungeon.

"Yeah. That makes sense. This is a dungeon."

I whistled. Long and slow.

"By the nine kings of hell."

"You're telling me," Gil said, rubbing his bald head. "Most of the dungeons have been claimed by the Alliance, and the Cardinals routinely clear them. I've never heard mention of a dungeon this far north."

"That's because no one has entered this dungeon in over eight hundred years," a voice said, echoing through the stairwell.

Footsteps sounded against stone in rhythmic descension. Slow, methodical. Each step sent a tinge of fear through me. Because I knew the voice, and I was furious at being played by her.

"There's no missing children, are there?" I asked loudly.

"Oh, they're very much missing," Morgan said, walking down the steps to join us in the small stone hallway. "They're just not here."

"Godsdamn it, Morgan. Why the ruse? Why lie to get us here?"

"Because it was the easiest and most direct method to get you to do what I wanted." Her smile deepened. "And I didn't necessarily lie. Both children of the clans are missing, and the two races will turn on each other soon if they aren't returned."

I threw my hands up. "So you had something to do with them disappearing? Why? And why lie to get us here? What do you want from us?"

She chuckled as she walked toward us.

Morgan smiled at me, and her eyes flashed. For a second they turned solid black, her pale features elongating, turning sharp as tar bled through her fiery locks, staining them midnight.

For a single split second, she bared her true form to us, as the goddess she was.

Her eyes were as black as Eris's, but soulless, empty. They terrified me.

Then she took a single step, and the illusion vanished. She slid me a wink as she walked to me, and I fought the urge to shiver.

"All excellent questions. With simple answers. I am going to need the clans very soon, and they are going to have to be able to work together." She paused and tapped a finger on her lips. "Now I can't directly force them to work for me, so I created a problem for them and then solved it, with your help as my emissary. Thus, putting them in my debt and feeling gracious enough to be willing to agree to whatever I ask of them in the future."

"That's cold, callous, and calculating...and ingenious." I sighed and shrugged. "Something I'm not even surprised about coming from you. But why lie to us? You could've told me the truth."

Morgan laughed and shook her head. "No, I couldn't. You" —she held her arms up and looked up, trying to remember something— "What's the phrase you humans are so fond of using? Ah! Yes. You have a terrible poker face."

She slipped past me and started walking slowly toward the door.

"And besides, I couldn't guarantee that someone wasn't listening in on us. Or that the bar owner wasn't a spy for our enemy. The deception was necessary. I've been planning this for months. I wasn't going to let an errant slip of the tongue ruin everything."

I exhaled, long and slow. And then took several deep breaths so I wouldn't lash out at her on principle.

I'd have done the same thing. I'm just pissed it happened to me. Get over it.

"Okay." I nodded. "Yeah. I get it. So why don't you tell us why we're really here?"

"First things first." She turned and glanced back at me and waved her hand. "I hope this is adequate compensation for tricking you."

Quest: Mediation Completed!
Prevent a war between the wolfmen and rabbitmen clans
Type: Unique
Difficulty: A
Reward: 35000 Exp!

"And both children will be returned to their families without a scratch on them. They're already on their way back, both with similar enough stories that paint your little group in a very positive light and also reinforce their eventual gratitude to me."

She pointed a long slender finger at the door, her wicked black fingernail resembling a talon. "And at the beginning, I promised you power, and I intend to keep my word."

She placed a hand on the stone door, and the rock shivered, almost recoiling at her touch.

"Behold, the Nymirian Dungeon."

I blinked and scratched my head. "The Nymirian Dungeon is nestled in the Badlands. There's no way it reaches all the way to here."

"Oh, but it does. The Nymirian Dungeon is actually quite a bit larger than most of you humans give it credit for. Though this portion has been sequestered away. It was hidden for a reason, and no one has set foot down there for a great many years."

I stared at the stone door that required blood, and a lump of dread filled my gullet. Dungeons were not to be trifled with. They were monster and trap-infested, designed solely to kill those who entered, even though they were always filled with riches beyond measure. An unexplored dungeon would have to guard a great prize indeed.

But is it worth risking our lives for? The treasure I couldn't care less about. I have more than enough gold. But I need more power. I need the power to defeat Magnus.

It's a risk to delve the dungeon, but it's certain death to face Magnus at half strength.

I don't think we have a choice here.

"All right, we'll go in," I said, turning to Morgan. "But no way is holding up your end of the bargain the reason we're here. What's down there that has you so invested?"

She chuckled and leaned against the wall, crossing her arms. "Can't I just be helpful?"

"Not a chance, so spill."

"So cynical." She laughed, giving me an approving smile. "There is more than one power down in the depths of the dungeon. Power for you and your bonded…and for me."

"We both grow stronger, eh?"

"Precisely." Her green eyes sparkled with wicked intent.

As much as I found myself liking Morgan, I needed to keep in mind that she was a goddess, a being with incredible power and someone not to be trifled with.

I nodded to her. "So how do we open the door?"

Morgan motioned to Eris. "With her blood, the blood of the Hive Queen." She quickly held up a hand as my eyes widened. "Just a few drops, nothing more."

"Okay." I turned to the others.

This wasn't just my call; a dungeon raid was a team effort. "All right, looks like we got set up for a dungeon crawl. It's not what we signed up for, so anyone who doesn't want to enter can stay behind."

Gil laughed. "You know me, always down for running a dungeon. It's been too long since we've cleared one. No way am I missing exploring a brand-new dungeon. I'm in."

I laughed and held my fist up. "Well, as raid leader, I expect nothing less. You're in charge while we're down there."

He nodded. "Course." Gil looked at the others. "As Sam said. Anyone wants to bow out, now's your chance."

"Hurry up and open the fuckin' door. I'd like to know what the hell we're walking into," Yumiko said. "Oh yeah, and good fucking luck having two archers in a godsdamn dungeon. Tight corners and little to no open space. I'm going to be fucking useless." She thumbed back to Eris. "So will Eris, although she's got a few close-range tricks now. Leaves me with my thumb up my ass for this excursion."

"You'll be in charge of carrying all the loot we pick up," I said with a cheeky smile.

Yumiko glared death at me, flashing her sharp fangs. "I will drain you dry."

"Oh, bite me." I winked at her. "But seriously. Don't worry about it. You still have your blood magic, right?"

She looked away, her shoulders sagging. "I'd prefer not to use that if I can help it…but if our lives are in danger, you can count on me."

With her and Gil on board, that just left Raven and Mika. I looked to them. "You guys down?"

"Hell yeah," Mika said.

"I've already followed you into the dark once before. Another time or two won't be any different." Raven gave me a kind smile as she finished speaking.

All right, let's get a move on then.

Morgan smiled. "If you will, Eris. Just touch your finger to the door."

Eris nodded and walked over to the door. I gave her hand a squeeze as she walked past me.

She reached out and touched the stone, her fingers trembling slightly as she did so. As soon as her hand touched the stone, she sucked in a breath. Her inhalation was audible in the small chamber.

At first nothing happened, then the door shifted slightly, warping like it was malleable. Then it grew still.

"Ow! By the void," Eris hissed, yanking her hand back.

A thick trickle of blood ran down her pale finger to drip to the ground. She stuck it in her mouth and then fanned her hand.

"That hurt."

I grabbed a potion from my inventory and let her have a small sip. As she handed it back, the door shuddered once more and started moving.

It descended, opening up to reveal another stairwell that continued even deeper into the earth.

"Who wants to go down the creepy tunnel first?" Gill asked, peering down into the darkness.

"I believe that honor falls to you as raid leader, bud," I replied with a chuckle and a wry grin.

"Fuck."

Gil grabbed a torch and potion from his inventory. "Torch or cat's eye?"

"I say go torch," Mika chimed in. "We can always switch to cat's eye later, but if there's a light source, then we'll have burned a potion for nothing."

"He's right. We can't risk potion sickness down there, not when we have no idea what's waiting for us."

"Torch it is, then." Gil stored his potion away and lit his torch. Even more light filled the cramped tunnel, and Gil started down the stairs.

"Good luck. I'll see you all when you reach the end of the dungeon," Morgan said and then vanished.

"Bitch can't even help us clear the dungeon but expects to take a portion of the reward. Now tell me what kind of fucking sense that makes," Yumiko grumbled to herself, following after Gil.

I went in after Yu, with Raven and Eris next while Mika brought up the rear.

It was a standard formation for a dungeon raid, although our party most certainly wasn't optimized.

Really wish Levi or Behemoth were here. We could use a tank right about now.

And so down we went, into the deep.

The stairs continued for a long time, at least fifteen minutes, and when we finally reached the end, it opened into a long hallway.

The stone differed here. Instead of the gray rock of the mountains, it was the tan of sandstone.

"Guess this is the official start of the dungeon," Gil said. "Let's see what it's got in store for us."

He walked slowly, each stride purposeful and precise. He only made it a few feet before he crouched.

"That didn't take long."

Gil stepped back, grabbing his axe. He pressed the handle to the tiled floor. Air whooshed loudly next to him, followed by the clink of metal.

We all followed the sound and found six arrows buried an inch into the wall on the opposite side.

"Traps, this early on." I sighed. "This is going to be a pain in the ass."

"You're not the one who's going to trigger them, so keep your complaints to yourself," Gil shot back.

From there it was slow going, because we had to check every tile for traps. Which took time. There were three more arrow traps in that hallway alone, but nothing more as we reached the wooden door at the other end.

"Ten to one odds the door's rigged," Mika said, poking his head around.

"Yeah, my money's on trapped, too." Gil shook his head. "Why couldn't Wilson be the one here? He loves disarming traps."

"Because someone had to stay and run the guild. We still have bounties on our heads, if you've forgotten, so let's hurry up and clear this dungeon. I don't like leaving the guild for so long," I said.

"Yeah, yeah."

Gil checked the door over and gave the thumbs up; it wasn't trapped. He pushed open the handle and was about to take a step when there was the snap of string.

A giant blade fell from the ceiling and embedded itself half an inch from Gil's foot.

"Holy fuck!" he shouted and jumped back. "I hate this dungeon!"

I had to agree. It wasn't uncommon for dungeons to be trapped, but this was going overboard, and it was the first level. Which was supposed to be the easiest.

If this dungeon held to logic, then it was setting out to be one of the hardest dungeons on Nexus.

And we had to clear it.

Hurray.

Gil kicked the blade aside, and we all entered the first room.

It was a rough square with a high ceiling that was lined with holes. The walls were also lined with holes, but the floor was not.

There was nothing else in the room but the door on the far side of the room.

"Spikes in the walls and ceilings?" Gil asked.

"That would be my guess," Yumiko said.

"Flip a coin to see who goes first?"

I raised my hand. "I'll do it." I smiled. "Don't want another axe to fall on you."

Though I enjoyed our banter, my smile quickly fell as I surveyed the room, trying to discern any pattern or pathway that would lead us to safety without getting shish kebabbed by the inevitable spikes in the floor.

The first step in a trapped room was always the worst, I moved slowly, crouched low to the ground as I walked. I checked over every inch of the floor as I went along.

But the good thing about pressure plates is that there was a weight limit. It was usually only a pound or two, which would instantly break if someone put all their weight on it. But if a person was careful, it was quite easy to tell which tiles were the loaded ones because there was just a little give to them.

I ended up on my hands and knees as I worked. And I'm sure I looked a little silly, but I'd rather look foolish than get impaled by spikes.

My fingers glided lightly over the stones, searching each one until I found the ones that didn't move. It was a highly tedious process, but the alternative was a very painful death.

It took about half an hour for me to clear the room, and by the end, I was dripping sweat, and my wrists and knees ached something fierce.

Once I reached the end, I checked the door for traps like Gil had done before, but this time, I took a pinch of flour into my palm and blew it in a fine mist over the door.

It cascaded down and revealed nothing to me so I assumed the door wasn't trapped and slowly opened it.

Another gloomy stairwell met me as the door slowly creaked open, but no blade descended from the ceiling to cut me in half.

I turned back to the others and slowly guided them through.

When we were all in the stairwell, Gil took point again.

He had the most experience with dungeons, but it wasn't fair for him to take all the risk, so whenever he and I delved together, we always split who cleared the rooms.

Though Mika is with us this time. We could probably rotate between all three of us.

If the dungeon dragged on for longer than I was expecting, then that is absolutely what I would do. But until then it would be just me and Gil who took turns.

This stairwell was a bit shorter than the first, and we came to another door.

"Get ready, guys," Gil said as he checked over the door for more traps.

It was going to get really annoying if this was entirely a trap dungeon. Though I'd never encountered one that was solely traps.

The door opened, and Gil cursed.

"What?" I asked.

"Drakelings, a lot of them."

"Silver or black?"

"Black."

I nodded. "Good, that makes this a lot easier."

Gil whirled around, shocked. "The hell you going on about, Sam? Black drakelings are highly venomous. One bite is lethal without antidote."

I grinned. "It's a good thing Eris and I are immune to all poisons and venoms...well, she is. I'm mostly immune." I looked back at her and winked. "I'd rather not get bit, though."

"Yeah, not while we have company present at any rate," she said, a faint blush to her cheeks as she came to stand beside me. "But Sam is right; the two of us stand the best chance to clear them out without suffering any casualties."

"Anyone got any antidotes? I didn't think to bring any since I can't be killed by them, but I really don't want the side effects right now."

"Take some of mine," Mika said, throwing a bottle my way.

I stowed it away and took Gil's place with Eris as the door opened.

"You ready for this?" I asked.

"Of course, my bonded."

I drew my sword, and the two of us rushed inside.

The room was darker than the previous one, and there were no tiles. It was plain rock, which likely meant there weren't any traps.

There were, however, a lot of Drakelings. Nearly fifteen of them.

They were long, reptilian creatures with thick black scales that extended all the way to their tails. Their bright yellow eyes flashed as torches instantly lit as we stepped into the room.

A sibilant hiss sounded from each of them as they took notice of us.

"Let's do this."

I activated *Hive Mind* and willed my chitin to form to my command. It encased me in thick armor, and I surged forward.

The first of the drakelings crouched and jumped at me. Its vicious fangs dripping poison as it sailed through the air.

I stopped, grounded my stance, and brought my blade in a sideways arc. Steel met scale, and my sword bit deep, slicing the drakeling's head off in one fluid strike.

Brackish, dark blue blood splashed out in an arc as the head hit the ground with a sickening wet squelch. I stepped to the side to avoid the mess of blood and engaged a second monster.

They were fast on the ground, agile and elusive, but they had a propensity to leap at their prey, which left them vulnerable when in the air.

Even in the Ouroboros project, Isaac Newton was a motherfucker.

The second beast jumped; its mouth unhinged as it leapt at me. An arrow from Eris took it through the mouth. The force of the arrow slowed the momentum of the drakeling. I caught it with the arrow still lodged in its mouth and yanked the shaft free with my left hand. With my right hand gripping its throat, I squeezed. My chitin encased fingers tore through its scales as I ripped out its throat.

I turned and hurled the dying lizard at a group of its friends who were circling around me. As they all dodged in different directions, I threw the arrow like a miniature spear and pieced one of the drakelings in the head, killing it instantly.

"Make sure to retrieve that when we're done, love." Eris fired at another drakeling, killing it. "I can't regenerate my chitin."

"I promise." I smiled and curb stomped one of the small drakelings as it attempted to bite through my leg.

The others were easy to dispatch since they couldn't get through our armor to harm us. It was basically child's play. Eris and I picked them off with ease.

"Ready?" I asked.

"Pull."

I tossed the squirming drakeling into the air. It hissed in defiant rage before Eris's arrow stuck it in the belly. She'd angled the shot nicely, and it had nicked its heart. A gush of blood poured from it as it died.

"Your turn," she said laughing.

"All right, but make sure you pick a good one."

We took turns killing them, and though we did take longer clearing the room than Gil or the others might have wanted, I hadn't had so much simple fun in a very long time.

Eris and I enjoyed ourselves while we slaughtered a room full of lethal, venom-filled monsters who wanted nothing more than to rip us to pieces.

When they were all dead, I sagged back and heaved a sigh of exhaustion as I let my chitin fade.

"I'll go get the others. You grab a drink."

"Don't have to tell me twice," I replied and sat down, leaning back against the wall.

I tried to pull my flask of whiskey out, but I was met with nothing but air.

Oh, right, I'm giving up drinking. No matter how many times I had to remind myself, I couldn't stop the wave of disappointment that came over me each time.

Damn it. Quitting fucking sucks. Instead I grabbed a flask of spring water. The rabbitmen had a nice spring in the mountains, and they swore that it was the best water I'd ever taste.

And I had to admit it was. It was so pure and clean and I drank my fill but it wasn't whiskey.

Best get used to it; not going to change.

Once I had realized I had a problem, I couldn't go back, no matter how much I wanted to. I was trying to better myself, and it started by cutting out alcohol.

I put the water away as the others walked into the room and whistled.

"Damn, the hell'd you two do in here, have a fuckin' finger painting class? Make some abstract art? Picasso would have a raging orgasm if he stepped in here. Just look at all the blood!"

I laughed. "Sorry about that. We might've gone overboard a bit."

"A bit. I'm standing in an inch of drakeling blood over here," Mika said, a look of incredulity on his face.

Gil jutted his chin towards the door. "What's beyond it?"

I shrugged. "Not a clue, was waiting for you. Plus, I'm catching my breath. Breaks are healthy when clearing dungeons, you know."

"I'd heard that somewhere." He chuckled and went over to the door at the far end of the room.

We'd tried to keep the mess away from the door in case it was trapped, but a few splashes of blue marred the wooden door.

Gil opened it carefully after checking for traps and grinned. "Least it's not another stairwell." He raised his hand toward the door. "Got a long hallway instead."

"Traps?"

He sighed. "Probably. Have I mentioned how much I hate this dungeon?"

"Yeah, we know." Mika laughed. "You want me to have a go? Not fair to make the two of you do all the work."

I'd already had the idea, but it wasn't just my call.

"Gil?" I asked.

"Why not? Let's let the noob get some practice in."

"I'm only a noob in comparison to the guild. I know for a fact that I've died fewer times than our fearless guild leader over there."

I laughed. "Shut it, unless you want me to change that number for you."

He chuckled. "You wouldn't dare, not since we can't respawn anymore. That'd mean the end of this beautiful mug for the rest of eternity. I don't think you could cope."

His tone may have been jovial, but it stirred too much darkness, brought up too many negative thoughts for me to laugh it off.

We're down to one life left, and here we are delving an unknown dungeon. This isn't a time for laughter and games.

Though they made my heart swell with contentment, I couldn't afford to relax and forget that this wasn't a game anymore. It had never been that for me, but especially now. None of us could afford to let ourselves slip up.

I stood and wiped my monster blood covered hands on my black cotton pants. "Let's get a move on. Mika, you're lead for this section. Don't play the hero and do something foolish. Stay safe above all else. Understood?"

He sobered immediately. "Yes, guild leader."

"Good."

He took off down the hallway, careful of traps, but after several long moments of crouching low to the ground, he turned back, shaking his head.

"No traps that I can see. I'll keep to high alert as lookout as I go forward, but my gut is telling me that this section is clear."

It made sense. If the traps hadn't gotten us this far, it would be a mistake to keep laying them as thick as they were, but that didn't mean they wouldn't appear again at some point. We would still have to stay alert every step of the way which slowed our progress considerably.

Once Mika cleared the hallway, we proceeded. We all bunched together at the entrance to the next room while Gil checked it over. When it was clear that there were no traps on the door, Gil opened it.

A rush of cold air engulfed us as the wooden door slammed wide open against the rock, and we stepped inside. Heavy gray stone rose on both sides as we filed through the door. It continued in a narrow corridor before it opened about twenty feet away. Though there were no torches along the walls, light came from ahead of us and allowed us to navigate.

As we slowly moved forward still tightly bunched together, the heavy foreboding that lingered in the air settled deep in my chest. As we reached the end of the hall, it opened into an enormous cavern easily a hundred feet high and wide. It was so large and dark that I couldn't tell where it ended.

As soon as we all stepped out of the hallway, there was a tug in my chest, like my heart was yanked forward an inch. It sucked the breath from me and nearly floored me.

I shook it off and turned to the others, who were in similar straits. All of them wore pained expressions on their faces except for Eris. She had a look of lazy contentment on hers.

"That was rather pleasant," she muttered before looking up at me, her smile faltering as she noticed my pained expression. "What's wrong?"

"I'm fine," I replied.

Eris opened her mouth to respond, but before she could, there was another rush of air, but this time it came from behind us. It rolled through the cavern, and with it came light. Hundreds of torches lit up one by one along the walls and from down below us.

We all peered over the edge and gasped.

Below us lay an expansive stone maze, stretching from one end of the corridor to the next. It was tall, winding, and the howls of monsters rose from its unfathomed depths.

The very air around us grew cold as we took in the monstrous labyrinth.

"So," Gil began. "Who's going first?"

Chapter 7 - The Maze

Staring down at the maze was terrifying. The previous warmth that had filled my chest vanished in the face of such oppressiveness. For some reason, the maze called to me, but I didn't want to answer. It reeked of malice and deception.

Its very construction was a warning to those who looked upon it. I wanted nothing to do with it. But that wasn't my call to make.

I chose to be here, chose to stand by his side. That means I don't get to run just because I don't like the look of the place. I have to stay and fight, no matter what.

The others glanced around, and Gil, being his usual self, broke the tension with a joke.

I chuckled. "Not me."

Sam frowned. "I'll go first." He turned to me. "Any other volunteers?"

My hand rose on its own, despite my desire to stay where I was. I had to have the resolve to fight, or I could never truly call myself queen.

Mother holds the title of queen, and the mantle is shared by both of us, but I can't let her and Magnus win. Even if she is my mother, I will not let her take the title of queen from me. Not when she was the reason for our people's destruction.

The fate of the Hive was sealed, but if I was to be the final queen of the Hive, I would do everything in my power to make sure mine was an honorable rule, even if there were few left for me to govern.

Sam smiled down at me when I raised my hand. "Glad to have you on board." He turned to the others. "Guess Eris and I will check out the maze and come back. I don't like that idea of just the two of us traversing the maze by ourselves, so we should travel in groups."

To our right were a set of steps leading down to the entrance of the maze. They were carved from the rock that surrounded us, as was the maze itself.

We descended down the steps, only to be greeted by another door like the one to the entrance of the dungeon itself. It sat waiting for my blood.

"Guess I know what I have to do." I walked up to the door and pressed my hand to it.

As soon as my flesh touched the cold, coarse stone, there was another jab, and my blood smeared across the rock. I bit back a shout and dealt with the pain.

When my blood touched the rock, it shifted, forming words along the stone. As they appeared, I knew at once what they said, but Sam stepped forward and scratched his head.

"I can't read that. Do you know what it says?"

I nodded. "It's Entoma, the language of entomancers. It says that this is a trial for the monarch of the Hive…that others are not permitted to undertake the trial."

"Trial? What trial?"

"I don't know, but I can't have any companions with me while I undertake whatever it is. It'll be just me in there."

Sam cursed. His mouth set in a hard line that quickly turned to a frown, he shook his head. "Then we don't take the trial. We abandon the quest, go home…" he trailed off, knowing as well as I did that we couldn't just leave.

There was only one option available to us; I had to take the trial because we both knew what loomed over our heads.

"I'm going in." I grabbed Sam's hand and pulled him down for a soft kiss. I held his lips with mine for a long moment, pouring how much I loved him into my kiss. "I love you, Sam. For now, until eternity."

I wasn't saying goodbye, just letting him know for the thousandth time how much he meant to me. *If this is a trial, then it means to test me. Which means I could die. Which means I need to prepare for that eventuality.*

It wasn't hard. The specter of death had been looming over my shoulder ever since Magnus had told me he needed my life to save the world.

"Love you too, Eris…be careful and give the trial hell for me."

"I promise."

With our parting words, there was nothing left to say, and I turned to go in.

My heart pounded in my chest as I walked into the maze of stone. A soon as I crossed an invisible threshold, the stone door rose up and sealed me off from the outside world.

Well, I guess this is it.

Rock torch sconces sat above me, lining the walls. They flared to life with a roar of flames; the cackling spark writhed as if angry, casting twisting shade along the floor.

I sighed, quieting my racing heart, and took a single step, ready to face this maze by myself.

There was a rush of wind and the flapping of feathers. And a new shadow appeared over me.

She dropped from the sky, letting her raven-black wings shift back into her skin.

"What are you doing here?" I shouted.

Raven turned to me with a smile. "Didn't think I'd let you go alone, did you?" She peered up at the top of the maze. "Well, now that I know that it worked, just stay right there, I'll go grab the others."

Her self-assured grin and fiery attitude made my heart swell. As she shifted to her bird form, I stepped back and gave her plenty of room. My back hit the stone entrance, and a wave of chills crawled up my spine.

Raven took off into the sky, only to fly headfirst into a shimmering clear dome. She slammed into it at speed, and there was the sound of cracking glass as the barrier shimmered with a pulsating blue light. A crack appeared where she'd struck.

Even as I stared at the crack, the blue light flared up over the damage, and in the blink of an eye, it disappeared.

As Raven hit the dome, she rebounded with a high-pitched shriek of pain, locking up as she fell back to the ground. She automatically shifted to her human form and lay in a crumpled heap on the ground, blood pooling from a severe gash in her arm. It was broken from what I could tell, and the bone sticking out from her skin. I quickly took off my pack and pulled out a health potion.

I ran over to her and shifted her onto my lap. Her breathing was ragged, and her eyes were closed. I forced open her mouth and slowly poured the red liquid down her throat. She swallowed, and bit by bit, I gave her the entire vial.

Almost immediately some color returned to her place cheeks, and her arm stitched itself back together. When the damage to her body had been healed, she opened her eyes. They were bleary, unfocused.

"That was painful."

"And very stupid of you. Why didn't you stay with the others where it was safe?"

"Because I wasn't going to let you take this trial alone. I love you just as much as I love Sam, and I couldn't sit still and do nothing. Was going to grab Sam next, but it seems the maze won't let us cheat again."

I cradled her head against my chest and wrapped my arms around her, trying not to cry. "I'm glad you're here with me. I didn't want to admit it to Sam, but I'm terrified."

She sat up, kissing me softly once before she stood, and her claws elongated. "Well, let's kick this maze's ass and get back to everyone." Raven tensed up, staring down the long hallway. "Though neither of us are really meant for close combat. Huh. Well shit."

I stood behind her and reached into the Hive Mind, pulling at the chitin buried under my skin. I willed it to form and let it cover me from head to toe.

"No, we're not. But I don't think we're exactly being given a choice here."

Since my bow was going to be useless in the confined spaces, I summoned two long daggers in my hands. Sam had been teaching me martial arts, and both he and Raven had taught me knife fighting. I was only so-so with either of them, but it would have to be enough.

I handed one of my knives to Raven. "Here, you can use this."

She nodded. "Decent blade." She held it in her palm, checking the weight. "It's balanced perfectly, so I can throw it, too, if need be."

"Good, then let's get going. I want to find out what this place has in store for us."

The two of use crept forward as quietly as we could, though it was a wasted practice. The hallway we came to was empty. It was a T junction, two paths, one right, the other left.

"Which way do we go?" Raven asked. "Left? I think we should go left."

"Hold up." I crouched. Pushing my consciousness out as I opened myself to my magic, I searched for any of my little ones that might be lurking around. Hiding in the small places of the world. "Let me see if I can find out the correct route with my insects."

Raven shuddered; she, like Sam, didn't exactly enjoy my little ones.

I smiled at her and pushed my mind out as far as it could go but there was nothing.

Not a single insect or spider could be found within my radius, which was impossible. I'd never encountered a place that didn't have at least a few insects. But it was like this place was entirely void of them.

Not one insect in a maze built for the Hive. Is this part of the trial? It had to be, but I had no idea how it could keep out the insects.

Maybe that barrier keeps them out? That makes sense. But it doesn't help me in the least.

Regardless of the barrier or the fact that we were walking into this essentially blind, I had to continue. Had to see this through.

Something was tugging at my head, an innate desire to keep going forward. Deep down, there was something that wanted me to undertake this trial, needed me to undertake it.

The two of us started down the left-hand path, the smooth walls stretching out ahead of us before it veered sharply right.

"Let's keep our eyes peeled, eh Eris?" Raven said. "I'm betting this hallway isn't just a hallway."

I nodded. Considering the rest of the traps in the place, it made sense. I wasn't adept at ferreting them out like Sam and Gil but I did have one advantage over Raven—my chitin.

"Just stay behind me. My armor should hold up under all but the most severe of traps, so I don't want you getting hurt when I can take the brunt of the damage."

"True, but I'm betting my eyes are better than yours."

She grunted in pain, and I turned to face her. Raven's eyes had changed from the solid blood red to the beady eyes of her bird form. They stared at me, unblinking.

"I didn't know you could do that," I said.

"Yeah, well. It hurts like a bitch and gives me a massive migraine after a while, so I don't like using it too often, but it beats getting impaled by a random trap we didn't see coming."

"All right, we'll both keep an eye out. I protect you, and you protect me."

She flashed me a fierce grin. "Deal."

We both kept going, keeping low to the ground, our movements precise as we searched for traps along the floor and walls.

After twenty feet of this, we were only halfway down the corridor and hadn't discovered a single trap. I was starting to get tired of staying so low. It put pressure on my knees, and they began to ache.

From my few furtive glances at Raven, she wasn't having too much fun either.

I was about to speak up and suggest quickening our pace when scratching came from overhead. I looked up to see shadows shifting and twisting on the ceiling above us.

Almost as if they sensed my gaze, fifty pairs of eyes opened at once.

Air whistled as streaks shot toward us at breakneck speed.

"Look out!" I screamed and threw myself at Raven, tackling her at the waist and taking her to the ground.

I landed atop her as jagged shards of rock rained all around us. Sharp, vicious pain flared to life on my side and my leg, and I fought to keep from crying out.

As soon as the barrage ended. I rolled off Raven and stood, agony burning up my legs as they shook with fatigue.

"You okay?" she asked, not looking at me.

"Just…great" I huffed, trying to catch my breath.

Raven glanced over at me, her eyes widening in shock. "You're bleeding!"

I shook my head. "Doesn't matter now. Here they come."

Whatever the creatures were that attacked us, they dropped from the ceiling in front and behind of us.

They were small gray beasts about the size of cats. Their thin bodies resembled rock and seemed just as craggy and impenetrable. Six long, spindly legs scuttled on the ground while a long tail rose from their backs.

As I got a better look at them, I realized I knew them. I'd just never seen them before.

"What the hell are these things?" Raven shouted.

"Rock scorpions!"

They were vicious monsters that only vaguely had anything to do with the creatures they resembled.

The scorpions were created by a entomancer mage centuries before I was ever born. They were meant to be mindless golems, but they were made with mana-infused rock and took on a mind of their own. They were a plague and could multiply as long as they were near rock and there was mana in their surroundings.

What are they doing here? Mother told me they were eradicated ages ago.

Having them be here was terrifying because I didn't know how to fight them. I vaguely remembered the stories but trying to remember a bedtime story in the middle of battle was far more difficult than I'd imagined.

"Don't let them swarm you. Take to the air."

Raven didn't argue and sprouted her black wings once more. She rose just off the ground but stayed far away from the glowing translucent barrier overhead.

She swept her wings out in front of her, using her feathers as throwing knives. They flew through the air and sank deep into the scorpions' stone carapaces but did nothing. Not a single scorpion dropped from her volley.

"Shit!" she cursed, floating toward me. "Grab hold!"

She held her arm outstretched and lowered, flapping her wings urgently as she flew lower to the ground. I leapt into the air and took her hand. I was jerked off the ground just as the mass of scorpions converged on where I'd been seconds before.

Raven flew as high as she could without slamming against the barrier. When we reached the peak, we stopped and hovered. I held onto Raven as tightly as I could while I stared down at the creatures; their many eyes remained locked on us.

We're not safe yet!

"Move!"

To her credit, she didn't hesitate and flew to the side as more shards of rock projectiles flew past us. They slammed into the barrier and shattered on impact, sending shards of rock and dust raining back to the ground.

I had to do something. There was nothing Raven could do to harm them, and this was a test for the Hive Queen. Which meant there had to be a way to win. I just had to figure it out.

"How long can you fly and hold me?"

"Not long." Raven grunted and shifted to get a better grip on me. "No offense, sunflower, but you're very heavy. And I'm not strong enough to hold you for long."

I nodded. "Can you hold me for two minutes?"

"Guess we'll find out."

Before she finished speaking, I let my chitin armor fade under my skin and entered the Hive Mind at the same time.

It'd been a while since I'd delved into the mind. After I'd gotten my weapons, I hadn't really spent much time there. And that was my fault. I should've been strengthening myself and exploring, but even now, my mana wasn't strong enough for extended forays.

The warm emerald smoke swirled around me as I submerged myself into the whirling vortex that was the Hive Mind.

"Greetings, my queen. How may I assist you today?" my Aspect asked.

"Rock scorpions. I need to know how to defeat them!"

"Right away, my queen."

There was a tug on my soul, and I was pulled deeper into the mind. Almost immediately, the drain on my mana was palpable. Flashes and whispers from the shades of the past drifted past my ear, whispering long-forgotten words and secrets to me. Things I had no use for at the time. The only thing I needed was knowledge about how to beat my current foe; I didn't have the strength to stay longer than that.

But as I went deeper, my strength weakened until even keeping my eyes open was a challenge. Deeper and deeper I slipped, until at last I slowed and came to a stop. In front of me was a fragment of a memory.

It was of people that I'd never seen before, but they were clearly entomancers. One had silver eyes, while the female had eyes as black as mine but with a crimson shine to the glossy black.

Both of them stood over a rock scorpion body. Along its back was a deep crack, and the hollow insides were visible. Inside the fissure was a small glowing blue stone. A mana stone.

That's right! Adam told me that all constructs either need a mage to supply the mana or a mana stone embedded in their bodies.

He'd told me while standing at the entrance to the loot room in castle Gloom Harbor. Standing on either side of the entrance were two crystalline golems that Adam had built. He spoke with nothing but pride in his voice while he told me the complex process he'd gone through to build them.

I didn't much care about them, but I very much cared about Adam, and after Evelyn's death, I'd been trying to spend more time with him to help keep his mind off losing his sister.

A wave of fatigue came over me and snapped me out of my thoughts. I was running out of mana, and I'd found the information I needed.

I hastily exited the Hive Mind; my consciousness was being tugged out rapidly. I snapped back into my body and my limbs shook with fatigue. *Need a mana potion.*

But my needs would have to wait. Raven struggled to keep us airborne. She dipped, her arms trembling with strain.

"Raven, fly back to the entrance and set us down. I know how to beat them!"

"Gotcha!"

She dropped, angling away from the numerous beasts and flew back to the start of the maze. When we were back, she set us down, and I quickly pulled out a mana potion. I greedily drank the contents to ease my shaking body. I wiped the mass of sweat from my forehead before it dripped into my eyes then quickly tied my thick hair back.

The both of us had to get ready. They were coming.

"They have cores in the center of their bodies. We'll need to pierce them to destroy them."

Raven turned to me with eyes wide. "They're made of stone, though. How are we supposed to do that?"

"Quick, hand me back my chitin dagger."

She did so immediately, tossing me the dagger. As soon as it touched my skin, I absorbed it along with the one I'd made for myself. They just wouldn't cut it.

In my vision I'd seen a weapon in the hands of the male who'd brought back the rock scorpion. It was a twisting cylindrical knife meant for puncturing. All I had to do was copy it from memory and will my chitin to form to its shape.

Glossy black ink pooled into my hands and I reconstructed what I'd seen. Two wicked black daggers came to life in my hands. Both of them like a corkscrew that looked strong enough to even pierce through rock.

I handed one to Raven as scuttling echoed off the walls. They were nearly on us.

"Get ready! Here they come. Remember to stab the center of their bodies."

As the first of them rounded the corner, we raced down the hall to meet them. I reached them first and stabbed downward with all my might. My chitin blade struck rock, and heavy vibrations radiated up my arm. For a second I feared it wouldn't be enough to penetrate, but as soon as I struck, the rock gave way and splintered under my attack.

The blade sank deep into the rock scorpion and struck the glowing mana stone within the beast. There was a sharp crack, and the stone shattered like glass, releasing a thick tendril of blue vapor. It rushed across my skin and invigorated me, filling me with mana.

I breathed in and once more willed my chitin to form around my body. The dagger had given me the idea, and the defeated scorpion had given me the mana to use them.

Four long arachnid limbs protruded from my back along with the scorpius tail. The tips of each I willed to shape to my desires and mimic the dagger that was in my hands.

It bent to my will, and in a blink I didn't have one weapon to fight with—I had six. I launched myself into the mass of creatures, striking out all at once with my chitinous limbs to attack the rock scorpions' weak points. My reinforced chitin limbs splintered their outer rock bodies and shattered the mana stones with ease.

My mana dropped rapidly from the massive expenditure I was using to keep up this form, but six vapor trails of mana filled the air, and I breathed in deep, refilling my limited mana pool with each sweet inhalation.

Raven was next to me, having killed one scorpion on her own. But she wasn't moving, just staring at me in shock. She stared at me as I tore through six beasts in one attack.

She smiled widely. "I'll be on the sidelines…watching."

It was the right move, as glad as I was to have her here. This was my trial, and I had to take care of it myself, but her being here was the greatest gift she could give me.

She banished my fear of being alone, and more importantly, she gave me a reason to fight. I'd fight to the death to protect her, and I needed that savagery in the moment. The same savagery Sam unleashed when he went to battle.

I didn't understand it at first, but now I did. He showed no mercy in battle because his enemies would show him none. Sometimes evil begot evil and you had to match it.

With a fierce cry that rose from my throat, I tore through the beasts with ease.

They swarmed around me, stabbing with their sharp stingers and snapping at my flesh with their claws, but each time they got close to me, I struck with my limbs, skewering them. I breathed in, letting their mana fuel me as I attacked. I slung their empty shells at the remnants of the others who advanced on me. But I stabbed out with my Arachne limbs and kept pushing them back.

I had a superior reach, and they couldn't get close enough to strike me. But they were clever creatures and they possessed some semblance of animalistic cunning. When they saw they couldn't reach me without dying, they backed up and started flinging their rock shards toward me. A few pinged harmlessly off my chitin, but with the limited amount chitin in my body, parts of my armor were weaker than the others, and a few shards got through.

Sharp flashes of pain struck me, but I ignored them and grabbed at two of the bodies of the golems.

I held them out in front of me like shields and brought them in front of my chest to protect myself from further projectiles.

Their rock fragments were made from the same material as their bodies, and they couldn't pierce through.

I'd taken away their main methods of attack, but they still outnumbered us dozens to one.

If each one I'd killed hadn't given me a burst of mana from the stones, we'd have both died in minutes. But as it was, I was able to kill each and every one of them and keep pushing my mana to the limits and refilling it.

The parts of the chitin I used to pierce the shells of the rock golems got weaker with each strike, and I had to reform the tips a dozen or more times as they continuously dulled, but I eventually destroyed all of them.

As the last rock scorpion died, I sagged to the ground, letting the chitin fade out of me. I leaned against the stone wall, my chest heaving as sweat dripped from every pore.

Even if my mana filled itself, I'm still not used to fighting for so long. I'm exhausted.

I raised a trembling hand to wipe my sweat and failed as my strength left me.

"Here," Raven said, holding out a waterskin.

I grabbed it and took a long drink, polishing off the entire contents. It was delicious and soothed my parched mouth.

As soon as I was done, I let the skin fall to the ground and just leaned against the wall, letting my breath calm down.

Raven came and sat next to me, leaning her head on my shoulder.

"That was incredible, Eris. I had no idea you could fight like that."

"Neither did I." I chuckled. "I think that was mostly Sam's teaching coming out."

She laughed with me. "Love him, but he doesn't go easy on us during training, does he?"

"Not even kind of."

We both sat and let ourselves rest. Raven hadn't fought the scorpions, but she'd used a lot of her strength, just keeping me afloat. She wasn't that strong in her human form, and the barrier didn't allow enough space for her to use her bird form well.

After about fifteen minutes, I'd recovered most of my strength, or enough of it that I felt confident to proceed. I stood and then turned and helped Raven up. We walked around the corner and started back down the long hallway that had been filled with scorpions half an hour ago.

"You think that was the last of the enemies?" Raven asked.

"I hope so, at least for the moment, but I don't think that was the final test by far. Not even close."

"You too, huh?" Raven nodded. "Yeah. I feel like this maze is going to get a lot harder before we get through it."

I reached over and took her hand. "I'm glad you're here with me though; it makes all the difference in the world."

"No place I'd rather be. Now let's stop stalling and find out what else this bullshit place has in store for us."

Right. No choice, but to keep going.

At the end of the corridor was a sharp right turn. We followed it and found another choice: to go straight or turn left.

"Left again?" I asked.

She nodded.

"Left it is." I took the left and we came to a hallway with half a dozen exits. One on the left. Two on the right and another T junction.

"You think the maze is just fucking with us now?" she asked.

"I really hope not."

I sighed. *Which way to go? My gut says to keep sticking with left turns, but if I stick to that plan, I'm not going through the other hallways, and maybe my gut is wrong here.*

There really wasn't a good option. But I had to make a choice.

I looked up, at the top of the maze and the barrier over our heads. When my gaze fell back down, I lingered on the tops of the walls, an idea forming in my head.

There's no way that could work right? That seems too obvious.

Even if I was a long shot, I still had to try.

"I've got an idea. Catch me if I fall."

Before she could respond, I ran forward and willed my hands into claws. I sank them into the wall and used them to haul myself up to the top of the wall. The wall was thin and barely a few feet across, so I'd have to be careful as I walked. As I stood on top of the wall and waited for something to happen, nothing did.

I grinned. "I can't believe that worked." I turned and looked down at Raven. "C'mon, why don't you climb up?"

She smiled and used her wings to fly towards me and land. "I had the same thought, but after the barrier, I didn't figure it would work. Same for me using my wings to scout ahead, but if that worked, then maybe I should fly ahead and find the route for you?"

I shook my head. "Definitely not. As easy as that would make things, we don't know what kinds of dangers are still lurking around the corners. I don't want to get separated from you and you get hurt or worse because I wasn't there beside you. If we do this. We do this together."

Raven grinned, showing her brilliant white teeth before leaning down and kissing me.

When we pulled back, she kissed me once more and turned, balancing on the wall. "Let's get started, then. We'll stick to the left and work our way through this forsaken hellhole."

I returned her grin with one of my own.

"Let's get started."

Chapter 8 - What Lies at the Center

We took off, both rushing ahead along the wall. Raven jumped first, sailing over the maze to land precisely on the other side. I ran after her, leaping and aiming for the small wall that continued for what seemed like forever.

I landed and crouched, finding my balance before standing.

"That wasn't so hard."

"Nope, easy as skipping when I was a child," Raven replied. She turned her gaze from me to the rest of the maze. "You think there are more rock scorpions?"

I shrugged. "I don't know. But I'm thinking that if this is a trial rather than a trap, then having me fight the same enemy after I proved victorious against them once doesn't make sense. I figure there will be different challenges in store for us."

She nodded, peering over the edge at the ground. There was nothing below us, and I cast my eyes upward to the cavern ceiling far above us, but I could not see anything. Or there was nothing for me to see would be more apt.

"All right, I'm not seeing anything, but that doesn't mean much. We can't exactly stay here, can we?" Raven asked.

"Nope. We have to continue."

The two of us rushed along the walls, running and jumping in sync with each other. As we ran, we both watched below us for monsters or traps, but there was nothing, which told me that either the rock scorpions were the only enemies in the maze, or there were others, but by staying on top of the walls, we could avoid them.

I rather liked the idea that there were no enemies, not that we were just skipping over them.

It didn't take us long to find the center of the maze with us scaling the walls like we were. Ten minutes of running later and we arrived. The center of the maze was a rough circle with several entrances that led to different parts of the maze. In the middle of the circle was a small crystal orb. And there was nothing else around it. A barren room with a small pedestal containing the orb.

Both of us perched on the walls.

We looked at each other. "What do you think we should do?" I asked.

"I think we only have one option here. Go down and touch the orb."

I chuckled. "I was afraid you'd say that."

With nothing left to do but gather my courage, I hopped off the wall and landed in a crouch, my ears attuned to any change. The only sounds I could pick up were Raven's breathing and the empty echo of the cavern.

"I think we're clear but stay up there and be prepared to grab me if this is a trap," I said, summoning a dagger to my hand.

Raven arched her back and let her wings burst free. They spilled inky feathers over the ground as she flapped them and prepared to launch herself at me if things went wrong.

"I've got you."

If nothing else, it made me feel better. I smiled and turned back to the orb.

As far as I could tell, it was just a sphere of glass, but if it was lying here at the end of the maze in a forgotten part of the world, then I knew it wasn't that at all.

I approached it slowly, taking each step with caution while I checked for traps. There was nothing, and step after step the orb grew closer.

Before I was ready, I stood before it.

What am I supposed to do with this? Do I pick it up? Or just touch it?

I reached out a hand and placed it on the glass. It was smooth and surprisingly warm despite being in the rather frigid underground cave. My entomancer blood kept me from shivering, but even I knew that it was nearing an uncomfortable amount of cold.

The orb shouldn't be warm, yet it was.

As soon as I touched it, there was a yank on my mana pool, and without my consent, tendrils of my magic poured out of me. My smoke filled the orb with emerald mist that writhed and swirled endlessly.

There was a flash of light in the center of the orb, and it shattered, sending rainbow shards scattering in all directions as my smoke drifted down to the ground.

"Eris, you okay?" Raven asked, panicked.

"I'm fine. But I don't know why it reacted that way."

The smoke drifted around my feet, swirling and breaking over my ankles. The mist spread over the ground before settling on the floor.

There was a low thump that vibrated through my feet before the thunk of a lock disengaged, and the floor shifted.

"What the hell?" Raven said.

The floor shifted, opening slightly as my magic was sucked down to the depths.

What's going on?

As the floor shifted, so too did the walls. They began to descend beneath the ground. Raven, sensing the change, leapt off the wall and landed beside me.

"Have you any idea what's going on?"

"Not a clue." I shook my head.

The walls of the maze descended into the ground in minutes, leaving a plain, smooth floor that stretched all the way back to the entrance of the cavern.

In the distance, I could just make out the flickering flames of the guild torches.

I knew the rest of the team would be joining us as soon as the walls went down, and my heart sped up at the thought. I wanted nothing more than for Sam to be by my side next to Raven. I didn't know what was going on, and I didn't like the profound sense of unease this place instilled in me.

There was movement once more behind us. I turned and watched as a section of wall rose from the ground creating an opening to a stairwell that led deeper into the Nymirian Dungeon.

Whatever this place was, this trial, wasn't over yet.

"A queen, yet a cheater. How disappointing," a feminine voice said.

What?

The voice came out of nowhere, yet it sounded like someone was right next to me. I turned to look at Raven, who was as wide-eyed as I.

"You heard that, right?"

I nodded. "Hello, is anyone there?"

"Imperceptive too. This one is right next to the queen and she doesn't even realize. Disappointing indeed," a different voice said, this one masculine in tone.

I whirled around, but yet there was no one in sight.

"Show yourselves!" I demanded.

Whoever it was snickered, a light chortle that sent a chill up my skin.

"As you wish."

"Ugh!" Raven choked. A gargled cry slipped from her.

I turned around and found her held by a shadowed figure, a hand gripped tightly around her throat.

"This one is very disappointed in you, queen. Innumerable years we've waited for you, and you disappoint us." He stepped closer, allowing me to get a proper look at him.

The man was tall and thin, with pale green skin. He peered around Raven to stare at me. His head was elongated; he had sharp, razor thin lips and a small nose. But his eyes drew mine.

They were large and nearly the same size as mine, but on the man's lanky frame, they were almost bulbous. Bright yellow eyes stared back at me with only a miniscule black pupil.

Two small antennae stood out from his gray hair.

My breath caught when I took him in because I hadn't seen someone like him in a very long time.

"I feared you'd gone extinct," I said, breathing a sigh of relief.

"We have not," the female voice said, right next to me.

I titled my head to find the girl right behind me. She looked similar to the man, yet younger, with red hair rather than gray.

She took me by the wrist and wrapped her other hand around my throat. "Such a shame. When the blood seal finally opened, this one thought her prayers finally answered, but you have failed."

"Failed? Why because we used the walls?"

"No." She shook her head. "The maze was there to be accomplished by any means, but you failed when you brought a companion to the trial of the Hive. She should not be here. Yet she is."

"A failure, dear daughter, or perhaps not."

"True, Father." The girl nodded. "That one was of middling use. And didn't contribute much. Perhaps not a failure after all."

"You were watching us?"

She nodded. "We see all."

Before I could respond, pounding footsteps heralded the approach of the Gloom Knights.

Our assailants hissed and retreated, still holding onto us. They stood next to one another and turned as the Gloom Knights arrived.

There was a collective intake of breath as the guild caught sight of our captors.

Sam stepped forward, fury in his eyes. "Let them go."

The female chittered, laughing. "A human. Many centuries still must pass before this one would ever concede to a human." She gripped my neck tight enough to hurt. I whimpered as her sharp nails cut into my skin. "A human does not belong here. Leave."

Sam took another step, his anger building as his features hardened. His longsword cleared his sheath, and he levied it at the woman.

A heavy aura surrounded him as he glared death at my captor. The air cracked, and wind whipped around him like the moment right before a thunderstorm. His amber eyes flared with golden light and lit up the darkened cavern. His skin paled, turning as white as a corpse as the metallic scent of ozone burned in my nose. Wind tore at his once copper strands as they turned to silver and broke free from the tie holding them in place.

His radiant eyes narrowed. "Let. Her. Go. Right now." It wasn't an order; it was a declaration that if they didn't release us instantly, there wouldn't be anything left of them when Sam was finished.

It was a declaration of war.

The one holding me flinched and turned to the other. "Not a human. A godling. What should this one do, Father?"

The male sneered. "Human. Godling. Does not matter. This is a trial of the Hive. Those not of our kingdom do not belong."

"What the hell are you, anyway?" Raven asked, turning her head to look at the man holding her.

"They're mantearians. Part of the Hive," I said.

"Look like fuckin' praying mantises to me," Yumiko said, her tone harsh and biting.

"Other way around. Praying mantises look like mantearians. They came first," I said.

It took a moment, but what I'd said a second caught up to me. I'd panicked since they arrived and hadn't been thinking clearly, but I'd jogged my own memory.

I didn't need Sam to escape, and I couldn't have him attacking the mantearians and killing them.

"Sam. It's okay, I've got this." I held my hand up, forcing a smile on my face.

He turned to me, the fury in his golden eyes softening, though he maintained his grip on his sword. "You sure?"

"Of course."

Sam nodded and stepped back, stowing his blade.

"The queen thinks she can escape me. This one is amused," the girl said.

You keep laughing, because weak or not, I am still the Hive Queen, and you will obey me.

I tugged at my magic, opening myself up to the pulsating warmth that flowed through my veins. I let it trickle down my hands as I pushed my consciousness out and felt for my subjects.

Though stronger than my little ones, the mantearians were members of the Hive, bound by the magic that flowed through our veins and connected us.

And I was the Hive Queen, the monarch of the Hive.

I would not be denied.

Just as I did with Misumena, I pushed against their consciousness and smothered them with my will. What I was doing was dangerous, because if they didn't yield, I would destroy their minds, break them and reduce them to empty, broken husks.

But that was their choice. Misumena was too proud. She was an old god and refused to bend to my will. If the mantearians refused to bow, I would break them.

Either way, I'd be free.

I didn't like doing this. It pained me, but at that moment, they were my enemies, and I couldn't allow an attack against me to stand.

My will blanketed them like a vice, and I squeezed. They resisted at first, but their command of magic was woefully inadequate, and even as weakened as I was, they couldn't measure up to my power.

Bit by bit, their will crumbled, and try as they might, they fought against me in vain. Just before I would have broken them, they submitted, and my will flowed over them. They were mine to control.

"Release us," I commanded.

At once their limbs retracted, and they backed up, standing side by side, looking down at the ground.

"This one is sorry, Queen. We meant no disrespect," the girl said.

I didn't care about their excuses. I had proven myself stronger; that was all that mattered to the Hive.

"Kneel before your queen!"

Both of them dropped and bent their knee to me.

A satisfied smile broke over my lips. "Good. Now tell me your names."

"This one is Beru," the girl said.

"And this one is Merran," the man said.

Beru lifted her head and grinned at me. "This one is proud to admit she was wrong. The queen has returned. This is a day of celebration."

I was about to respond, but footsteps thudded behind me, and Sam stood behind me. He wrapped his arms around my chest and pressed his lips to my head. He kissed me and leaned down next to my ear.

"I didn't doubt you could do it for a second. I'm so proud of you."

"Love you."

"As I you."

He let go of me and went over to Raven, making sure she was okay. He would make sure she was all right, so I didn't have to worry about it. I wanted to check on her, too, but I had to deal with the mantearians right now. The rest could wait.

I walked over to them, my shadow hiding their frantic, terrified gazes.

"What was the point of this trial?"

Beru lifted her head, her eyes widening. "Oh, My Queen. This was not the trial. This was just to prove you were strong enough to take the trial and that you were the true Queen of the Hive."

"What?" I crossed my arms under my chest. "This wasn't the trial?"

"No, My Queen. But if you would permit this one to show you to our home, we could explain."

The maze and traps were hard enough, but if that was just the prelude, do I actually stand a chance at completing this trial?

I turned to Sam and the others, who were eyeing our guests with suspicion. "What should we do?"

Sam shrugged. "We came all this way already. Might as well see it through." His eyes shifted to Beru. "But let's get one thing straight. She's my queen. Anyone else lays a hand on her, they die."

Both mantearians nodded furiously. "We understand, knight godling. We will respect our queen."

He frowned scratching his stubbled chin. "Godling. That's the second time you've called me that. What does it mean?"

Merran looked up, confused. He tilted his head side to side. "This one doesn't understand. Godling is godling. A half divine. A guardian. We know of your kind. Keepers of the peace. Power beyond mortality. Godling is godling."

"Damn, that doesn't answer anything I didn't already know," Sam said.

"Wait," Gil interjected. "Didn't Adam talk to you about it?"

Sam nodded. "A bit, but besides the guardian stuff, he didn't really know much. Just that now I'm supposedly half god. Whatever the hell that means." He shook his head and muttered to himself. "By the nine kings of hell, Evelyn. What were you thinking?"

It was soft enough that I was one of the few who actually heard what he'd said.

There wasn't anything I could do to help Sam figure out his new abilities, but I had to admit, I kind of liked the way he looked. Not that I didn't like how he looked normally, but the golden eyes and pale skin gave him an exotic look. It didn't take away from his ruggedness, but it refined those features.

I liked it.

But my thoughts about his appearance aside, we had to descend deeper into the dungeon.

"All right, lead us to your home."

Merran and Beru stood at once, heading toward the raised stairwell where the orb had once resided.

"This one would like you to follow us if it pleases you," Beru said.

"Where's Merran going?"

He turned and bowed to me. "This one is going to scout the entrance to the dungeon and reset our traps."

Without even a whisper, Merran vanished in front of our eyes.

The others gasped at his sudden disappearance, and I chuckled.

"Get used to it. The mantearians are the best at stealth. Even entomancers have a hard time spotting them, and if they don't want to be found, you won't find them."

Gil whistled. "And I thought Wilson was scary."

"You're telling me," Mika replied, pulling at his ponytail. "I've worked with some of the best players who specialized in stealth. That wasn't *Shadow Walk,* or *Invisibility.* That was terrifying."

The others nodded in agreement, but having seen Wilson move, I knew he could keep up with the mantearians he if wanted to.

Their optical camouflage isn't that impressive once you know how it works. All they do is cloak themselves and mimic their surroundings.

The skill itself wasn't that amazing, but where they excelled was their training. It wasn't just the fact they could turn themselves invisible. What really made them impressive was their dedication and training. The mantearians trained nearly from birth in the art of stealth and sabotage.

They were the Hive Kingdom's spies and assassins.

Though I didn't really want to go deeper into this place, didn't want to undertake more tests, I had no choice.

I longed to feel the sunshine on my skin once more, but instead, I ventured even deeper into the damp and the dark. Beru led us down hundreds of steps. During the descent I thought the stairs would never end when they finally deposited us out into a long stone hallway.

"Forgive this one. We've grown accustomed to the dark but allow me to light the way for you."

Beru vanished and reappeared with a torch in hand. She held it aloft, and the flickering flame lit the way as we made our way down the hall.

It ended at a doorway much like the ones we'd seen previously in this dungeon but, unlike those which were written in Script and Entoma, this one was written in the language of the mantearians, and I had to admit that I was rusty.

I squinted, as if that would make the words suddenly have meaning. "This door doesn't require blood does it?"

Beru shook her head. "No, queen. It merely requires the touch of this one." Beru reached out with her green hand and touched a finger to the door.

There was a heavy clunk of a lock disengaging, and the door retracted below the ground.

Beru stepped back and with a sweeping bow, motioned for us to continue. "Welcome, queen and knight, to this one's home. The Nymirian Dungeon."

I stepped inside and gasped.

"How is this possible?" I whispered as I stared, mouth agape at what I was seeing.

We were hundreds of feet underground, yet a lush forest rose up in the cavern.

Gray stone was all around us, along the floor and ceiling, but there, too, were trees and grass. Birds chirped, and the buzz of insects filled my ears.

There was a beautiful forest inside a cage of stone.

The others walked behind us and let out gasps of surprise. It was just a forest, but it was such an unexpected sight that we all reacted out of shock.

Beru nodded, giving me a small, wistful smile. "This one is glad you can enjoy the forest." Her tone matched her voice, and it was filled with longing and regret, but I didn't understand why.

"Beru, what aren't you telling me?" I asked.

"The forest," Sam said, coming up behind me. He wrapped his arms around my collar and looked at Beru. "It isn't real, is it?"

Beru sighed and nodded. "As much as this one wishes otherwise."

"What?" I gasped. "How is that possible?"

On instinct, I pooled my magic and pushed it toward the sound of insects. But there were none. The presence of the mantearians in the cavern lit up in my mind, I could sense them, but there were no insects, none of my little ones.

Sam was right. This forest isn't real.

My shoulders drooped as I came to the realization. After wishing for sunshine and the forest, to have it and then have it immediately taken from me was a painful blow that hurt more than I cared for.

"Apologies, My Queen. It was not this one's desire to fool you, but this one just wished to give you a glimpse of the forest for a moment."

"You still didn't answer my question. How is this possible?"

"Illusion magic," Sam answered for Beru. "It's also how you camouflage yourselves, right?"

She nodded. "But how did you know?"

Sam reached into his tunic and pulled out a small amulet. It was silver and nothing more than a circle with script on it. I'd never seen it on him before. "*Detect Life* amulet. A must-have when running dungeons. Mimics are a bitch."

Beru laughed, long and hard. It was a hissing laugh that grated on the ears, but I endured it as I endured it so long ago.

They really haven't changed much, have they?

"This one is amused. Clever godling."

Sam stowed the necklace back under his shirt and leaned over to speak gently in my ear, "Would you mind if I borrowed your hair tie? Mine snapped."

"Of course."

Sam kissed the tip of my ear and ran his warm fingers over my scalp. He took the tie and quickly tied back his silver hair.

I turned to him and smiled. "Are you going to stay like that for a while?"

He looked down at himself and back up. "What? In my demigod form?" He shrugged. "I guess. I don't really care for it, but it's not like it's harming anything." His golden eyes lit up with deviousness. "Why, do you like it?"

"Very much so." I grinned at him.

"What she means is it's sexy as fuck," Raven chimed in, walking over to us.

Sam blushed, a hint of red tinged his cheeks and he grinned sheepishly. "Well, then I guess I can suffer in this form for a little while. But don't get used to it. I'll change back when I have the time."

Raven draped herself on Sam, leaning heavily on him while her mouth met his. It was a quick kiss and when she pulled back, she grinned. "You say that, but I know the only reason you keep your beard is because Eris likes it.

If we both said that we liked you better this way, I bet you'd stay that way, just to keep us happy."

He laughed. "You give yourselves way too much credit. I'm not that much of a pushover."

"Yeah, right!" Gil shouted over to us. He, Yumiko and Mika were watching us with barely contained laughter. "If Eris asked for our heads, your first response would be 'Which would you like first?'" he said in a high-pitched mocking tone.

Sam jabbed a finger at Gil, a wide smile on his face. "Just for that, I'm taking yours first."

"Man, I thought we were bros?"

"Them's the breaks." Sam shrugged. "Bro code's been dead for over a thousand years."

Both Sam and Gil cracked up after that, devolving into laughter with Mika and Yumiko. As usual, some of their humor was lost on me, but I understood the gist of what they were saying.

I was just glad they were laughing. I think we all needed it. I took Sam's hand in mine and looked out at the fake forest. I couldn't stop the sigh of regret that slipped through my lips, but I could at least put a smile on my face in front of my beloveds.

"All right, all right," Sam said, giving my hand a squeeze. "Enough joking around. Let's not forget that we're still inside a dungeon. And safe zone or not, this place is still an unknown." And just like that, the smiles fell away, and the others returned to their business-like attitudes.

Through all our jesting, Beru had stood to the side, watching us, taking it in. What she thought of us was something I couldn't begin to guess. Her bright yellow eyes were unreadable, as was her blank expression.

"If it pleases you, this one would take you to the mantearian king."

"Please, escort us," I said, letting go of Sam's hand.

As much as I wanted to keep holding it, I had a responsibility to appear strong in front of the Hive. A little girl holding the hand of her lover for comfort didn't convey strength.

Beru turned and began walking toward the forest. I followed her, my head held high.

If I am to be queen, then I need to start acting like it. Though in the deepest part of myself, I felt like a fraud, I couldn't let doubt eat at me. Whether or not I felt like the queen, I was. The mantle that pulsed through my veins was proof of that.

It was the same mantle that flowed through Aliria. *Two queens ruling over a dead kingdom. It's almost ironic.*

With a heavy sigh, we marched through the false forest to meet the king.

Chapter 9 - Queen and Knight

Sampson

The forest inside the cave had been surprising to say the least, but after seeing the creepy mantearians' tricks up close, I wasn't fooled by what awaited me as we stepped into the cavern. Watching Eris's shoulders slump when I told her the truth had been hard to see.

I hated taking that away from her, but I didn't want the forest of illusions to get her hopes up and then be dashed when she stepped into it.

Better to hurt her quickly and get it over with than set her up for greater disappointment later.

As Beru led us into the forest, Eris declined the invitation to hold my hand. She instead walked with a purposeful stride and kept her head up and shoulders back as she followed Beru.

I couldn't help but smile inwardly, though I would never laugh out loud, not when I could tell at once what she was doing.

Forcing herself into the role of queen. I love you, Eris. But you're trying too hard now. Just be who you were back in the maze when you stood up to the mantearians. That is what makes a queen, and you're a natural, love. Just get out of your head for a second.

For the first time since our bond had been severed, I wished we still had our connection. I would pour all my love and acceptance for her into it, let her know that I knew that she didn't need to put on airs, that she was a natural queen.

I'll talk to her later, tell her exactly what she needs to hear.

"Lost in thought?" Raven asked from beside me.

"Just thinking about Eris," I whispered, though it was kind of pointless. On two counts. Either Eris heard me, and considering how good her hearing was, there was no way I could get away with whispering, but she also was focused on her charade and was likely not paying attention to anything but keeping up appearances, so my whispering was kind of a moot point.

"She's trying too hard," Raven whispered back. "Although I haven't spent as much time with her as you have, it's obvious she's trying to fit into a mold that isn't exactly meant for her."

"What do you mean?" I asked, tilting my head toward her.

Raven paused, placing a single slender finger on her red lips. "How to put this..." She hummed under her breath for a moment. "I think the only things she knows of being a queen came from Aliria, and she's trying to emulate her mother, but not replicate her, if that makes any sense."

I chuckled. "You're saying she knows that her mother is a cold, uncaring bitch, but that's all she has to go on when it comes to ruling, so she's trying and failing to adapt to that but also make it her own."

She nodded. "Exactly, but it's unnatural. She just needs to be herself. Who she is is good enough."

I'd like to think so, but the Hive doesn't exactly operate by standard rules. Eris has what it takes to be queen. I've seen it for myself, but the Hive doesn't conform to human standards.

That thought sent a wave of anger coursing through me, and I tried to immediately quash it. The anger and hurt Eris had left in my heart was slow to heal, but it was healing. I'd forgiven her, but actually forgiving her in my heart was a different matter. I was working on it, and Raven was helping. More than helping. Without her, I doubt I'd have been able to get over it, and that would have ruined me.

She stuck close to me as we walked through the forest, and even I had to admit that it was amazing. If I hadn't been looking for the telltale signs of illusion magic, I would have almost been fooled. *The mantearians are quick, and their camouflage skills are impressive. Adding their skill with illusion magic on top of that…Wilson would have an aneurysm, or more than likely, he'd freak out and demand to know their secrets.*

I shuddered at the thought of Wilson having command of even a dozen mantearians. They'd probably be the best thieves Nexus had ever seen.

I chuckled. *Good thing he's back at the castle. He doesn't need any more ideas in his head.*

"Whatcha laughing about?" Raven asked.

"Nothing, just thinking about home."

"You don't like being away from the castle, do you? For all your gruffness and anger, you're actually a big ol' softie, aren't you?"

I growled at her under my breath. "Don't make me hurt you."

She leaned closer with lust in her crimson eyes. "Is that a promise?" Her warm and sultry voice rolled over my skin like a touch, prickling my hair and sending shivers down my spine.

"Didn't you get enough of that last night?"

She shook her head. "Not on your life…but next time, let's go somewhere with more privacy."

My cheeks reddened at remembering Yumiko's comments at breakfast this morning, which seemed like ages ago.

"Deal," I said with a wink.

Our conversation had gone on long enough that, before I knew it, we arrived at a small wooden hut that seemed to be made from the bark of the surrounding trees. It had a thatched roof that was made of straw and leaves from the foliage surrounding the hut, but the forest was just an illusion, which meant the hut was an illusion as well.

Eris and Beru stepped inside, and the rest of us filed in after them.

More surprises met us when we entered the house. It was a lot bigger on the inside. What seemed like a ten-foot square hut opened into a massive living space. Rough wooden tables and chairs lay dotted around the room like some form of conference room. All the chairs faced the back of the wall where a man sat at a small round table.

Although he was the only one who appeared to be in the room, my *Detect Life* charm told me otherwise. It was a necessary spell, and one that I was incredibly thankful I had with me.

Two mantearians hid under illusion spells next to the man I assumed to be king, though the aura he gave off was anything but regal. He seemed more like an elderly librarian than king of assassins, but judging by the guards hidden away, he was no fool and, if all of this was an illusion, his very appearance could be fake as well.

Beru led Eris to the table where the old man sat, and I followed them, but I only made it halfway before the invisible mantearians moved to intercept me. They thought themselves hidden, and Beru had yet to reveal that I could see them, so they came at me with false confidence.

The flickering humanoid light on my left tried to grab my arm, likely to put me in a hold. I stepped back as his hand closed around empty air. I grabbed him by the elbow and flung him into the second shadow that approached from the right.

Not expecting resistance, the two couldn't react in time and collided with each other. A crack sounded through the hall as their heads bounced off each other. They fell to the floor with pained groans as their camouflage collapsed.

My sword cleared its sheath and I rested it against the neck of a plain looking mantearian with brown hair. The only exotic thing about him was his mantis eyes and green skin.

"That was foolish of you," I said, staring at the king.

"My apologies, my king." Beru bowed, sinking to one knee. "That one can see through our invisibility."

The king turned his wide eyes to me and smirked. "A godling. Forgive this one's soldiers. They're rather protective of this one."

I removed my blade from the man's neck and walked forward, my naked sword still in my hand. "I understand. I'm rather protective of my queen, and I'd recommend not attempting something like that again."

"Sam!" Eris hissed, turning to glare at me, her obsidian eyes lit up with a tinge of anger. "Let me handle this. You don't have to react to everything with violence, you know."

"They started it." I shrugged.

Eris tried not to laugh, but a smile graced her pink lips as she turned back to the king. "Greetings. My name is Eris. I'm an entomancer and the Hive Queen."

"Well met, Queen Eris. This one is Maloran, and it is humbling to be the one who greets the first entomancer in hundreds of years." He smiled; his pronounced crow's feet crinkled at the corners of his eyes. "You've kept us waiting a long time."

Eris opened her mouth to respond but, before she could, Maloran turned to me. "And well met, knight godling. This one applauds your resolve to protect the queen."

I nodded. "As long as you respect us and do not attempt violence upon us again, I'll behave myself."

"As expected of a knight." He smiled. "Though much as this one wishes to stay and converse, I imagine Queen Eris did not travel all this way merely to have polite conversation."

"We were sent by the Morrigan to clear the Nymirian Dungeon and claim the treasure that lies there."

Maloran's eyes lit up at that. His mouth sat agape for a second, but he quickly composed himself.

"Of course. This one is pleased by the news. It has been too many years since last contact with our goddess. But if you are here, it means the end is coming, yes?"

"What do you mean?" I asked, interrupting.

Maloran's eyes turned to me as I spoke. He looked back to Eris and then to me again before replying. "After the destruction of our kind and the whole of the Hive, our kind were placed here and given very specific instructions. Our kind were to guard this place for the Monarch of the Hive and wait for their return. If you are here, it must mean that our goddess's prediction is now coming to pass and the end is upon us."

"Not if we can help it," I said, coming to step closer to Eris. "But we do need to know what waits for us at the end of the dungeon."

He shook his head. "This one does not know. This one only knows what was passed down from his father before him—to wait for the monarch to return. This one is supposed to show you to the entrance."

Maloran rose from his chair.

He looked at Gil and the others before turning back to us. "This one wishes to know if the queen and her knight are going to bring the humans with them?"

Eris glanced at me and then the others. "Of course, I am. They are my friends. Why wouldn't I bring them along?"

"Because the dungeon was meant for the Hive—and only the Hive. This one shall not stop you from taking them, but this one must warn that one of the dangers it poses."

I scoffed and turned back to the others. "Who's up for exploring a highly lethal dungeon where we might die at any moment?"

Every single one of their hands shot up instantly. I turned back to find Eris with her hand up, smirking up at me.

"So what's the issue again?" I asked, glancing at Maloran.

He shrugged, a smile teasing his cracked lips. "Very well." He shifted his eyes to the far end of the room where his guards now stood. Maloran nodded to them.

A sudden wave of vertigo hit me as the room shifted and grew hazy, roiling like a mirage before it vanished, and we found ourselves in a large stone cavern rather than the wooden hut.

I knew it was an illusion.

The vindication that bubbled to the surface was short-lived as Maloran walked over to the wall and a door appeared.

It was the same door that had appeared at the end of the corridor under the cabin we first came to. The same blood seal locked the door.

"So what was the point of the dungeon before the dungeon?" I asked.

"It was a trial for the Monarch of the Hive so that only a worthy monarch could reach this door. It was a test. The real challenge begins once that one steps through the door. This one wishes both queen and the knight the best of luck."

Before he left, he stopped and turned to Eris and me.

"One more thing," he said, bowing his head low. "A gift and a token of loyalty to the Monarch of the Hive. As the first queen in generations, this one bequeaths the will of the mantearians to you. May it aid you in the trial to come."

As he spoke, he dropped to one knee, and a rush of air flowed from him. A warm current brushed over my skin and seeped into my chest.

Alert! Mantearia's Blessing Unlocked

+15 to Wisdom and Agility

Unlocked (Hive Mind) Special: Mantis Blades

The *Agility and Wisdom* bonus was useless since I was at max for one and didn't use the other, but this wasn't just a power for myself, and the added *Agility and Wisdom* for Eris would only strengthen her. That was what mattered more than any personal power.

After he gifted us his will, he bid us good luck once more and walked out of the room and the small cavern leaving us alone.

"Okay, got a question," Gil said as soon as Maloran and the rest of the mantearians had left. He thumbed back the way they'd just left and lowered his voice. "What the hell was up with the way they talk?"

Eris turned to Gil and stared at him for a solid second before bursting into a fit of giggles.

"It's just the way they speak. It takes some getting used to, but they are very polite and honor bound. Despite being assassins and spies, we can take them at their word."

Gil shrugged. "Still a fucking weird way of speaking," he muttered as we marched over to the door.

Without hesitation, Eris touched her hand to the door and winced as her finger was sliced open. Her ruby-red life dripped over the door before bubbling and hissing.

The door opened with a click, and we all filed inside.

"Oh great. More stairs," I said as I peered down into the descending darkness.

There was a small shove from Eris. "Come on, don't be a baby. Let's get this over with."

"All right, all right. Don't be so pushy. Don't want me to take a tumble down the stairs now, do we?"

I grabbed a torch from my inventory and lit it as the others did the same. We marched down the stone steps for a few minutes in silence until we came to another door.

"What the hell is with this fuckin' place and all the godsdamn doors?" Yumiko asked.

"Think I'd rather have the doors than whatever's behind them," Mika replied.

It wasn't a blood seal door, so I opened it and stepped through into a large room made of stone. It was stone, but it wasn't crude rock; it was built like a castle, with large stone blocks that rose to an arched ceiling high above us. As we stepped inside, torches lit up the space. Hundreds of them flickered to life, bathing us in lambent light.

"Okay. I take it back. I think I'd rather have the fuckin' doors. Holy fucking hell, look at this shit."

I had to agree with Yumiko. This place was insane.

"It's like a castle, but for giants," I said.

"But giants haven't been seen on Nexus since we arrived," Gil said.

"Yeah. Would've said the same thing about the mantearians until an hour ago," I fired back.

He quickly closed his mouth.

"Well, no point standing around. Let's find out where this place leads."

I turned toward the only exit in the room, which was a long corridor that curved away, snaking its way out of sight. With trepidation building in my veins, I drew my blade and had *Chitin Armor* on the tip of my tongue.

There were no rugs or decorations on the stone floors or walls. Just torch sconces. It gave the place an even creepier vibe. The whole place was nothing but dancing shadows, twisting and writhing as they stretched along the halls.

As we approached the bend of the first hall, I paused as subtle noises came discernible. I held my hand up for the others to stop moving and hold up so I could take a look. I crouched low and peered out.

It was a longer hallway lit only by torches, but there were humanoid figures shambling about in chaotic disarray. The putrid heavy stench of rot drifted my way and was so strong, I wondered why I didn't smell it before.

I pulled back with a sigh of relief.

"Roamers, about thirty of them."

But as they approached, I found them to not be human roamers. They each had sickly gray-green skin and bulging yellow eyes.

"Mantearians?" Eris gasped, her hand going to her mouth.

"What they are doesn't matter." I shrugged. "They're still roamers."

The others relaxed as I spoke. Roamers were never a challenge.

"Just make sure you have ample footing this time, darling," Raven said with a cheeky smile.

"You're never going to let me live that down, are you?"

"Not on your life."

I chuckled and stepped around the corner.

"You guys know what to do." As I levied my sword at the horde, I whistled loud and long. "Yo, zombies! Fresh meat!"

They turned as one and let out a horrendous groan and began stumbling toward me.

There was a flap of wings as Raven, Eris, and Yumiko bolted around the corner. Raven flew just over my head. She folded her wings in front of her and fired off a round of her throwing-knife-esque feathers. They flew end over end and stabbed into the weakened roamers' flesh. Raven landed a few kill shots with one single volley.

At the same time as Raven fired off her first attack, Yumiko and Eris both had their bows out and nocked. They loosed straight and true, taking two of the dead in the head with their first shots.

In under two seconds, nearly five of the roamers dropped to the ground permanently dead.

I charged into the fray with Gil and Mika on my heels.

My sword came down in an arc as I severed the first roamer's head from its shoulders. My superior shadowsteel bit deep into its rotten flesh and sliced through its weakened spine with ease. The roamer's head fell to the ground as I engaged a second one.

I kicked it in the chest to keep some distance, and as it stumbled back, I lunged forward and slid my steel though its nasal cavity and into its rotten brain. With a flick of my wrist, half its head came off and poured brackish gray matter over the slate tile floor.

I leaned into the strike, letting the momentum carry my sword into the next closest roamer. A former guard with stringy black hair rushed me as I killed the second and my blade intercepted him. I cut through his jaw and nicked the side of his neck as I swung. Brown, nearly coagulated blood burst from the gash and dripped thick and viscous as the roamer tried to lunge at me.

Its grimy, decayed gray fingers clutched at my tunic before I brought my fist up and smashed into the side of its head. It rocked back from the blow, careening to the side. It didn't have the motor function to stop itself from falling. It leaned against another roamer, and both of them crashed to the ground.

I stepped over them and ended them both with a single swing of my steel.

There was a thump as metal struck flesh from beside me. I turned my head to find Gil next to me. He swung his mighty axe down and nearly cleaved the damn zombie in two.

"Mika, take over!" he shouted as he hefted his axe up.

The samurai rushed in, his sword bursting into cobalt flames that brought a heavy warmth to the surroundings as Mika launched into a group of three roamers. He set up a combination of swings as his blade came down perpendicularly to the first zombie on the far right. He took it through the shoulder, and as the blade came out the other side, the top part of the roamer caught flame in an instant. It burst into flames even as it slid to the ground and let out one last dying moan as its decayed flesh blackened and turned to ash.

He chained his downward slash into a side strike that severed the legs of the second zombie at the knee. It cut cleanly through both legs with ease, and the torso of the roamer fell back even as one leg took one last stop before falling over. He didn't kill the creature but took it out of commission as he dealt with the final zombie.

Mika brought his blade up in his final movement and severed the roamer in two from the groin to the crown of its head.

With one last flick of his blade, Mika cast his blue flames out over the bodies of the zombies he'd killed and the one he crippled, burning them to a crisp before they turned to ash.

His movements had been fluid and precise, and I was impressed. *He's gotten better since we last fought together. And I don't even recognize him from back when we were both in the swords together.*

Eris and Yumiko rained death on the last few zombies, and Gil chopped his way through a few more stragglers.

As the last roamer fell, I wiped my blade on the shirt of the closest corpse and cleaned the blood and bits of brain from it.

Combat Results!
8 Killed (Roamer): 2400 Exp!
Total Exp Gained: 2400 Exp!
Exp: 5900/7200

I closed the notification and sheathed my blade.

"Well, that was fun," Mika said, wiping his brow.

Unbeknownst to him, however, a bit of blood had landed on the back of his hand, and he'd only succeeded in wiping a streak of brown gore across his head.

Yumiko looked over to him and sighed. She pulled out a clean white handkerchief from her inventory and marched over to him. "You've got a bit of brain stuck to your thick skull," she said, tossing him the cloth.

Mika smiled wide as he deftly caught it out of the air and quickly wiped his forehead. "Ah, you do like me. I knew you'd warm up to me eventually."

She scowled at him. "Don't make me drain you dry." She flashed her elongated canines.

"Speaking of." Mika walked over to her and offered her the handkerchief. "Why don't you use your blood magic?"

Her face scrunched in disgust. "Keep it."

Mika stared at her for a second and opened his mouth once more.

"Hey, Mika, why don't you take over as point man?" Gil asked in a too-loud voice.

He turned away from Yumiko and looked at Gil and then back at Yu. A lightbulb went off in his eyes, and he nodded. "Sure thing." He turned back to Yu. "Sorry. Didn't mean anything by it."

"It's nothing. You're forgiven."

Eris went over and began speaking to Yu while Raven, Gil, and I walked away from the stench of rotting corpses.

When we were far enough away, Raven leaned on me and whispered. "Sore subject I guess?"

I nodded. "Yeah. Yumiko doesn't like to talk about her vampirism. Doesn't want anything to do with it really."

"Why?"

"It's…it's a long story." I paused, about to say more when I stopped and shut my mouth. "Sorry. Not mine to tell."

Raven nodded. "I can understand that all too well."

I placed my hand on her shoulder and pulled her closer to me. "I know." I leaned over and kissed her. "Love you."

"Love you, too."

"All right, let's go kick some more ass!" I shouted loud enough for everyone to hear me.

"I'm always down for a hunt. But Sam, if there are zombies first thing…Gill trailed off, but I knew what he was getting at.

152

"It means that we can probably expect the spectral undead as we go along," I finished for him. "Which means that everyone needs to carry some quicksilver."

I should have plenty in my bag. I opened my inventory and pulled out three vials. Less than I thought I had. *I mean, I know it's been years since I've had need of silver, but I thought I always carried at least four vials? Damn. It's not enough.*

"Anyone have any vials?"

"I've got two," Gil said.

"Three for me," Yumiko replied.

"Well, I didn't bring any. But I've got *Phantom Blade* if I need to cut a ghost in half," Mika said.

Eight vials. Should be enough depending on how long the dungeon is.

I handed a vial to Eris and kept two for myself. Raven wouldn't have any use for them, considering she normally didn't fight with a weapon.

Well, she does have the knife strapped to her back, but she fights with her claws and feathers more often than not. I'd rather keep it for myself. Besides, if she's in a situation where she needs quicksilver, then we've already failed and are likely dead.

"Okay. Keep the vials on hand, but don't use them just yet. I don't want to waste our silver on zombies or skeletons if I can avoid it."

A torrent of affirmations echoed through the stone corridor, and we pushed forward, Mika as point man.

The halls were sparsely lit and gave off an oppressive vibe as we continued.

It didn't take us long before we found more roamers. Using our teamwork, we dispatched them as quickly as the first round and we kept going.

I killed four of them myself.

At first, I didn't notice that we were walking in a spiral. The floor declined ever so slightly, but we were definitely descending. The air grew increasingly colder as we walked, killing zombies by the dozens every few minutes.

Nearly twenty minutes of this went by in a flash before we reached the end of the hallway and found a crossroads waiting for us.

Stone identical to the rest of the castle greeted us but offered no indication as to the way to go. It was a toss-up on the correct path.

"Okay. Hear me out here," Mika began.

I held up my hand and stopped him from speaking. "Hell no. And fuck you for even thinking it."

"So that's a no from the guild leader." Mika chuckled. "Are you sure? We'd clear the floors much faster."

"No. We're in a haunted dungeon and that's what you give me!? Do you want to die? Because that's how we die."

"Fine. Fine," Mika relented giving up on his monumentally stupid idea.

Eris held her hand up. "I'm confused. What are we talking about?"

"Mika wants us to split up. Cover more ground, yada-yada," Gil said. "It's fucking stupid and would likely wind up with us all getting picked apart."

"Okay. Holy hell." Mika threw his hands up. "I'm all ears if anyone has any better ideas."

"We stick together and clear each room one at a time."

"Okay," he said. "So which room is first?"

"Left." Eris pointed. And began heading in that direction.

Raven laughed at that and followed her.

I shrugged. "Well, you heard the lady. Left it is."

We soon found ourselves in a large open room with thick stone pillars supporting the ceiling. Heavy square coffins filled the room, lined up in neat rows, covering the entirety of the floor. As soon as we stepped into the room, the torches along the walls shifted and stuttered, the orange flames disappearing and replaced by flickering effervescent green lights.

"Son of a bitch!" I cursed and forced my eyes away. "Mage lights, don't look at them."

As soon as the mage lights flickered to life, a low, haunted wail echoed through the silent tomb and from the sarcophagi lining the stone room.

Before we could move, a dozen ethereal hands shot up from each coffin. Spectral clawed hands gripped the sides of the stone and hauled themselves out of their resting places.

In the span of a few seconds, the room filled with a dozen floating, hooded creatures.

Wraiths.

Just when my day couldn't get any creepier. Perfect.

Chapter 10 - The King Who Walks in Shadow

The wraiths resembled the mantearians only in the vaguest sense of things. Their faces were each hidden by a ragged torn cloak that covered them from head to toe, showing only twisted and malformed hands which resembled claws.

They were transparent and glowing a sickly green from the mage lights around the room.

As one, they turned to face us and let out a horrendous moan that rattled me to my core.

"Use the quicksilver," I shouted and hastily dumped the vial over my sword.

I tossed the vial to the ground as I finished emptying it and charged into the mass of floating wraiths. I didn't bother using *Chitin Armor*. It would only slow me down and would do nothing against a creature that could ignore any armor that wasn't backed with silver.

If the wraith reached me, its claws would shear through my flesh like butter and would curse me, causing necrosis in seconds.

While not the most annoying of the spectral undead, they were fucking terrifying to fight en masse.

The first one floated toward me, its hood flapping in an invisible wind as it swung its decayed hand toward me.

I brought my sword up and intercepted the hand before it could reach me. The silver parted the wraith's incorporeal flesh with ease, hissing like grease in a pan as silver-white smoke billowed up from the wound. I cut through the wraith's hand, and as it arced off its arm, it fizzled and evaporated before it could even reach the ground.

The wraith let out a horrendous scream, a hissing wail that gave my heart pause as it rattled around my ears.

I ignored the pain as blood trickled down my cheek and plunged my sword into the wraith's heart. It shuddered, stopping its horrendous screeching as it burst into a thousand strands of ectoplasm that fell slowly to the floor and lay in a congealing puddle.

One down. A lot more to go.

As I turned, air whistled over my shoulder and I found myself face to face with a wraith who'd crept up on me. It was too close and I couldn't back up in time. Its hand was an inch from my face when it stopped and shuddered. It groaned and then disappeared as it turned into even more ectoplasm.

As it dropped to the ground, so did an arrow coated in silver.

I turned around to find Yumiko grinning like a madwoman.

"Saved your ass, didn't I?" Her crimson eyes lit up in humor as she turned, drawing another arrow and launching it at another wraith.

Eris stood with Raven behind her. Neither one of them could fight since they didn't have any silver, but both had health potions and curse repellent in small bags around their shoulders, compliments of Yu. They stood ready to heal any wound or injury we might sustain while fighting.

It may have been selfish of me, but I was grateful for them to be out of the fight. As capable and strong as they were, I still worried about their safety, especially when dealing with wraiths which were lethal to unsuspecting adventurers and made carrying quicksilver and curse repellent mandatory.

I turned away from the girls to engage another wraith, that had gotten too close to Mika.

"Mika, behind you!" I shouted as I rushed to him.

He didn't even flinch. He dropped to his knees and turned, whipping his blade in an arc behind him. It glowed blue, pulsing translucent every second or so. As he cut, his *Phantom Blade* struck the wraith and severed it at its torso. It disintegrated as Mika's sword passed through it.

He stood up, flashed me a smile and shrugged. "What's behind me again?"

I laughed. "Don't get cocky. We still have half a dozen to deal with."

"I know! A little help over here!" Gil shouted.

We turned as to witness that Gil, for whatever reason, had drawn the ire of four of the wraiths, and each one was spread out enough that if he swung at one, the others would swarm him.

"Yu, take the ones on the left!" I shouted and shifted my grip on my sword.

I didn't much like throwing things that weren't meant to be thrown, and my sword definitely counted as something that should only leave my hand when I was either out of battle or dead. Unfortunately, circumstances required that I know how to throw my sword as I would a javelin, so that's exactly what I did.

I reared back and launched the silver-coated blade at the closest wraith. It flew straight, and with my increased Strength, it instantly sank through the wraith's back like it wasn't even there and took out its heart before passing an inch from Gil's shoulder as it struck the stone wall and clattered to the floor.

Yumiko took the one beside mine, and Mika struck down the one on the far right. Gil launched into action and sliced the last remaining wraith in two with his axe.

With that, we'd cleared the room of undead.

"Thanks, guys," Gil said, slumping to the floor.

He toppled over, his head cracking hard against the stone floor.

"Gil!" I shouted, rushing over to him.

At once I found the problem. Along his left arm were three long gashes. They were shallow, superficial wounds, but that was never the problem with wraiths. The claw marks were a deep purple on Gil's dark skin. Tendrils of purple mist rose up from the wound and crawled up through Gil's veins as his skin blackened and rotted away in seconds.

"Curse repellent. Quick!"

A bottle was forced in my hand, and I quickly poured it over the wound. It bubbled up on his skin, frothing and sliding away, taking the purple haze with it. The more I poured, the more the curse lifted. I emptied the entire bottle over Gil's wound, and then as soon as it was empty, I tossed it away and grabbed a health potion.

I forced it to Gil's lips and made him drink the entire bottle before I backed off.

Almost at once, the color returned to Gil's cheeks, and his breathing steadied. Curse magic was a pain in the ass to deal with, and if we hadn't had the repellent, the health potion would have been all but useless.

When Gil was healed, I turned, grabbed my blade from next to him, and leaned back against the stone, resting my head on the cool stone for a long moment.

The fight hadn't been all that taxing, but we'd been in combat almost nonstop since we'd arrived in this cursed castle or wherever the hell we were inside the Nymirian Dungeon and my battle fatigue was high. Even with all the points I'd allocated the past few months, I still had to be careful in prolonged fights.

"Okay, let's take a break and let everyone recover before we continue," I said.

Gil weakly raised his hand and gave me a thumbs up. "I'm all for that plan."

Good.

I hadn't checked my notifications since the first fight with the roamers. After dealing with the wraiths, there wasn't a better time.

Combat Results!
4 Killed (Roamers): 1200 Exp!
2 Killed (Wraiths): 1800 Exp!
Total Exp Gained: 3000 Exp!
Exp: 7200/7200
Level Up!
Exp: 1700/7300
Level: 73
10 Stat Points Available!

I added five to *Battle Fatigue,* bringing it to fifty-five, while the other five went to *Attack Damage,* taking it to an even seventy.

Eris and Raven came over to sit beside me on the floor while everyone else stowed their weapons away and sat back as well. We'd all earned a breather. Eris leaned her head on my shoulder and her warmth instantly took the slight chill from the stone. I rested my head against hers and closed my eyes for a moment.

I didn't mean to fall asleep, but I was exhausted and so warm that I couldn't help it. What felt like only moments after I closed my eyes, someone shook me awake. I jolted up, awake instantly.

"I'm up, I'm up," I said, my eyes going wide as I remembered where I was.

I glanced around the room and found it empty. There were no enemies, except for the remains of the wraiths.

I was also alone. No one else was in the room with me.

The others were gone.

My eyes went wide as I searched the room and found not a single trace of them. The vials of curse repellant and health potion were on the ground where I'd tossed them, but Eris, Raven, and the others were nowhere to be found.

"Guys?" I called out and received no response.

Where did everyone go? I wondered, and then froze as a thought stuck me and froze the blood in my veins.

If everyone is gone, and the room is empty. Then who shook me awake?

I turned around, staring at where I'd fallen asleep and found nothing. There was nothing there. With fear in my heart, I stumbled over to one of the sarcophagi and shoved it open, hoping beyond hope that I wasn't about to find my family's corpses in the coffins.

As the lid scraped against the stone and crashed to the ground, I heaved a sigh of relief. There was a skeleton in it, but it'd obviously been there for a very long time and wasn't one of my friends.

I shook my head and leaned back against the stone.

Where did everyone go?

I didn't like this. The whole haunted castle already made my skin crawl, but this was stepping into a realm of things I hadn't experienced before.

With my sword clenched tight in my fist and the quicksilver still coating my blade, I had a choice to make.

Either I stay here and wait on everyone, or I leave and try to find them. Both were risky, but I knew for a fact that everyone wouldn't leave without waking me, and if they were attacked, I'd have woken up immediately.

No. Something else was going on here, and I couldn't afford to wait around and find out what.

Aspect, give me Chitin Armor.

"Of course."

And while I'm at it, do you know where Eris is?

"Unfortunately, not. As we are Errant, I have no connection to the queen anymore."

"Damn it." I quickly pulled up my character page and scrolled to the very bottom. There I found the boost to my stats that I received when I was in close proximity to Eris. It was still active. *So Eris is still close by.*

Twenty meters wasn't that big of a range.

"Eris!" I called out. "Can you hear me?"

There was only silence in the tomb which meant I didn't have a clue.

I rubbed my eyes, still fighting the tiredness that wore me out. I yawned and scratched my chin, trying to figure this out.

If Eris is nearby, then maybe I just can't see her? But neither *Detect Life* nor anything else reveled anything to me.

Am I dreaming, then?

Before I could tell myself what a bad idea it was, I brought my hand up and slugged myself across the face.

Chitin bit into my flesh and knocked a tooth loose as pain flashed across my jaw.

"Ow, godsdamn it," I cursed and spat out my tooth. "Okay. So I'm not dreaming, and I'm an idiot. At least I can confirm both of those things in the name of science."

I rubbed my aching jaw and finally decided I'd have to leave the room if I wanted answers. I stood up from the coffin and moved out into the hall. I quickly found myself back at the crossroads and had a second decision to make.

Which way to go?

Even as the thought formed, the flickering flames of the torches sputtered and died out to be quickly replaced with a bright blue flame.

It wasn't the bubbling, frothy green of mage lights, and my head didn't spin when I looked at them, so I assumed they were safe to look at. They lit up along the right passageway, indicating which way to go.

Normally, my instincts would have been screaming at me to go any other way but that direction, but my friends were missing, and I didn't have a choice. I had to find them.

I began walking down a very long hallway, and after ten minutes I found a set of wrought-iron stairs, spiraling up a tower that rose as high as I could see.

"Guess the only way is up." I shrugged and began the climb.

The only sounds that accompanied me were my heavy footfalls and my increased breathing as I climbed step after step for what seemed like an hour. I was in pretty fantastic shape, but my legs were burning after the mile-long climb up the thousand stairs of doom, and I wanted nothing more than to sit down for a few minutes with a nice cold bottle of water and relax.

Or better yet, a godsdamned ale.

I sighed and ran a hand though my silver locks.

164

"Cold turkey can kiss my ass!" I shouted at the top of my lungs.

Again, I received no response. After a few moments of catching my breath I slugged onward. Eventually, I reached the top of the stairs, which deposited me into a small hallway.

After walking for a few minutes, I found myself in front of a set of double doors. They were wooden with iron hinges, and before I could even take a step to open them, they opened at my approach.

They creaked open, sending panic coursing through my blood as blue flames flickered to life on either side of them.

I sighed. "*Deep into that darkness peering, long I stood there, wondering, fearing, doubting, dreaming dreams no mortal ever dared to dream before.*"

I chuckled. *What is with this place that brings out the gothic literature side of me?*

The silence of the tomb held my answer, and with the wisdom of Poe at my back, I stepped inside a throne room, not unlike the one Magnus had for himself. The room was long, and filled with heavy stone pillars that held up a high vaulted ceiling. Along the wall were numerous windows, but beyond them was nothing but gray, craggy stone.

Situated along the far wall was a heavy stone dais that rose to tower over me. Situated at the top was a writhing shadow. Blue fire cast sickening light over the shade.

The shadows twisted and curled, looking like nothing more than obsidian fire.

I had no clue what was going on. But the oppressive atmosphere that came from the shadow was overwhelming. It was fear, paranoia, and pain rolled into one heavy aura that settled over me like a cloud and tried to force me to the ground.

Though it took everything I had, I withstood the pain and took a single step forward. Then another and another until finally, I stood before the raised throne, staring up at nothing.

The shadow shifted, and though it had no features, I could tell it was staring down at me. Slowly it rose from the throne and stood. The writhing shadows shrank down, turning into a humanoid figure that walked slowly down the stairs.

Each step sent terror flowing through me, and I couldn't fight it. I could do nothing but stand absolutely still, for if I did anything else, I'd run screaming from the room.

As the shadow stepped down the final step and stood eye level with me, two pinpricks of blue fire lit up where its eyes would be, and a gruesome blue smile formed where it should have lips.

"Impressive, for you to stand before me without your heart stopping," a male, sibilant voice said. "I'd normally attribute it to your blood." His smile grew wider as he spoke next. "But we both know the kind of man you are. You'd stand your ground even before one of the nine kings of hell, wouldn't you, Sam?"

"Who are you?" I managed to choke out.

"I am the Shadow King."

What? I shook my head and frowned. "Bullshit. The Shadow King is a myth—a horror story criminals tell each other—a legend. He doesn't actually exist."

"Oh, I can confirm that I very much exist." His wide smile fell away to form a light smirk. "But I will admit that the Shadow King was never one for the spotlight, so I'm not surprised you don't believe. But come now, Sam. After everything you've been through, you still doubt the word of a god?"

"Maybe I've just exceeded my quota of shit I believe these days. And as for you being a god, I find that word doesn't mean as much as it used to. The word of a god means even less."

He chucked and nodded. "Fair enough. But if you won't accept the word of a god…" The shadows around the figure peeled back, and the heavy, oppressive aura dissipated like it had never been there at all, "then how about the word of a friend?"

The shadows faded and revealed the face of the Shadow King.

It was a face I recognized. He looked a little different. There was more light to his eyes, and his black, once long and lanky hair had been cut and combed back from his gaunt face. It was the face of the man I'd met in Tombsgard Prison—a man who had become a friend and helped me escape that awful place.

"Maus?" I asked.

"Been a while, Sam." He grinned at me. "I'm digging the new look. Very god-like, though not as cool as living shadows, amiright?"

"Maus! What the fuck?"

He laughed, heartily. And for a second, the man I knew in the prison returned. We hadn't exactly been friends before we left, but we'd fought side by side to escape the depths. That counted for something in my book, and even if we may never go have a beer together, he was someone I couldn't just ignore.

Especially now.

"How are you the Shadow King? And if you're a god, what were you doing in prison?"

Maus held up a hand to stop my onslaught of questions and smirked at me. "Hold your horses, Sam; one question at a time."

He paused and leaned against the armrest of the throne he once again sat in, crossing his legs.

"One, I wasn't the Shadow King when we were in prison together. This has been a recent development. Two, how I became the Shadow King is a long and frankly very complex story that would take more time to tell than we have here. But suffice it to say that the Shadow King is a mantle, just like your Hive Knight class or the mantle of Hive Queen. It can be transferred."

I crossed my arms, scratching at my beard. "Is it the same for the other gods?"

He shook his head. "No…well, I don't know. I don't think so." Maus held his hands up. "I'm not exactly best friends with the rest of the gods, given I only met them a few weeks ago, and they weren't exactly thrilled that I killed the former Shadow King."

What the actual fuck is going on?

My life kept going from one insane, crazy thing to the next with barely any time for me to process what the hell was actually going on.

I didn't like it. It felt as if I was being pulled in four separate directions at once, and sooner or later, it'd tear me apart.

"So what are you doing here? This is supposed to be a test for the Hive."

"And it was until the former Shadow King struck a deal with Magnus. They were working together. I only found out about it after we'd met, so I couldn't warn you, and by the time I could, I couldn't find you. Figured you were coming this way, so I did my best to intercept you…and here we are."

"So you saved us?"

"Precisely." He grinned.

"And what do you want in return?"

Maus shook his head and hopped up from the throne. He walked down to me and sat back on the stone steps. From his inventory, he pulled out a large silver flask.

"Want some? It's dwarven whiskey—strong."

My mouth watered at the mere mention of whiskey, and I sat down beside him. The voice in the back of my head telling me Raven and Eris would be disappointed in me was quiet as I took the flask and tipped it back.

Warm fire spilled delicious heaven down my throat and after a large swig, I passed it back and sighed deeply.

"Godsdamn, that was excellent."

As soon as the whiskey settled in my stomach, the guilt that had been silent flared to life and instantly made me regret taking the drink.

Raven would be frowning at me right now, and Eris would have that so-cute pout on her lips. They'd both be incredibly disappointed.

Maus took a drink and passed it back to me.

I held the flask in my hands, wanting so very much to take another drink, but my hand wouldn't let me bring it to my mouth. Shame and self-hatred crept up each time I tried. I stared at the flask for a minute before I handed it back to Maus.

"Thanks for the drink, but I'm good."

"More for me then." He chuckled and took another swig before storing it back in his inventory. "So what are you going to do?"

I shrugged. "Keep going down this cursed dungeon. I have a quest to deliver the treasure to the Morrigan. It's not something that I can easily ignore."

"That's your choice. I just came to warn you. I figured I owed you that much."

I shook my head. "You didn't owe me anything. We both paid our debts to each other when we escaped, and if anything, I owe you. You saved me when I collapsed next to the knockers. I'd say our debts have long since been paid."

He turned to look at me and grinned, bumping his shoulder against mine. "That may be true, but still, I saw a chance to help a friend and I took it.

Didn't cost me anything but a little time, and I got to screw over one of the most dangerous men on Nexus. It's been a good week."

Magnus.

"What was he doing here?"

Maus shook his head. "Personally, nothing. He never even stepped foot in the dungeon, but he sent his men to clear it and recover whatever lay at the end of it. I just happened to be waiting for him when he did, and my minions were more than capable of slaughtering the force he brought."

"Minions?" I raised an eyebrow before my eyes widened. "The roamers and wraiths? They're yours?"

"Yep." He nodded, his eyes twinkling. "Seems one of my abilities is the command of the dead. I'm like the world's strongest necromancer. Badass, yeah?"

"I'll say. So could you get rid of them?"

"I could, but I won't…consider it a second gift. You've got quicksilver, so nothing you come up against will be able to do much damage against you—well, that's not true, but you could really use the levels. So have some fun slaughtering my minions as you work your way to the bottom of the dungeon. Just follow the corpses."

With that, he patted my knee and stood. "Well, as fun as this has been catching up, I have other things I must attend to. The schedule of a god is busier than you'd think. But consider everything I've done for you as a favor. And maybe I'll have need of you in the future…you know, barring the world ending, of course."

"Wait! Where are my friends? I woke up and they were nowhere to be found."

Maus laughed. "Don't worry. They're fine." He turned back to me. "Be seeing you Sam. Sooner than you think."

His eyes flashed blue, and then he vanished.

"What the hell, Maus?"

Before I could turn around to go back, someone's hand was on my shoulder, shaking me.

My eyes flew open and I rose to my feet instantly.

Gil stood in front of me, with his hand on my shoulder. "There you are; I've been shaking you for a good few seconds now." He grinned down at me. "Guess you really needed the sleep, huh?"

"What?" I looked around. "Where am I?"

I blinked and found myself back in the sarcophagus room. Everyone stood in front of me, looking down at me.

"You all right, man?" Mika asked.

Eris's warm hand wrapped around my arm. "Sam?"

I rubbed my eyes, shaking off the dream, for it could have been nothing else. I rubbed my cheek, trying to feel where I'd punched myself and there was no pain.

That wasn't like any dream I've ever had before. Seriously, what the hell, Maus?

"Yeah. I'm fine. Just slept hard I guess."

"Good." Gil clapped me on the shoulder and laughed. "Then let's get a move on. Not all of us got an hour nap you know."

An hour? I had been tired earlier, but from past experience knew that an hour nap would have only worn me out even further. I felt as if I'd gotten eight uninterrupted hours of sleep and was as refreshed as I could be.

"All right, then let's get back to it." I grabbed my sword and we all slowly walked forward listening intently for any enemy threat.

I didn't bother telling them about my dream meeting with Maus. I knew for a fact it had been real—had actually happened—but I didn't think the others would believe me. They would have chalked it up to a fever dream and most likely would have dismissed it.

Even if they believed me, it didn't really change anything. I didn't learn anything that would help us in the moment, except that whatever awaited us at the bottom of the Nymirian Dungeon was valuable enough that Magnus either wanted it or didn't want us to have it.

That was good enough for me.

We all left the room and continued through the cursed dungeon.

CHAPTER 11 - AT THE BOTTOM OF THE DUNGEON

Eris

Sam had been acting strangely since he'd woken up. It wasn't so much in his words, though they lacked his usual tone, but his actions were off. There was something that I couldn't quite put my finger on other than he just didn't seem like his usual self--Like the Sam who had gone to sleep and the Sam who had woken up were different.

Maybe he had a bad dream? That would explain his behavior. He has a lot going on right now. So maybe that's it.

I walked with Raven and Yumiko while Sam, Gil and Mika led. We returned to the crossroads and stopped.

"Which way do we go?" Gil asked.

"Not that way," Sam replied, thumbing at the right walkway. "That leads up."

Gil snorted. "Kay, when did you suddenly develop psychic powers?"

"Trust me, that's not the way we want to go."

Gil looked back at us. "Anyone else have anything to add?"

All of us shook our heads no.

"Well, guess that only leaves one option. Straight it is."

Gil took off and we followed, but I kept stealing furtive glances at Sam as we passed the crossroads. He turned his head and stared down the right passageway as if he'd been down it before and had a strange look in his golden eyes.

I let go of Raven's hand and sped up to join Sam and ruining our formation, but I couldn't hear anything, so I figured it's be okay for just a second.

As I reached him, I wound my arm through his.

"Sam?"

He looked down at me, his eyes widening for a second before they relaxed, and he smiled at me.

"What is it?"

"Are you okay? You don't seem like yourself."

He shook his head, his smile growing even wider. "Don't worry, love. I'm fine. Just shaking off my nap. I'll be right as rain soon."

I frowned. "Okay, if that's all it is."

"It is." He gave my arm a squeeze and drew his sword. "Now get back in formation. We have company."

"What? I can't hear anything. How can you tell?"

"*Life Detect.*" His eyes widened and he shoved me to the side as a near-invisible hand shot through the wall to my left and nearly took my head off.

I fell to the ground with a jarring crash as half a dozen creatures appeared from the walls.

"Phantoms!" Sam shouted.

"Of course. We'd have to fight fucking phantoms," Mika said. "Who else has magic?"

I had no clue what was going on and why magic had anything to do with it, but I stood and shouted, "I have magic."

Mika looked at me and shook his head. "No, actual magic, like elemental magic. Phantoms can't be harmed by physical weapons, even ones coated in silver. It takes magic to kill them."

That left me stunned. I didn't have access to any offensive or purely magical attacks; all I had was hive magic, which was very limited in what I could do with it.

And if they couldn't be harmed by physical attacks, then my chitin was useless.

"I've got nothing," I said.

"I've got antimagic, which would get rid of them, but I can only use it once every forty-eight hours."

"Well shit, Sam. You want me to take them all by myself?" Mika asked.

The sword in his hands was now coated in a thin layer of ice and frost rose from the edge of his blade as he stepped forward and sliced through a phantom.

It didn't even make a sound as it cried out in pain. It opened its mouth wide, but no sound traveled from its maw. It died, bursting into motes of light and disappearing.

"I can't keep this up forever," he said taking a step toward the next closest phantom.

"Oh, for fuck's sake, get outta the way," Yumiko said, coming to stand beside me. "I'll take care of them."

She drew her bow and nocked an arrow.

"Fuckin' get behind me, quickly!" ordered Yumiko.

Everyone did as she said and filed in behind her as the phantoms drifted toward us.

Her arrow glowed a ghostly blue as she drew it back. Yumiko released the arrow, and it flew through the air, glowing even brighter as a trail of ice formed in its wake.

As it reached halfway between them, the arrow stuttered, blinking out of existence and then reappeared as seven arrows instead of one. Four of the arrows struck phantoms. As they landed, they stuck to the phantoms' incorporeal bodies. Ice formed in an instant and covered them. With a heavy gust of frosted wind, icebergs rose from the arrows, carving through the phantoms and ripping them to shreds. They burst apart, turning to flickering lights as they died.

Yumiko killed the remaining phantoms in one further attack, but it had an unintended side effect.

The arrows that missed the phantoms struck the walls and floor, causing ice to form and completely block the way forward.

As Yumiko lowered her bow, she chuckled. "Whoops, might've gone a bit overboard there."

Sam laughed with her. "*Tempest Shot* and *Multiply*. Always a classic." He shook his head and held his hands up. "But yeah, I'd say you went a little above and beyond there, Yu."

"Fuck else was I supposed to do? Sit around with my thumb up my ass and let the ghosts haunt our asses? You're welcome, by the way."

He grinned at her. "Thanks."

"Fuck you," she said, but she was smiling at him.

"Well, now that we don't have to worry about the phantoms, how the hell are we going to get through this ice?"

Yumiko shrugged. "Ask the magic swordsman over there." She pointed at Mika. "Hey, samurai. Make with the fire and cut through the ice."

Mika laughed and performed an over-exaggerated bow. "Right away, mistress. Anything you need, mistress." He muttered to himself while he walked over to the wall of ice. "Shine your shoes while I'm at it, mistress; get you some champagne? Whatever you need, mistress."

As he approached the wall, his ice sword changed to one of blazing fire as the blue flame lit up, and he began hacking away at the ice.

Steam filled the room, and we were forced to step back as Mika swung at the ice over and over again. In less than a minute, he had cleared a hole wide enough for us to squeeze through.

But when he turned, he had steam burns over his face and arms.

"Someone get me a damn health potion before I pass out. I can't feel my fingers."

Sam leapt into action and handed Mika one from his inventory. Mika guzzled it down, and soon the burns began to disappear.

When Mika was back to normal, he nodded his thanks and blinked his eyes. They were heavy, like he was trying hard to stay awake.

"Dammit, now I want a nap, too," Mika muttered as he slid his sword back into its sheath.

"Tough, we've got to keep moving. The aftereffects of the health potion should wear off after a while if you keep moving."

He waved Sam off. "Yeah, I know. Let's just go already." Mika shook off Sam and worked his neck back and forth. He slapped his cheeks, and his eyes went wide. "All right, I'm up. But hell, I want coffee."

With Mika back to his usual self, it took a few minutes for each of us to climb through the dense ice. When we were all gathered on the other side, we ventured further down the hallway.,

More of the roamers met us as we rounded the corner but, thankfully, we didn't encounter any more phantoms.

Gil and Sam quickly dispatched the group of roamers, and we kept going.

It seemed like the stone hallway would never end, but after fighting through more of the undead, we reached an arched doorway. An iron staircase spiraled down, deeper into the dungeon.

I took one look down and gulped. It seemed like it descended forever.

"So, who wants to be the first down the staircase into hell?" Gil asked, standing beside me.

"Might as well be me," I said, raising my hand. "I haven't done much since we got here, and I feel like I'm relying on everyone else to fight my battles for me."

Gil shook his head. "Nonsense. You've been kicking ass since we left Gloom Harbor. Saved my ass at least once, so don't go thinking you aren't helping, Eris. Don't make me knock some sense into you."

He grinned at me and patted me on the shoulder.

I grinned back. "Thanks for being the best older brother I always wanted."

Gil blushed scarlet and turned away, rubbing the back of his head. He muttered something, but I didn't quite make it out.

I smiled at the sight of a flustered Gil and stepped onto the staircase. My foot clanged loudly against the iron and echoed for what seemed like forever before it faded from my ears.

I don't like this, but it's time to step up and do my part. I owe it to everyone here to contribute.

Just before I was about to descend, Sam grabbed my shoulder, and I turned.

"Here," he said, handing me a small dagger coated in silver. "In case you run into anything and I can't reach you in time. And watch out for traps. I don't think we'll run into anymore, but I've been wrong before."

I took the knife with my thanks and turned back to the stairs, my heart in my throat. With only a hint of fear, I took a single step and started down the stairs.

We all walked down for what had to have been twenty minutes straight. I stopped counting at a thousand steps, and for a while, I thought we'd actually stumbled into a trap and we'd be stuck in the staircase for all eternity.

It was pitch black in the stairwell; absolutely no light except that from our torches accompanied us. It gave the place a very oppressive atmosphere that seemed to constrict my breathing every time I inhaled. I hated the place, hated the cramped stairs and darkness. It reminded me too much of the void, and if I didn't focus, I'd find myself slipping back there, reliving those memoires.

At the moment I was ready to give up and succumb to the darkness, the stairs abruptly ended and opened onto another hallway.

This one was slightly smaller than the mammoth halls up above, but only just. Thick slabs of stone lined the floor and walls, arching at the ceiling. As soon as I stepped out, the torches along the wall burst to life and filled the space with warmth and light.

It was such a contrast to what we'd just experienced that it gave me whiplash. I was ready for more gloom, but the atmosphere changed with the fire. It became warm and welcoming.

"I don't like this," Sam said.

"You felt it too," Gil replied.

I turned to both of them. "What are you talking about?"

Sam stepped forward and gestured with his sword. "This place has been nothing but hostile to us since we arrived, and now, even deeper into the dungeon, it gets warm and cozy." He sighed and his golden eyes searched the surrounding space for anything that would confirm his suspicions. "I don't trust this."

"Well, trust or not, we can't exactly stand around in the hallway forever. We need to keep moving," Mika said. "I'll take point if you want."

Sam shook his head. "I've got it. About time we switched off anyway." He thumbed back at Gil.

"Unless you want to take a crack at it."

Gil held his hands up. "I'm good. I don't want to be up front alone when the walls start to bleed."

With it decided, Sam took his position as point man. I fell in line behind him with Mika, Raven, Gil, and Yumiko following behind us.

It was quiet. No one was inclined to speak, but the quiet only unnerved us even further.

"This place makes my skin crawl," Raven said.

"Ditto, but I'm not entirely sure it's not because of Mika here," Yumiko said, laughing.

"I heard that!"

The others joined in laughter, except for me and Sam. He was too focused on his job to pay much attention to the others, and my stomach was in too many knots to be up for laughing, but I understood the impulse.

This place was terrifying, and it only seemed to get worse the further we went. I would want to do anything to take the tension away if I could, as well, but I needed to be sharp and alert.

I gripped my knife tightly and followed Sam. We turned a corner, and he stopped so suddenly that I nearly ran him through from behind.

"What the fuck?" he breathed, letting his curse slip out in a gasp.

I peered around him and nearly dropped my knife as my hand went to my mouth.

"What? How?"

In front of us was another hallway, but this one wasn't straight; it broke off into other hallways at irregular intervals. Over a dozen separate hallways formed on either side, leading I had no clue where.

And if that wasn't bad enough, the entire place was filled with several hundred roamers.

Gil stepped up beside Sam and stared for a long moment at the sea of undead before he whistled long and slow.

"Holy mother of fuck, that's more zombies than I've seen in any horror movie, ever."

"You're telling me," Sam replied. "What do we do about them?"

Gil looked sideways at Sam, smiled and held up his fist. "We go to work."

Sam responded by brushing his knuckles against Gil's fist and smiling. "Let's go to work."

***

Three very long, very bloody and gross hours later, we had finally cleared the hallway of roamers.

They kept coming, hundreds at a time, from all the hallways, forcing us to work in teams to kill them all individually or in small groups. According to Sam, these hit and run tactics worked best for dealing with them.

But the downside was that it took time, a lot of it. And we were forced to fight in shifts to let the others recover from their battle fatigue.

During the fight, the others suffered minor cuts, scrapes, and bites from the undead, but nothing serious. Sam and I were saved from any injury because of our chitin, but that also meant we both exhausted ourselves—me from using my magic and him from battle fatigue.

At the end of the fight, all of us slumped to the ground and nearly passed out we were so tired.

"All right, guys. We've been fighting for hours—and hours before that. We've been in the dungeon for nearly a full day already. We need to get some sleep and rest or we're all going to collapse," Mika said.

Though I was loath to sleep in the dungeon, I couldn't deny how wonderful rest sounded. I'd never been so tired. Even during training when

Evelyn had beaten me black and blue, I'd still had the strength to cuddle up with Tegen and Cheira.

I grinned at the thought of them, despite my exhaustion. *I wonder how they're doing? I hope they're well.*

Maybe I can convince Sam to go to the Darkwoods after we get done with this cursed place. It'd be a nice little distraction for us.

I lost myself in the daydream and leaned against the stone wall while I rested.

"Mika's right. We need to set up camp," Gil said. "Let's camp, get a fire going, and make some food. The snack I had in the sarcophagus room wasn't very filling, and I just burned through a whole bunch of energy."

"Me too," I said. "I'm starving, though I did level up twice during that fight, so I can't really complain."

Yumiko nudged me. "Where'd your stats go?"

I paused, searching for the information. I'd only halfway paid attention when I'd received the notifications so I wasn't entirely sure.

"Looks like Strength, Agility, Wisdom, and Durability." I tapped a finger on my lips, fighting a yawn. "Not bad. I'm just glad my magic is starting to go up. It's still pretty weak."

Though I was still bone tired, I had to get up and help the others set up camp. We decided to fall back to the stairwell and came in the entryway. It gave us cover and only one direction to defend in case we missed any of the roamers.

I helped set up the sleeping pallets while Sam and Yumiko got the fire going and food prepared. I hadn't known that Yumiko was actually a very good cook and she could make delicious food in a style referred to as Old Japanese.

Whatever it was, it was full of flavor and utterly delicious. It was my first experience eating rice, which was rare on Nexus. I loved every bite, and before I knew it, I'd eaten three helpings.

I sat back on my hands, feeling like my stomach was going to burst.

"That was delicious. Thank you, Yu."

"Yeah, don't mention it. This place had me feeling a little homesick, so thanks for letting me indulge myself."

"What was your home like?" I asked.

"Busy." She smiled. "Before the Night-Fall, it was a crowded, chaotic place full of light and life." Her smile fell. "Then one day it wasn't. Those damn ghouls showed up and tore the world apart."

She got quiet after that, and I realized my mistake.

I shouldn't have opened my mouth. I know from Sam that people don't like talking about their old home.

I wanted to apologize, but I caught Yu's eye and she smiled, letting me know she didn't hold it against me. I mouthed my thanks and curled up next to Sam and the fire. Raven was on his other side, and we leaned against the wall.

Before I knew it, I was struggling to keep my eyes open, and I leaned heavily against Sam. My hand found his and was soon joined by Raven's. The three of us fell asleep holding hands, and we slept deeply.

I dreamed deeply. Flashes of my life and Sam's mixed together from my own memories and the ones I'd seen in the Mnemosyne. They formed a chaotic mixture of Nexus and the world Sam came from. I was running through the streets of the Compass Kingdom at night, chased by the abhorrent creatures known as ghouls. Their ice-blue eyes haunted me, and I stumbled, tripping over cobblestone. I turned as one opened its jaws wide, revealing thousands of silver needlepoint teeth that closed over my skull.

I woke with a start, my heart hammering in my chest. Sweat ran in rivulets down my forehead and stung my eyes.

As I calmed down, I took a look around to find several of the other Gloom Knights up and alert. Gil looked over at me and gave me a reassuring smile.

"Bad dreams too?" he asked.

I nodded.

He motioned to Sam and Raven, who were still sleeping. Their eyes flickered under their lids, and Sam twitched, his face pained. He was having a nightmare, and Raven, too.

"What's going on? I don't believe we'd all just have nightmares at the same time."

"You're right, we wouldn't. "He shook his head and sighed. "There's only one thing that can cause this level of powerful mental magic over us."

"What?" I asked.

"A lich."

I shuddered, my skin crawling with goosebumps at the mere mention of it.

"Are you sure?"

"Positive. It makes sense given the level of undead in the dungeon. I'm betting we find one at the bottom of this cursed labyrinth. But what worries me is that it's already starting to affect us."

I sat up and crossed my legs, easing away from Sam so I didn't wake him. "What does that matter?"

"Because I don't think it's aware of us yet. If so, the nightmares would be a whole lot worse. I think this is just the residual energy cast off by its insane aura. And if that's the case, it means the lich is stronger than any I've faced before."

"That's a fucking problem," Mika said, joining in on the conversation. "Liches are notoriously difficult to kill."

"Well, they're immortal right? Shouldn't it be impossible to kill them?"

Gil shook his head. "Incredibly, painfully difficult, but not impossible."

"All we have to do is find its phylactery and destroy it. That would kill it pretty quickly," Mika said.

The phylactery was a vial that contained a lich's soul, so I'd been told. They were the only thing keeping the lich alive, and to destroy one was to destroy the lich.

Because they were the lich's one weak spot, they were notoriously difficult to obtain. Liches hid them well because their lives depended on them being hidden away.

"Good news is that liches can't be too far away from their phylacteries. They'll wither away and die if they get too far away. And if this lich is as powerful as I think it is, then the phylactery has to be in the dungeon," Gil said.

"We just have to find it," Sam said, sitting up. "While also fighting off an immortal being who can cast magic better than almost anyone except Magnus. It's not going to be a walk in the park."

"When has it ever been easy for us? We've been fighting with the deck stacked against us since we formed the Gloom Knights. Hell, if things started getting easy now, I'd really worry something was wrong with the world." At that, Gil stood and went to rouse the others.

We quickly packed up camp even though no one was eager to leave the security of the camp site and continue forward to fight the denizens of the dungeon. I wasn't looking forward to facing the end of the dungeon. It wasn't going to be easy, and I didn't want any of my friends to get hurt.

But that isn't something I can stop from happening. We'll get hurt whether I like it or not. I just hope all of us can come out of this with our lives at the very least.

I must've made a face, because Raven came over to me and poked me with one of her fingers. "Whatcha brooding about over there, pouty?"

I shook my head. "Nothing. Just worried, I guess."

"I am too." She leaned over and placed her chin on top of my head. "But it'll be all right if we watch each other's backs. I've got yours."

I smiled. "And I've got yours. Now let's go and finish this dungeon."

Chapter 12 - The Lich

Gil led the way down the many hallways while we searched for the correct pathway that would lead us out of this miniature maze and to the final chamber of the dungeon.

It took about an hour or so of walking until we discovered the correct passage.

"All right, I have no clue how far until we reach the lich, so keep your guards up, okay?" Gil said.

We all stood ready to fight, nearly jumping at every shadow that danced along the stone walls. But after days of this, I'd long since grown used to the cramped quarters and heavy air.

I stayed close to Sam and Raven. Sam had his sword in hand, and Raven had her claws out; she'd finally caved and dipped her fingers into the quicksilver. Though she hadn't been happy about it.

She'd complained that it was going to be a nightmare to clean off, but personally I'd rather her be alive to have something to complain about.

We continued to find more and more undead as we went along. Dozens of undead, wraiths, and even a few more phantoms popped up here and there. After nothing but undead, we'd seen all the tricks they had to offer, and Gil, Sam, and Mika slaughtered them all with impunity.

Hours turned into another day as we walked, going this way and that following the never-ending paths that comprised this level of the dungeon and breaking the monotony with random bursts of hyper violence sparsed throughout, until we reached a final hallway.

This one was different than the barren and uniform stone I'd grown so used to. One major difference was the moss and lichen growing through the cracks and chipped portions.

It was worn and run down, obviously left to crumble and fall to pieces.

Sam walked over to the wall and touched it. His hand came way mossy. He wiped it off on his pants and frowned.

"Why is this section different than the rest? It shouldn't be—the rest of the dungeon has been the same, or at least similar. This is a deviation, and I don't like it."

"Not a clue, but can you feel the presence of the lich?" Gil asked.

He nodded. "Yeah, this one is tremendously powerful. We need to be very careful when dealing with it."

Sam stepped away from the wall, and we continued onward. This whole situation unnerved me to no end, and eventually, even I began to feel the overwhelming aura of the lich. It was something I'd never experienced before and was different from anything I'd ever experienced, which is why it took my senses so long to be able to distinguish what it was.

The aura was the same heavy atmosphere that had been surrounding us since we entered the undead dungeon, but it grew heavier with each step, and after a while, I realized it was subtly different. It was twisted and malevolent—a vile presence that weakened me with every step I took.

We eventually stopped a few dozen feet in front of a set of double doors.

We had reached the end of the dungeon.

"I don't like this," I muttered to myself, but my voice carried, and everyone heard me.

"I know, but we don't have much choice. We need to complete this dungeon and grab the treasure for the Morrigan," Sam replied.

"Doesn't mean I have to like it. This place is evil."

"Evil, maybe." He shook his head. "But we still have to kill the undead bastard up ahead, so let's stop talking and start doing."

Sam opened his inventory and took out a number of potions and other vials of equipment. He laid everything out in neat rows on a sheet of canvas cloth.

As I looked around the others were doing the same. Each of them took out items from their inventory and began sorting them into piles.

"What are we thinking here?" Mika asked. "*Tincture of Undeath* and *Decoction of the Archmage?*"

Sam rubbed his chin, tugging at the small hairs covering it. "Both good options. We'll need to counteract the lich's passive aura so *Tincture of Undeath* is a must. But *Decoction of the Archmage* is a bit much. We don't even know what kind of magic the lich possesses yet."

"Which is why we go ahead and counter every possibility." Mika grinned. "One-stop magic resistance and we're good to go."

"True, but that puts all of us at our potion limit. If we get injured and have to heal with a potion, that means potion sickness."

"I'd rather fight under the threat of potion sickness than have my appendage blasted off by a bolt of lightning," Mika replied.

Sam shook his head and shrugged. "You have a point there. And it's better to be safe than sorry. So yeah. Those two with a health and recovery potion waiting as backup, just in case."

With everyone in agreement about the potions they'd take before the fight, Sam and Gil passed around the extra potions they had and handed them to those who didn't have any—namely me and Raven.

I took both potions and downed them quickly. The *Tincture of Undeath* was bitter and brackish and I had to fight to keep it down. The decoction was rather smooth in comparison, having a hint of fire from the alcohol, but also a cool refreshment from a blend of different sweet flavors like peppermint.

After I'd drank both, my head swam with a rush before my body acclimated to whatever I'd just put in it.

As I handed the empty bottles back to Sam, he handed me one more vial containing another bit of quicksilver.

"Get some arrows from Yumiko and back us up. Raven will guard both of you from any close-range attackers while Gil, Mika, and I keep the lich occupied. When only the lich is left, grab your knife and start searching for the phylactery, okay?"

I nodded. "I'll do my best."

"I know you will." He smiled, a wry smile that lit up his eyes. "Just remember that our lives are in your hands. No pressure or anything."

He said it as a joke, but the weight of his words hit me hard enough to hitch my breathing for a second. I recovered before he noticed anything, thankfully.

If I mess up, then everyone dies. I can't afford any mistakes; everything has to be perfect.

I didn't have time to wonder what I was going to do about the situation, because before I had a chance to respond, Sam and the others drew arms.

"Ready?" he asked.

"Let's do this!" Gil shouted back.

The six of us rushed into the room.

It was unlike any other room I'd seen in the dungeon. Although it was mostly barren, cracked slate tiles with weeds growing up through them made up the floor, while crumbling pillars supported nothing. In cubbyholes along the walls were hundreds of lit candles with melting wax slipping lackadaisically to the ground.

In the center of the room stood a stone altar, with a thick crimson sash draped across it. Long-stemmed black candles sat in iron candelabras at all four corners.

Lying on the altar was the lich.

Its gray flesh was stretched too tightly across its bones, giving it an emaciated, hollow appearance. It had long, knurled fingers with fingernails shaved into wicked points. Its skull was bald, its eyes long since putrefied and fallen out, leaving empty sockets.

The lich wore a long, moth-eaten robe with more holes than fabric.

As we entered the room, a rush of wind swept around the room and made the candle flames flicker. The lich stirred at our presence and slowly sat up on the altar.

As he rose, he began floating off the floor, supporting himself with wind magic. His bony, sightless skull turned to us, and his eyes flared to life with twin points of blue flames.

"Who dares disturb my rest?" it croaked in an aged, wizened voice. It snarled as the flames grew brighter. "Humans, and a demi-human. It has been so long since I've had fresh meat. You'll do just fine. I'll tear your hearts out and walk in your skin."

He spoke a quick chant in Script, and with a flourish of his palm, a sapling tree burst from beneath the ground, writhing in chaos as it grew and twisted, forming a long stave. The lich took the staff, and the tree returned to the earth.

· His magic was fast, and we hadn't had much time to react to him casting before it had already finished. But as soon as he spoke again, Gil, Sam, and Mika rushed the lich.

They were fast, but the lich was quick with his spells, too. He recited another quick chant, and a ball of fire appeared at the end of the staff. It launched toward Gil, who was the largest target.

Gil didn't even flinch. He took the blast of fire in the chest, and it erupted with a heavy explosion of fire. He shook it off as if it were nothing and kept charging, his battleaxe raised.

He swung with all his might and took the lich in the chest. His weighted axe sheared through the lich as if it were parchment and bisected him neatly in half.

Even as Gil carried through with his strike, the lich laughed. His torso hung in the air before tendrils of flesh rose from his lower half and stretched toward his stomach. In an instant, the lich was whole once more as his body melded itself back together.

"Foolish human. Even with silver, I cannot be harmed."

He raised a bony hand and began chanting, low and guttural. As he finished, a dozen hands burst from the ground.

Roamers rose up from beneath the earth in droves and quickly separated the Gloom Knights. Their disgusting, rotten flesh sloughed off even as they hauled themselves up and began shambling forward.

I raised my bow and began firing, trying to kill the ones closest to Sam and Mika. I dropped three roamers quickly, but it seemed like they kept on coming. Every second more and more of them rose.

The lich laughed, a twisted cackle that sent shivers up my spine.

"Fools, hundreds have tried and failed to kill me. Now I'll add your bones to my collection."

Soon I had nearly exhausted my supply of chitin and could fire no more without weakening my exoskeleton.

"Eris, find the phylactery. Raven and I will hold off these bony fucks," Yumiko shouted.

I nodded and drew my dagger. It was coated with silver and would cut cleanly through any of the roamers that tried to get close to me.

I rushed to the side as the undead closed in around Raven and Yu. Raven leapt into the horde with her silver claws gleaming and tore into the roamers with a savagery I hadn't seen from her yet. Her claws elongated even further, and with a single swipe from her claws, she killed three of them at once.

Their flesh parted with a sizzle as it cracked and blacked under the touch of silver.

The others were keeping the lich busy while also killing more of the roamers. I knew I didn't have long to search. As soon as their potions wore off, they'd be vulnerable to magic once more and then the lich would tear them apart.

Their lives and mine rested on me solving this demented scavenger hunt.

I gripped the knife tightly and went to the most obvious place first, the altar.

Gil's massive body protected the lich from seeing me and I quickly tipped over the candles and other semi-religious artifacts that littered its surface.

None of them are the phylactery. Sam told me it's a small glass vial filled with a bright blue light.

All I found were candles and a few totems carved in the likeness of the lich.

With my search of the top of the altar having failed, I ripped the tapestry off the mantle and found a spot between the stone.

It seemed like the top of the altar could come free. If I was going to hide something that kept me alive, then placing it under the thing I slept on would probably be my first thought.

The lid was unbelievably heavy, even for someone of my strength. I summoned every ounce of strength I had and shoved the lid as hard as I could.

It creaked and groaned, scraping against itself as it moved inch by inch. Finally, after nearly exhausting myself, the lid reached the edge of the altar and slid off with a massive crash.

As soon as the lid was off, I peered into the coffin and searched for the vial. I found nothing but darkness. It seemed like the hole went on forever; it was so dark.

Then two bright crimson balls of light flared to life. Then they blinked.

That's a—

Before I could react, a large bony fist flew up and crashed into me. Agony robbed me of my breath as my nose burst, and a mess of blood ran down over my mouth and chin to stain my clothes. I flew back from the force, only to cry out as my back slammed into the wall behind me and even more pain radiated through me.

There was a horrendous shrill screech that emanated from below the altar.

A large, skeletal hand grabbed the lip of the altar, and then another appeared. Slowly, the head of the creature peered over the stone.

It was large, like a giant, easily a foot or more taller than Gil who was already a mountain of man. This skeleton was black from head to toe. Like it had been in a fire and burned to a crisp. Its eyes were two large pools of bloody crimson.

It climbed out of the altar and towered over me. It ignored everything else in the room. As the crimson eyes stared down at me, a flicker of recognition passed through them. The skeleton blinked, and its eyes began writhing.

The eyes dimmed, then they melted. The crimson slowly bled from the eyes to drip over the skull's cheekbones and down its face to coat its collarbone and ribs.

"Eris, run!" Sam shouted from far closer than I thought he'd be. "You can't fight that monster!"

"Yes, run, run as fast as you can! But you won't be able to escape the clutches of my bloody bones!" the lich said, laughing.

As the bloody bones stood before me, the blood that poured never-ending from its sockets coalesced where its heart should be. Behind its ribs, a ball of crimson blood pulsed, and tendrils of the blood made their way over its arms and legs, staining the black bones red.

It let out another horrendous shriek that made my ears bleed and then it lunged for me.

Sam couldn't save me; he was busy fighting the lich with the others. Raven and Yu were taking out the roamers, leaving me alone to fight this monstrous creature.

I gripped my knife tightly as bloody bones swiped down at me. I stepped back, narrowly dodging its wicked fingers.

"I won't lose to you," I said, staring it down.

Never again would I lose. It was time I stood on my own two feet and faught.

As its hand gouged deep rents into the earth, I darted forward. I brought my knife in an arc as I angled for the skeleton's elbow.

My knife struck the crimson bone and hewed a small divot from the bone as it passed by. I stepped through the monster's legs and tried once more to slice through the bone. I cut toward its ankle, doing nothing more making than a shallow, superficial gash.

Its hand came back, bending at an unnatural angle as it came for me.

I rolled out of the way just as it passed over my shoulder. Wind ruffled my clothes and whistled passed as its fist glanced off the stone altar and chipped it.

I can't get hit with that, not when I'm not even wearing armor.

It was clear that I needed my exoskeleton, but with my chitin drained from my arrows, I wouldn't have enough to form a proper defense. At best, I could probably withstand a blow or two before my chitin cracked and failed.

Better than nothing.

I summoned my chitin and willed it to form over my body as the bloody bones turned once more and clacked its mouth together in the approximation of a laugh.

When the black chitin oozed over my hands, I formed long claws on each finger. It was painfully obvious that my knife wasn't going to be enough. And I didn't have the chitin to form a proper weapon. Even using the claws meant I had to take away some of the thickness of my chitin from the rest of my body. But I believed it was a worthwhile tradeoff.

Either I killed the thing or I died. A little extra padding wasn't going to stop that thing's strength.

My armor fully formed instantly, but it was still a second too long to stand still.

Bloody bones came after me with both hands clenched together like a massive hammer. Its bones creaked as it raised them above its head and crashed them back down on me.

I was forced to dodge. I threw myself into a forward roll and came up just as its fist struck. The force was enough to send me flying. My feet lifted off the ground, and I sailed toward bloody bones. My head struck the bottom of its ribcage and spun me around before I slammed into the ground.

My chitin had mitigated the impact, but barely, and my head rang as my vision swam.

"Ow…" I muttered, trying to come back to myself.

It took everything I had to stand up. Chips of black chitin fell off me like ashes and skittered over the cracked and broken stone.

As I stood, I was still inside bloody bones's space. It stood from its massive attack, and I knew I didn't have much time.

I jumped even as it bent its knees and stood up. My hands gripped the bottom of its ribcage and I used them as rungs on a ladder to climb up to its shoulder.

Its skull turned to look at me, its lidless, sightless eyes somehow conveying a sense of utter delight that I was so close to it. Its jaw clacked open, and it surged toward me, snapping its mouth closed right next to me.

The sharp sound shattered my concentration as terror pounded through my veins. I'd never been so terrified of anything in my life except the void, and the pitch-black eyes of the bloody bones were reminding me all too well of that.

My grip loosened on the bones as I panicked and dropped a few ribs down, trying to keep away from its jaws. As I was about to climb back up, its left arm began to move, and I spied a blood sac where its shoulder should have been. It was dark, and it blended in well with the blackened bones so I had missed it at first glance.

This creature wasn't like the skeletons I'd encountered before, they were held together solely by magic and didn't require the need for muscles to help it move. For some reason, bloody bones wasn't like the rest of the skeletons. It was sentient to some degree rather than a construct like most skeletons. It was also held together with blood that somehow simulated muscle tissue and allowed it to put greater than normal strength behind its blows.

Its strength even rivaled my own, or even surpassed it.

But as I noticed the blood sac, I had an idea that could save me, and hopefully everyone else.

We were running out of time, and the longer I fought with bloody bones, the less time the others had to deal with the lich. We'd only been fighting for a few minutes, but it seemed like a lifetime and that time was running out.

I had to act fast.

As bloody bones lifted its arm, I leapt from its ribcage and clung to its arm like it was a lifeline. My clawed fingers dug into its bone, and I gripped it tight, holding onto it with everything I had.

With my left hand, I reached up and grabbed hold of the large blood sac.

I dug my fingers deep, putting every ounce of my considerable strength into it. Bloody bones let out the loudest scream yet, its high-pitched shriek of agony locking my body up for a spilt second. It overrode my nerves and froze me in place.

It stopped me just long enough for it to bring its other arm around and punch me as hard as it could.

My world went black as its heavy fist slammed into me. When I came to, I was lying on the ground a dozen feet away. I must have only been out for a second, but it was long enough.

The attack had shattered my chitin. It crumbled to nothing, and I was pretty sure I had a few broken ribs. With how much it hurt for me to breathe, they were at least broken. As I stood, I raised my hand. Something squishy lay in my palm.

It was the bloody sac from the skeleton's shoulder. I looked up at bloody bones and found it where it had been. It hadn't moved and was now missing its arm.

I'd torn the one thing holding it's arm in place, and it lay in a scattered pile at its feet.

I stood, despite the pain, and willed the rest of my chitin back under my skin except for my clawed hands. My chitin was too weak to stave off another hit, and I'd rather use what was left to bolster my claws.

Bloody bones was down an arm, and I knew how to defeat it now.

As it shook off the shock of having its arm torn off, it regarded me with an expression I could only describe as pure malice. It hated me for what I'd done.

Good. Because I hate you. I hate you with my entire being because you and your master are risking the lives of my family. I won't let you harm them.

I gritted my teeth against the pain and rushed bloody bones for one final attack.

It stepped toward me and slammed its fist down. I rolled to the side and came up on my feet. I kept running and passed its legs. I went around behind bloody bones and turned, jumping up. I grabbed hold of its pelvis and wrapped my legs around its thigh. I dug in between its leg and hips for the blood sac that had to be connecting its leg. After some careless pawing, I had it in my hands, and I pulled with all my might.

I ripped the blood sac free and pushed off its leg as soon as it came loose. With nothing attaching the leg to bloody bones, it went flying from the force of my jump. Bloody bones shifted and crashed to the ground.

It tried to compensate and managed to balance for half a second before it came crashing down next to its discarded body parts. It landed on its ribs, and there was a sharp crack as a few of them broke from the force.

I walked over around it and met its cold gaze one last time.

It stared up at me with undisguised hatred on its face, but with its left arm and leg missing, it could do nothing but crawl towards me and snap its jaws.

I stepped to the side and up onto its back as it began crawling. Residing in the center of its chest was the largest blood sac, right where its heart would have been. I gripped it with both hands and pulled.

It resisted for a long moment, but I sank my hips and yanked with every last bit of strength I had left.

The blood sac burst under my fingers and came free with a sickening squelch as it turned to mush even as I ripped it from bloody bones's chest.

The monster gave one final howl of rage and misery, raising its head up once more before it died and crashed against the stone floor. Bloody bones lay still, and then crumbled into ash under me.

A warmth spread through me, letting me know that I'd leveled up multiple times after defeating the skeleton.

As proud as I was, I didn't have time to waste dealing with my level up. I had to find the phylactery before everyone died.

The battle had raged around me, and no one had made any headway. Raven was covered in brackish filth from the roamers, and her breathing was ragged and stilted, but she was fine. So was Yumiko, who hadn't let a roamer near her long enough to take a swing at her.

The rest of the Gloom Knights were a bit bloody and worn down, but they were all still alive facing the lich who hadn't stopped casting spell after spell at them.

I searched the remains of bloody bones but found nothing. If it wasn't inside bloody bones, then it had to be in the altar. I raced to it and once more peered down.

A large hole dropped into what seemed like a cave. If the phylactery was anywhere, it'd be there.

I vaulted the lip and jumped down. I hung in the air for less than a second before I landed on rocky ground and stumbled as my knees buckled. I tried to roll with the impact but just wound up face planting on the rock.

"Ow. That hurt," I groaned and rubbed my aching face.

I was bloody all over, some from me, but mostly from bloody bones. I shook my head and stood. It was pitch black in the cave, but my eyes could still pick out shapes in the dark. I continued forward for a few feet until I reached a hand-carved alcove.

There was only one item situated there. It was a small glass vial that shimmered with a bright light that almost seemed like a liquid. I picked it up, and it sloshed around, growing brighter.

From up above, a scream of rage blasted through the cavern loud enough to make my ears ache.

The lich knew I'd found its phylactery.

I closed my clawed hand and crushed it.

There was a heavy thump of pressure, and I found myself falling. Darkness crept into my vision, and then there was nothing but the desire for me to sleep.

When I came to, I was back in the altar room. I recognized the ceiling. I was warm, and I didn't ache anymore. In fact, I was very comfortable.

I shifted, and as soon as I moved, Sam's smiling face entered my field of vision. He grinned down at me.

"About time you woke up, sleepyhead."

"I guess I needed a nap," I replied, snuggling closer to him. "What happened?"

"Well, after you destroyed the phylactery, the lich died, and so did all of his minions which was just in time, too. We had mere minutes at most remaining on our potions."

He beamed at me and ran his hand through my hair.

"I told you to run from bloody bones, and that was a mistake. I didn't think you could defeat it. Even high-leveled players sometimes have trouble dealing with them. I underestimated you, and for that I'm sorry. I'm so proud of you, Eris."

I tilted my head, and he caught my meaning. His lips met mine, and I wrapped my hand around the base of his neck. Our kiss was brief, but passionate. When we broke apart, our lips lingered on each other's for a moment longer before he leaned back, and we stood.

As I checked myself over, I found my clothes were a mess, but nothing that couldn't be salvaged. The others were looking much more refreshed, if a little bloody.

"Why haven't you guys healed your injuries?"

"Can't risk potion sickness. We decided to rest here for a few hours and let the potions' recovery time lapse before we heal ourselves and continue."

"Continue?" I shook my head. "I thought the lich was the end of the dungeon?"

Sam stood next to me and pointed at the far wall. It had been just rock earlier, but now the rock had crumbled away and revealed a doorway that led to even further in the dungeon.

"I'm getting really tired of this place," I said.

"You and me both," Raven said, coming over to me. "But what can we do. Let's rest a bit before we do anything else. C'mon, you deserve it."

Raven led me over to the far wall, where she'd set out blankets and had a small fire going. After a cup of hot tea that Yumiko had made, I laid my head in Raven's lap and promptly fell asleep.

Chapter 13 - Dungeon's End

Sampson

As Eris and the others took a much-needed break, I sank back against the stone altar and heaved a sigh of relief.

The fight with the lich had been taxing, to say the least, and I was grateful to be done with it. It had turned into a stalemate at the end, with none of the attacks on either side doing much permanent damage. In truth, the roamers were more trouble than the lich.

I was just glad it was over, and we could all rest and recover. We'd been down in the dungeon for a couple of days at this point, and I was starting to miss the sun.

While I was resting, I pulled out a skin of water and downed it along with a few bits of food before I started dealing with my status.

After a full day of fighting all manner of undead, I'd stopped even opening it, letting it all pile up. It was a nightmare.

Combat Results!
187 Killed (Roamers): 56100 Exp!
18 Killed (Wraith): 16200 Exp!
1 Killed (Lich): 15000 Exp!
Total Exp Gain: 87300 Exp!
Exp: 7300/7300
Level Up! (x11)
Exp: 3200/8400
Level: 84
110 Stat Points Available!

1 Ability Point Available!

I whistled, long and slow.

"You too, huh?" Gil asked from across the room.

"The experience? Yeah. I just gained a mountain of it."

He nodded and fiddled with his interface in front of him. "Never thought I'd ever gain as much experience at one time than when we fought the elder dragon, but I'm surprised once again." He rubbed the back of his head. "A shame it all went to waste though. Can't do anything with it after I hit max level."

Most of the Gloom Knights were level one hundred. Because of the mantle of Hive Knight, I was the lowest leveled player in the guild; even with the leveling booster, I was still playing catch up.

Well, I doubt I'll have a chance to earn as much experience like this again, so I can't count on leveling up past ninety before I have to face Magnus. Which means I know what my next ability is.

Without any hint of regret, I chose *Return to Zero.*

I read the description and smiled.

That'll even the playing field nicely.

But I knew that even with the ability, it wouldn't guarantee anything. Magnus had a thousand years on me, had more power than I could imagine, and one ability, even one designed to counter his power, wouldn't be enough to beat him on its own.

I still needed to get stronger.

Which means I need to allocate my stat points carefully.

I added thirty to *Attack Damage,* taking it to one hundred. Twenty went to *Battle Fatigue,* bringing it to seventy-five—an adequate number—which left me sixty points to play with.

Though I wasn't a Blade Master any longer, my old playstyle reared its head. I wasn't as strong as I used to be in terms of pure damage output, but I was by far more durable than I'd ever been. I had a good deal of strength and defense, but I wanted more speed, to attack and react faster. My training could compensate for some of it, but I was slower than I had been before I became a Hive Knight.

Against Magnus, who could cast magic in a blink of an eye, I needed speed.

With my mind made up, I put thirty points into *Attack Speed,* taking it to fifty-five, and the last thirty went to *Movement Speed,* bringing it to an even fifty.

As I accepted my changes, my body grew hot, and my fingertips and toes burned as muscle shifted and my body grew a bit lighter, my movements slightly more assured.

It was a feeling I had nearly forgotten about, but I could tell the subtle difference in my body from the added points. Strength and speed flowed through my body for the briefest moment before my body acclimated to the change, and the pleasant tingle faded, leaving me exhausted.

After I dealt with my stats, I let the tiredness roll over my body and closed my eyes for a few moments.

It must have been more than my body could handle in such a short time coupled with the near constant fighting we'd been doing for over two days, because I slept for nearly eight hours.

When I finally got up. I was stiff, my muscles were shot, and my mouth was as dry as a desert. Most of the others were still asleep.

We all fought hard, and we definitely needed a nap.

After I drank an entire waterskin, I got up and went over to where Raven and Eris were. Raven leaned against the wall while Eris used her lap as a pillow. A blanket had been thrown over both of them, but I bet that Eris did more to combat the chill than any blanket.

Raven looked uncomfortable, so I sat down next to her and leaned her head onto my shoulder. She awoke at the subtle shift, her bright crimson eyes lighting up as she looked at me. She yawned and then gave me a sleepy smile.

"Sorry I woke you," I whispered, "You looked uncomfortable."

"It's okay." Raven scooted over, being careful not to wake Eris, which was pointless because she could sleep through thunderstorms.

She scooted over and into my lap, leaning her head in the crook between my neck and shoulder. When she'd gotten comfortable, she reached over and grabbed my arms. One she wrapped around her waist and intertwined our fingers, but the second, she slipped under her shirt to cup her breast while she held it there.

"Much better," she murmured and then her head lolled to the side. Her hot breath prickled my neck and chest.

I snorted softly and kissed the top of her head and brushed a few errant locks of her pitch-black hair away from her forehead. I was sure we looked fairly ridiculous with Raven using me as a bed and Eris using Raven as a bed, but I loved seeing both of my girls resting comfortably. Even in this dark dungeon it made me smile.

We stayed like that for a couple of hours, and I got another short nap, but by the time morning came, it was time to get up.

Gil jumped up with a shout of fright before calming down.

"Godsdamn it, I forgot to turn off my alarm."

It was such a mundane thing, even more so in a place like this that it caught me completely off guard. I laughed. I laughed long and hard, a full bellied laugh that woke up not just Raven and Eris but the others as well.

"Yeah, yeah. Keep laughing, won't be so funny when I put a snake in your tent," Gil grumbled.

"Go right ahead." I chuckled. "Snakes have never bothered me. It was bugs I was afraid of, and well, Eris kinda fixed that fear."

She turned and beamed at me. "Morning, love."

"Morning," I replied.

When everyone was awake, we got up, made a quick breakfast and readied ourselves for the battles to be faced today.

Eris had reclaimed all of her chitin arrows from yesterday's fight, but I was hoping we wouldn't have to fight.

Logically, we'd beaten the dungeon boss. There shouldn't be anything else but the treasure room left, and we had been too tired to find out the previous night just in case we were wrong.

"This dungeon has subverted expectations at every turn, so we should be careful."

"Agreed," Mika said and drew his katana.

The rest of us drew arms and stepped through the hole in the cavern wall.

Almost immediately, the ground sloped down. It wasn't sudden enough to make us fall, but it was enough to make our balance precarious at best.

"Don't slip," I said. "You'll take us all out like bowling pins if you do."

That garnered a few chuckles, but everyone became too focused on their footing to laugh.

We made our way down the mile-long slope, and only once we were halfway down the damn thing did I have the thought.

"Uh, guys. How the hell are we going to get up again?"

"Son of a bitch," Gil said, stopping.

"Did none of us really think about that before we jumped down this fuckin' rabbit hole?" Yumiko asked, her voice bitter and annoyed, likely at herself more than us.

"You can be Alice in this scenario," I said. "But I don't think we can get back up, so I'm hoping we didn't just fall for one last trap from the lich."

"Well, I can always fly back up with a rope, if it comes to that," Raven said, which would save all our asses.

"Oh, thank the gods." Gil beamed at Raven as relief spread across his face. "I've said it before, and I'll say it again: you're too good for us."

We all laughed, and it helped ease the tension quite a bit as we once more tackled the steep incline.

Soon we all had reached the bottom. We stood in a small corridor that was fundamentally different than anything we'd seen in the dungeon yet. The dark castle layout up above and the labyrinth maze were both different types of architecture than what surrounded us now.

It was sandstone. The walls, floors and ceiling were thick slabs of tan sandstone. Carved into each of the blocks were words in a language I didn't speak. It resembled the language I'd seen on the blood doors, but it wasn't exact.

"Eris, any clue what that says?" I asked.

"Uh, kind of." She paused, her finger tapping her lip, tugging at it while she was lost in thought. "It's a mixture of all the languages of the hive in one. But it doesn't exactly translate into the human tongue very well. The best I can do is: blood of the Hive returns to the Hive. But that doesn't exactly make a whole lot of sense."

"Is it another blood door?"

She shook her head. "I don't know. This is something I've never seen before."

Eris walked forward and ran her fingers along the words. As she did so, she whimpered and pulled her hand back. A heavy drop of blood covered a section of the wall, partially obscuring the letters.

It seemed there was something sharp enough to cause her to bleed, but as we stood and waited for something to happen, nothing did. Half a minute turned into five and still, nothing happened.

"Any ideas?" I asked.

"Not a one," she said. "Anyone else have a thought?"

"Nope. This freaky magic is way above my pay grade," Gil said. "You need me to cleave some skulls, I'm your guy. But figuring out ancient puzzles is more Wilson or Adam's speed. I'm just a brute with a battleaxe."

Eris turned, laughing. "But you're our brute with a battleaxe, Gil. And don't you forget it."

"Maybe it needs more blood?" Yumiko said, thinking out loud. "Or maybe the mixture of languages means it needs more than one type of blood? I don't fuckin' know."

"Well, there's a thought," I said. "Why don't we try adding my blood to the mix, since I am technically part of the Hive."

Eris shrugged. "That's as good a thought as any." She stepped aside and motioned for me to give it a try.

I stepped up and placed my hand where hers had been. There was a sharp slice of pain as my skin split open and my blood spilled out to mix with Eris's.

I stepped back with a curse as my fingers stung, but I shook it off and waited next to Eris for a moment.

As before, nothing happened.

"Well, that was a bust," I said.

Gil and the others laughed, but I'd already run out of ideas.

Eris stood there, staring at the words with intense concentration on her face. I had nothing else to offer her in hopes of solving this puzzle. I was out of my depth in this situation. I was neither the smartest nor dumbest person I'd ever met, but puzzles had never been something I was extremely good at.

My lateral thinking was average at best. I dealt with my problems head on. It was who I was. Maybe it was a simplistic way of viewing the world, but it was what I had to work with, and it hadn't let me down so far.

I stood next to Eris with my hand resting against hers while she tried to work out the hidden meaning of the writing. It took her about ten minutes to figure it out. And when she did, her obsidian eyes lit up in delight. She turned to me with a wide smile on her face. "I've got it!"

The others stood up from the game they were playing in the corner and came and joined us.

"Well, don't keep us in suspense," Mika said. "Tell us. I want to get the hell out of this cave."

"I mistranslated it. Well, I didn't and I did at the same time." She pointed at the first word. "Blood in Rachnaran can also be written as life. Which is another word for spirit in Entoma. It requires not just blood, but spirit. Mana."

"So it just needs some of your magic?"

"Exactly." She nodded.

"Well, make with the magic already. This cave is already starting to reek," Yumiko said.

"You don't exactly smell like summertime roses yourself, Yu. Not our fault we all smell like rotten flesh."

"Yeah, but I'd kill Mika here for a hot shower." She chuckled.

"Hey!" Mika protested. "No…I get it. I'd at least sacrifice a pinky for hot water and some soap."

Eris ignored the laughter of the others and stepped towards the door. She held her arms aloft and let her magic dribble out. The still air changed to heavy gust as she poured out more magic than I'd ever seen her produce before. It quickly filled the room with the heavy scent of the forest. Hints of pine, rose, wood rot, and earth brushed past my nose, and I inhaled deeply.

The others weren't wrong—we all need baths.

I basked in the pleasant aroma for a moment before the smoke drifted to the walls. As it touched the sandstone, the words lit up and pulsed with green light. There was a distinct click of a lock disengaging and then a deep rumble as the far wall began to descend.

"Looks like that did the trick," I said.

We all moved forward behind Eris as she exited the hallway and went through the door.

As we stepped through the door, we found ourselves in another tomb instead of a treasure vault. However, it was not the dead castle variety we had just spent over two days traversing.

This place held a quiet reverence to the space, as if the soul resting here was at peace. I knew, somewhere in the back of my lizard brain, that the dead in this place would, in fact, stay dead.

The tomb was rather small, comprised of the same sandstone that lined the hall. It was perhaps only slightly larger than my bedroom back at Castle Gloom Harbor. A single sarcophagus lay in the center of the room, surrounded by hundreds-of-years-old items from people wishing to pay their respects.

"Eris, what is this place?"

"It's an ancient burial chamber for entomancers. But we haven't buried people like this in many centuries. Preserving a corpse in stone was seen as disrespectful, considering our connection to nature. Most of the Hive were buried in the earth to give our bodies back to the land which means this has either been here long before we started burying people in the ground or this was used as a form of punishment."

"Punishment?" I scratched my chin. "What do you mean?"

She shook her head and crossed the room and placed her hand on the coffin. "To put a body in something like this was to completely cut them off from nature and the earth. It was marked as a punishment for those who committed heinous crimes. They were buried far away from the forest, and their spirits weren't allowed to join the Hive Mind. They were banished."

"Do you know who this is?" I asked as I came to stand beside her.

As I glanced down at the coffin, I found more writing carved into the stone. I couldn't read it, but Eris could.

While she stood, deciphering what the writing said, I looked around the room. Besides the sarcophagus and the trinkets, there wasn't anything else in the room that I could see. Which left me very confused.

We were sent here by the Morrigan, yet there is nothing here of value besides the corpse—no treasure or power here like she promised.

I turned and glanced back at the raised coffin. It was large, large enough to fit a full-grown man and then some.

Maybe the coffin is the treasure, or at least what lies inside it.

After I was finished checking the room, Eris had figured out what the text said and ran her fingers over it.

"This is the tomb of Kalidan Petraeus. A former monarch of the Hive."

"Why was a monarch buried in such a disgraceful way?"

"According to what's written here, he betrayed the Hive by challenging the previous monarch to a duel, and besting him."

I shook my head. "Why is that a bad thing? Isn't that exactly how your mother assumed the throne?"

She nodded. "Yes, but it wasn't how things were normally done. She only got away with it because there literally was no one stronger than her to contest her ascension. Normal transitions of power happened when either the monarch died or were offered something extremely valuable in exchange for the mantle."

I whistled. "Buying the monarchy—your race really did exist on buying and selling favors."

"And look where it got us," she replied, her shoulders slumping.

I wrapped my arms around her and kissed the top of her head. "None of that now, love. It will only make you sad." I stepped back and motioned to the coffin. "Looks to me like whatever we came here for is inside the coffin. Let's take it and get the fuck out of this nightmare maze."

"Fuckin' seconded!" Yumiko shouted next to the others.

"All right." Eris nodded. "I'd like to go home, too."

We all placed our hands on the lid and shoved it off. The lid crashed to the floor and broke into a dozen large chunks of rock.

Lying inside the coffin was a skeleton. But it wasn't any normal skeleton. It was humanoid, but that was where the similarities ended. The bones were a stark, glossy black. They shimmered from the light of our torches, and it took me a moment to realize what it was.

"Chitin. The skeleton is coated in chitin."

I remembered what the Aspect had told me after I fought Jasmine, that absorbing one's chitin was a sign of respect. That it was a way to honor the dead. I didn't think it exactly applied to this situation, but Eris definitely needed access to more chitin.

I nudged her with my elbow. "You should take the chitin for yourself."

She turned to me and shook her head. "I don't know. I did not best this man in battle. To take his chitin in such a way would be dishonorable."

"Honor." I scoffed. "Fuck honor. Honor won't keep you alive when everything is stacked against you. I'd much rather you be the most dishonorable person alive, rather than say you lived honorably to your corpse. Take it, not because of honor or ceremony, but because it will keep you alive. That's all that matters."

Eris hesitated. Her eyes flicked to mine and then back to the corpse. She shook her head again and sighed. "Perhaps you are right. I'm holding onto the ideals of the past, but it's not like there is anyone left to call me out on them. The Hive is broken and scattered; there are only two entomancers left alive. The Hive is no more, as much as I wish otherwise. Holding onto my ideals of what the Hive should be won't bring them back."

She reached out and placed a hand on the skeleton. It took a second, but the rigid, glossy chitin melted and then turned into a liquid. It crawled up Eris's arm and then sank under skin in a matter of seconds.

When it was over, she let out a quiet gasp. "Oh, that was a lot more chitin than I previously had access to. I feel heavy now. This is going to take some getting used to."

Despite the weight the chitin added, she still looked as tiny as usual. I grinned at her and then turned back to the coffin.

"There has to be more than just some chitin in there. We still need to find whatever Morgan needs."

Once the chitin was gone, I found two more items in the coffin. One was a small, glowing green stone that rested in the back of the skeleton's head. It actually looked like it had been inside his skull and had burst through the back. I shuddered at the thought and went to pick up the stone.

Eris shot her hand out and grabbed my wrist. "Don't touch that!"

I quickly pulled my hand back and turned to face her. "And why not?"

"Because that's a fragment of the Hive Mind. It's like a collection of memories from whoever this person was, but far stronger. Even as a member of the Hive, it would probably overwhelm you if you were to absorb it. I don't know if I'm even strong enough to withstand it."

"Oh, I think you're perfectly capable of wielding the knowledge, little one," a feminine voice said.

We turned in unison at the sultry voice to find Morgan leaning negligently against the wall seemingly without a care in the world.

She'd changed slightly; her outfit was unlike anything I'd seen her wear before. It was gray leather armor, but it contoured to her like it was painted on and left little to the imagination. Her hair was done up atop her head and pulled back out of her face.

"How the hell did you get here?" I demanded.

She chuckled. "I am a goddess, after all," she said as she walked towards me. She reached out a long, slender finger and tapped the necklace I wore. "But if you must know, it's because of that little trinket I gave you. It not only allows the denizens of this world to travel with you, but it lets me travel to you at will."

I clenched my teeth tight as my nails dug into my palm and rage burned in my throat. "So, you used us to clear the dungeon for you."

"Yes. I can travel to most of the world with ease, but there are certain places even a goddess must traverse with caution. I made your role in this clear from the beginning and you did such a good job. I figured it would take you five days, but you cleared it in under three. Bravo."

Morgan paused and smirked at me as I tried not to strangle her.

"And don't give me that look. I still plan on upholding my bargain. You and Eris have already received power, and once she uses that little bauble in there, I imagine she'll gain even more."

Morgan walked over to the coffin and peered over it. She reached down and plucked the other item from the coffin. It was a small ring in the shape of a honeycomb with numerous diamonds accenting the white gold metal.

It seemed a trivial bit of wealth, but I was betting it was anything but if the Morrigan wanted it.

"It seems our bargain is complete," she said as she pocketed the ring.

"Hold up." I held my hand out to her and then immediately thought better of the action. "All of this for a trinket, and you're not even going to tell us what's so special about it?"

She shook her head, a smile brimming on her lips. "What does it matter what it does? I wanted it, and you helped get it for me. A courier doesn't ask what's inside the parcels he delivers, does he? I've upheld my end, and you have upheld yours. Our business is concluded for now."

"For now?"

Morgan nodded. "We will see each other again, but the when and where are not known to me yet. If you wish to know more, you'll have to ask Edna. She refuses to answer me, so good luck getting her to answer you."

"Any idea how we're getting out of here? Is there a hidden door that leads back to the entrance?"

Morgan laughed. "No. Who in their right mind would build what amounts to a fortress and then put in a shortcut that anyone with half a brain could find and exploit?"

With that she bid us farewell and vanished.

I sighed and sat back against the sarcophagus.

Great.

"Well, I guess we should retrace our path to get out of here." The others groaned at the prospect of traversing back through the entire dungeon, but at least it would take less time since we wouldn't have to fight any monsters this time around.

Eris ripped a bit of her shirt and picked up the fragment of Mnemosyne in the coffin and tucked it into her pocket.

"I'm ready to go when you are," she said.

I sat up with a groan and sighed as I took the lead and walked out of the tomb.

This isn't going to be fun.

***

It took us another full day and a half to get out of the dungeon. We stopped for a few breaks and rested only when we had to, but it was still covered nearly forty miles, and no matter the pace we set, we couldn't cover that much ground in a single day.

By the time we climbed out of the dungeon and reached the cabins atop the mountain, we were all so tired that the prospect of traveling even more that day was immediately rejected.

Yumiko and Eris went hunting for some wild game while Gil, Mika, and I cleaned the cabin and Raven got the wood fire stoves going.

We all decided to camp in the largest cabin, which was the one that housed the entrance to the dungeon. We dragged a few mattresses from the other cabins and though it was cramped with everyone in one building, and I much preferred it to if we were spread out, it was easier to share one fire.

It took Eris and Yumiko no time at all to bag a few rabbits, and after I prepared them, Raven cooked them to perfection along with a few dried potatoes and other rations we had left. The meal was savory, if a little small, and once we finished eating, we kept the stove going for the warmth and quickly fell asleep.

The next morning, we packed up and decided to return to the rabbitmen town. I wanted to give the wolfman town of Jole a wide berth, since we had killed a few of their men, and from what Morgan had said, the king's son would have been returned to him. As far as I was concerned we'd upheld our word, and I saw no reason to stir anything up by entering their city, especially when they no longer had a use for us and would likely attack us.

We bypassed Jole and changed course to make our way back to the rabbitmen city.

We squeezed back in through the small mountain pass and were back at the city gates in a few hours.

One of the servants went to inform the Aminah clan leader of our return, and we were shown back to our temporary quarters in the meantime.

I was nearly a hundred percent certain it was because none of us had showered in damn near a week and we had filth all over us. I knew for a fact the clothes under my amor were ruined, and the armor would need to be cleaned and polished.

As Raven, Eris, and I stepped back into our room, I quickly stripped out of my armor and tossed my soiled clothes to the floor. I ignored everything else, opened the sliding door to the hot spring baths, and slid in until I was totally immersed.

Eris and Raven followed my lead and stripped as well. Soon, the three of us were neck deep in steaming hot water.

"Godsdamn, I'd almost say this whole excursion was worth it just for this moment right here."

I was always one to appreciate a good bath, but after not having one for over a week and then stepping into one was nearly transcendent. I brought out my soaps and rags and spent at least half an hour scrubbing every inch of my body and washing my hair three times just for good measure.

Raven and Eris did the same, until we used up most of the soap, but it was well worth it.

When we were all done, I leaned back against the rock edge and sighed with contentment.

"That was wonderful."

"Agreed," Raven said, wading over to me. She mirrored me by leaning back and wrapping her arm through mine. "I don't think I've ever gone so long without a bath before and would prefer to never go that long again."

I chuckled and placed my arm around her shoulder, pulling her into me. "I can get behind that."

"Speaking of getting behind things," she said, a smirk on her lips and lust in her eyes. Raven quickly scooted onto my lap, pressing her backside into my groin. "It's been over a week now. And I really don't think I can take another minute of this pent-up need."

"That's understandable." I let Raven pull my hands around. One went to her chest, while the other slipped between her legs. "But as I told you when we entered the dungeon that dungeon sex is strictly forbidden."

It was mainly about the danger and lack of privacy that created the "no having sex in a dungeon" rule, but it was also a hygiene thing with me. I loved both Raven and Eris, and if we'd been alone and they'd asked, I might have given in, but when you've gone days, sometimes over a week like this raid had been, without bathing and while fighting all kinds of monsters, having sex afterward was just gross and incredibly unsanitary.

Plus, we slept in the same room with the others, and I didn't want it bad enough that I was willing to subject them to a peep show.

But now that we were clean and had some alone time, there was no reason to deny her request. I pressed against her with my fingers, and she let slip a moan of delight.

Eris splashed over to us as soon as Raven opened her mouth.

"Don't you two start without me," she said, pouting.

"Wouldn't dream of it…but let's keep it down and make it fast. We do have a meeting to get to," I said.

Raven tilted her head to look at me, her porcelain skin delightfully flushed, and lust abounding in her crimson eyes.

"I can keep it down, but I don't think I can rush this."

Eris crept closer, and her lips found mine before she began kissing her way down my chest. Raven mirrored her, and before I knew it, rapturous bliss engulfed me, and all previous engagements became meaningless.

Chapter 14 - Kincaid

After a brief meeting with the Aminah clan and vaguely describing what we'd found beneath the cabins near the wolfmen city, we accepted her thanks for returning her daughter. I happily accepted the completion of the quest that I had in no way earned, but I wasn't going to turn down the experience.

Quest: Return
Ensured the safe return of Rhoa Aminah's daughter.
Type: Unique
Difficulty: A
Reward: 30000 Exp!

I accepted the quest and closed my interface, not wanting to deal with my level ups at the moment.

We said our farewells, and after accepting a personal gift from Rhoa, we took our leave from the Pale Everlands.

"I do have to say, these fur coats she gave us for rescuing her daughter are amazing," Gil said as we walked through a six-inch snowfall.

She'd given us each a hand-crafted fur coat after we'd declined their offer of gold. I knew for a fact that the clans didn't have much material wealth since they very rarely ever traded with the other races, so I didn't feel right taking what little money they had for a job we technically didn't complete.

To allow her to save face we all accepted a fur coat, and that was ample enough payment, especially for Gil, who was two men in one.

It was a thoughtful and timely gift, especially considering the massive blizzard that kicked up just as we left.

Wind whipped at my reddened face and chilled even my eyelashes. My silver hair swept around me nearly invisible against the white backdrop.

Raven shifted inside my shirt, her sharp talons dug into my skin ever so slightly as she maneuvered herself, trying to stay warm and comfortable.

She'd realized as soon as the blizzard started that she wouldn't be able to move very well and her core temperature would drop if she tried to make it on her own, so she'd shifted and once more nestled against me. I didn't mind; I'd do anything for her, and her feathers were actually warm as she kept nuzzling her head against my neck.

Eris walked beside me, seemingly unperturbed by the racing wind. I mean, it wasn't that much of a bother to me—my body temperature was more than enough to handle it—but it didn't mean I still didn't feel the chill that clawed over my skin. She walked like it was a warm spring morning, and I had to applaud her ability to be completely able to adapt no matter the weather.

The others, however, were having a much harder time in the snow. Gil and I took turns breaking trail in the deepening snow and the others struggled along behind. It was freezing, but they each took a drink of a potion that raised their body temperature and let them walk in the snow without risk of damaging their bodies.

The potion, *Phoenix Flame*, lasted nearly a full day and was rather mild, so one could drink it without fear of potion sickness if they needed to drink another potion or two. I didn't need it anymore, but the others were still human—something I wasn't any longer.

I shook off those thoughts and focused on staying as warm and dry as I possibly could. The trek through down the rest of the mountain was relatively uneventful but exhausting.

We stopped only once as night came quicker than we thought because of the time it'd taken us to get through the blizzard. The six of us huddled in a small cave around a fire for the night, and after a meager meal of dried rations, we curled up around the fire and went to sleep.

In the morning, the blizzard had disappeared, and bright blue sky shone high above us. We packed up camp and set off again.

The town of Wyston came into view a couple hours later. The sleepy village was a welcome site and unchanged from when we passed through what seemed a lifetime ago.

"I don't know about you guys, but I could use a drink," Gil said.

"Same here," Mika replied.

"Well, why don't we stop at the Crystal's Drip and have a pint or two?" I asked, my mouth watering at the prospect.

Despite my fake drink in the dream with Maus, I was having a hard time fighting the urge to drink. I was tempted to grab an ale with them to celebrate a job well done.

Nothing wrong with grabbing a celebratory drink with my friends after a dungeon raid. It's tradition. One drink won't hurt anything.

Raven's claws dug into my skin as she poked her head out and stared at me with her beady crimson eyes. Her black beak nudged my chin.

"I mean, why don't you guys stop and have a drink." I sighed as Raven winked at me. "Yeah, yeah."

With a plan in mind, we picked up the pace towards the town and the tavern.

The Crystal's Drip hadn't changed much since I'd been there nearly fifteen years ago. It was a quaint tavern with mostly wooden accents and a stone tile floor. Long banquet tables dominated most of the space with the bar tucked into the far corner.

Nearly a dozen people sat around the tables, most of them crystal miners.

The owner, a grizzled old man who had the hunched frame of a career miner, leaned against the wooden counter as we sat down at an empty table.

"Wha' can I ge' ye'? he asked in a rough tone, as if speaking hurt his throat.

"A round of ale for them and a mug of mana tea for me," I said, pulling out a single gold coin. I held it up to him and laid it on the table next to me. His brown eyes lit up at the sight of gold. I couldn't blame him. Wyston was a small town of miners who made good money hauling up the crystals, but even they probably weren't used to seeing very many people paying with gold.

"Righ' away."

Eris nudged me with her finger, prodding my ribs. "What's mana tea?"

I smirked, and playfully swatted her finger away. "Quit that, unless you want to poke a hole in my side." I grinned as her compound eyes lit up with humor, my face reflected back at me a hundred times in her many facets. "But to answer your question, it's a mixture of black tea that's been filtered through crushed up mana stones. It infuses the drink with a rather pleasant flavor, and it also acts as a stimulant, which perks you up. It's not as good as coffee, but it's as close as we can come on Nexus."

After a few minutes, the bartender brought our drinks and swept the coin into his hand. I told him to keep it and keep the drinks coming.

As I took a sip of my cup, I was rewarded with a pleasant bitterness that was replaced with a tingly rush as the mana hit my tongue. It swirled around my mouth and went down smoothly. While not being a replacement for alcohol, it had a certain reminiscence about it that eased some of my withdrawal.

Too bad mana tea is about three times as expensive as a bottle of my favorite whiskey. Though it might almost be worth investing in the equipment needed to make it myself, especially since I'm quitting. What else am I going to spend my money on?

We all talked and drank, basking in the quiet glow of our victory. As our cheer dwindled away, I opened my character page, finally having the patience to deal with my stats.

Exp: 8400/8400
Level Up! (x3)
Exp: 7700/8700
Level: 87
30 Stat Points Available!

I had enough speed for now thanks to my recent level ups, so I didn't want to add even more to it just yet.

Let's add a bit more health just in case things get past my chitin.

I used all thirty points to bring my *Health* up to fifty-five, giving me a significant boost. With the added stat points from the wills of the other races of the Hive, I was actually stronger than I should be. And once I reached max level, I'd have more power than nearly anyone on Nexus.

Once I dealt with my stats, we finished off our first round of drinks and ordered a second round. But before the bartender could deliver them, someone new joined us at the table.

A man wearing an expensive black suit that was tailored to his frame and radiated a quiet thrum of magical power sat down in front of us without a care in the world. He was tall, on the thin side, but there was enough muscle to denote him as a fighter. He had short, brunette hair and a thick goatee.

His bright blue eyes regarded me with interest as he brought his arms up and laid them on the table. On his hands were two obsidian gauntlets that covered the back of his hands. Embedded in them were two polished mana crystals, shining brightly with blueish white mana.

I'd never seen a design like them before, yet they seemed familiar to me, like a half-remembered memory that I couldn't quite place.

The man was impeccably dressed and his movements precise. He unnerved me almost at once.

"Can I help you?" I asked.

His eyes sparkled as he tilted his head. "You most certainly can, Duran, though you do look quite different than the last time I laid eyes on you."

I paused, pushing my empty teacup away with my left hand while my right gripped my sword.

"Do I know you?"

He shook his head. "No, we've never had the pleasure of meeting face to face, but I've heard much about you and your Gloom Knights. You've become a bit of a scary story told around the Merchants Guild. The Gloom Knights, the scourge of Nexus. Only fools would risk straying into your territory uninvited."

His words gave me pause, then they sent a chill up my spine.

He said the Merchants Guild, and that could mean he can be only one person.

"Fuck! You're Kincaid, aren't you?"

He just smiled, his bright white teeth giving me my answer.

The others around the table sucked in a breath at the mere mention of the leader of the Merchants Guild.

"How'd you find us?" I asked.

"Oh, I have my ways," Kincaid said. "Now, we both know that most of you have rather large bounties on your heads, barring your exotic ladies and the vampire, of course. They're free to go; I have no quarrel with them, but it's long since time that we have a chat, eh, Duran?"

I slammed my fist on the table, biting my lip hard enough to bleed. *Damn it. This isn't good.*

I turned to the bartender and motioned for another round of drinks. "If we're going to talk, might as well do it over drinks."

Kincaid laughed, the corners of his mouth raising, making crow's feet appear at the edge of his eyes. "Yes, let's do this like gentlemen. It saves so much time and effort."

The bartender quickly returned with another round, and I slid him a large pouch of gold coins. He paled at the sight of the proffered money, clutched it tightly to himself as he fled, running out of the bar as if it were on fire.

Kincaid smiled at the money and the antics of the bartender. He leaned across the table ever so slightly, grinning at me.

"Your drug empire has complicated a great many things in my life and, as much as I can appreciate good entrepreneurial spirit, you and yours spat in the face of the Merchants Guild. If you had only paid your dues like the rest, this could have been avoided. I could have protected you from the Alliance, but, no, you had to be greedy—you and your distributor both."

My eyes widened. "Miguel?"

He nodded, his sapphire eyes radiating superiority. "He was quite troublesome, a fighter it seems. It took hours to get him to give you up." His eyes darkened and narrowed. "But they all break in the end. He died screaming."

"You son of a bitch!"

Before I could stop myself, I was halfway over the table, about to choke the life out of the man.

"Gotcha." Kincaid smiled.

He spoke in Script, but even as I registered that he was casting a spell, it completed, and a blast of force took me in the chest.

I went flying back, my leg caught on the back of the chair I had been sitting in, and then I slammed against the back of another table. The air exploded from my lungs as pain radiated up my back. As I tried to stand, I used a chair as a support and just managed to right myself as Kincaid stood.

He rose from the table in a single fluid motion and adjusted his suit with a nonchalant grace about him. He was completely unperturbed by the fact that he was about to go into battle against four of the strongest players on Nexus.

But he had reason to be confident. Although I'd never gone against him before, his fighting style was legendary.

Kincaid raised his gauntlet and spoke again. Another blast of wind magic rushed toward me. It sliced through the wooden table with ease, and I threw myself to the side as it struck next to me.

The others had quickly gotten up from the table and drawn their weapons to engage the mage.

Gil's axe glowed silver as he used *Steel-Breaker* to try and cleave Kincaid in two. The axe struck Kincaid's shoulder and stopped cold. Gil's axe was hero-tier, one of the best weapons he could own, backed by his single strongest attack, and yet it didn't even scratch Kincaid's suit.

As Gil's weapon landed, particles of light radiated from Kincaid's shoulder across his chest to his right arm. It flowed into his gauntlet and he brought his hand up to Gil's chest.

"Release."

At once, there was a snap of pressure, and Gil's eyes bulged out of their sockets as he paled and went flying back. Numerous spurts of blood rose from his chest, which looked like a spiderweb of crimson as if his body had been crushed. He flew back and hit the edge of the bar and lay still.

Shit! Gil!

I grabbed a handful of potions from my inventory and tossed them to Raven and Eris. "Heal Gil, and don't get involved."

As I spoke, I drew my sword and leapt over the table towards Kincaid.

"Leave my friends alone, you bastard!"

As I was in midair, Kincaid turned to me, a smile on his face. He raised his gauntlet and opened his mouth to cast a spell.

"I don't think so!" I roared, and activated *Aura of the Antimage*. It billowed from my skin and swirled invisably around the room engulfing Kincaid in a bubble of antimagic.

He finished chanting his spell, but nothing happened. His words echoed hollow and died powerless.

"Antimagic," he said in wonderment just as I landed.

I brought my sword down across his chest. This time, his suit couldn't withstand my attack. I sliced through the thin material before meeting resistance as my blade cut down his chest.

He winced in pain and backed up. A flash of glossy black chainmail shone through his shredded suit.

Shadowsteel chainmail. Of course.

Kincaid was richer than just about anyone other than Magnus. He could afford the highest quality weapons and armor available. Even taking out his magic, he wouldn't go down easy.

Kincaid grinned as he stepped back, gliding away on the balls of his feet. "Impressive. I wasn't expecting antimagic. You surprised me."

He brought his gloves up and flicked his hands out. The mana crystals embedded in the gauntlets flew out and crashed to the ground, shattering like glass now that they weren't filled with mana.

As they hit the ground, he reached into his inventory and pulled out two more fresh crystals.

"Oh, like hell I'm just going to let you reload like that in the middle of a fight."

I rushed him, thrusting with my sword. I was fast, but so was he. Kincaid stepped out of the way as my thrust sailed by him. I turned and pivoted with my sword, catching one of the fresh, replacement crystals with the tip of my blade.

A shrill tone rang out that was followed by a sharp crack as a web of lines sprouted from the crystal.

Kincaid's eyes widened in alarm.

"You're insane!" he shouted.

"Fuck you!"

He reacted quickly, tossing the cracked mana crystal into the farthest corner of the room.

"Everyone get down!" I yelled and dove for Eris and Raven who were crouched by Gil, feeding him a potion. I covered all of them and mentally asked the Aspect to bring out *Chitin Armor*. I willed *Chitin Shield* in my right hand, passing my sword to my off hand.

Just as I brought the shield over us, there was a loud crack as the crystal broke in half. Then there was only white noise as it exploded in a humongous wave of magic. It slammed into us at full force, and for a second and an eternity, I swore my arm was about to be ripped from my body.

The chitin grew hot and began cracking under the explosion. It passed over us in a second. Once it was over, there was a groan of wood, and I risked a peek.

The wall where Kincaid had thrown the crystal was gone, vaporized under the explosion, and most of the tables and other items scattered around the place were nothing but hunks of ash. Yumiko and Mika had taken shelter behind the bar since it was a solid piece of wood. I think that, and the fact I had helped disperse some of the impact with my body, was the only reason we were still alive.

The roof cracked and pieces began falling down around us. It was weakened, and I was betting the entire thing was about to come down.

"Anyone dead?" I asked.

"Just peachy!" Mika shouted back.

"Then run, this place is falling apart!"

As I got up, Raven and Eris both helped Gil stand. They were fine except for some minor burns and a few scrapes.

I searched for Kincaid and found that he'd been thrown back from the force of the explosion and had just managed to use his one remaining gauntlet crystal and cast a barrier before the broken crystal detonated.

It appeared that he'd taken a bit of a knock. He had a few cuts along his face, and his hair was singed.

I didn't let him move. I pulled out a few smoke bombs and one that was filled with a poison gas. I tossed all three into the room while Mika and Yumiko retreated with Gil and the girls.

There wasn't much time, and I had to act fast. The poison and smoke would disorient and debilitate, but I didn't know if it would be enough.

Kincaid wasn't a pushover, wasn't even close to that.

Once the others were free and clear, I charged him once more. I formed my arachnid limbs and scorpion tail as I burst into the smoke.

He'd just cancelled his barrier and took a deep breath when I reached him. He coughed as smoke and poison seeped into his lungs. I brought my sword to bear, and he reacted by firing off a small *Fireshot*. It sailed toward me, and I easily batted it aside with my shield.

There wasn't enough time to form a second spell before my sword reached him. He tried to parry it with his gauntlet, and it caught the side of it as I struck.

I let him throw my sword to the side and used the momentum to bring my leg up and strike his knee. It connected with a solid crack as I broke his leg and put him off balance.

Kincaid cried out in agony but fought through the pain and brought his gauntlet up to my face. I hadn't recovered from the kick and I was off balance. I hadn't expected him to be able to push away having his leg broken so easily.

His mouth formed a spell, and whatever it was, I was about to take it head on. I didn't like my chances.

There was only one option left to me. I used *Will of the Immortal*. The world around me grew still, and the color washed away to nothing but hues of gray. Time had completely stopped. Nothing moved.

It was my first time using the skill since Magnus had given it to me. It was surreal; even if I'd grown used to using *Dance of the Immortal*, this version was far more powerful.

It gave me twenty seconds of complete time stop, and I could maneuver objects and people at will. I stepped away from Kincaid and was about to bring my sword across his throat when he turned and grinned at me.

"You're just full of surprises, aren't you?"

"You've got to be fucking kidding me," I said, exasperated. "Why does everyone I fight in this world have a counter to time magic?"

Kincaid's eyes flashed purple and he stood. "I'd actually wager few people can counter this. But Magnus has many allies, and he likes granting them power in exchange for obedience."

I scoffed and spat, "So even you work for Magnus?"

Kincaid shook his head. "Oh, no. I don't work for him, but I have worked with him on occasion. Even I'm not foolish enough to go against him. In exchange for a few favors here and there, he's granted me certain gifts. But I am not one of his Time Wardens, as he calls his lieutenants."

"But you can still manipulate time?"

He shrugged. "Manipulate? Hardly. I'm just not affected by your ability to stop time."

I gripped my sword and prepared to attack. "Regardless, I aim to see you dead, Kincaid. Your ability to move during this doesn't change what has to happened here."

"Ah." He grinned. "I disagree. I'm rather partial to my life, you see. And I know when I'm evenly matched. Don't think I'm willing to risk my life for the pitiful amount your head is worth. You surprised me with your abilities this time, but don't think this is over. I'll go about this another way."

His grin widened. "Be seeing you, Duran."

Before I could stop him, Kincaid held his gauntlet up and spoke a single word in Script. A bright white light filled the room in a second and blinded me.

On instinct, I stepped back and covered my vital areas with my shield as the light dimmed and my eyes adjusted.

When I could finally see once more, Kincaid was gone. I glanced around the ruined bar, but couldn't find him.

The gray world flashed, letting me know my time was up. I looked up at the crumbling ceiling and beat a hasty retreat before the entire building came crashing down around me.

Bright colors filled my vision as *Will of the Immortal* faded, and I sagged to the ground as my battle fatigue raised to nearly max.

Darkness swam at the edge of my vision, and my strength waned. I fought to keep from passing out as my sword dropped from my hands and the chitin that encased my body sank beneath my skin.

It wasn't much, but it allowed me to stand once more as I grabbed for my blade and dragged it from the building just as there was a wooden groan and a heavy snap. The Crystal's Drip collapsed in on itself, and a cloud of dust and smoke rushed over me.

I stepped out of the cloud and reached the opposite side of the street where a small house sat. I leaned against the wall and sank to the snow as I reached my limit.

"Sam!" Eris cried, as she and the others ran to me.

Without waiting, she flung herself into my arms and crushed me in a fierce hug. Raven was next, though her affection was much more subdued. She rested her hand on my shoulder and gave it a small squeeze.

"I'm glad you're both all right," I said as I laid my head against the frosted wood.

"You good?" Gil asked. "What happened to Kincaid?"

I shrugged. "He decided the risk wasn't worth it and retreated. I don't know where he went."

"Damn, was hoping you'd gotten him."

"Me too," I said with a sigh. "He's not going to let this go. We're going to have to be very careful in the future."

"Damn straight," Mika said, sidling up to me. He sat down next to me, forcing Eris to practically crawl into my lap, which I suspected neither of us much minded. "The Alliance is one thing, but the Merchants Guild is not something to be trifled with."

"Yeah." I nodded. "Regardless of anything else, I'd say our Gloom Shroom business is well and truly dead."

"Yeah, yeah. Woe is us; life is fucked. Can we get out of this fucking weather? I'm freezing my tits off here," Yumiko said, shivering.

I could see why. Her fur coat had several large holes in it and a bunch of tears.

Did that happen during the fight or the escape?

"Here." I took my coat from my inventory and tossed it to her. "Might be big on you, but it should keep you warm."

"Thanks."

With great force of will, I attempted to stand. Eris hopped off me and took my hand, helping me up.

"All right, we can gossip once we're back at Gloom Harbor. I'm tired of the snow. Let's go home."

Chapter 15 - Home Again

After the fight at the bar, we tended to our wounds and prepared to return home. It was once again strange to step into the teleporter that would take us to Gloom Harbor.

As I stepped inside, I couldn't help but feel like I didn't belong. It was a profane sensation that crawled over my skin and clawed at my mind.

But as quickly as it came, it faded away, and I stepped out of the white marble doorway of the teleporter and stared up at the gray stone walls of Castle Gloom Harbor.

A stiff breeze tumbled over the sparse grasslands and brought the sharp stench of brine and fish to my nose from Lake Gloom.

I turned my head and stared out at the plains that led to the Rolling Hills. It still bore the scars of a battle that had recently been fought. I didn't know all the details because it was before I had been freed from my prison, but I'd seen some of it when Sam had touched the void crystal that I had resided in.

An army had marched onto their lands, and they'd defended themselves. The battle had been over in a couple of hours, but the consequences of the battle would linger on the land for years to come.

It was a sad thought that spoke to the nature of humans. Something that took years to build could be destroyed in seconds. Still, the earth would endure; the earth would always endure.

Raven stepped out of the teleporter after me and she was swiftly joined by the others.

When at last Sam stepped through, he made his way to the gate and stopped.

A man atop the battlements called down to us.

"Passphrase?"

"To the—to the king who walks in shadow," Sam stuttered.

I frowned. *It's not like Sam to trip over his words. Maybe he's just tired.*

In truth, I think we were all beyond tired. The trip to the Nymirian Dungeon had been harrowing to say the least, and I was glad to be home.

The gate guard nodded at Sam and whistled to lower the gate. Once inside the walls, we entered the inner bailey, and then from there we trudged to the main hall. As always, Amber, the head maid, was there waiting for us.

"Welcome home," she said in a cheery tone. "Wilson requests your attention, sir."

"Of course, he does." Sam sighed. "Over a week away, so I'm sure there's lots he wants to discuss."

"Shall I bring refreshments to the guild hall?"

I nodded. "Might as well get this over with."

Mika chuckled. "You know, for one of the most infamous guilds on Nexus, you sure have a lot of bureaucracy and red tape."

"Blame Wilson. He used to be the head of some kind of government agency. Fifteen years I've known the man, and he refuses to tell me which three letter agency he worked for...but he does keep the guild running like clockwork."

Sam and the others turned toward the guild hall, and I followed them.

When we stepped inside, Sam went and took his seat at the head of the round wooden table, while I sat beside him in the seat that had once belonged to Gil, and Raven sat beside me.

As we waited for the others to arrive, I laid my head on the table.

"Tired?" Raven asked.

"Exhausted," I replied, and used my arms as a pillow.

She laughed and placed a hand on my back, rubbing with just the right amount of pressure. Her hands soothed me, and I sighed contentedly as she reached my neck and worked out the tension lingering in my shoulders.

"I love you," I moaned.

Raven chuckled at my words and increased the pressure just a tad. "As I love you, sunflower. But if you keep making those kinds of noises, people will get the wrong idea."

"Let them; it's not like I have anything to be ashamed about."

Sam placed his hand on my thigh and squeezed. His hand was warm, and though my body heat more than banished the slight chill that lingered in the stone room, I enjoyed his touch and his warmth.

He rubbed my thigh affectionately, and even without looking up, I knew he had his wry smile plastered on his lips.

"You did a wonderful job in the dungeon, Eris. I'm so incredibly proud of you."

I smiled despite myself. I knew how Sam felt about me, but it was nice being told regardless. Despite myself, I basked in the touch of the two people I cared about more than anyone else in the world and quickly fell asleep.

When I awoke, the room was filled with people. I didn't know how long I'd slept, but when I poked my head up, there were a few laughs.

"She wakes," Makenna said, smiling at me.

Her bright red hair was tied in pigtails, and she had some kind of stain across her pale face that hid the freckles on her nose. She looked at me with bright emerald eyes and tried not to laugh.

"You snore in your sleep, Eris," she said, holding back a laugh.

I frowned, which just set her off in a quiet chuckle.

"Do I really?"

"Yeah, but it's cute. Like whistling more than snoring," she replied.

Wilson quickly cleared his throat. "As fun as this conversation is, we have very important topics to discuss." He turned to me, and I thought I noticed a hint of a smile grace his hard-set face. "Sam just finished telling us about the dungeon. I'm glad that you all returned unhurt."

It was as close to a compliment as I had ever received from Wilson.

"Thank you, Wilson." I smiled at him.

He didn't like me when I first arrived, and I couldn't blame him for that, but I think he had started warming up to me. Given his usual frosty demeanor, I figured that was the best I was ever going to get from him.

"What'd I miss?"

"I just finished telling him about our encounter with Kincaid," Sam said.

"To think you fought the head of the Merchants Guild and not only survived but caused him to flee. I wouldn't have believed it if anyone else had told me the story, and even now, I have a hard time believing it was that simple."

Sam shrugged. "It was far from simple, but Kincaid is a magic user. Thanks to Evelyn, I've gotten several abilities to directly counter magic and I didn't even have to use my trump card."

I looked over at Adam. At the mention of his sister, his face grew solemn. It was just for a second, but I knew that despite the cheery attitude he put on, he was still deeply grieving for his sister.

Aren't we all grieving for her?

Things had been chaotic these last few weeks, and I hadn't had much time to reflect on it, but I missed Evelyn dearly. I hadn't known her long, but she had made a huge impact on my life in the short time that I had spent with her. It was only due to her training that I was even alive now.

I owed her my life, and even in death, she still saved me every time I fought.

I hope you can rest, Evelyn. For how much you endured in your life, you deserve a chance to be at peace.

"Speaking of…" Wilson began after taking a sip of his beer and turning to Sam. "Are you planning to stay in that…state? Form? I don't fucking know!"

Sam looked down at his alabaster skin and fingered his silver hair. Even now, his golden eyes glowed, casting a bright sheen onto the table.

"I don't know. It kind of just happened in the dungeon and I never got around to turning back." He paused, running his hand over the scar on his palm. "I think I'll stay like this for the time being. When all is said and done and this is all over with, then I can go back to being myself."

"I still think you look hot, but that's just my opinion," Raven said with utter nonchalance, breaking the tension in the room in an instant.

A round of laughter went around the room, but it quickly died.

Sam sighed and drained his glass of water before refilling it. "I think it's time to implement our evacuation protocol."

"Are you sure?" Wilson asked.

"It seems like a smart move, especially considering the heat that's on us. We're sitting ducks here, and even if we've held this castle before, I don't want to trust in our defenses against the might of the Merchants Guild."

Wilson nodded. "As much as I hate to agree, it might be time and, worst case, if nothing happens all we lose out on is time."

"Time?" Sam scoffed. "A few months ago, I'd have said that time was the one thing we could afford to lose…but now, I think it's our most precious resource and one that's swiftly running out."

He paused, looking around the room at each of his friends before his eyes settled on me.

"Get the safehouse ready, Wilson. Markos, Gil, Levi, and Behemoth, get ready to move the contents of the loot room. Wilson is the only one who can know the location of the safehouse until it's time, so when it's ready, let him know.

"Makenna, Yumiko and Adam, you know what to do. Get the castle and surrounding lands prepared. Overkill."

Makenna's eyes lit up, a dark and wicked glint that was out of place on the kind and innocent girl I'd come to know.

"With pleasure," she said.

Oh right, she is an assassin, after all. I forget that because of how sweet she is.

Sam nodded. "Get it done as quickly as you can. We leave tomorrow at the latest. I know it's an overreaction, but I'd rather be paranoid and alive."

After that, Sam closed the meeting, and everyone went about their assigned tasks.

There wasn't much I could do except for packing up everything I wanted to take with me, so I climbed to the third floor and stepped inside our room. It had been only a week or so since I'd been in the room, but I'd missed it terribly. It was not the same bare room anymore. Raven and I had added to it since we'd started living with Sam. There was a bit more furniture now than there had been.

Although I knew we were on a deadline, I wanted a few minutes to myself, so I quickly stripped out of my clothes and went directly to the bath.

Just as my hand reached for the handle, a voice stopped me in my tracks.

"Hello, my little fly."

My blood ran cold as I slowly turned towards the voice of my mother.

She stood in the entrance to the balcony, with Magnus just behind her. He looked at me, blushed slightly, and turned his head.

"I'll be on the balcony. You have five minutes, Aliria. Make them count."

As soon as Magnus turned his head, I rushed to the wardrobe and threw on a robe, also grabbing my sword that Gil had forged for me.

The blade was whisper thin and shimmered under the crackling light of the candles. The guard was also thin, but Gil had engraved the silver metal. A pattern of hexagons crossed the guard, matching my eyes perfectly. The hilt was wrapped leather over wood with a small stud for the pommel. It was cute and dangerous at the same time, and I'd fallen in love with it at once.

I hadn't ever had need of it, but I'd kept it as a keepsake. It would be little better than a club in my hands against my mother, but I wanted something, at the very least, to give me the confidence that I could defend myself.

I was going to save my chitin until I needed it.

As I turned, I drew the sword and pointed it at my mother as a slew of mixed emotions tore my heart in two separate directions.

"What do you want?"

Aliria smiled at me, the same soft smile she'd used on me when I was a little girl—the smile that told me everything would be all right. She stepped out of the doorway to the balcony and walked over to the bed. She sat down in a single fluid motion.

For some reason, I didn't want her on the bed that Sam, Raven, and I shared. It was for us, and she didn't belong on it.

"Is that any way to greet your mother?"

"Mother?" I seethed as rage burned in my mouth. "What kind of mother sacrifices their own daughter! You'd have given me to Magnus without a second thought!"

Her smile faltered, then fell. She dropped her gaze and stared at her hands. Her slender fingers played over each other and she picked at her nails, something that she only did when she was nervous about something.

"I—I don't have a choice. If there was any other way, I'd take it. I would. But there isn't." She sighed and brushed an errant lock of her golden hair from her face, her black and gold eyes looking anywhere but at me. "Despite the pain in my heart, it's the only logical thing to do. One life, for the lives of millions. Even if it's my own daughter's life, I can't sacrifice the lives of the world for one person."

The sword in my hand quivered, my fingers trembling as my emotions burned in my throat and tears filled my eyes.

"We'll find another way. Sam promised me that he'd find a way, and I believe him. He's been in my life such a short time, but in that time, he's shown me more love and kindness than you ever did. If someone I've only known for a few months has more faith than my own mother…I don't know what that says." My sword slipped from my hands as I threw my hands up. "You didn't even try to fight for me. You just handed my life over without pause. Sam fought for me. Evelyn fought for me, and she died so that we could continue to fight. And if you won't fight for me, I will. I will fight for my life as hard as I can."

In the depths of my heart, an emotion so rare to me I couldn't place it welled up in my stomach and burned through my body. I gnashed my teeth as my skin itched, and I gripped the bedframe hard enough to crack the wood.

"You, who were supposed to protect me, threw me to the wolves. I loved you like the sun my whole life. I worshipped you, even when I knew that what you were doing was wrong. I entrusted my life to you, and all I received was suffering for it. I watched you die and then was thrown into the void. I suffered in cold silence for centuries because of you!"

Hatred. What filled me was nothing short of absolute hatred.

In that moment, every bit of love I held for my mother burned away, and I was left with one undeniable truth that tore at my soul.

I hated my mother.

She was evil. I had known that from the day she ascended the throne, but I had never wanted to admit it.

I stepped back from the bed. In the back of my mind, I didn't want to break something Sam had carved himself. But I couldn't control my anger, and it opened my connection to the Hive Mind on instinct.

Chitin formed at my command and covered me from head to toe. Four arachnid limbs and a scorpion tail formed at my back. My hands turned to claws as I stalked towards her.

"Get out. Don't come back." My voice tore in my throat and bile burned in my stomach. "If I ever see you again, I'll kill you. I won't ever be your sacrifice. We'll find a different way."

Aliria stood and nodded. She walked to the balcony and stopped, her hand on the frame.

"I'm—I'm sorry, little fly. You deserved a better mother than me, but I do, and always have, loved you."

"Get out!"

My voice broke and I could barely hold myself together.

She left, and as she reached Magnus, they both just disappeared.

As soon as they were gone, I let the chitin fade away under my skin and fell to my knees. I couldn't stop the tears that streamed down my face as my heart broke in two. I sobbed inconsolably for what seemed like forever.

I didn't even notice the door opening until soft hands wrapped around me. I looked up into Raven's smiling face. She brushed my hair back from my face and cupped my cheek.

"It'll be okay."

She couldn't have known why I was crying, but all she knew was that I was falling to pieces, and she was trying to do anything to keep that from happening. Her arms wrapped around me and pulled me into her lap while she brushed my hair and whispered that everything would be okay.

Raven held me until I had nothing left to cry. When I was done, I clutched at her, grabbing handfuls of the back of her shirt. She held onto me with all her strength and refused to let me go.

It was exactly what I needed.

"Thank you," I finally managed to say after what had to have been an hour of me just holding onto to her.

"Whatever you need, whenever you need it. I'm here for you, Eris. So is Sam."

I wiped my eyes and sniffed, trying to breathe normally again. "He didn't see me like this did he?"

It wouldn't have been the first time Sam had seen me fall to pieces, but he always maintained the strength to hold himself together, so I didn't want him to always see how fragile I really was.

"No, love." Raven kissed the top of my head. "It was just me. And I won't say a word."

I lifted my head and Raven smiled at me once more before she leaned down and kissed me once more. Her lips were soft, while mine were chapped, but she didn't care.

It was a simple kiss, but it was enough. It told me exactly what I needed to know at that moment, the thing that Aliria had stolen from me.

That I was wanted.

I kissed her back with abandon, my sudden ferocity surprising her for a second before she returned the kiss with just as much passion.

Raven and I hadn't been together just the two of us before, because I didn't think Raven was all that comfortable with it, but this time, she didn't back down.

She picked me up, our lips still locked together, and brought me to the bed. Only then did she break the kiss, and it was to undress herself. She stripped and climbed onto the bed next to me.

Raven helped me to undress as well, and then her flesh pressed against mine as her lips travelled up my body. She kissed her way from my thighs to my breasts and then my lips.

Her hands found mine and intertwined.

Raven then showed me just how much I was wanted, and I basked in every delicious second of it as she took away my pain.

Chapter 16 - Hive Mind

At some point after our lovemaking, Raven pulled the blankets over us and we fell asleep holding onto one another. She held me like I was a stuffed animal, clutched to her chest, and I napped in her arms.

When I came to, another, stronger pair of arms were wrapped around me. I rolled onto my back and found Sam asleep next to me. He was on his side with his arms around me.

It was probably the happiest and saddest I'd ever been in my life. I'd lost my mother, but I had gained both Sam and Raven, who I loved more than I could express in words.

I honestly didn't know if I would make that choice. To have my mother be the mother I always wanted her to be, or to have the both of them.

There never really was a choice. I was just happy I had them in my life.

I snuggled into Raven's chest and pulled Sam closer to me.

He woke up just barely, his golden eyes bleary as they stared into mine.

"Afternoon, love," he whispered.

"Afternoon?" I shook my head. "How long have I been asleep?"

"A few hours if I had to guess. I came to check on you after seeing Wilson off and helping Levi and Behemoth with the loot room. I figured we're going to be working late into the night, so I decided to grab a quick nap. Besides, the two of you looked so peaceful sleeping.

I grinned at him. "I don't want to get up."

"I don't either, but we have to. We have too much to do, and I don't want to waste any more time." He scooted closer to me on the bed and buried his head in the nape of my neck. "Believe me when I say that I'd rather lie in bed with you for the next week."

I rested my cheek on his and just breathed in his scent. It had changed since he'd gone back to his demigod form. It still had the same musky scent as always, but here was a hint of something sweet to him now. It was intoxicating, and I longed to be closer to him.

Of course, it was the same scent that had lingered on Evelyn when I was near her as well, so I assumed it had something to do with his inhumanity now.

"I love you, Sam."

"As I love you." He paused as his hands wrapped around me. One went under my back, while the other went over my chest. "Did you and Raven have fun?"

I nodded, clutching his hand tight. "It was a little awkward at first, but once Raven let go of her inhibitions, it was wonderful."

"Raven can hear you two, you know," she said from the other side of me. "And yes, it was good. I was just unsure of myself for a bit at first." She kissed my neck, her warm breath pulsed against my skin. "Now, let's get up and get to work. As much as I'd rather do anything else like sleep some more."

"Not going to argue there," Sam said. "I could sleep for a week." He sighed and sat up. "Actually, how about the two of you get some rest? There isn't much you can do to help. No offense, but we have our inventories that can carry a few hundred pounds of gear. You two don't, so there isn't a whole lot you could help with."

Sam got up and pulled on some clothes while Raven snuggled against me.

"I won't argue, but if you need us, come get us," she said.

After that, we all fell back to sleep clutched against each other. I held onto her as sleep clawed at my eyes, and before I knew it, I was asleep.

Sunlight streamed through the dark curtains and fell across my eyes, waking me. I slowly got up and stretched, working the tightness out of my muscles. After everything that had happened, it was wonderful to sleep in.

Neither Sam nor Raven were next to me which meant I had the bed to myself, but as I turned, I caught a whiff of myself and frowned.

Definitely need a bath.

With everything that had happened yesterday, I hadn't had a chance to bathe since we left the Pale Everlands.

I climbed out of bed and went to the bathroom.

Steam rushed out when I opened the door, along with splashes and voices. I stepped inside and found Raven and Sam in the stone bath together, both of them soaked head to toe.

Raven dipped her fingers into the water and splashed a handful of water at Sam, grinning madly. Her porcelain skin flushed with the heat of the water, but her crimson eyes glinted with mischief.

"Don't make me start a water fight, Raven. I'll show you no mercy," Sam said with a laugh.

"Bring it on, darling. I accept your challenge."

Sam retaliated by shoving both hands in front of him and sending a tidal wave of water crashing into Raven. Her midnight hair fell into her face, and she spit out a mouthful of water. With her soaking hair streaming water down her face, she looked like a wet mop.

It was kind of the cutest thing I'd ever seen.

"Oh, you've done it now," she replied, her voice serious, but there was a smile tugging at her lips as she tried to maintain her composure.

Raven shifted and brought her wings out. Obsidian feathers rained down into the bath as she flapped them and swirled the steam around the room. She dipped them into the water, preparing to use them to launch a massive wave at Sam.

I grinned at their antics and was surprised to see this playful side of them. Things had been too serious lately for much levity and despite, or maybe because of, everything that had happened yesterday, I wanted nothing more than to join them.

They were too absorbed in their play to notice my presence, so I grinned and, backing up to the wall, took off at a sprint and leapt into the bath face first, arms spread wide.

"Splash!" I shouted.

I landed in the middle of the bath and submerged for a second before I floated to the surface. I rolled over onto my back and groaned.

"Okay, that wasn't my smartest plan. My stomach hurts now."

Sam stared at me for a second before bursting into laughter. Which Raven swiftly joined in.

"You shouldn't have done a belly flop then, you dummy," Sam said, wading over to me. He kissed me, trying to hold in his laughter. "But it was pretty funny to watch, so I won't dock you points for style."

"I think the surprise attack deserves bonus points," Raven said, laughing as she brushed her sopping hair back.

As quickly as it came, the slight pain in my stomach faded, and I leaned back in the piping hot water.

"Why didn't you two wake me?" I asked.

"We tried," Sam said. "I came back up for a breather and to get a bath after sorting through about a hundred chests of junk in the loot room. Raven woke up when I opened the door."

"Yeah, we tried to wake you up, but you were out of it," Raven said, smiling at me. "I figured you needed to sleep, so we let you rest while we took a bath together."

I frowned, but it was a fake one and I couldn't keep it on my face as both Sam and Raven looked to each other and laughed.

To hide my embarrassment, I soaked my head and proceeded to clean myself. I combed my fingers through my hair before I waded over to the stone shelf carved into the stone at the far edge of the bath. I procured a washrag and my favorite of Sam's soaps. The one that smelled of cherries and cream.

Yumiko had made a bunch of it when I mentioned how much I loved it and had given some to me as a gift. It was such a small thing, but it was one of my most favorite of the gifts I'd ever gotten.

As I brought it back, Sam leaned over and plucked the large bar of soap from my hand. When I turned to him, he leaned over and stole the washrag from my other hand.

I'd forgotten how fast Sam was, and he'd taken both items from me while I stared at him.

"Sam!" I fake pouted, trying not to laugh.

He lathered up the cloth and smirked. "I'll give them back, promise."

As he finished, he placed the soap out of the bath and came over behind me. He brushed the washrag over my shoulders and neck, even going up and scrubbing behind my ears for me.

"Makenna made some oil for you to use on your ears," he said, his breath hot against my skin as he cleaned me. "I put it on the shelf above the sink."

"I'll have to thank her."

I would have said more, but I was actually enjoying having Sam wash me. It wasn't sexual, but it was incredibly intimate, and I basked in the shared moment between the two of us.

But of course, we couldn't leave Raven out of it.

She went and grabbed another washrag and joined in on the fun, going around in front of me while Sam washed my back.

When I was done, we switched places and washed Raven, and then it was Sam's turn.

And as we finished, we just stayed in the hot water, letting the soap lazily drift around us.

"What are your plans for the day?" Sam asked.

"Uh, I think I'm going to help Adam and Makenna with their preparations," Raven said. "I might not be able to do much, but I can at least offer to help them."

"And I'm going to pack up the room and then explore the Hive Mind shard we found in the dungeon. If it does contain some sort of power, then we're going to need it. And soon," I said.

I bit my lip as I finished speaking, debating whether to tell them that Magnus and Aliria had come by. After a few moments of hesitation, I decided against it, knowing it wouldn't help anything and would just cause them to worry about me.

If I could help it, I wanted to keep their worries as small as possible.

"Okay, just stay close by. I'm going to finish helping the others get everything ready to move. I'd also advise refilling your packs if you get a chance. We can't take half of everything we've got stored in here, so if you don't take it, we're just going to leave it behind. We're leaving today as soon as we get everything we absolutely need. So we don't have all the time in the world to spare."

"What happens to all the stuff we leave?" I asked.

"Nothing if the castle stays under our control, but if someone takes the castle, it all becomes theirs. So we're trying to gather up our coin and things of value. That and our personal stuff. We can always retake the castle if it comes to that, but I'm not going to risk our lives trying to defend a bunch of stuff."

I shook my head. "You really think something is going to happen to the castle?"

"I don't know." He shrugged, brushing his wet hair out of his face. "But I do know that we're a well-known target, and with the bounties on our heads, I'm actually surprised more people haven't showed up trying to claim them. It's not a risk I'm willing to take with our lives, now that we can't respawn, so we leave and then, when this is all over, we can come back. We took this castle once; we can do it again."

"This didn't always belong to the Gloom Knights?"

"Nope. When we first started out, this place belonged to a guild of player killers—people who took contracts on other players—basically assassins, but for people like us. Gil, Levi, Behemoth, and I drew the attention of the main group of players and lured them out while Adam and Alistair dealt with the guards, and Wilson, Makenna, and Evelyn snuck in and killed the leader of the guild. We took the castle out from under them."

It made me feel better after hearing the story. Even with the short time I'd been here, Castle Gloom Harbor had become my home, and I didn't want to give it up so easily. It was the first place I felt truly welcome. But Sam was right, it was just a place. As fond as I was of it, it didn't matter compared to the people who made it home for me. We could make a new home for ourselves anywhere in the world.

I held my hands up and noticed how pruned they'd become, and I sighed.

"As much I love the bath, we'd best get out before we shrivel up."

Both of them laughed, and we climbed out and quickly dried off. I left the bathroom and went to my wardrobe to change. I donned a pair of black cotton pants that were soft to the touch and easy to move in. After that, I pulled on a golden shirt with a slight V-neck that fit my small frame perfectly.

As I finished dressing, I leaned down and carefully picked up the cloth bag that now held the fragment of Mnemosyne. It was cold to the touch and weighty, despite how small it was.

"You want help with that?" Sam asked, coming to stand beside me.

He wore a forest green tunic that stopped at his waist and a pair of brown pants. Both articles of clothing were much finer than any I'd seen him wear before.

"No. Thank you. I have to do this alone." I shook my head, and then smiled at him. "You look nice," I said.

"Thanks." He grinned sheepishly. "Magnus actually gave them to me when he abducted me. He may be a callous bastard, but the clothes are nice, so might as well wear them." He tied his silver hair back with the leather strap at his wrist and nodded once more at the gem in my hands. "You sure?"

I nodded, clutching it to my chest. "It's my responsibility. Besides, you have your own job to do." I grinned wide, trying to hide my apprehension at what I was about to do. "So you best get back to it."

"Right." He turned away from me and left the room with Raven at his heels.

When they were both gone, I went over to the bed and sat at the edge. I pulled the crimson comforter over my legs despite the fact that I wasn't cold. I stared at the small bag in my palm and hesitated.

I didn't know what I would find inside, and I wasn't sure I wanted to know. So much of the Hive was different than I remembered. Or maybe I was just viewing my culture through the eyes of an adult and not as a child any longer.

In spite of everything wrong with the Hive, they were still my people, and I was still their queen.

Ha. Guess I answered my own question. I let out a quiet laugh and pulled at the drawstring holding the bag closed. *I have no choice. No matter what I find inside, I have to be the one to do this. No one else can.*

I tipped the bag out, and the bright green crystal fell out into my palm.

It was cold to the touch, and the chill bit into my fingers. I sucked in a breath, but before I could exhale, my mind swam, and I found myself falling.

As I fell back onto the bed, I expected the softness of the mattress, but what I landed against was hard stone. I sat up and looked around. I was in a strange chamber comprised of rough gray rock. High above lay hundreds of jagged stalactites that looked poised to drop and skewer me at any moment.

Below me lay more rough and uneven stone floor. Not man-made, but natural, eaten away by erosion.

"How long has it been?" a rough, male voice asked.

I whirled around, searching the circular room as I tried to find the source of the voice. But there was nothing but darkness in front of me. I had better night vision than any human, but even I couldn't see more than a few feet in front of my face.

"Where are you?" I called out.

Silence stretched for a time before the voice spoke once again.

"How long has it been?"

"I don't know what you're asking." I scrambled to my feet and turned in a circle. "I can't see you!"

As I turned once more, I froze as my blood ran cold, and my heart leapt in my throat.

Just a few inches in front of me stood a man who hadn't been there a second before.

I had to tilt my head to meet his eyes. He was thin, and emaciated with dark, ruddy skin and thick, shaggy hair that fell to his shoulders. His entomancer eyes were a bright green that shifted to black in the light that came from no detectable source.

His eyes were wide and frantic, and even as he stared at me, he was looking through me, like I wasn't even there.

"How long has it been?" he asked once again.

When I didn't immediately answer, he suddenly lunged forward. His face closed the distance between us, but he suddenly stopped, half a centimeter from my face.

The rattling of chain accompanied him as his chilling breath burned in my nose.

I glanced down and was finally able to see the rest of his body. He was garbed in soiled rags that only covered him enough to protect his modesty. His arms and legs were bound by manacles. They stretched out, the chains taut as they vanished into the darkness.

There was even an iron band around his neck that I hadn't noticed.

When I refused to answer, he slumped against the chains, defeated.

"Please. How long has it been since I've been trapped in this place?"

My voice failed me for a moment, and I stepped back. Even if he was bound, I instinctively didn't want to be close to him.

"Are you Kalidan Petraeus?"

"That name means nothing to me anymore. Now I'm just the Prisoner. That is who I am. Why won't you answer my question?"

I shook my head. "Because I don't know the answer. Centuries at least. Maybe even longer. Time is warped, and I'm not sure how long I was sealed away either. I can't give you an exact answer. I'm sorry."

He sighed, a deep, aching sigh that rolled over me like a touch and caused me to shiver. "Centuries. That's good enough for me." He paused and then glanced up, his eyes trying and failing to track my voice. "I can't see you. But I can hear you. You said you were sealed away. Are you like me?"

"I don't think so. This isn't the void."

"The void." Kalidan smiled wide, a psychotic smile as a dark laugh bubbled from his throat. He laughed in a broken, twisted way. "The void. Heh, you must have done something far worse than I to have been consigned to the vanishing maw."

"You're wrong, but regardless of what I did, I came here because I was told what lies inside this place would grant me power." I stood my ground, crossing my arms over my chest. "That is the only reason we are even conversing right now."

"Power." He strained against his chains, his wild eye staring at where he guessed my voice to be coming from. "Yes, I can give you power. But you must give me something first."

"No." I shook my head. "I can guess what you want, and I won't do it."

Kalidan laughed even harder. "That's too bad. If you don't release me, I can't grant you what you seek. Now what was that word that the dwarves and humans were so fond of using? Oh yes. Impasse. I believe we're at an impasse."

I bit my lip, tapping my finger against my chin, resisting the urge to pace. I knew he was right. But I didn't know what would happen if I released him. I had no idea what crime he had committed to be sealed away in the Nymirian Dungeon in the first place.

Eventually I worked up the courage to ask, but he just stared at me, his mouth set in a hard line.

It was clear that he wouldn't tell me, because his crime was either so horrible, or he didn't want it affecting my decision.

If I did nothing, neither of us gained anything; but if I did nothing, I didn't lose anything either.

"How can I trust that you'll uphold your bargain?"

Kalidan chuckled, gripping the chains with his hands and pulling as hard as he could.

"Just look at me! I'm dead. Reduced to nothing but a ghost, forced to guard a reliquary as punishment."

"A—reliquary? Are you sure? I thought this was just a fragment of Mnemosyne."

He grinned in victory.

"Piqued your interest now, haven't I? What I am is just a fragment, but what I guard is much more than that. I hold knowledge lost to time, power beyond anything the Hive could hope to remember. And it can be yours if you just release me."

"What would you do if I released you?"

He didn't speak for a long moment. The chains clinked against one another as he shifted, looking away from me. Water dripped from somewhere behind me and splashed into a puddle on the ground.

I fought the urge to turn around in the darkness. I didn't want to take my eyes off of Kalidan. I didn't trust him, and I didn't want to free him. I didn't know what could happen if he was free. He was dangerous enough to have part of his mind sealed away. But if what he was saying was true, and he did guard a reliquary, then that fit with what the Morrigan had said.

A reliquary was power.

But forbidden power.

Power that the previous generations of Hive thought too dangerous to absorb into the Hive Mind but still wanted to keep in case it was ever needed again. So they used a spell and removed the memories and placed them into a willing—or sometimes unwilling—sacrifice. Upon that person's death, they would become both a prisoner and a warden, guarding the knowledge, but also being unable to pass on.

I imagined it was very much like what I experienced in the void.

And on that alone, can I leave him in here if I could save him? Could I make that choice?

The void was aptly named the Devourer. It had eaten away at me for too many centuries, and I didn't know if I could willing let anyone else suffer like that if I could help it. Doing nothing would be the worst thing I could do. Even if it was a risk, I couldn't live with myself if I just walked away.

I sighed, knowing my mind was already made up. I was going to help Kalidan. And if he tried to harm me, then I would deal with it. I was still the Hive Queen, and that power meant something.

"You didn't answer my question, Kalidan," I said.

His head dropped and his hair fell in his face, obscuring it from me. Another drop of water sounded, but this time it came from right in front of me. I looked down as a drop of water fell from Kalidan's cheek.

He was crying.

"I just want to die." He choked out a sob, and even more tears fell freely. "I've been here for so long that I can't even remember what fresh air smelled like, what my favorite foods tasted like. I'm nothing but a shell of a dead man—a half-remembered dream—and I just want to wake up or to sleep the endless sleep of the dead."

Kalidan glanced up at me, and for the first time, it actually seemed like he could see me, his eyes stared into mine as tears ran down his face.

"Help me," he begged.

I'd already made up my mind. I was going to help him, despite the voice in the back of my head warning me that it was a trap. I had to do something.

"I'll help you," I whispered.

"Thank you." He turned his head and motioned toward the chains. "Break them all, and I'll be free."

Trepidation and fear eased into my nerves, and my hands shook as my heart pounded loudly in my chest. I walked slowly toward the chains on his right side. A single step at a time. One foot after the other.

As I reached the first chain, I wrapped my fingers around it. The metal was biting, a frigid cold that didn't belong. It was too cold to be natural.

To be bound like this must be torture; every second of every day, he'd be freezing.

The void was colder than this at times, but I had slept through most of it. I didn't think Kalidan had such a luxury.

I gripped the chain tight and pulled as hard as I could. It came with a yielding screech as I tore the metal in half. It clattered to the stone and disappeared.

After the first one, I moved to the others, tearing them apart before I reached the final one. The collar around his neck.

It forced me to get close to him as I slipped my hands under the band to be able to grip it. The stench of rot filled my nose. The stench of the dead.

With a tug, I broke the collar and fell back. I hit the ground hard and scrambled up, my chitin already forming into my armor and sword.

Kalidan hung in the air. Despite the fact that he was no longer held up by the chains, he was still suspended, his feet just shy of the ground.

His head jerked down, and he stared at me, his eyes having lost the luster of madness.

"Ah, I'm free from my chains at last." He let out a heavy sigh as a bright smile blossomed on his face. His body lowered to the ground, and he inclined his head to me. "Thank you."

When he took me in, he chuckled.

"What's so funny?"

Kalidan pointed at me. "You are. I can feel it now. The last flicker of life that resides in my chest is drawn to your will." He bent down on one knee and lowered his head. "Your Majesty. I, Kalidan Petraeus, thank you from the bottom of my heart."

He raised his head, and a smirk teased his lips.

"But if you would permit me to give you some advice, from one monarch to another?"

I nodded, my apprehension easing up. It didn't seem like Kalidan had any ill will towards me, and I heaved a sigh of relief.

"Please. The—the last monarch didn't exactly leave me with instructions on how to be queen."

Kalidan rose and walked over to me, his footsteps light on the stone. He stood in front of me and slowly raised a hand. He made very clear, precise and slow movements to show that he meant no harm. He reached out and touched my chitin at the shoulder, running his fingers over the jagged black material.

"As I thought. No one's taught you how to use your chitin properly, have they?"

I shook my head. "What do you mean?"

He flicked the edge of my shoulder. "I mean this." He stepped back and gestured at me. "The way you use your chitin is highly inefficient. You're not maximizing its effectiveness like this."

"I don't understand?"

Kalidan chuckled and stepped back one more step. "That's obvious. Watch me, and I'll show you how it's done."

Before my eyes, chitin came at his call. It didn't travel up his skin like mine did; instead, it came from every pore on his body and wrapped him in chitin in seconds. The chitin wasn't like what I'd been used to seeing. It wasn't jagged or rough. It was smooth, forming like bands of muscle over Kalidan, like an actual second skin. There was no wasted inch of chitin; it all served its purpose in the most functional and efficient way possible.

"This is what the true capabilities of chitin are. Not only does it minimize the amount you use, but it increases your speed, agility, and strength even more than normal."

My eyes lit up at the causal display of power. It was effortless for Kalidan, but I could tell at once how much better his armor was compared to mine. Learning from him would increase not just my abilities, but Sam's as well. It was exactly the kind of power I needed.

"Will you teach me?" I asked.

He shook his head and walked over to me once more. "There is no need to teach you." Kalidan smiled as he strolled across the cavern. "The reliquary holds my memories as well as the secrets of the Hive. There's no need to teach when you can just understand."

As he got within a few feet of me, he flickered, turning translucent for a moment.

"My time is up. I have to go now. Thank you once more, Queen. And a word of warning. Use the power store here with caution and restraint. There's a reason the Hive locked it away."

Kalidan kept walking, and as he reached me, he walked right through me, disappearing into a thousand motes of light. He disappeared, and the last sight of him I had was his smile as he stared straight ahead.

When he was gone, a piercing pain flooded through my head, along with flashes, memories, and knowledge that I had no recollection of learning; I just knew it. As I knew how to breathe, it was instinctual.

My hands lit up with verdant smoke as my body accessed the Hive Mind all on its own. I had no control over my actions as I plunged deep into the swirling green abyss. Memories filled my thoughts. Things I hadn't experienced myself played through my mind as I fell deeper and deeper.

A flash of green light shone down on me and blinded me. When I opened my eyes, the same green fragment of the Mnemosyne floated in front of me.

I reached out and grabbed it. As my fingers closed around the stone, it crumbled to dust and floated through my fingers like grains of sand. The dust swirled around me, and as it flew away, understanding came over me.

Dozens of spells and the memories of how to use them crashed into me, and my head pounded with the influx of knowledge. The reliquary had been passed to me, and I understood why some of the Hive thought it best to lock the information away.

It was too much at once. And my mind shifted, straining under the weight of what it had been granted.

My body itched, and before I could stop it, chitin burrowed from my back, forming without my command. Wings of an apocritan burst from my back and began flapping. The buzz of a wasp in flight accompanied my wings.

The apocritans were the only members of the Hive innately capable of flight, and their lightweight bodies made them extremely agile.

As I absorbed the reliquary, I was somehow granted the will of the apocritans. After the mantearians had granted Sam and I their will, the apocritans' will had been the only one I lacked. And despite there not being any of them left alive, I still obtained the will.

I had the wills of every race of the Hive now.

The influx of information into my brain slowed and then stopped all together. When it ended, a weight settled over me as the Monarch of the

Hive and the inheritor of the reliquary. I had to safeguard it to the best of my ability and not let it fall into the wrong hands.

But despite the danger using such magic presented, I knew it would give us an edge in the fight against Magnus and that was good enough for me.

When I'd finished absorbing the reliquary, I could move my body once more. I slowed the magic connecting me to the Hive Mind and began to rise to the surface once more. I came out of the magic slowly, letting myself return to reality as carefully as I could.

Prolonged diving in the Hive Mind could drive even the strongest of people insane with the sheer amount of information that resided there, and I had to be careful so I didn't lose myself.

I opened my eyes and was back in our room.

My body ached like nothing I'd ever experienced before. I was sweaty, and my heart raced. I gingerly sat up and shook off the fatigue that had set in. I had no idea how long I'd been out, but from how high the sun was overhead, I'd guess it had been a couple of hours.

In my hands was the remnants of the fragment of Mnemosyne. It was nothing but dust now. I wiped my hands and stood up.

"Well, that was…something."

My head swam with the memories I'd gained, and a few spells came to me automatically.

Let's see how they work.

I willed the spell to come forth and cast it.

Light swam in front of me, and then it stabilized, and everything turned back to normal. I held up my hand, but it wasn't there.

There was only a vague shimmer where the outline of my hand should be. The rest of my body was nearly invisible.

"So that's what *Camouflage* looks like when you use it."

I grinned and canceled the spell.

My body came back into view along with a small wave of exhaustion. My mana still wasn't large enough to use all the spells for an extended period of time, but it was still incredibly useful for what it was.

I brushed my hair back and was about to take a quick bath to clean myself off when the door flew open.

It slammed against the stone with a resounding thud as Raven burst into the room.

I turned and smiled when I saw it was her, but the panicked, frightened look on her face stopped me in my tracks.

"What is it?"

She panted, her hands on her knees, unable to speak. Instead, she pointed out towards the balcony.

I opened the door to the balcony and walked out.

The sight below me rendered me speechless.

There, massing on the Rolling Hills, heading towards Castle Gloom Harbor, were thousands and thousands of soldiers.

An army had come to our home.

Chapter 17 - Betrayal

I finished loading the largest chest of gold into a storage container and stowed it in my inventory. It was only about thirty thousand gold. Less than a tenth of the amount of wealth we kept in the loot room, but it was all I could personally carry.

Damn it. I knew I'd regret not putting more points into Carry Capacity.

It would take days to load the spoils of fifteen years and get them transported to the safe house. Time that I knew we didn't have.

I looked around the small stone room laden with wooden chests filled worth millions of gold worth of treasure and sighed. We'd been at this for twelve hours and we hadn't even made a dent. We'd gathered the most valuable and easy to carry items, but even with all of us, we were leaving a lot of gold on the table.

I leaned against the worn brass table in the center of the room and tugged at my ponytail. "I doubt Kincaid will put off attacking us. Since his first attempt failed, he's going to try and overwhelm us," I muttered to myself, lost in thought. "He has the full backing of the Alliance and the Adventurers Guild at his disposal. He's going to come at us hard."

"We should be long gone before then," Harper said.

"Yeah, Wilson just sent a message saying the safehouse is good to go. So let's start loading up what we can and head over," Gil said, storing two chests just as big as the one I had into his inventory. "I don't like leaving, but we have to."

"I know." I sighed, tuning around and hopping up on the table. "You know, as long as we've lived here, this place didn't start feeling like home until Eris showed up." I pointed at the edge of the table where a red rug lay under the brass. "Right there is where we met, and my life irrevocably changed."

Gil chuckled and thumped me on the shoulder. "For the better. Best friend or not, you were a handful to deal with. She's mellowed you out, let you regain a semblance of your humanity. She and Raven both have done more for you in a handful of months than any of us could do in a decade."

"You're not wrong about that."

I had changed. And though I hadn't wanted it at first, I couldn't imagine my life going any other way.

Just as Gil was about to respond, a notification flared to life in my interface.

Alert! Apocrita's Blessing Unlocked!
+15 to Strength and Agility
Unlocked (Hive Mind) Special: Wasp Wings

Oh, wow.

"Huh, how about that?"

"What's up?" Gil asked.

I closed the notification and smirked at Gil. "Guess Eris figured out the memory stone we took from the dungeon. Because I just received a powerup."

"Good. We fucking need it." He sighed and leaned against the table next to me. "You have any idea how we're supposed to stop Magnus?"

"Not a one." I shook my head, frowning. "Not only do we have to stop Magnus, but we also have to figure out a way to keep the system from collapsing."

"That's a tall order for a group of thugs."

I snorted, tapping him on the arm with my knuckles. "You're telling me. I'm the least qualified person to deal with this shit. But it's the hand life dealt us, so we have to play with what we've got."

"Hey," Harper said, looking up from his interface. "I'm gonna go ahead and meet up with Levi and Behemoth."

I nodded. "We'll be right behind you."

After we finished talking, we stood up and got back to work. Gil and I lifted a few chests and began to move them from the loot room to the base of the stairs. It took about fifteen minutes to move all the chests we were going to take with us.

When we were done, I stepped out of the loot room with Gil right behind me carrying the last of the chests. Levi and Behemoth already had their inventories full and were a few minutes ahead of us. They'd wait for us at the teleportation gate so Gil and I could lead them to the safehouse.

The two of us passed by the massive crystalline golems guarding the loot room. Their sapphire skin shone in the candlelight as they stared straight ahead with their greatswords in their hands. They hadn't so much as moved since Adam created them nearly eight years ago. The stalwart guardians of the loot room.

We dropped the chests at the stairs and went up to the first floor and outside. I didn't bother saying goodbye to the others. We'd be back in a couple of hours anyway.

From the message Wilson sent me and Gil. The safehouse is an hour outside Aldrust. In the unclaimed forest between Aldrust and Yllsaria. I chuckled. *In between the elves and the dwarves. I wouldn't think to look for us there.*

With our trade contracts with both countries, the Gloom Knights held cordial relations with both races. *Well, the elves at least. The dwarves still hate me for stealing Lachrymal's Heart.*

But as long as they didn't know we were there, we'd be fine.

A stiff breeze rolled through the bailey as we stepped outside. It was tinged with the usual scents of Lake Gloom. The stench of fish and brine, but also something else.

I took a deep breath and stopped in my tracks.

No. That can't be what I'm thinking.

"Hey Gil, you smell horses?"

He stopped and sniffed. "Yeah, barely over the fish, but why? The stables are close—" Gil froze, his dark skin paling as he realized what I was thinking. "Can't be. It hasn't been two days since we got back. There's no way they'd get here that fast."

"They would if Kincaid had them in reserve, just in case his first plan failed."

Gil and I looked at each other and then out towards the Rolling Hills. We looked back at each other for a split second before we both sprinted out of the bailey and to the ramparts. As we double timed it up the stone steps, we ran into one of the men-at-arms coming down. It was the rabbitman, Lyahgos.

His gray rabbit ears were down, and his face held a sheen of sweat.

"Boss! I was just coming to get you." His breath came in great gulps.

I nodded. "How bad is it?"

He looked over his shoulder and turned. "It's bad." He motioned us to follow him as he went back up the stairs.

When we reached the edge of the wall. I stared out over the fields as a strong off feeling of déjà vu came over me.

Well, this is fucked.

I counted two full battalions of Alliance soldiers, over two thousand troops. Not to mention the assorted groups of thirteen scattered in between them.

It was such overkill that I couldn't almost comprehend it. The only thing I could do was laugh.

"Two battalions and a handful of player guilds. I mean, our bounties are high, but that's taking it to the extreme."

"We can't fight them," Gil said.

I shook my head and leaned on the merlon as a breeze ruffled me hair. "Nope. Not at all."

After a moment of letting the fear and panic run wild in my head, I snapped out of it and turned to Gil.

"Guess my paranoia was warranted after all. Go get everyone! We're getting out of here!" As Gil rushed off, I glanced at Lyahgos. "Gather the men. Get them armed and ready to fight."

"Sir!"

He ran off behind Gil. And I hated that I had to give that order.

There was nothing I could do to save the NPCs here. With the amulet, I could only teleport a few with me, not nearly the hundred or so of them that resided in the castle.

I hate it, but they knew the deal when they signed up with us. I paused, trying to think of any way I could get everyone out alive and I came up empty.

Nothing I can do. Time to move. Get Eris and Raven and teleport out of here with the others.

We'd burn through our teleportation scrolls, but if there was ever a time to use them, it was now.

Harper stood a dozen feet away, staring at the army. He'd changed into his armor, a sleek set of black leather armor with red accents at his chest and going down his side. He pulled his leather hood over his bright orange hair and glanced down below the ramparts and then at me. I cursed as I realized what he was looking at.

Levi and Behemoth!

I rushed over next to Harper as I leaned over the stone to the both of them.

They stood next to the white marble teleportation gate and were looking out to the Rolling Hills. Levi turned back to me and then to the gate.

"Boss! The hell's going on? I can't see nuthin' from this angle."

"An army. Looks like the Alliance got here quicker than expected. Teleport to Aldrust—we'll meet you there."

Levi shook his head, his thick brown hair curled atop his head. "Can't! The gate is down. Someone used nullification magic."

What!

"Shit!"

We were in trouble. With nullification magic active, no magic could work in a certain radius. And without knowing from where it came, there was nothing we could do to stop it.

Even if I can dispel null magic with antimagic, if I don't know where the source is, it won't do anything.

"How did they manage to sneak up past our guards close enough to use null magic?" I asked aloud.

"That's a problem," Harper said.

"Yeah, no shit."

I paused, lost in thought for a moment as I tried to figure out how we were going to get out of this one.

We had a very limited window of escape and get clear before the army was close enough to start doing damage. Which meant we didn't have time to stand around deliberating; we had to act.

I turned back to Harper.

"We've got to go! Tell the gate guard to lower…"

I trailed off as Harper stood still, not looking at me as he pulled a crimson bow and a quiver of arrows from his inventory and slowly nocked an arrow and drew back his bow.

The army was at least a mile or more out. Even considering Harper's unbelievable skill with a bow, there was no way he could land a shot at that distance.

"Harper, the hell are you doing? I know you're good, but you can't make a shot like that."

He turned to me, gave me a wide grin that raised the acne scars on his cheeks and nodded.

"Oh, I'm well aware."

Harper turned back out, leaned over the stone merlon and lowered his bow.

Aiming at Levi and Behemoth.

"What the hell are you doing!"

As I moved to grab him, Harper released his arrow.

The black shaft of the arrow glowed bright red as it flew through the air and impacted a second later. There was a soft thump as the arrow embedded itself in the grass. Then, before I could react, a rush of sulfuric air washed over me, and there was a sharp crack as Harper's *Explosive Arrow* activated.

White light bathed me, and there was an intense wave of pressure followed by a massive explosion.

I stumbled by the sudden force of the blast, and my ears rang as bits of rock and dirt scattered all around me. My vision swam and blood pooled in my mouth and I fought to right myself.

As I blinked my eyes clear, a flash of orange hair was all I could make out before something struck my chest.

I looked down at the arrow halfway embedded over my heart. There was no pain, not yet. I stumbled back as another two arrows hit me, and then my balance was robbed from me and I hit the ground hard.

My head slammed back against the pavestones, and my consciousness waned.

All of this happened in seconds, and I was so stunned that I couldn't form a counterattack as I faced a stark reality.

Harper had betrayed us.

He'd always been an abrasive hothead, but he'd been one of us. Or so I thought.

Sharp footsteps clacked as Harper made his way to me. He stood over me, his bow drawn back and an arrow pointed at my face.

"You really are a tough sonuvabitch aren't you? Three arrows to the chest, and I still didn't get penetration." He shrugged and spit. "Well, let's see how your face does."

Always were one for melodrama. Fool.

The single greatest rule of fighting was never gloat over an enemy before they were dead. Yet Harper, a veteran player, was making a grievous mistake.

One that I fully planned on capitalizing on.

As he shifted his aim, I swept my leg and caught Harper's ankle. He cried out and lost his balance as he fired, sending his arrow off target. It sliced a groove along my cheek and cut through my earlobe before it ricocheted off the stone floor.

I ignored the burning pain and threw myself into the kick, taking Harper to the ground. His head cracked against the side of the rampart, and he let out a groan as he tried to stand back up.

Harper was the best shot I'd ever seen. Hell, he'd landed three arrows in nearly the same spot in under three seconds. But he was a trash close range fighter, and he knew it.

He threw his arm out to break his fall and rolled away as my foot came down where he'd been standing. Harper popped up and tried to go for another arrow.

As he nocked it, I summoned my *Chitin Shield*. And it bounced harmlessly off my reinforced chitin.

"How the hell am I not getting through?" he shouted, drawing another arrow.

I raised my shield and deflected the next two arrows as I walked towards him. My rage built with every step.

"Oh, fuck this," he said, and his bow started glowing.

Recognition flashed through my eyes; I couldn't let him get off his next shot. I activated *Aura of the Antimage*.

An invisible current swirled around me in a circle and dispersed all around me. It rushed out and over Harper in an instant, destroying his *Phase Shot*. One of the few abilities that could negate my chitin's defenses and pierce right through me.

He wasn't expecting to have his ability shattered, and when he released his arrow, it glanced off my shield, and I was in his space before he could line up another shot.

I didn't call it, but jagged chitin rose from my skin and covered me in seconds. I reached out with my clawed hand and ripped his bow from his hand and tossed it aside while my other hand grabbed Harper by the throat.

He and I hadn't spent a lot of time together. He was young, perpetually an eighteen-year-old and though mentally, he should have been a middle-aged man, his personality had, like his body, been stuck as a teenager.

It made him annoying at times, but I'd called him a friend, and I would've gone through hell for him. We may have not gotten along all the time, but he was family, and I couldn't understand why he'd tried to kill us.

There hadn't been time to check on Levi and Behemoth, but they were tough, and I had to hope that they withstood Harper's sneak attack.

I closed off his airway as rage overtook me and brought him close to my face. Without his bow and the distance to use it, Harper was helpless against me.

"You haven't fought with me in a long time, so you haven't been aware of the few new tricks I've picked up. Let me show you the newest one."

Though I hadn't used it before, it—like the others I'd acquired—was instinctual. I willed my wasp wings to form, and they sprouted from my back. They were thin, glossy black from the chitin. As soon as they materialized, they began to beat faster and faster, and I rose off the ground.

It was surreal, as I just had to think about flying upward and the wings moved on their own. I was and wasn't controlling them.

We flew high above the castle until I was level with the third story and could see the balcony that led to my room.

Harper struggled against me before he realized how high we were, and then he got really still. His movements became very deliberate.

I ignored him for a moment and stared out over the Rolling Hills at the advancing army. It was too much, and I knew we had to go. Our time was quickly running out.

There was just one thing I had to do.

"Why?" I asked. "Why did you betray us? How could you?"

Harper laughed. "I never betrayed you." He shook his head. "Was never one of you in the first place."

"What?" I asked, my eyes wide.

He scoffed and looked down. His face paled before turning slightly green. "Was a plant from the moment we met." Harper chuckled to himself. "That man, don't know how he knows so much, but he does. Paid me a fortune to infiltrate your little group and wait."

"Who? Magnus?"

"If I tell you, will you let me go?"

I let out a harsh bark of laughter. "You want me to let you go after what you've done? You know that's not how I do things."

"It is if you want to know everything. I'll tell you, but I want a guarantee."

I wrestled with the decision for a moment before deciding to give Harper exactly what he asked for.

"Fine. I'll let you go, but I want to know everything."

He nodded. "Yeah. Magnus hired me. Was just meant to keep an eye on Evelyn and Adam, help bring them to him when the time came, but then you went and screwed things up; turned all this into a shitshow. He dismissed me after Evelyn died."

"He did? Why?"

"Had no use for me anymore," Harper said, his eyes wide as he glanced down. "After everything, I was just going to walk away, but then we all got bounties on our heads. I reached out to the Merchants Guild. Offered to make a deal."

"To what end?" I squeezed his neck tighter and held him aloft, the chitin helping to support his weight as he dangled a hundred feet in the sky. "What did Kincaid want in exchange for your freedom?"

"He wanted me to sabotage you. To stop you and the others from being able to teleport and to take out a few members if I could. Said he'd split the bounties for all of you if I helped. I used a hero-tier nullification scroll."

Damn. That means that they'll be out for at least an hour. If not more.

I shook my head and sighed as my arm trembled with the strain of holding Harper. Even with my strength as high as it was and the chitin's support, humans weren't meant to be able to hold someone up one-handed.

And Harper had told me everything about his involvement. In the back of my head, pieces aligned that I hadn't known connected until Harper told me. it made sense that he was a traitor; I just hadn't seen it.

None of us had.

I don't have any more time to dwell on this. It won't change anything, and I need to check on Levi and Behemoth and start getting everyone out of here.

The window of our escape was rapidly dwindling. So we had to go.

"You betrayed us. Those who looked at you like family."

"Family." Harper scoffed. "A self-destructive guild full of psychotics led by you, a self-loathing drunkard. Just because you may have grown the past few months doesn't change anything. You're all still a bunch of freaks."

"Maybe so. But they're my freaks, and I won't have anyone disrespect them like that. Goodbye Harper. I'll see you in hell."

"You said you'd let me go," He began before he cursed and looked down. "Oh, godsdamn it."

"Fell right into that one. And speaking of falling."

I dropped him.

Harper hung in the air for a fraction of a second before he dropped, and a few seconds later hit the ground with a gut-wrenching squelch.

I ignored his broken, twisted body that lay in chunks over the rampart as I drifted back to the ground and leaned over the railing to check on Levi and Behemoth.

"Hey, you two all ri—"

Levi and Behemoth were dead.

Both of them had been right next to where Harper's *Explosive Arrow* had landed, and without time to prepare their defenses, had been completely vulnerable when it detonated.

The concussive force had been enough to twist their steel armor until it was barely recognizable, and the fire had done the rest of the work. Their bodies were broken, deformed husks, and the ground around them was scorched earth.

Two of my oldest friends were dead, killed by someone I'd considered an ally, a friend and part of my family.

Bile burned in my throat at the sight of my friends' corpses, but I couldn't stop and mourn. I had to go, to warn the others and get them to safety.

With a final glance at them and the promise to make Kincaid pay for his part in their deaths, I turned and went back to the keep.

Chapter 18 - The Cardinals

With Harper having sabotaged our ability to teleport, that left escaping the castle by lake. The others were tough and I had to believe they'd be fine, but I had to grab the girls before anything else.

I took off and headed back to the keep. I shouldn't have wasted time with Harper, but it had only been a couple of minutes, and if a couple of minutes decided whether we lived or died, then we were already screwed.

The army still had a mile or so to go. That would take time, time that we would use to flee. When the army arrived at our doorstep, I wanted us to be long gone.

The men at arms would hold the castle until it was breached, and then they would surrender. It was a plan that would cost a few of them their lives, but it would keep most of them alive. If in trouble with the Alliance.

Worry about legal trouble later. After we survive.

I sprinted to the castle and found Raven and Eris running down the stairs with Yumiko and Adam right behind them. Gil and Makenna quickly joined us in the entrance hall. A door opened to my right and Markos and Mika joined us as well.

As soon as they entered, I spoke.

"There's no time to explain, so ask questions later. Harper was a plant by Kincaid. He betrayed us and used null magic to take out the teleporters. We can't get out through the gate."

"What?" Gil asked, nearly shouting.

The others all started talking in tandem, asking all the questions we didn't have time for. We really had to go.

Gil was about to say something else when he stopped and looked around the entrance hall. "We're missing two people. Shit, where are Levi and Behemoth?"

I shook my head and tried not to think of their mangled, burning bodies as a chill rose up my spin and my stomach turned.

"Dead. Harper killed them, then tried to kill me."

Gil blanched as rage crossed his face. "He's been with us for years, why would he turn on us now?"

I held my hand up. "We can talk later. We need to get to Aldrust, and Wilson will guide us to the safehouse from there. We just have to get out of the castle first."

Even as despair chilled my bones, I had to give Kincaid credit. He'd trapped us but good, and the Alliance and guilds would soon surround the castle with their numbers.

The troops were a concern, but we could handle a good portion of them. If it was just the soldiers, we could punch a hole through the men and make a break for it, but with the guilds, there was no way we could fight.

A single guild would give us trouble. Five of them would crush us.

Even as I accepted Levi and Behemoth's deaths, the realization that even more of my friends might not make it out of here hit me hard enough to take my breath away and made my knees go weak.

"All right. Let's head to the gate and get the fuck out of here," Mika said.

The others nodded, and we raced toward the doors. Just as we opened them, Lyahgos raced toward us.

"Thirteen riders just broke off from the main army and are heading here at speed. They'll be here in minutes."

I stopped and cursed as a stiff breeze rolled through the bailey.

It was a smart plan; a single guild could stall us from leaving long enough for the army to arrive. There was still a way for the others to get away.

But someone would have to stay behind.

I turned to the others. "So unless someone has a better plan, I think our only move is to cause a diversion long enough to let most of you get far enough away to use teleportation."

"You can't fight them," Mika said, grabbing my arm.

"Yeah, I know. But I can stall them." I turned to him, placing a hand on his. "I saw the banner of the Cardinals, so you and I can both guess which guild is likely heading our way."

Mika turned and spat. "Lonny."

"He probably came here just for a chance at my head." I smiled. "Well, I plan on giving it to him. Let you guys have a chance to get away."

Everyone erupted in protest, which made my heart swell with pride, but I wasn't going to ask any of them to die in my place. If someone had to give their life to save everyone, then it should be me.

But I didn't have a death wish, not anymore. I wanted to live more than anything, but I couldn't live with the knowledge that one of my friends gave their life for me when I could have done something.

I couldn't help Evelyn, and I refused to be in that position again. That being said, I wasn't going to walk out and hand them my death.

I had a plan.

"Okay, settle down. Everyone meet up at the grotto beneath the castle and take the boats there. Get across the lake and head toward the ocean. Should be far enough out that their null magic can't reach."

When I finished the first part of my plan, I turned to Raven.

"I hate to ask, but I'm going to need your help. I want you to shift into your bird form and make sure the others get away clean. When they do, I want you to come to me and let me know. Then you and I break away from the army and fly to the safehouse."

Gil shook his head, coming over to me. "That plan is suicide. No way do the Cardinals let you stall them long enough for all of us to get away."

"You don't know Ascalon. The man's got one hell of a bone to pick with me. Trust me, I can stall them long enough for you guys to get away."

"Bu—"

"Gil." I threw my hands up. "If you have any other plan that gets us all out alive, then I'm all ears, but if not, then I'm going to settle for the plan that gets most of us out alive and only puts me in danger."

He still didn't like it, and neither did I, but we didn't have time to argue or sit down and figure out a better plan. It was what I could come up with on short notice, so it would have to be enough.

Gil opened his mouth to protest, but we couldn't argue, not now.

"Shit! Go!" I wasn't going to waste any more time that we didn't have. "I'll stall them!"

I turned, not even having the chance to say goodbye to them. We had seconds to spare, and I was going to do everything I could to make sure they escaped.

We all rushed to the front gate. If we were going to leave, we had to do it quickly.

"Eris, you and Adam grab the horses. Take Lacuna and ride out as fast as you can when I draw the attention of the Cardinals!"

"It's not going to fuckin' work!" Yumiko shouted as we ran. "Last I remember, Nolan is still a Cardinal, and he has a wide area of effect magic. We step out, and they'll blast us."

"Well, what else can we do?" I asked.

"We give them one hell of a fight, and then while they're catching their breath, we run."

The problem with trying to come up with a plan, was the Cardinals. If we could quickly take them down then we might stand a chance before the rest of the army arrived.

It would all rely on how they reacted. We could try to hit them hard and fast, like Yumiko suggested, but we weren't at full strength and that put us at a disadvantage when fighting. *Will of the Immortal* was still on cooldown, so unless I downed a recovery potion, I wouldn't be able to use it.

"Fuck it." I pulled one out of my inventory and downed it. A sweetness filled my mouth as I drank it down and tossed the bottle away. "Okay! New plan, we hit them hard before the rest of the army arrives and then run the fuck away!"

Gil grinned at me from beside me. "Now that's a plan I can get behind. Either we all escape, or we go down fighting!"

The front gate was blocked by whatever the guards could find. Wood, stone, and even sacks of grain. Anything that would slow down the invaders.

It would take too long to get through, so I shifted and turned, heading up the stairs to the ramparts.

I glanced down and found both Levi and Behemoth's remains had vanished. Which was a good thing. I didn't want the others to see what had become of our friends. I shifted my gaze and looked out at the field. The Cardinals were close now and would be here in less than thirty seconds. The Alliance army was about ten minutes out, not leaving us a large window to get away.

It'll have to be enough.

"Okay, I'll go and stall them for a second, and when I attack, that's the cue to join me," I said, turning to the others.

My friends stood behind me, each of them decked out in the best gear we had, all of them looking every inch the warriors I knew them to be. As the wind rolled through and brought a few leaves swirling around them, my heart ached with fierce pride.

I couldn't have asked for a better family.

"I just want to say that it has been an honor and a privilege to know each and every one of you," I said. "You're my family."

Gil stepped forward and clapped me on the shoulder. "Yeah, well. As a guild leader, you kinda suck, but I couldn't have asked for a better brother."

"Love you guys." I grinned. "Now let's go show the strongest guild on Nexus that they should've brought a hundred times the men to take on the Gloom Knights!"

Gil gave me a fierce smile. "Sound off."

I nodded, matching his smile as adrenaline pulsed through my veins.

"Gloom Knights, to war!" A cheer rose from the lips of every member.

But despite our enthusiasm, our words died in our throats as the Cardinals arrived. They were regarded as the most powerful players on Nexus for a reason. We couldn't underestimate them. If we did, we'd all die.

The Cardinals arrived on pure white steeds with perfectly groomed manes. Each of them wore identical armor—gleaming red plate mail with their emblem embossed on their chests. The only difference among them was Lonny who wore a golden cape, which signified him as the guild leader.

For all our history, the pain that lingered in my chest refused to leave. I held such conflicting emotions for Lonny that I didn't know whether to weep or throw something in rage.

But despite that, Lonny had a problem with me. His rage was supposed to be directed at me, not at those I held dear.

He would relish the chance to kill me, and it didn't matter who stood in the way of that.

I sighed as I picked him out from the crowd.

Well, best get this over with.

I vaulted the ramparts and landed into a roll. I'd already donned my shadowsteel plate mail, and I rested my hand on my sword as I marched over to the thirteen players in a semicircle in front of me.

Lonny stood at the center while the others remained astride their horses. His thick, chestnut hair was a few inches longer than last I'd seen him, and some of the curl had been tamed. His rugged face was set in stone, and when his eyes landed on me, they narrowed in confusion before a spark of recognition shone through them, followed swiftly by rage.

"Duran," he said. "The hell happened to you?"

"Long story. But if you're going to address me, I stopped going by Duran. It's Sam now."

He let out a hollow laugh. "Sam." He scoffed. "Sophia was the only one who was allowed to call you that. What changed?"

"I did, Lonny. I'm not holding onto all that bitterness and self-loathing anymore. I refuse to blame myself for Sophia's death any longer."

He drew his sword in a flash. The large ruby set in the pommel of his silver and gold blade reflected the sun and cast blood red light into my eyes.

"She died because of you!" he screamed.

I shook my head. "No, Soph died because she refused to live in this world of misery and blood for a second longer." I walked slowly towards them. "You can twist that fact into whatever you want. You can blame me till the day you die, but it won't change the fact that neither of us could have saved her. If we had, it would have only prolonged her suffering, and I think you know that."

"No!" He levied his sword at me. "It was because of you!"

As the echo of his words died around us, the silence was deafening. Blades of grass rustled in the wind, and the heavy breathing of the horses were the only other sounds around us, as Lonny attacked.

"I'm sorry," I said and activated *Will of the Immortal.*

The world came to a complete standstill as the color faded from around me. Nothing but graywashed landscape rose around me. Lonny and the others were completely frozen.

And for once, none of them could counteract my ability.

I heaved a mental sigh of relief and stepped toward Lonny. I had twenty seconds of time stop to make my moves. Twenty seconds didn't seem like that much time, but to a warrior, it was all the time in the world.

Chitin came at my call, pooling black over my skin as I focused on summoning my arachnid limbs and scorpion tail. I needed the extra limbs if I was going to pull this off.

Lonny stood frozen in front of me, the sword he'd held for fifteen years raised. It was the same blade that had taken my life all those years ago.

I left Lonny alone. Whether it was compassion, or just because he used to be my best friend, or because I wanted a chance to face him in combat again, I didn't have it in me to kill him without looking him in the eye.

But the other members of the Cardinals were fair game. I cared nothing for them and would dispatch them quickly.

Every member of the Cardinals was Paladin class. And as I knew well, that wasn't the be all end all.

I had been a Swift Paladin before I became Blade Master, the class I had held before Hive Knight. But there were many different playstyles for a Paladin.

Rushing to the left, I engaged the first of the guild. The Cardinals were legendary, but I still didn't know all of them by heart. I'd heard all of their names and stories of their exploits but putting faces to names was something I couldn't do.

The first man I went after was tall and well built. He had short hair and stern eyes. I could tell at once he was a tank. I used my back limbs to push off the ground and propel me forward. I unsheathed my sword as I flew through the air and brought it down across the man's throat.

Resistance met me as crimson rain spilled into the gray world. I took his head off his shoulders as I landed on the leather saddle behind him.

As soon as my feet hit something solid, I used my limbs to stabilize myself and pushed off again. I shot toward the second guild member. The petite woman was a mage from her robes and the staff clutched in her hands. I angled by her and punched through her heart with my scorpion tail.

Two were dead in less than three seconds.

No matter how powerful the Cardinals were, no matter how fierce their reputation, if they couldn't defend themselves or use their abilities, they were nothing but cannon fodder.

I circled the guild, using my powerful limbs to keep me moving at high speed as I slaughtered each one of them. Their hero-tier armor was nothing as I ripped through each of their necks or punched through their hearts. I killed them all as quickly as I could, not standing still for a moment.

When I was done, there were twelve dead Cardinals and too much red in a sea of gray.

There was a singular moment, one second out of twenty where I stepped back and just marveled at what I'd done.

I'd single handedly decimated the most powerful guild on Nexus.

I'd cheated in the worst way imaginable. It wasn't fair, just, or honorable.

But it was spectacular.

And then, with seconds to spare, I had a choice to make.

I ignored my handy work and stood in front of Lonny. His sword was a centimeter from my throat. A place that we had both been in once before.

As I stared into his hate-filled eyes. I had to choose.

To indulge in my selfish desire to have a fight with him. Prove that I had grown and could best him in an honorable duel. That just because he'd killed me once, it didn't mean he could do it again.

Or I could deal with him like I'd dealt with the rest of his guild.

I knew the choice I'd have made six months ago. Duran, at the height of his game, a level one hundred Blade Master, would have done anything for the chance to prove to Ascalon that he was better than him. To inflict the same humiliation upon Lonny as had been done to him.

I'd have fought him to the death regardless of the risks it placed on the others. I'd have given in to my rage and anger and sacrificed everything in hopes of putting to rights something that I hadn't yet forgiven myself for.

Durandahl was a fool.

But I was Sampson Acre.

"I'm sorry, Lonny. For the part I played in your pain. Truly, I am." I took the shining blade from his hands and turned it around. I stared into his eyes as I pressed the sword to his heart and shoved it through his chest. It was the highest quality blade and backed by my strength it cut through his armor and into his heart with minimal resistance. "Maybe now you can find your peace."

With the sword still lodged into his chest, I stepped back. Regret pooled in my throat as I bit down the bile that filled my mouth. I wanted to turn away, but I couldn't. I had to witness the choice I'd made.

Lonny had been my friend, but if it was the choice between a man who had been a friend or the lives of my family, or even my selfish desires and the lives of my family, there was no choice.

I'd sacrifice Lonny for them in a heartbeat.

Which is exactly what I'd done.

The world flashed into color. My time was up. I had the barest of seconds left, and I had one more thing I had to do. I took a recovery potion from my inventory and took a single sip.

It was risky, considering that I'd drunk a whole one before the fight, but I didn't have a choice. Potion Sickness was guaranteed, but I had three hours before it kicked in and I needed the strength to keep the others safe.

I just hoped I wasn't pushing past potion sickness and into system overload.

With the potion in my mouth, I waited until the world turned back to color until I swallowed.

Hues of green flooded all around me as the Rolling Hills came into view. The blue sky sparkled, and clouds drifted past as thirteen people bled out an ocean of blood into the grass.

My body seized up as my battle fatigue rose to near max and teased overflow. At the last movement, the mouthful of recovery potion kicked in and brought it back down. I was still over seventy-five percent of the way to max, but I could swing my sword a few times before I dropped.

As I stumbled, Lonny dropped to his knees in front of me.

I cancelled my chitin armor and moved over to Lonny.

He stared at me with blood pooling in his mouth. He managed one glance back to his comrades and back to me, his eyes wide.

"How?" he gargled as his lungs filled with blood.

"I wish it didn't have to be this way, Lonny," I said, kneeling next to him.

He shook his head. "Doesn't matter." He choked and spat a mouthful of blood. "This just makes us even. I won't lose next time."

"There won't be a next time." My voice was nothing more than a whisper. "Not for you and me. The system is failing. There are no more respawns for us. This is the end. I'm sorry."

Lonny looked into my eyes trying to find any hint of deception, and when he found none, he sighed. He stopped fighting and let himself fall to the side.

"We shouldn't have been allowed a second chance anyways, Sam. The things we survived on Earth—we should have just been allowed to die in peace. This place is just purgatory for us, and if it's coming to an end, so be it." He coughed again, his voice failing him. "This world lost all meaning for me a long time ago."

"Yeah." I sighed, searching his face for any semblance of the man I'd known. I came up empty. "Tell Sophia I know why she killed herself, and that I understand."

Lonny turned to me as sorrow filled his eyes before it was replaced by fire.

His head shot up as he glared at me. "Tell her yourself, bastard!" As he fell back down, he started laughing, but it was wrong, half choking, half gargling as he died.

He raised his hand and pointed his finger at the sky, still laughing. "The Cardinals. Handpicked by the high priest himself to serve as his right hand. The best guild in this accursed world, and we were just the distraction."

He kept laughing as I followed his hand as it pointed towards the sun. When I was looking near straight up, I stopped and froze.

My blood turned to ice in my veins, and my mind refused to comprehend what I was seeing in front of me.

296

There's no way. That's too much. It's too much.

High above us, well past the highest point of Castle Gloom Harbor, past the clouds and birds in the sky.

Thirteen massive script circles formed in front of the sun.

The first and closest to the sun was the largest and least complex. It was a near translucent blue. The next was smaller, finer and more intricate. It was also lighter in color. It went that way for all of the spell circles. Each of them smaller and increasing in complexity until it reached the very last one which was solid white, and script formed, dissolving and reforming at increasing rates as the spell built to its finality.

It was a spell that I had never seen performed before, but I knew of it. *Sunburst Oblivion.*

Cataclysm class magic of the highest caliber.

Castle Gloom Harbor was doomed.

But I couldn't do nothing.

The others hadn't realized the sword of Damocles hanging over their heads.

"Jump!" I shouted at them, standing up and running towards them. "Get clear of the castle!"

Eris and Raven, not to mention the rest of them, were still atop the ramparts. They didn't know what was going on, but they trusted me enough to do as I said without question.

Gil stepped back and leapt as far as he could while the others did the same. Raven sprouted wings, grabbed Eris, and took off towards me.

Just as I shouted, one of the most powerful spells in existence completed. There was a blinding pillar of white light that slammed into the ground like the judgment of a god and then a thump of pressure before the world exploded in front of me.

Chapter 19 - The End of the Gloom Knights

My teeth rattled in my skull as my bones shook, and blood ran from my eyes and nose. A high-pitched whine ripped through my skull as my heartbeat pounded too loudly in my ears. Even with my eyes wide open, there was nothing but white as an intense heatwave rolled toward us.

I screamed Eris and Raven's names, but my voice was lost to the thunderous rumble around me. Although I couldn't see, something soft and warm crashed into me.

Even without most of my senses, I couldn't mistake Raven and Eris for anything else. With only the barest hint of the direction of the blast, I covered them both and formed my chitin armor and shield to cover us.

I didn't know how long *Sunburst Oblivion* lasted, but the explosion seemed to stretch on for eternity as I huddled over my girls and fought to keep from passing out from the pain.

Shards of stone struck all around us. One of them even gouged a chunk of meat from my left arm. Another took a bite out of my shoulder, and one sliced through the side of my head. Half an inch to the left and I'd have died then and there.

After the close encounter, I willed more chitin around my vital areas.

Eventually, an eternity and a half later, the blistering heat abated, and the rumbling stopped. My ears still rang from the concussive force, but it was manageable as the edge of my vision cleared.

As soon as my sight retuned, I glanced down at Eris and Raven.

Both of them were alive. Eris had covered herself in chitin like I had, and we'd both instinctively protected Raven. She was by far the worst out of the three of us. Burns covered her back, and one of her wings had been torn off, leaving a bloody stump. Numerous cuts ran down her pale skin and her eyes were unfocused.

I pulled a health potion from my inventory and poured it down her throat. Her wounds stitched themselves closed, and her wing began to reform as her breathing stabilized.

When I knew they were both going to live, I double checked to make sure Eris didn't have any wounds, and then I handed her a small bag filled with potions while I grabbed a second bag for myself.

"We need to check on the others!" I shouted.

And finally, I glanced up to survey the damage that had been done.

As I gazed at the place that had been my home for over a decade, my heart broke. Castle Gloom Harbor was gone.

It had been reduced to rubble and glass. The keep was ash, blasted to a glossy wasteland that refracted light from the scorched glass that lay scattered around where my home had been.

Even the very edge of the ramparts hadn't been spared, and when the explosion had blasted apart the keep, the stone impacted and obliterated most of the structure.

My home.

Not just my home, but the people who lived there too. Lyahgos and Charlotte, Amber, Ruby, and Jade. Our guards, maid staff, cooks. Everyone. Over a hundred NPCs had just lost their lives.

Lacuna.

My horse was dead. I'd had Lacuna for nearly as long as we'd held Gloom Harbor. She was stubborn, nearly as prideful as I was and smarter than me by an order of magnitude.

And I would never see her again.

It was too much. Far too much to lose at once, yet I'd lost it all the same.

And I couldn't stop and mourn any of it, because more lives than mine hung in the balance. I had to check on my friends, had to make sure they were all right.

The area around the blast was scorched. Huge swathes of grassland around the castle were blackened and torn; burnt grass lifted up and swirled around us in the rush of wind from the lake, but it wasn't enough to get rid of the acrid stench in the air.

I spotted Gil first, lying face down next to a large chunk of stone. Blood splashed across its surface.

Oh gods, no!

I rushed over to him as fast as my legs would carry me. I threw myself to the ground, a potion already in hand as I turned him over. I didn't bother checking for life signs, I just poured the health potion into his mouth as fast as it would go down.

When it was empty, I tossed it aside and checked his heartbeat. I waited. For years I waited, that single millisecond stretched for a decade until the faint tremor of his pulse flicked through my fingertip.

He was alive.

But he was also in bad shape. The boulder had ripped his left arm off completely and crushed half his body. The potion would heal him, but he wasn't waking up today or the next couple of days, more likely.

I poured another one down his throat to help speed up the recovery, not caring if he went into system overload.

When some color returned to his body and my racing heart calmed, I placed a hand on his shoulder, promising him that he would be okay.

I stood and went to check on the next person.

Mika was next, and he was mostly fine; half his hair was singed to a crisp, and he was bleeding heavily, but he was on his knees already drinking a potion as I ran past him. He gave me a sorrowful look as I ran past him.

"Sorry about Lonny."

I was too, but I didn't have time to worry about that when my friends could be hurt. I was close to where the teleportation gate had been and where nothing but cracked and shattered marble remained. When I passed it, a voice called my name.

"Sam! Help!" Adam shouted.

I turned and found him with Yumiko and Makenna. All three of them were alive and mostly unhurt. Nothing save for some cuts and scrapes.

But they stood in front of a large part of the rampart that had crumbled under the blast. Trapped in the rubble was Markos.

This day of losses wasn't done with me yet.

As I approached, I found the problem.

Markos was pinned beneath a large mass of rubble; the lower half of his body was under a thousand pounds of wreckage.

His thin frame made even smaller by the massive hunk of stone. His mop of brown hair was slick with sweat and brushed back enough that I could see, for the first time in years, his eyes. They were two crystal clear pools of water.

Blood pooled from out of the stone and around the corners of his mouth.

He was dying.

I reached him and knelt, knowing at once the issue.

A health potion was useless here because half of his body was still trapped under the stone. If we healed him, his body would just be crushed all over again. But we also couldn't lift the heavy chunks off of him.

They simply weighed too much, and it would take too long to lift all of the stone to free him. He had a handful of minutes left, and it'd take us hours to shift the stone enough to get him out.

I knew there was nothing we could do to save him.

Markos was going to die.

He lifted his head and moved his fingers. I took his hand and squeezed.

"Hey, bud. Don't worry. We'll get you out of there in no time," I lied. "You're gonna be all right."

He laughed and spat up some blood. "We both know that isn't true. The thread of fate has run out for me. I'm sorry, Sam. This is my fault. My idea to produce the gloom mushrooms, and my idea for the gloam. I brought all of this on us, and I'm sorry."

I shook my head, squeezing his hand even tighter. "You can't hog the blame, Mark. Not this time. Not when there's enough to go around for the both of us. We both did this, not just you. And I won't let you take that on yourself."

Markos looked up at me, and for the first time in a long time, the quirky mage had clarity in his face. He smiled at me through bloody teeth, gripped my hand tight.

"My friend, for too many years, you've been a sin eater. Devouring the blame and shouldering it yourself. Let me do that for you. Just once before I die, let me eat the sin so you don't have to."

He sighed, and his grip on me relaxed. His eyes grew dim, and Markos the healer, the man who single-handedly created a drug empire so powerful that it threatened the entirety of the Compass Kingdom, died.

I let go of his hand and closed his eyes.

"Goodbye, my friend."

I turned and stepped back. The sight of him like that was more than my stomach could bear. I turned and vomited into the grass. I doubled over and heaved until there was nothing but acidic bile that burned in my throat.

When I came back up, tears streaked down my face.

It was too much. In the span of a few seconds, I'd lost more than I could comprehend. And now I was staring at the dead body of a friend, a member of my family who would never return.

I didn't know what to do, what I could do.

There was nothing to do but weep for the dead.

I couldn't bear seeing him like that; my excuse was that I had to check on the others, but that was a half lie. I just didn't want to look anymore.

I'd seen more death and pain that I could remember, but something like this hit too close.

I wiped my eyes and stood, turning to the others. I coughed, tilting my head as I stopped and dried my eyes once more.

"Is everyone else alive?" I asked.

"Yeah," Mika said, stepping over to us. "Eris and Raven are with Gil. He's stabilized and is recovering. They are tending to him." He sighed and pointed towards the teleportation gate. "Everyone besides Levi, Behemoth, and…and Markos, are fine."

I nodded, swallowing a couple of times as I stared down at Markos. "Okay. The plan hasn't changed. We still have an army baring down on us." I turned and looked out at the encroaching troops.

They were about five minutes away; they had stopped when *Sunburst Oblivion* launched. It wouldn't take them long to start moving again and they'd be on us before we knew it.

304

"Get down to the grotto and get the boats. We need to hurry and get out of here before we get trapped."

The others stepped into action, picking themselves up and heading over to Gil. Mika and Yumiko, with the help of Eris, carried him to the edge of the stairs leading down to the lake.

With everyone moving and focused on escape, I needed to do the same, but I stopped, turned, and stared at the ruins of my home one last time.

Too many memories lay within. And as much as I'd hated them, I'd have given anything to sit in on one of Wilson's guild meetings again, with all of us around the table.

Alistair, Evelyn, Levi, Behemoth, and Markos gone.

The lives of my friends that I'd have given almost anything to see again. The body would start to vanish in a handful of minutes, and with Levi and Behemoth already deleted from the world, it seemed a good final resting place as any other in this world.

I sighed and shook my head, and I turned to leave. As I moved, so too did something else. In the ruined remains of my castle. Something shifted in the distance where the keep had been; something moved under the rock.

For a second, I thought it was some of the staff, that they had survived, but logic quickly told me that there was simply no way for anything living to have come out of that unscathed.

There was a heavy crack, and a massive sapphire hand burst through the stone, sending chunks flying in all directions.

It took me a moment to recognize the hand. It was one of the crystalline golems. It broke through the rest of the rubble with its massive greatsword, knocking rock away as fast as it could as it pried itself loose.

When it was free, it turned as a second hand reached up from below. Both crystalline golems were intact. As the first golem pulled the second free, Adam came over and stood next to me.

"I didn't expect the golems to have survived," I said.

He chuckled, but it lacked all emotion. "What can I say, I build to last."

As we watched, both golems began walking towards us, moving quickly despite their size. They didn't care what was in their way. They moved through it with ease, breaking out of the castle and coming to stand before their master.

"It's been a wild ride, hasn't it, Sam?"

"Yeah." I nodded. "The best."

Adam sighed and shook his head. "I just wanted everyone to survive. That was my goal. Joining up with Windigo Industries and helping to build the Ouroboros Project, I just wanted to help as many people survive as possible. So did Jess, in her own way. She was never the most social person, but the apocalypse made her cold. Made us both cold."

"I know."

And I did know. Surviving in that world gone wrong was a nightmare, and people couldn't survive and come out the other side unscathed.

"None of us weathered that storm unscathed." I turned to him and shook my head. "But what does that have to do with anything?"

He smiled at me. His wry smile that told me he was cooking up something. "Just an old man rambling." He sighed and clapped me on the shoulder, glancing back at the approaching army. "You know the hardest part about all of this?"

"What?"

"The fact that after every system reset, everyone lost their memories, while we kept ours. It's a hard thing, to make friends knowing that they are only going to forget you in a hundred years. It made life difficult for the both of us—hell, even Magnus, I reckon. He didn't used to be that way, you know.

Nick was a kind man, helpful even when doing so cost him. He was there for his friends, no matter what."

"What the hell happened to him then? The man I know isn't anything like that."

Adam turned to the castle and smiled. "The same thing that happened to the rest of us. Survival. Coming through that nightmarish world alive took something from all of us."

He laughed softly to himself and held out his hand to me.

"I'm just glad I got the chance to know you again, Sam. It's been…it's been fun."

"Wait, what?" I whirled around and stared at him as he spoke. "Run that by me again."

He winked at me. "Did you ever wonder why Evelyn was nice to you when she generally hated everyone else?"

"Uh, I just figured she had a thing for me." I shrugged. "Evelyn was, for the most part, generally uncomplicated. If she saw something she wanted, she took it. And I fed into that from time to time."

Adam laughed and once more eyed the troops, a small, sad smile on his lips. "You're probably right about that, but that wasn't all. This isn't the first time we've been friends, Sam. We were good friends a few hundred years ago. A simpler, less complicated era. But that's a story for another time. And we've run out of it, I'm afraid."

I turned and stared at the army coming down over the hills in the distance. He was right. We had to go.

But his words hit me, and I understood their meaning.

"You're not coming with us?"

He shook his head. "Afraid not." Adam tilted his head towards me, scratching his chin. "Someone has to make sure the army is distracted while you escape." He paused and stared down at the ground. "Besides, Sam. I'm tired. A thousand years is more than humans are supposed to live. I could handle it with Jess. It was easier with the two of us, but now…now I have nothing left."

"No." I grabbed him by the shoulder. "Let's go, Adam. I can't do this without you. I can't fight Magnus alone! You can't give up, not until we make that bastard pay for what he did to Evelyn."

"You'll be fine. Edna will help you; she was always smarter than me anyways. Besides, I don't think I can deal with watching Nick die. He is the way he is, but for most of my incredibly long life, he's been my best friend. I'd rather leave this world in your hands. Jessica trusted you with her will. The least I can do is trust you with mine."

Adam stepped away from me and pulled out a small knife from his inventory. He placed it against his palm and dug in. He winced as not-quite-human blood poured from the wound. He ripped his *Shard of Divinity* from his hand and held it up to the sun.

"Such power in a small thing." He reached into his inventory and pulled out a small cloth bag. He dropped the shard in the bag and then tossed it to me.

As I caught it, his golden eyes flared bright before they faded, and color returned to Adam.

His fine hair that swept down over his forehead faded from the bright silver to a deep black. His golden eyes turned a dull jade. And his skin tanned to heathy hue rather than the pale of a corpse it had been.

Like Evelyn, his persona fell away, replaced by who he really was.

"James, right?" I asked.

He nodded. "Jameson Alexander Bell." He motioned to the bag in my hand. "Break it in half and give it to your girls. It will make them stronger, for the battle to come."

James turned to face the army who was really close now.

"Give him hell for me, Sam. Do what I don't have the strength for. Make Nick regret taking my sister from us."

"I will," I said, my voice caught in my throat.

James stood tall in his leather armor as his hands went into his inventory and pulled out his summoning crystals. The crystalline golems lumbered over and stood on either side of him.

"It's a shame you have to miss this. I haven't been able to let loose like this in a long time."

He started tossing crystals down as fast as he could pull them out of his inventory, dozens of them.

More than any summoner could control at once.

But he summoned them regardless.

A hundred different kinds of monsters. And I realized then that James had been hiding his strength from us for a very long time, as he summoned an elder dragon. It was easily twice as massive as the elder storm dragon I had fought so many months ago.

This one was a bright green. A wind dragon. As it was summoned, it let out a deafening roar and summoned a massive tornado to hound the incoming army.

The final creature he summoned was his void golem. The gaping black hole in the center of its tall, humanoid body was already ripping what little grass remained around it and devouring it.

"Go," he said. "I'll keep them busy for a long damn time."

And I believed him. With his power, he could take on the whole damn army himself, and I thought he had a good chance of succeeding against them.

But the other players, the dozens of them—he wouldn't be able to hold out against all of them.

Sooner or later, they would overwhelm him. It took mana to summon a creature. Not much, but when he summoned them by the hundreds, he would be running close to mana depletion no matter how much stronger he was than a normal player.

James was still going to die.

I knew that to be fact. But he was going out on his own terms, and I understood that better than most. I had no right to interfere with his decision.

Even if he was leaving me to save the world on my own.

"Give 'em hell, James."

He turned back and grinned. "You know it."

With that, he marched his summoned army forward, giving me a final parting wave.

I wanted to stay and fight with the man who'd been one of my best friends, but I couldn't. I had to protect the others.

Goodbye, James.

That word had been said too many times today. I'd lost too many friends, and I was numb to the emotions waiting just under the surface. I knew I was going to break down as soon as I let myself stop and rest for a moment, but that moment wasn't now.

I turned and headed for the grotto, and just as I reached the steps, the beginning of the Alliance's assault on the one-man army Jameson Bell commenced.

With a heavy heart, I forced myself not to look back and took the wet, mossy steps two at a time as I reached the end of the path

To the right was the mouth of the cove that led to our supply of narcotics, but to the left was a small, wooden dock. A handful of small boats, which were little more than canoes, sat in the water. Half of them were missing, and as I glanced out at the water, I found the few remaining members of the Gloom Knights paddling out to the center of the lake.

Of the boats that remained, only one had any occupants in it. Raven and Eris sat in the boat closest to the water, waiting on me.

I crossed the dock and boarded the boat in seconds, my need to get them out of there outweighing everything else.

As I sat down, they leaned towards me.

"Is Adam not coming?" Eris asked.

I shook my head as I untied the boat and shoved off.

"Oh. I'm sorry," she said.

"Me too."

We began rowing to meet the others in the center of the lake. I focused solely on the oars, making sure to keep them level and paddling as fast as I could as they sluiced in and out of the water.

It took about ten minutes of rowing to reach the middle of the lake.

The others sat clustered together in the handful of rowboats.

None of them spoke.

I stopped rowing and just stared out at the greenish water as it crashed against the side of the boat. We rocked gently back and forth as the wind carried the distant sounds of battle to us.

We need to get moving. We can't stay here.

"All right, everyone grab your teleportation scrolls and teleport to Aldrust."

Mika stood, shouldering Gil. "See you guys on the other side."

He held his scroll up, and as it activated, he disappeared in a shower of light. Soon, the others repeated the action, and half a minute later, it was just the three of us next to a bunch of empty boats.

There was so much I wanted to say, but I didn't have the right words for any of it. I clutched the amulet I'd taken from Gil in my hand as I stared back at the ruined remains of Castle Gloom Harbor and imagined, for just a second, that my world hadn't just crumbled…That my home still stood; that I could go back to my room, have a stiff drink while I stood on the balcony and stare out at the world; that I could take a bath in the tub Adam and I had built together.

That my friends were still alive.

That all was right with the world.

But nothing was right with the world, and it wouldn't ever be again.

The bodies of my friends would already have been deleted from the world. And as that fact settled over me, I realized an undeniable truth. No matter if I stopped Magnus and helped save Nexus, the Gloom Knights were finished.

Nothing could change that.

I sighed and turned away from my home, knowing I'd never set foot there again. I shook my head and pulled out the scroll.

"Let's get out of here."

Chapter 20 - Regroup and Recovery

Eris

As Sam reached out his hand, he turned his head away, stealing one last glance at his home. It was an involuntary reflex on his part. He just couldn't let go, and I understood that.

I reached a hand into the rippling water by the edge of the boat and enjoyed the cold water as it brushed along my skin. By the time I brought it back, Sam was ready to leave.

We held hands and teleported to the outside of Aldrust.

I stumbled as we stepped out of the gate, and the cool moisture on my hand quickly dried under the beating sun.

Behind us loomed the massive walls that surrounded the dwarven city. The massive slabs of earth had both been formed and were now being held together with magic.

Grassland stretched around us, but as I turned to my left, a forest stood at the very edge of my vision.

The others were waiting for us when we arrived. They'd changed out of their armor and now wore more casual clothes. I couldn't help but notice that each one of them wore black, despite the heat.

"We need to get out of this heat," Mika said, thumbing back towards the forest.

Gil was still slung over his shoulder and seeing him easily carry the larger man reminded me that I'd underestimated Mika's strength.

"Yeah. You're right," Sam said, brushing his silver hair back. He looked toward the sea of trees and nodded. "Let's get moving. We have a number of miles to cover in this heat. Hope everyone brought water."

He strode off without another word, and I knew better than to try and talk to him now.

He's just lost friends, family. I wouldn't want to talk right now either.

More than that, I knew he hadn't yet processed their deaths, because I hadn't either. I hadn't known them long, but each of them was still my friend, too. Especially Markos and Adam. They were two of Sam's closest friends, as well, and losing them was going to be hard to accept, for all of the Gloom Knights.

So I said nothing as Sam walked ahead of the others. No one was inclined to talk right now and focused on their own thoughts and emotions.

I hung back with Raven as we walked, but neither of us cared to speak.

We walked in silence for a few hours until the sun finally faded under a canopy of dense foliage. A mixture of coniferous and deciduous trees stood tall above us. As the sun's merciless gaze receded, I heaved a sigh and wiped my brow.

A soft breeze whispered over my skin and chilled the sheen of sweat that lingered on my skin.

"Thirsty?" Raven asked.

She held out a canteen, her ruby red lips wet as she offered me a drink. I took it and drank deeply. It was slightly warm from the heat, but I didn't care. I hadn't realized how dehydrated I actually was and greedily slaked my thirst.

When I was finished, I handed it back to her.

"Thank you."

She nodded, her crimson eyes downcast as she looked anywhere but at me.

I understood that she didn't want to talk, and neither did I really. We were all pushing down our emotions because we'd all break down and start sobbing if we let what we were feeling out.

As we got deeper into the woods, Sam made a slight direction change to the right, heading into even thicker brush.

After another twenty to thirty minutes of walking, we stopped.

Before us in the middle of the woods was a tall log cabin. But it was huge, two stories, and it spanned for a while in either direction. Nestled around and on top of the cabin was green netting filled with fresh green leaves, and thick brush lay around the perimeter of the land, hiding it from sight unless you knew it was there.

Even the wood the cabin was made from was meant to blend in, and there was a chaos to the structure, to break up the shape of the house.

"Is this our new home?" I asked.

Sam turned back to me and nodded, sadness in his eyes. "For now, at least. It will do."

With that, he walked up the steps to the porch, past a long wooden bench by the door, and raised his hand to knock. He held it there for a long moment before he sighed and rapped three times, then once, then twice more.

"To the king who walks in shadow."

The door opened and Wilson walked out, leaning against the frame. He was dressed impeccably as usual, his steel-gray hair slicked back and his gray beard neatly combed and trimmed.

"About time. What took you—"

He stopped as he stared at Sam's face and then looked closely at the rest of us. He counted in his head quickly, noticing the missing members of the

Gloom Knights at once. Realization dawned on his face, and it quickly fell as he hung his head.

"What happened?"

"Harper." Sam choked, his words coming out stilted as he tried to keep everything bottled up. "He betrayed us, used null magic to trap us, and killed Levi and Behemoth. Alliance took care of the rest. They destroyed the castle. Killed…killed Markos. Adam…He stayed back…To buy time."

After that, Sam fell to his knees, wracked with sobs. He let go of everything then and there. My eyes welled with tears of their own as my heart tore seeing him like that.

The others joined in, letting their emotions out.

For a long time after that, the only sound that could be heard was crying.

***

It was still night when I woke up. Night sounds of nature buzzed all round me as the sway of trees in the wind reminded me where I was and what happened.

I was lying down, and despite the fact I was outside, I was very comfortable. As I shifted my head, I found I was laying in Sam's lap. He was fast asleep sitting up, his head lolled to the side, propped up by his hand.

We were on the porch of the cabin, lying on the bench. Raven was on the other side of me, propped up just like Sam was.

The rest of the Gloom Knights were scattered around the porch, lying on makeshift sleeping bags as they clustered together.

Acrid smoke wafted past and burned in my nose. Wilson sat on the front steps, a wooden pipe in his hand. He took a long puff and blew the smoke into rings, three at a time as he stared up at the stars.

He turned and glanced at me as I sat up. His steely eyes were puffy and red.

"Evening, Eris," he whispered.

I got up and went to sit by him, pulling my legs up and wrapping my arms around them. "Evening, Wilson. Couldn't sleep?"

"Don't know if I'll ever sleep again," he muttered, to himself more than me. He sighed and ran a hand through his hair. "I should've been there. Maybe I could've done something."

I shook my head. "I don't think you could've done anything but die along with the others. There just wasn't enough time. I don't understand the magic humans use very well, but the others do, and they're all incredibly smart. If there was a way out, they would have found it."

"Yeah, I know. But we should've thought ahead, should've known the Alliance and Kincaid would pull a stunt like that. We knew he'd try again, and we should've been prepared for something like that. It was smart, what I would've done in his shoes, and I should've thought of it."

"That's not on you, though. We did what we could. We were already preparing to leave." I paused, trying to find the right words. But there were none.

He shook his head. "We could've just left that day. Up and abandoned everything. It was just stuff, and it's all gone now anyway. We killed our friends to protect our wealth. That's on us."

I sighed. There was nothing I could say that would make anything okay for any of them. Loss was like that. It wasn't something words could fix, no matter how good the words were. He was right, but he was twisting the facts to punish himself. I couldn't say anything to ease his mind, but I had to do something.

I opened up the Hive Mind and willed magic into my fingers. This was something I didn't know I could do, but I had acquired the spell for it in the reliquary, so I had to try.

The tendrils of magic flowed from my fingers to the grass, and the blades rose, stretching and multiplying as they reached six feet off the ground. Thousands of strands of grass bent to my command and began shifting, changing into four figures.

I used my memories of each of the fallen Gloom Knights and reconstructed their likeness with the grass. It took a few moments, but when I was done, Levi, Behemoth, Markos, and Adam were standing in front of Wilson.

The wind rustled through the trees and caused the grass to shift and move. In the dim moonlight that shimmered through the clouds and the wind that blew, for a brief moment, it was as if they really were alive again.

Wilson stared at them, his eyes wide and his pipe forgotten in his mouth. At that moment, a cloud parted, and a beam of light illuminated his face. A single tear reflected in the light as it fell down his face.

The spell cost a lot of magic to use and even more for the precise control it took, and I couldn't hold it. I let it go, and the figures unraveled. The blades of grass got caught in the wind and scattered throughout the forest, leaving us alone again.

He reached up and wiped his eye with a casual brush of his hand. He stood and turned to go back inside. As he passed by me, he stopped and placed his hand on my shoulder.

"Thank you."

At that, he went inside, and I remained, staring up at the moon for a long time.

I must've dozed off again resting my head on my knees because when I came to, Sam was next to me, drinking a cup of mana tea. He sat beside me staring out at the trees while taking the occasional sip of his drink.

"Morning," I said.

"Morning, love."

He set his cup down and wrapped an arm around my waist. He pulled me to him, and I scooted into his lap. He held me tight, his chin on my shoulder.

Sam held me like a lifeline. Like he was drowning, and I was the only thing keeping him tied to shore.

I understood the feeling, because Sam had been my lifeline when I'd first come out of the void. I clung to him because he was the only thing that kept me sane. I was more than willing to do the same for him.

"I love you," I said.

"As I love you." His chin shifted as I leaned back into his chest. I held his hands in mine and just sat there as we both stared at the rising sun. He eventually picked up his cup and took another drink. When he set it down once more, he sighed. "What are we going to do?"

"About what?"

"About any of this. This wasn't supposed to be my fight. You and I weren't supposed to be caught in the middle of this war." His voice rose with every passing second. He gripped his cup tightly in his hands as anguish filled his words. "None of this was supposed to happen. This was Evelyn and Adam's war. And what do they do? They leave! They abandon me, leaving me to face Magnus alone!"

He threw the cup as hard as he could. It sailed through the air, the remnants of tea scattering in the sunlight before the cup shattered on a tree in the distance.

"Damn it," he cursed.

Air whistled behind him before something cracked against Sam, and his head flung forward.

"Ow! Godsdamn it."

I turned and found Raven standing over him. She'd changed clothes and now wore loose-fitting black pants and a gray sleeveless top that showed off her porcelain skin. Her hand was balled into a fist, poised over the back of his head.

Sam turned his head, glaring before his eyes softened when he realized it was her. "The hell was that for, Raven?"

"You're being an idiot, so I thought I should smack some sense into you."

"Smack?" He rubbed the back of his head, wincing. "More like a right hook."

Raven folded her arms under her chest and smirked down at him. "Well, you have an abnormally thick head, so I wanted to make sure I got my point across." She knelt and pressed her forehead to his. "You know you're not alone in this, so don't pretend for a second that you are. It's not you against Magnus alone. It's all of us. Don't forget that."

"I don't know," Sam whispered. "It feels like everything rests on my shoulders, even more so now." He held up his hands and stared at his incredibly pale skin. "This power that Evelyn gave me. I don't know what to do with it, how to use it to beat Magnus."

I shifted and got out of Sam's lap, moving to sit beside him. As he and Raven continued to press their heads together, I reached over and flicked his nose. It wasn't hard, just enough to get his attention.

As he turned to me, I spoke.

"You're moping again, love." I placed my hand atop his and smiled. "Whatever happens, as long as the three of us are together, nothing else matters. I know you're hurting; we all are. But just because we're in pain doesn't mean we can give up. We have a world to save, after all."

He sighed, shaking his head slightly as his wry grin teased his lips. He pulled back from Raven and nodded.

"You're right. I just...I just never thought I'd lose so much at once. It still doesn't feel real, you know—that our home is gone; that my friends are dead." Sam hung his head, running his hands up and down his arms. "Even if we save the world, they aren't coming back. None of them."

As he spoke, he stood. He pulled something out of his inventory and sat back down.

It was a small cloth bag, with a single object inside it.

Sam held it carefully, like it held immense value. He turned it over in his palm, staring out at the leaves that blew in the wind.

"Adam gave me this before he went into battle. Told me to give it to both of you, and that it would make you both strong."

He pulled out a small ball-peen hammer and opened the bag. He tipped the contents out, and a small sparkling orange gemstone landed on the wooden porch with a thunk.

I instantly backed up from it. I knew what it was.

It was a *Shard of Divinity*—the object that had given Adam and Evelyn their godhood; the same divinity that Sam now had. It was power, but I still didn't know what it did.

"Adam told me to break it in half and give it to both of you. It must be something important if he wanted you two to have it."

Sam brought the hammer down on the shard, and it cracked with a sharp retort. It spilt down the middle as the hammer slammed into the wood, creating a barrier between the two pieces. Dozens of minute fragments scattered across the porch before stopping. The slivers of orange stone began wobbling before they were drawn back to the larger pieces like magnets.

Instantly, two small fragments of divinity lay before us.

"One for each of us?" Raven asked.

"Yep. I don't know why, but Adam told me once he'd tried combining both his and Evelyn's shards, and that one person having all of them didn't change anything, so there's no point in me holding on to both shards if it won't do anything. I'd rather the two of you have them."

Raven didn't seem to mind taking one, but I had some reservations. I'd seen the trouble these things had brought Adam and Evelyn back on Earth. They were cautious of the shards, but that was over a thousand years ago, and I guess they got used to them.

My fingers trembled as I reached out and took the shard in my hand. The stone was freezing, despite the warm air that ruffled our hair. The chill bit into my fingers as it slid towards my palm, and as soon as it settled on the meat of my hand, it started burning.

The pain sucked my breath from me as the shard buried its way to the center of my hand. It melted into my body and dispersed through my veins. It was a similar feeling to the Hive magic in that way.

As it reached the center of my chest, my mana well exploded.

A surge of power ran through me like a current, setting every single one of my nerves on fire as the new power changed my body. Eventually, it settled down and the pain vanished. I heaved a sigh of relief as I leaned back against the stair rail. Sweat poured down my face as I looked over at Raven, who wasn't doing much better than I was.

Her eyes were closed in pain, and she was breathing heavily, her chest rising and falling in chaos as she tried to control the pain running through her.

Then, as it was with me, the pain stopped, and her face relaxed.

"Holy hell, that was—"

"Intense," I finished for her.

"Yeah, I'll say." She turned to me and smiled. "Though I'm kinda glad you still look the same Eris. I don't know how silver hair would look on you."

Oh, right. Sam's appearance changed. But as I looked at Raven, she looked as she always did. Her normal self. *Huh, wonder why we didn't change?*

The answer was obvious. Because Sam broke the shard in half. Whatever power it held, we didn't get enough of it to fundamentally change us. Sam was a demigod, but I knew that we were not which I was kind of thankful for—not that I didn't like how Sam looked, but I couldn't imagine myself with the same look. I'd just gotten around to loving how I looked. I didn't want to change that.

But even with only half of the shard, my magic had nearly doubled. It was an instinctual feeling, but I just knew that I had grown much stronger than I was previously.

"I agree. But even so, it was worth it for the increase to my magic."

"You're telling me," Raven said.

"Wait a second," Sam said, holding up his hand. "Your magic increased?"

Both of us nodded at the same time.

Sam rubbed his stubbled chin. "Odd. My magic didn't increase in the slightest, and I have a full shard."

I shrugged, not knowing much more about the inner workings of the shards than he did. The memories the Mnemosyne had shown me of Evelyn hadn't told me how they worked, just that they were supernatural in nature.

"Maybe it's because magic is a fundamental part of us?" Raven asked, shaking her head. "I use a form of faery magic to transform, and Eris is deeply connected to the Hive."

"Faery magic?" Sam asked. "I thought it was a race thing that lets you transform."

"Yes and no. Shapeshifters can transform without chanting or casting spells, but the ability that lets us do that is magic that comes from the Alice. Magic is a part of us." She pointed at Sam. "But you don't use magic. You're a fighter. Maybe the shard gave you a different kind of power? I dunno."

"I don't either," he replied. "And there's no one to ask anymore."

Sam sighed and brushed his hair back. "I'm just glad both of you are stronger. Having that will come in handy when we take on Magnus…together."

"Speaking of together," a deep baritone voice said. "What's our plan?"

We all three turned around and found Gil's massive frame standing behind us. For such a large man, I hadn't heard him approach, but then again, I was occupied with my thoughts and hadn't been paying attention.

My eyes shot up as he smiled down at us. I know he was Sam's best friend, but I couldn't contain my happiness as I bolted up and went and hugged him.

"I'm so glad you're all right!" I shouted, burying my face into his stomach.

He laughed and patted me on the head. "Yeah, I'm all right. Thanks for worrying about little old me." As I stepped back from him, he turned to Sam. "Hey, bud."

The look of relief on Sam's face warmed my heart. He took a step toward Gil and grabbed him in a massive bear hug. To see Sam, who was small by comparison, pick him up was very funny.

I chuckled at the sight of Sam holding up Gil before he set him down and clapped him on the back.

"I'm glad you're all right!" Sam said.

"Yeah, I'm good. Now get off me before Kenna stabs us both."

There was a short bright laugh from behind them both as Makenna stepped out from the cabin. "I think I can overlook the bromance just this once. We were all worried about you."

"Yeah." Gil rubbed his bald head. "I'm just sorry I couldn't be of use. Maybe if I'd been awake, I could've helped save Markos." Gil turned his head and cursed. "Godsdamn Harper, I can't believe it. I can't. He was always brash and abrasive, but a traitor?" He breathed, long and slow. "Fuck."

"Yeah," Sam said sitting back down on the first step.

"So, as Gil asked, what's the plan?" Wilson asked, coming out along with the rest of the guild who arranged themselves along the wide porch, all eyes turned to Sam.

He sighed and rubbed the back of his head. "I don't know what you want from me, guys. Any way you look at it, the Gloom Knights are finished. I'm not your guild leader anymore."

"Bullshit," Wilson said. "Long as it says Gloom Knights in my guild tab, you're the leader." He knelt and stared Sam directly in the eye. "We've followed your foolish ass this long." He smiled. "So don't for one second thing we're going to allow you to give up now."

Wilson held out his hand and offered it to Sam.

Sam took it with a smile on his face. Wilson hauled him up, and Sam glanced at each of us crowding the porch before he leaned back against the railing and chuckled.

"Well, if you believe in me that much, how can I refuse?"

"Don't get the fuckin' wrong idea. We have absolutely no faith in you as a leader, but it's not like any of us rejects can fuckin' do it better," Yumiko said, smiling at Sam.

"I'll drink to that," Gil said, holding up a large bottle of whiskey that he pulled from his inventory. He tossed everyone a glass and quickly poured a very large portion into each of them. When we all had a drink, he raised his glass to Sam. "To the best of the worst."

Sam smirked at Gil, looking down at his glass of amber. He stared at it for a long moment before he raised it high. "To our fallen friends. Save us room in the nine hells—we'll see you there!"

Everyone toasted their friends and Sam downed his glass in a single gulp. I looked down at mine and threw it back. It burned going down, but I found I didn't mind it so much.

As the toast ended, Sam fiddled with the nearly empty glass in his hands. A speck of whiskey lingered inside and rolled this way and that as Sam played with the glass.

"With a speech like that, I should have answers for you all, but I don't." He shrugged. "I've got nothing. Magnus gave me two months, but that was nearly a month ago. And I'm no closer to figuring out what to do now than I was then."

We all lapsed into silence. I didn't have any idea what to do either. We'd completed the Morrigan's request, and I'd gained power, and then even more power at the reliquary. But I had no idea if it was enough to stop Magnus.

No, I know it's not enough to stop Magnus. That much is fact, but I shouldn't worry about him. He won't be my opponent.

I didn't need the power to defeat Magnus. I needed the power to defeat Aliria.

Sam would try to protect me from having to fight her. He wouldn't want me to have that on my soul, but he will need my help so she didn't aid Magnus. I will have to fight her. I'm the only one who can.

It hurt to think about, but I was ready to fight my mother, prepared to kill her. Some part of me still loved her, but it was the part of me that knew she could have been different, had the coin landed on the other side. She could have been an amazing mother, but she chose her own selfish desires over her child.

And that part of her I hated.

But Aliria aside, we still needed some kind of plan, and I had no idea.

"Sam, any thoughts?" Wilson asked.

He shook his head. "Not a one. Magnus isn't someone we can best in a head-on confrontation. He's too powerful, too connected. He's been building his empire for a thousand years and I'm betting it runs deeper than even we can comprehend. He's a god."

"Well, then it should take other gods to best him, wouldn't you say?" a familiar sultry feminine voice said.

We all turned and found the Morrigan standing at the edge of the trees. The speckled shade from the canopy over her cast chaotic strands of light over her slim, black dress as she stepped onto the grass.

Her black heels matched her dress, and her fiery hair was loose, whipping around her shoulders like a raging inferno. Her emerald eyes latched onto Sam as she strode toward us.

"What are you doing here?" he asked, standing up.

"Oh, simmer down, I'm here to help." Morrigan flashed him a smile.

Sam growled under his breath and marched down the steps. "You know, I've lost too much to be in the mood for games, Morgan. So why don't you get to the point before I lose my temper."

There was a gust of wind and a singular pop as a new figure joined the Morrigan. She was short, with deeply tanned skin and dark, curly hair. Her bright green eyes met mine before she shifted her gaze to Sam.

"I'd advise against violence, Master Acre. The Morrigan is a valuable ally that I'd rather not have squandered," she said.

He turned to the new arrival and scowled. "Edna. About damn time you showed up."

Edna curtsied, her head dipping slightly. "My apologies, Master Acre. I have had too many preparations to complete to respond to you."

Sam cocked his head to the side, scratching his chin. "The hell you calling me master for? I'm not your master."

"That is factually incorrect. As of four o' clock yesterday afternoon, ownership transferred to you, Sampson Acre. Making you my master."

"Who the hell authorized that?" he asked.

"Master Bell. Just before his death."

The anger in Sam deflated in an instant. He hung his head, sighing as he pinched the bridge of his nose.

"Adam. Of course." He looked up at Edna. "Why did he give you to me?"

She shrugged. "Per United Nations AI Ownership Laws of 2057, all unbound AI must have an owner, or they will be terminated. I must have an owner, and Master Bell chose you over Mr. Parks."

He shook his head. "What does that mean for me?"

Edna shook her head. "Not much, I'm afraid. I'm still cut off from most of the greater system. But I think it was meant as a symbolic gesture—that was something I can see Master Bell doing."

Sam sighed again, clenching his hands at his sides. "Did…did he suffer?"

"Master Bell?" Edna asked, placing a finger on her lip as she looked to the sky. Her eyes flicked to Sam's before they went to the ground. She paused, clearly trying to figure out the best way to answer Sam. Eventually she let out a very human sigh and nodded. "He…went down fighting. Master Bell managed to defeat one thousand two hundred and fifty-three Alliance soldiers and thirty-two players from four different guilds before he was brought down."

Sam nodded, turning away from Edna for a moment. "Yeah, I told him to give them hell, and of course he'd take that literally." Sam smiled to himself and turned to Edna. "Okay. So if you're here, then you must have a way to fix the system?"

Edna shook her head softly. "I am afraid not yet. I have considered six thousand four hundred and seventy-one scenarios to attempt to halt or reverse the damage done to the system, but I have millions more to consider. This is a process that will take time, perhaps even years."

"Which we don't have," Morrigan said, raising her hands.

"So why are you here?" Sam asked. He crossed his arms over his chest and frowned at the two arrivals. "I'm sure it's not to just bring us bad news."

"Of course not, Master Acre. What we need is simply time—time to formulate and execute a plan that will save this world. We can't do that with

Mr. Parks going against us. He is a threat that needs to be handled so we can buy time to figure out a solution."

Sam paused. "We're going after Magnus?"

The Morrigan smiled, and her true persona flared. Her monstrous, bird-like appearance came over her face as she smiled. "Not just you and your guild, but everyone. Even the gods aren't sitting this out."

He laughed out of nowhere, a bright smile on his face. It wasn't the happy smile he so often wore. This one was cold, cruel.

"So this isn't a siege. This is a knock-down, drag-out, no-holds-barred fight to the death."

Morrigan nodded at Sam, her smile matching his.

"I think the word you are looking for, Sam, is war. This is war."

Chapter 21 - Council of the Gods

Sampson

Morgan held out her hand to me, still holding her callous smile. For once, I liked it. It mirrored the cold rage that boiled in my chest.

All of this was because of Magnus. Because of his goals. Even the attack on our guild. We'd brought that trouble on ourselves, I wasn't going to deny that.

But having Harper as a planted spy was the reason my friends were dead. Harper might as well have slit their throats himself.

Magnus is going to pay for what he's done. Even more now. I'm going to make him suffer.

I took Morgan's hand, and suddenly I wasn't standing in the woods of the Emerald Ocean. I'd been teleported to a place that I'd never been before but I recognized it from the memories I'd taken from Raven.

We stepped out onto a huge garden terrace. Flowers of every variety bloomed in patches of grass around a white stone walkway. I followed the curved path to the entrance of a monstrous castle. It was made of the same polished white stone as the walkway and could have been marble for how it shone. A flower-shaped stained-glass window hung above an archway, which led to a set of dark rosewood double doors.

"Ah, this is… this is," Raven stammered from next to me.

I hadn't realized that both she and Eris had accompanied me when Morgan teleported us. I turned to her, and her normally pale skin was deathly white. Goosebumps rose up her uncovered arms, and true panic filled her eyes.

Raven was one of the strongest people I knew. And to see how petrified she was reminded me of the dangers of the being whose home we'd just intruded on.

I leaned toward her and took her hand, staring at the door at the far end of the garden like it was about to catch fire.

"This is the Crystal Court. The home of the Alice, Queen of the Faeries."

Morgan turned around to us and chuckled. "Let's go and say hello. It's rude to just stand here when our guests are waiting."

With that, Morgan strolled forward, unperturbed by the heavy atmosphere of the place.

I gulped as Raven's heartbeat slammed against my fingertips. I gave her hand a squeeze and a reassuring smile.

"Don't worry. I'll be right here the entire time."

"You promise?" she asked.

I nodded.

Eris stepped to the other side and took her other hand. "We both will."

Raven nodded. "All right. Let's go meet her."

We followed Morgan and just managed to catch up to her as she reached the double doors. She pushed them open without a care and marched into the castle like she owned the place.

I don't know if I should be reassured by her confidence or concerned.

The Alice was not a name; it was a title, granted to whomever became the Faery Queen. It, like both the Hive Knight and Queen titles, was a mantle. The person with the mantle of the Alice became a god.

Wonder if the other gods are mantles then? It would make sense.

332

I'd done my best up until I met Eris to stay out of the gods' way. But it seemed that wasn't an option any longer.

The doors opened reveal a large throne room. The room was huge, but it was mostly comprised of empty space. The only things in the room besides the throne were a number of crimson rugs leading from the many doors to the throne itself.

The throne was wood, a rich rosewood that matched the doors. It was a child's throne, hand carved with flowers running up the side and back.

On the throne was the Alice. A bored-looking girl of nine or ten. She had long maroon hair that fell down her back and over her large dragonfly wings that shimmered and cast a rainbow of hues down their length. Her oceanic eyes regarded us with detachment, and she casually fiddled with the hem of her pale blue dress.

When we approached her, she shifted, leaning to the left and propping her head on her fist.

"Morgan. You're late. The others have been waiting for hours already."

Morgan scoffed. "Sorry, things came up. Besides, they're probably having a blast. You know how much the others so love to gossip."

"Like children, yes, I know." The Alice tilted her head and glanced at Raven. Her bored face changed, and a wicked smile formed as she licked her lips. "So, the pretty bird returns to me. My power suits you, little shifter. Would you care to make another pact? I'm sure I have something that would interest you."

Raven stiffened next to me at her words, and fury roared in my chest.

I stepped in front of Raven and broke the Alice's sight of Raven, my face set in stone.

The Alice smiled at me without showing her teeth. "Oh, the demigod wishes to bargain instead. How amusing. What do you seek from me?"

Edna, can you hear me?

"But of course, Master Acre."

I heaved a mental sigh of relief. I wasn't sure if I could communicate with her telepathically, but since I'd been able to with the Aspect, then I hoped I could with her as well.

You said your power is limited, but you're still this world's governing AI. Do you hold dominion over the gods?

"In a manner of speaking. Why? What are you planning?"

I didn't even have to say anything as Edna's presence filled my mind. It was a very familiar feeling. It was the same as the night Eris and I bonded ourselves to each other. Edna as Ouroboros had been in my head then, too.

She read my thoughts like a book, and then her presence receded a bit, but not before a hint of approval and amusement leaked out. *Yes. I can do that, but do not abuse this. We need them…but this incarnation of Alice has been a bitch for a couple hundred years."*

So she's an adult who just choses to look like a creepy child to fuck with people. I can work with that.

As Edna faded away, I strolled toward the queen of the faeries. The crack of my footsteps through the silent room was deafening.

The Alice smiled sweetly at me. "Cat got your tongue, demigod?" She leaned forward in her throne, still holding her gaze of superiority. "That look in your eye would be frightening were I anyone else."

When I got halfway to the throne, the Alice rose out of her chair and floated toward me using her wings. She lifted off the ground as she was eye level to me. She may have looked like a child, but I recognized the glint of evil in her eyes. She was someone who delighted in the suffering of others.

She leaned in close, close enough that our lips were nearly touching. She grinned. "Tell me, godling. Before I pluck your eyes from their sockets for daring to look at me like—"

"Restrain her," I said.

Before the Alice could finish her threat, she literally froze in place. Her wings stopped mid beat, but she hung in place. The only thing she could move was her eyes, and they went from superior to outraged and then panicked.

I willed chitin into my hand and gripped her across the throat. I bit into her flesh with ease and caused black blood to run down her pale throat.

"Listen here, you pixie bitch." I pressed my fingertips into the sides of her throat drawing even more blood. My voice was low, frigid, and filled with hate. "Do not speak to Raven; do not even look at her. Ever again. Because if you do, I'll rip your wings from your spine and devour your beating heart while you watch. Do I make myself clear?"

She couldn't nod, but she blinked twice.

"Good." I released my grip of her and wiped my fingers on her dress. "Now if you'd be so kind as to wait right here while the rest of us deal with business, that'd be great."

I left her stuck in midair while Morgan walked over to me, her eyes wide, and it was clear that she was doing everything she could not to burst out laughing at the sight of the Alice, one of the most terrifying beings on Nexus, helpless.

"As much fun as it would be to leave her there, teach her a lesson, we do need her to be a part of this council. Her strength isn't something we can ignore."

"Strength? What strength?" I grinned wide.

"That was quite humorous, Master Acre. But she has a right to sit in on the council. And we do need her power. I'm going to release her, and besides, your point was made."

I sighed and shook my head. "Fine."

There was a small snap, and the Alice dropped to the ground, blood running from the gashes along her neck. It dripped down her neck to her hands and then to the white stone under her. She coughed and stood, glaring at me as she did.

"How dare you!"

I stared down at her, my golden eyes alight with cold fury. "Remember what I said. I won't hesitate."

The Alice nodded, looking away from me. The wounds on her neck closed as quickly as they had appeared, and she again rose off the ground. She turned to Morgan and motioned toward one of the doors on the opposite end of the throne room.

"The meeting is being held in there. Follow me," she said, all previous hints of cruel joviality gone.

I smiled to myself as she and Morgan began walking while I waited for Eris and Raven.

Both of them took my hands and we started followed.

"That—that was. That was incredible, Sam," Raven said. "I can't believe you did that for me."

"I'd fight anyone in this world or the next for the two of you. I may not be much, but I can fight. I can fight anyone. Doesn't mean I'll win, but I'll at least try."

The gods led the three of us through the doors into a large rectangular room. It was comprised of the exact marble as the throne room, but it was much smaller and was filled with a small array of furniture.

A large wooden table was surrounded by thirteen chairs. In the far corner of the room was a bar with every spirit or liquor I'd ever seen in my life and quite a few I knew I'd never laid eyes one before.

My mouth watered at the mere prospect of trying them, but I shook my head and focused on the table—more specifically, at the people who sat around it.

Half of the chairs were filled, and each member had a drink of some kind in front of them. Just from being in the room for only a second, the overwhelming aura in the room caused my heart rate to spike. Ozone burned in my nose, and small spikes of pain danced along my brain.

I was in the presence of the gods of this artificial world, and their auras were palpable.

"My head hurts," Eris whispered from beside me, her voice small.

"I can barely breathe," Raven said.

Even I wasn't immune to the feeling, but it wasn't that bad for me. I was also a demigod and a guardian, so I assumed those gave me some innate resistance to the gods.

I looked at each god and could make an accurate guess as to who they were.

The Morrigan and the Alice took their places at the table, and I looked at the others. Maus was here, half his body wrapped in shadow.

He gave me a wide smile and a thumbs up.

The other gods, however, I didn't know.

At the head of the table was a thin, incredibly beautiful woman with golden tanned skin, dark gold eyes, and hair as black as Raven's. She wore a lustrous golden gown, that dipped at her chest, and around her mouth was a strip of black cloth.

She was, without a doubt, the Whisper—the patron goddess of the Church of the Penitent Whisper, and the ruling religion of the human NPCs.

Next to her was a man in a black robe. He had sharp cheekbones, incredibly pale skin, and long green hair. His eyes were the exact shade of emerald as Lachrymal's Heart, and the streaks of black tears running down his face gave him away.

Lachrymal. The Weeping God.

To the Whisper's right was the god of the elves. He wore a simple forest green tunic and made it look stunning. He was a beautiful man with long golden hair, blue eyes, and pointed ears. He had the refined grace of the elves, and that meant he was the final god. Sylvanus.

All of the gods were here.

And it set my teeth on edge.

They turned and stared at us as we entered and none, save Morgan and Maus, looked friendly. Sylvanus was indifferent at best.

I smiled at both the Whisper and Lachrymal. "Ah, guess I can understand why you two hate me."

"You stole my heart!" Lachrymal shouted, standing as he slammed his palms on the table.

"And you broke your oath of service to me, claiming the title of Paladin without earning it," the Whisper said, in, well, a whisper. Her voice was muffled by the cloth around her lips.

I shrugged and strolled over to the closest seat. I sat down and kicked my feet back. "Get over it. We've got much bigger things to discuss."

"Can I kill him?" Lachrymal said, turning to Morgan. "I'd really like to kill him."

"Seconded. But I'd like to torture him first," the Alice replied.

Maus snorted and took a sip of the ale that was in front of him. "You couldn't go five minutes without making enemies, could you, Sam?"

"You know I just love pissing people off." I smiled at him. "Besides, how many chances will I get to piss off the gods ever again? Might as well rub it in while I can."

"Fair enough. And they are a little insufferable. I've only been one of them for a few weeks now. It's weird getting used to."

"Wait." I sat up. "So when we met, you really weren't the Shadow King?"

Maus shook his head and grabbed his ale. He took a heavy gulp and thumped it on the table. "Nope. But he is the one who sent me to Tombsgard in the first place, so when I got out, I snuck into his house and slit his treacherous throat while he slept. I had no idea that once I killed the fool that I'd become the next Shadow King. But, hey, I won't say it wasn't a perk."

I paused, rubbing my chin. "I was right, and the mantles are transferable." I grinned and turned to the Alice. "I'd recommend you start being a lot nicer to me."

She stood and scowled at me. "Why you—"

"Enough of this!" Edna shouted, appearing next to me.

Instantly all eyes were on her.

She turned to me and smiled. "You've had your fun but now it's time to get serious. We have much to discuss and a lot to get into place." She turned and glanced at the others around the table. "So no more bickering, is that understood?"

Whether it was the amount of respect the gods showed Edna or the gravity of the situation, the room sobered in seconds.

A round of yeas echoed around the room, and we all gave Edna the respect she was due.

When the room quieted, Edna came around and leaned against my chair leg. She turned to me and spoke while also addressing the rest of the room.

"Now, we have a few more guests joining us that will be instrumental in our plans. They should be here momentarily." She leaned down and whispered to me. "Now, I really don't want you to overreact, Master Acre. We need her, so I'm asking you to restrain yourself."

I shrugged. "I can handle it. Who is it though?"

Before she had a chance to respond, the doors opened, and three people strode in. Two I recognized.

One was Rhoa Aminah the leader of the rabbitmen. Her fine golden hair and sparkling blue eyes paired well with the flowing red dress that she wore.

The other was the old, silver-haired wolfman leader, Morn. Like the last time I'd seen him, he wore his black fur trimmed robe and looked as grandfatherly as ever.

The third was a mystery to me. I'd never seen her before.

She was tall, with rich brown skin and fine snow-white hair that fell to her shoulders. Her features were sharp like a razorblade and she had large, pitch black eyes.

As she walked closer, she turned and looked at me and then Eris. She smiled widely, showing rows of sharp teeth.

It was then that I got a better look at her eyes and noticed the red hourglasses in them. Like a black widow.

I couldn't stop the rage and heartache that rose to the surface at seeing her. I knew who she was, and cold righteous fury filled my chest. I blinked and I was no longer sitting at the table. I was on my feet halfway to the bitch who had slept with Eris.

"Reina!"

My hand was on my sword, and I drew it in an instant. I couldn't stop myself.

I'd convinced myself that I'd forgiven Eris for what she'd done, and I had, for the most part. Raven and Eris had both helped me get over the anger and betrayal I felt.

But it wasn't gone. It still lingered in the deepest part of my soul and as soon as I laid eyes on Reina, it all boiled to the surface.

She smiled at me. "So this is your human lover?"

There was nothing I could do to stop myself, and my blade arced toward her neck as I tried to take her head off.

As my sword slid through the air and reached her neck, it vanished. I swung my empty hands downward, and the lack of weight caused me to stumble. When I got back up, I looked around, wondering if I'd dropped my sword when I found it in Edna's hands.

She held it as if it weighed as little as a feather and she pointed it at me. "Really, Master Acre. I told you to restrain yourself. You didn't listen for a single second, did you?"

"I—"

"Is there anyone here you don't have a grudge against?" the Alice asked. "For a human, you sure manage to anger a good many people. I'd almost be impressed if I didn't want your entrails decorating my garden."

I paused and the anger flooded out of me in an instant. I sighed and thumbed over to the elven god. "Sylvanus and I are cool."

He scoffed. "I don't know you, godling."

I shrugged and sat back down. "In present company, that's as good as I'm going to get." I turned to Reina. "Edna is right. And besides, we have bigger things to worry about right now. But don't think that means you and I are allies. I will have my pound of flesh from you, got it?"

Her eyes narrowed and she plastered a frosty smile across her lips. "I welcome the attempt."

Edna held up her hand as our newest guests took their seats.

"Now that everyone is here, we can begin." She eyed me and smiled slightly.

She tossed my sword back, and I caught it easily.

"Seriously, Master Acre. Must you antagonize everyone? We need them as allies if what I have planned is going to work. So please, no more outbursts. We'll never get anywhere at this rate."

I grinned sheepishly. *Sorry, Edna. But that bitch deserves it.*

She sent a smirk my way. *"Be that as it may, we have little time and much to go over, so please?"*

I nodded. *Yeah, I'll behave. As long as that's all the surprises for the evening.*

Edna cast a sideways smile at me and walked around to stand behind the thirteenth chair at the table. "Now that everyone is here, we can begin. Most of you know roughly why we have gathered here, but for those who only have bits and pieces, let me illuminate.

"We are here to plan the death of Nicholas Parks, or as many of you know him, Magnus."

There were a few murmurs from around the table, and I for one didn't blame them.

What was being planned was in essence, declaring war on one of the most powerful beings in this world. And from the slight nervousness from a few of the gods, they knew of his power.

Yeah, I guess I'd be freaking out too if I were them. The gods are powerful, but as Maus proved, they aren't immortal. They can die. And going up against Magnus means a few of them might actually bite the bullet.

I ignored the other gods and kept my hands on Raven and Eris's thighs while we waited for Edna to continue.

She waited for the noise to die down some before she placed her palms on the table and looked at each one of us.

"This is not going to be easy. Magnus has been making preparations since the last reset. Getting to his castle is not going to be easy. And once there, getting in is going to be even harder. Magnus employs an army of soldiers, and since the recent assault on his castle by Master and Mistress Bell, he's increased his numbers tenfold."

"And teleportation is impossible correct?" I asked, raising my hand like I was in school again. "Because last time I was there, there was something blocking the use of teleportation."

Edna nodded. "That is correct. There is an artifact that is the mirror opposite of the amulet you wear. It cancels out teleportation and communication magic within a certain radius. None of us can get in undetected I'm afraid."

Yeah, that tracks. I removed my hand from Raven's thigh and scratched my chin. *I couldn't call out when I was there, and we couldn't use our teleportation to escape. Which led to Evelyn sacrificing herself.*

I sighed. *I need a drink.*

The bar in the far corner was tempting, and I stood and walked over to it.

"Don't mind me, keep going," I said as I perused the selection of fine spirits.

Eventually I settled on some more mana tea, though the urge to try some of the rare whiskeys was nearly overpowering.

I poured a large cup, snagged a bottle for Raven, and went and sat back down.

Contrary to what I'd said, Edna had waited on me. Which pissed off the gods. I tried to hide my grin, but it teased at the corners of my lips as I sat down.

Raven immediately leaned into me, kissed me on the cheek, and while I was distracted by her lips, snagged the bottle of whiskey from me.

"I'll be having that, thanks." She grinned wide.

"Got it for you in the first place."

I took a sip of my drink and slid it to Eris while I waited on Edna.

Her cerulean eyes twinkled as she sighed slightly and shook her head. "As I was saying. Because the subtle route is out, we must take the direct route. Which means we need soldiers, and a lot of them."

She turned to look at Reina first. Edna stared hard at her for a brief moment until Reina blinked her widowed eyes and inclined her head.

"As per my bargain with the Hive Queen, the Arachne forces stand ready. You will have your men." She smiled and shifted her gaze to me, giving me a wink. "I always keep my bargains."

"Oh, I'm going to enjoy causing you pain."

"A sadist." She licked her lips. "Lovely."

Eris tugged on my arm and I looked down at her. She pouted at me. "Sam, stop it. You're blaming her when it was my decision to say, yes. I thought we'd gotten past this, but if you're going to be angry at someone, be angry at me."

I shook my head. "Can't be angry at you. It'd kill me, so she's what I've got to work with." I spoke up louder. "But I'm guessing a few spider warriors isn't the extent of our forces?"

Edna shook her head and motioned to Rhoa and Morn.

They both stood, looked to each other and then to the room.

"For the safe return of our children and at the behest of our goddess, the rabbitmen will contribute to the war effort," Rhoa said.

"As will the wolfmen. We will put aside our differences for the time being and assist the best we can."

I just sat there, my mouth agape before I composed myself and shifted to glare at Morgan. I raised my eyebrow. I scoffed and smiled.

Forget the rest of the gods, you're devious.

Morgan returned my smile, and though she couldn't read my thoughts, my face gave away exactly what I was thinking, and she nodded, her smile growing deeper.

She knew exactly what she was doing the entire time. And she had us all dancing to her tune.

Morgan's smile shifted as she looked to Edna. "Is that all of our forces?"

"Not quite." Edna shook her head. "It's why I called Lachrymal and Sylvanus here. As the patron gods of the elves and the dwarves, they can call upon their races for the war."

Lachrymal nodded. "This is true. And my priests have already called upon my Chosen to assist. You will have nearly fifty of the best dwarven warriors at your disposal."

I whistled. "Lachrymal's Chosen are no joke. They are very hard to kill."

"You would know, wouldn't you?" Lachrymal asked.

I shrugged. "Sorry." I shook my head. "But that's beside the point. So we have the dwarves and elves on board as well?"

Sylvanus stood and nodded. "Yes. The elves have sent a few hundred of their soldiers to assist."

"Good," I said.

I hadn't fought elves much before, maybe a handful of times in the many years I'd been here, but every time I did, they gave me a run for my money. They were fluid and graceful, and that transferred into their combat styles.

With all the races except the humans with us, I thought we had a great chance of surviving. And even if we didn't, I had a feeling we'd be fine.

I looked up at Maus. "I'm guessing you're going to lend us the use of your undead?"

He nodded. "And I'll even resurrect the fallen members of the assault team." He grinned. "So even if you all die, you'll still be able to fight."

I chuckled, but it was good to know we actually had a fighting chance at taking the fight to Magnus.

But a thought hit me.

"Our army gets us through the gates of the castle. But that's it. I'm guessing that's where I come in?"

Edna nodded. "You, Eris, and Raven will have to face Magnus and Aliria by yourselves."

I gulped as all eyes turned to me. Sweat beaded on my forehead, and my mouth grew dry as my heart rate increased.

"So, it's up to me to face down Magnus." I sighed. "No pressure."

The rage and hatred I held for him boiled to the surface, and a part of me wanted nothing more than to begin the assault on the castle immediately so I could get my hands on him, but the cool, rational part of my mind was screaming at me to stop and use my head.

Magnus was the single most dangerous person I'd ever met. He even dwarfed the power of the gods. Evelyn, the best fighter I'd ever seen, who taught me everything I knew of the sword, was no match for him.

What chance do I stand?

I didn't know. I turned to Eris, who looked up at me with her big, compounded black eyes and smiled at me.

And it didn't matter that I didn't believe that I could win against Magnus. It didn't matter that his power overwhelmed mine.

I had to try.

For Eris.

"All right. I'm game. So let's get this party started."

Chapter 22 - The Assault on Castle Aliria

Sampson

The waiting was the worst. After the council, good or bad, I was ready to get the show on the road. But life doesn't work like that.

There was a lot to do before we could begin.

There were a great number of troops we had to manage and the supplies we needed to acquire.

Therefore, while the gods and the others dealt with their soldiers and logistics, Eris, Raven, and I went back to our safehouse to meet with the others and report.

Morgan teleported us back, and once more, we stood in the small clearing in front of the log cabin.

A stiff breeze blew through the trees as we landed, and I sighed as I stepped forward and turned back to Morgan.

She smirked at me. "Everything should be ready in a week. I'll come and let you know when we're ready to begin."

After that, she left, disappearing into thin air as the three of us stared at each other.

"So it's on us?" Raven asked.

"Looks like it." I ran my hand through my head and cursed. "Damn it, Adam. You and Evelyn both left me to clean up your mess."

"Hey, now." Eris wound her arm though mine and leaned on me. "Don't blame them. This is on Magnus, not them. They were doing the best that they could, and it broke them. I think they were both just ready to die."

I hung my head and rubbed my eyes. "Yeah. I know. I just feel like everything is resting on my shoulders and it's all going to come crumbling down."

"Well, you always have us to help you carry the burden," Raven said, kissing my neck. "We won't let you buckle under the weight of it all."

"Thanks." I glanced up at the cabin. "Now let's go tell everyone what's going on."

The three of us marched up the wooden steps and entered the cabin. The door squeaked as we opened it and stepped inside.

Unlike the rough camouflaged outside, the interior of the cabin was rather extravagant.

Rich hues of smooth wood lined the floor and the walls. Brass candelabras and a large chandelier hung overhead, filled with a hundred candles, which cast light over every inch of the space.

A large sectional made of black drake leather dominated the center of the living room and a roaring fireplace was situated in the center.

Gil, Wilson, and Yumiko sat on the sectional while Mika lounged with his head in Yumiko's lap. She looked torn between punching him and running her hands through his hair, but it was nice to see the rare, softer side of her.

As we entered, everyone turned to us.

Yumiko blushed, her too-pale cheeks turning the same crimson shade as her eyes. She quickly shoved Mika off her and stood.

"The hell took you guys so long? You've been gone nearly a full day," she said.

"Now, Yu. Let them at least sit down before we bombard them with questions," Gil said.

"Thanks."

I turned to the left and slipped through a doorway before I reached the kitchen. A large stone chest sat between two wooden countertops. I knelt and opened it. The chill of the numerous frost stones chilled me as I pulled out three bottles of ale and returned to the living room.

Raven held her hand out for one and the second I gave to Eris. I popped the top of the last on and took a heavy pull.

It was indescribably delicious.

"I thought you quit?" Raven asked.

"I'll quit after all this shit is over and done with," I said as I sat down and rested the ice-cold bottle against my brow.

"Okay. He's sitting, and he has a beer. What the fuck happened?"

Despite the headache pounding through my head, I laughed at Yumiko, but it quickly died as I sighed and turned to them.

"It's a long story." I motioned to Gil. "So grab Makenna because I only want to tell it once."

He nodded and went to retrieve his lover while I polished off my beer. When I was done, Eris handed me hers with a smile.

I took another drink of it, and by the time I was done, Gil had returned with the little redhead in tow.

They sat down, and I spent the next hour telling them everything that had happened with the council.

When I was done, they sat in stunned silence for a few moments before Wilson broke it with a low whistle. "Well, I'll be damned. That's one hell of a story and one hell of a quest we've been thrown into."

I shook my head and held up my hand. "I appreciate it, but the Gloom Knights have officially disbanded. You guys don't owe me anything more. And I'd say we've all given enough. This is my fight, not yours."

Wilson shook his head and sighed. "You dumbass. If it's your fight, that makes it our fight. Just because half of the Gloom Knights are no more doesn't stop making us family."

"Yeah, you fuckin' jackass. I didn't lose my home just to sit on my ass and twiddle my thumbs while the war for the end of the world happens. I'm in."

I chuckled at Yumiko's response before I turned to Gil. "What are your thoughts?"

He shook his head and rested a hand on Makenna's thigh. "I want to keep Kenna safe, and my head is telling me that we should all lie low until if or when this blows over. But that isn't going to happen, and I refuse to let my best friend go into battle alone. It's not going to happen. Not ever."

I grinned at the giant. "Thanks, bud."

Though I was thrilled beyond words that my friends were still willing to stick with me, I was terrified about losing anyone else. I hadn't had time to fully grieve yet; in addition we were about to face arguably the most difficult fight we'd ever considered.

There was a chance not all of us would come out the other side unscathed.

And that terrified me.

I sighed and finished my drink. Even the bite of the alcohol wasn't helping the situation.

"Well, we have a few days while everyone gets ready. We should be doing the same thing." I turned to Wilson. "How much did we manage to stash away from the loot room?"

He shrugged and tugged on his wiry silver beard. "Maybe a hundred thousand—if that. Enough to stock up on potions, but nothing we can do about our armor and gear."

"We've got what we've got, and it'll have to be enough," Gil said. "But we can always visit Aldrust and procure the potions we need."

Wilson cleared his throat. "I'll do that. I'll go tomorrow and pick up whatever we need."

I nodded. "All right. Do that, but potions aren't going to cut it."

"What do you mean?"

There was a good chance that Magnus would bolster his guards with players. There were plenty of mercenary guilds out there, not to mention the Adventurers Guild. I didn't like the idea of killing players, even now. But it was something that I had to account for.

After a few moments of contemplation, I had an idea.

"Grab the potions we need, but I'm also going to have you to pick up a few other things."

I told Wilson my plan and what to get. His eyes lit up as I finished.

"I can do that. Not a bad plan for once, Sam."

"Yeah." I shrugged. "I can use that brain of mine on occasion. So we have our plan in place. We gear up and wait for the others to tell us when the assault begins."

After that, we broke up the meeting and went to our rooms. The next day, Wilson left for Aldrust, and the rest of us passed the time training, sorting out our gear, and doing anything to keep from thinking about what lay ahead of us.

Whether we liked it or not, a week passed and the morning of the seventh day, there was a knock at the door.

I opened it to find Morgan standing there.

She'd changed into her black leather armor and wielded two shortswords on her waist.

"Is it time?" I asked.

"Yep."

"Are you fighting too?" I asked as I gave her the once-over.

She smiled, and her emerald eyes lit up with a bright glow. "Of course. The entire fate of the world rests on stopping Magnus. It'd be foolish for any of us to sit this one out."

"Right." I turned and whistled.

It took a few minutes, but everyone roused themselves.

They knew what the whistle meant and had changed into their armor. Even Eris had a set of black leather armor that looked nearly identical to Raven's.

When I looked over at Gil, he just grinned.

"All right, everyone ready?"

Each of them nodded.

I turned back to Morgan. "You heard 'em."

Her eyes sparkled and she leaned over and pulled a small item from her pocket. "I got what I needed from this, so I figured you probably need it more than I do." She tossed the small shiny bauble to Eris.

When Eris held it up, and I got a better look at it the ring Morgan had pulled from the tomb in the dungeon. The honeycomb pattern lit up in the candlelight.

As she slipped it on her finger, Eris gasped and shuddered slightly.

"What did you just do?" I asked.

"Gave her a boost to her mana," replied Morgan. "The ring enhances the amount of mana she can use, so she should be well equipped to handle the fight to come."

"And what did you need it for exactly?"

Morgan shrugged. "I didn't need it as much as Edna needed it. There was something stored within the ring that she had to have. I don't know what it was, nor do I intend to ask. She belongs to you now. You wanna know, ask her."

I snorted. "Maybe when this is all over, but right now, we have more important things to focus on. Let's get going."

Morgan smiled at me and nodded. She reached out and placed a hand on my shoulder. There was a sudden haziness, and then we were no longer in the house.

High sand dunes loomed, casting ample shade that was instantly banished by the beating sun that hung high overhead. I began to sweat as I turned around, and my jaw dropped.

I'd seen wars before, had been a part of a few small ones over the years. But those had been between no more than five thousand troops on both sides.

What awaited us was ten thousand soldiers. A heavy mixture of rabbitmen, wolfmen, Arachne, elves, and dwarves.

The Arachne numbered the fewest at two or three hundred, and I picked out the fifty of Lachrymal's Chosen standing at the front lines. The rest of the army was made up of mostly rabbitmen and dwarves, with wolfmen being a close third.

It looked like the elves had fielded about two thousand soldiers, and their tall, graceful beauty was magnified by the sharp golden armor they wore.

There were even a hundred or so fae. They had recurve bows and were using their wings to keep themselves floating off the ground which caused sand to whip around them.

All in all, it was the largest army I'd ever seen.

The gods stood in front like generals as we arrived and surveyed the troops. I shook off my amazement and marched over to them.

"Is everyone ready?"

Edna disengaged from the others and came over to me.

"They are."

Looking out across the sands of the Badlands, I couldn't tell where we were, but I assumed we were close to Castle Aliria.

I didn't have to ask as Edna turned to me and nodded. She pointed east. "We're about a mile from the castle. And it looks like Magnus knows we're coming. His forces number about three thousand soldiers, but he also has player guilds backing him up."

"Yeah?" I turned to Edna and nodded. "Figured he'd use players to fight for him. But he knows if they die, they won't come back." I shook my head. "That's despicable. And I thought I understood him."

I really did believe that. I understood that Magnus was ruthless, but it was a cold, logical ruthlessness that I understood better than I wanted to admit. He was unyielding in the pursuit of his goals, but I hadn't really considered what that exactly entailed.

Using people as shields when you know they won't come back. I scoffed. *He probably thinks that he's doing the system a favor by killing players.*

I understood my goal before this, but it finally hit home that Magnus had to die. His goal for the world would leave it barren and lifeless. If he had his way, there wouldn't be much of a world to save.

"All right. Get everyone ready," I said.

"Understood."

Edna walked off to converse with the gods, and I went back to my former guildmates. I stood before them and there was so much I wanted to say to them, but when I tried, my throat closed up.

My eyes burned, and I rubbed them.

"Thanks," I finally managed to say. "Thanks for being the best damn family I could ask for."

Gil came up and clapped me on the shoulder. "Couldn't have asked for a better one. Now let's go kick some major ass. One last time."

Wilson stepped up next to Gil and his silver eyes glowed brightly as he gave me a rare smile. "Magnus took down the Gloom Knights. Let's make him regret ever thinking he could cross us."

I looked at Raven and Eris, who looked resplendent in their armor with the beating sun bathing them in light and the wind tugging at their hair. I had never loved anyone as much as I loved the people standing in front of me.

"I love you all. Gil and Wilson said it best. Let's show the world what it means to fuck with the Gloom Knights."

We led the march to Castle Aliria.

The rest of the army matched us pace for pace as the gods and the Gloom Knights ran through the sand dunes towards the castle.

Running a mile isn't difficult. But running a mile through sand while wearing close to sixty pounds of armor and carrying a sword is enough to tire anyone out.

But it was a good run. It got my heart rate up, and with each step, my rage built and built. Until finally, we crested a hill, and the castle came into view.

Castle Aliria was situated on a large red rock plateau, with a man-made incline that led to the castle itself which was made of dark gray stone. It was built in a similar style of Castle Gloom Harbor and reminded me of the home that no longer existed.

Situated around the entrance to the plateau were thousands of troops and the player guilds. The troops were troubling, but what really concerned me were the players.

One player could kill a hundred NPCs easily. Such was the power gap, and even with our numbers, I didn't know if it would be enough.

It'll have to be.

As the rest of our army climbed the hill behind us it got quiet. Our two armies just stared at one another for a few moments, and the silence stretched on.

It seemed neither side was willing to break the calm before the storm, but it had to be done.

It was time to take the fight to Magnus.

"For everyone that bastard has taken from us." I drew my sword and raised it high. "For the best damn years of my life. One last time. Gloom Knights, to war!"

The shout that rose from their lips echoed through my soul, and we charged down the hill toward the waiting army.

Gil and Wilson were at my side as Raven shifted to her bird form and Eris leapt and hopped on her back.

The faeries followed them with their bows drawn.

I surged forward with the Gloom Knights at my back as the rest of the army spread out and followed our lead.

A cheer rose from the other army, and they advanced to meet our charge with the players leading the way.

Our two sides met with a thunderous clash of steel and blood.

As we reached the first of the enemy players, I put our first strategy into motion.

I activated *Will of the Immortal.*

The world ground to a halt as gray overtook the colored landscape.

I knew what I had to do, and I had to make it fast. As everyone froze in place, I turned and placed my hand on each of the Gloom Knights as I passed them, willing them to join me in the time stop.

The blinked as they adjusted to the colorless world.

"No time to enjoy this," I said. "Everyone know what they have to do?"

They each pulled out a fistful of small gray stones with Script engraved into them. I pulled out my own handful and willed what little mana I had into them.

The fire stones glowed a bright orange before the color faded and the stones went back to the lifeless gray of the rest of the world.

I grinned.

Glad we tested this before we began fighting.

I'd asked Wilson to pick as many of them up as he could when he went into Aldrust with the plan in my head, but no idea if it would work or not.

Once each stone was primed, I raced through the groups of players, dropping the stones at their feet as the others did the same. We only had twenty seconds of time stop, and we had a lot of ground to cover.

When the twenty seconds were almost up and the color began flickering back into the world, I stopped and started backpedaling toward our side of the field as I tossed the rest of my stones as hard as I could.

The world stuttered as time returned to normal, and I sank to my knees as my battle fatigue rose to near max. I didn't fight it this time and instead rolled with it and covered my ears.

For a second nothing happened.

And then the ground shuddered.

A sharp crack pierced the air, and a gust of wind swept over us before there was a cacophony of explosions, and the sky turned orange as the fire stones exploded into torrential infernos that rose to tower over us as they engulfed hundreds.

I looked up to nearly fifty rising tornados of fire.

Terrifying screams of those burning melded with the cries of battle as metal struck metal and formed into a unrecognizable drone as people died in droves.

I took a recovery potion from my inventory and downed it as I stood. My fatigue drained to zero as the three-hour timer began in the corner of my vision.

I had three hours to kill Magnus before I dropped, and we failed.

Three hours to save the world.

No pressure.

Our opening salvo had done its job, and we'd weakened the defending army considerably. It was absolutely worth me blowing through my trump card at the start of the battle.

It wasn't like I could use it against Magnus, so I'd found a better use for it, and we'd probably reduced the players to half of what they had been moments before.

A sea of bodies surrounded me, but I knew which ones were friendly and which weren't, thanks to the fact that this was a war instance.

It was like a siege instance, but different. It allowed members of the same army to see each other and it also reduced friendly fire damage to where it was nearly nonexistent. The instance was incredibly helpful, and I doubted that it had ever been used on such a large force before.

A faint green outline surrounded my allies, and red denoted hostiles.

I slipped through the bodies and cut down any enemies in my path. Against NPCs, it was incredibly easy to score kills, and we'd disorganized the players enough that they were having trouble forming a defense against us.

I lost sight of the others as we moved further and further into enemy lines, but I knew they were fine. We were some of the strongest players on Nexus. We wouldn't go down so easily.

Magic and skills activated around us indiscriminately. Dozens died in seconds on both sides as the players started fighting back. They had overwhelming power, but their numbers were few, especially after our surprise firestorm. So even if they managed a few good sucker punches, our side drowned them in bodies.

Blood ran over my boots as I skirted around a mage with his head cut off next to a giant stone pillar that had crushed half a dozen of Magnus's guards.

One of Lachrymal's Chosen gave me a wink before he raised his axe and buried it in the back of another nameless soldier.

I raised my blade to block a strike from a man in shining silver armor. I batted it aside and brought my sword up to his neck. I sliced through his exposed skin where his gorget and helmet ended, and his life splashed across my vision.

As he dropped lifelessly to the ground, a flickering shadow enveloped him, and his flesh rotted in seconds. He rose back up off the ground as a faint green outline surrounded him. He was a roamer now, an undead.

And even as he stood, a near translucent figure floated from his back and let out a horrific wail.

Maus could even summon phantoms from the corpses of the dead. Two undead rose from the corpses of each fallen member, nearly quadrupling our fighting strength even as both sides lost members.

There was a scream, and to the far left, a group of players were surrounded by a horde of scorpions. Thousands of them crawled towards the players, who froze in fear at the sight. They tried to fight them off, but there were so many.

One player cast *Fireshot* and killed a hundred in a single blast, but they kept coming. The scorpions crawled over the players and stung them again and again.

As they tried to defend themselves, a shadow passed overhead, and a flurry of arrows rained down from Eris and the faeries.

They killed the group of players in a handful of seconds.

Good job!

I surged through the gap Eris had made and engaged a few more NPCs. Six of them engaged me, and I fought them off by circling around them, never giving them a clear opening. My sword cut three of them down. I was about to go for the last three when my instinct screamed at me. I backed away as a pike slammed into the ground next to me.

A hulking player with a wide face and dark brown hair stood behind me.

As he tried to remove his pike, I stepped toward him and grabbed the handle of the wooden shaft with my off hand. I willed chitin into my hand and snapped the wood, breaking it in half. He stared at me, dumbfounded as his weapon broke.

I ripped the pike from his hand and shoved it through his thigh. The man let out a horrendous scream as he struggled to stay standing. I slipped around behind him and rammed the tip of my sword through the back of his neck.

He lurched, gurgling on his own blood as he fell to the ground and slid off the edge of my blade.

I didn't have time to bask in my victory, as the three guards I'd left ganged up on me. Air whistled as a mace sailed toward my head. I held up my left hand and used *Chitin Shield.*

The mace bounced off my shield and completely numbed my arm, leaving its wielder vulnerable. I shuffled to him and jabbed the edge of my shield to his unprotected throat.

His windpipe collapsed under the force of my blow and he sank to the sand, unable to even gasp for breath.

There was a whisper of wind behind the other two guards, and I smiled as my favorite silver-haired rogue appeared behind them.

His twin daggers flashed in the sun, and crimson blood rose only to fall and mix with the coarse grains all around us.

Wilson grinned at me. "Need a hand?"

"Won't say no," I replied. "How's the fight looking?"

We both turned as a new group of men attacked. Our steel clashed, and we quickly dispatched them.

As Wilson cut down his pair of guards, he gave me a thumbs up. "We're winning. By a good margin so far, but I think it's only because we decimated the players first. If they'd been allowed to use their full range of spells, we'd be fucked."

"I agree. So you think we can leave the battle to the army and head for the castle?"

Wilson thought about it for a second as he cut down an unaware solider whose back was to him. After a second or two, he nodded.

"Yeah. The hard part of the fight is over, and with your timer, we don't want to waste time. Get your girls and give Magnus hell. We'll handle things out here."

"Thanks."

I was about to head out when Wilson grabbed my shoulder.

"What's up?"

He shook his head. "Just in case. It's been a privilege, Sam."

I grinned and clapped him on the shoulder. "Likewise. I'll see you on the other side."

Wilson disengaged only to launch into an attack on a group of three players. He used one of his strongest abilities. *Mistwalk.*

He turned into living shadow that couldn't be harmed except by magic. But from the weapons the three players used, they weren't mages. He slipped around them, and his blades materialized out of thin air. He slaughtered all three of them in a handful of seconds.

And then he was gone, his shadow flying away to capitalize on the minute he could use his ability.

I left him to his devices and pulled out a flare stone. It was built on the same principle as a fire stone, but instead of a torrent of fire, it launched a single bright burst of fire into the sky like a flare gun.

As I willed mana into it, it lit up, and I tossed it high into the sky. It burst apart, and a single gout of bright orange flame shot up and then dissipated.

The signal had been sent. I just had to get to the front of the castle.

I cut a swath through the army as the enemy forces dwindled. It took a few minutes of rushing through and occasionally stopping to fight a guard.

But I finally reached the plateau and began to climb the incline. The rest of the troops were fighting, and they'd left the entrance unguarded.

As I reached the top and the large stone gates of Castle Aliria stood before me, something tickled the back of my neck, and a warning screamed through my head.

The air pressure changed and the ground beneath my feet shifted.

I jumped to the side as four massive slabs of stone rose from where I'd been standing seconds before and converged, forming a cage that quickly crushed in on itself. That would have been my body if I'd been a second slower.

"Ah, just missed you. That's twice you've surprised me," a familiar voice said to my right.

Sitting on a large red rock that was at least ten feet tall, was Kincaid.

"Figured I'd run into you again," I said, stepping back.

He hopped down and gave me a low bow. "Yes. You've proven worth every gold. I was surprised when you were able to fend me off, and even more surprised you escaped *Sunburst Oblivion*. If our men hadn't been held up by those damn golems, we'd have had you."

"Adam. The man who single-handedly held off your army was Adam. He was one of my best friends, and I'm going to make you pay for your part in his death and the deaths of every single one of my friends.

"I'm going to enjoy this," said Kincaid as he raised his gauntlet and spoke a quick chant in Script.

I was already moving as his quickfire spell finished. It was a blast of condensed air that burst apart with the force of a bomb and lifted me off my feet. I hit the ground in a roll and willed my chitin armor over my body.

It had taken me a lot longer to learn to implement the method Eris used to reduce the amount of chitin used to form her armor, but after a week, I'd managed.

Black chitin pooled out of my skin and over my armor and clung to me like a second skin. Instead of the blocky, jagged chitin I was used to, it was smooth, like bands of corded muscles that wrapped themselves over me in a second.

It formed over my skin, and I rushed forward.

Eris was right, and my speed increased considerably. I was much faster. Even with my Agility maxed from all the boosts, I'd never moved this fast before except for when I was a Blade Master. I crossed the distance as Kincaid built another spell.

He turned his black gauntlet toward me, and the mana stone inside it cracked and shattered as the mana was used up.

A flash of an orange spell filled my vision as I brought my left hand up and activated *Chitin Shield*. I placed the flat of my shield over his hand and braced myself.

His fire spell went off and struck my shield a split second later. The spell detonated, and a rush of burning pressure shoved me back, but I grounded myself and fought to keep standing.

Kincaid screamed, and there was a muffled thump.

I lowered my shield to find Kincaid had been blasted back by the force of his spell. His suit may have had damage resistance, but even he couldn't ignore physics.

I walked over to him, with my sword raised. Though his body may have been protected, his face wasn't.

The fire had reflected, and half of his head was a blackened mess. Kincaid kept screaming as he pulled out a health potion and uncapped it.

I stood over him and stepped on his hand. I crushed the health potion, and the glass shredded his hand. He whimpered and his one good eye begged me to spare him.

"Please. Wait!" he croaked.

My steel slid through to his chest. His mana-powered suit had absorbed too much and failed. It was no better than cloth now. My blade met flesh and punctured through his heart with ease.

"For one of the most feared man on Nexus, you really didn't live up to your legend. How disappointing. That was for Adam, and for the members of my family you helped murder."

Kincaid died choking on his own blood which was too good of a death for him.

I pulled my sword free and wiped it on his burnt suit.

As I finished, I turned and glanced out over the battlefield.

From the faint green glow over my allied troops, it was going well for us. We outnumbered the rest of the army five to one and were just playing clean up at this point.

I checked my friends list to find that they were all still alive, which was a weight off my shoulders. Just as I looked up, there was a rush of wind and a flap of wings.

Eris and Raven swooped down and landed next to me with a thump. Eris hopped off Raven and rushed over to me as she transformed back.

"Sorry we're late," Eris said as she wrapped me in a hug.

"Yeah," Raven said walking over to me. "We had to help the fae with a few things."

Raven scowled and looked away.

"Had to help the Alice?"

She nodded. "Bitch needed backup. A group of players broke through to the gods, and we had to provide archery support while they dealt with them." She scoffed. "Was five seconds from getting a blade in the guts when we showed up."

I chuckled and let go of Eris to step closer to her and wrap my hands around her waist as I pulled her into a hug.

"I'm proud of you for being the bigger person and helping her." I leaned down to kiss the top of her head. I trailed my kisses to her ear, then her cheek, and finally her lips. I pulled her close as my hand went to the back of her neck, and her mouth parted. She welcomed me and met my passion with her own.

When we broke apart, I kissed her lips once more and smiled.

"But as the king of not being the bigger person, we'll make that bitch pay when this is all said and done."

We were still in the middle of a battle, and I knew we should be getting into the castle, but I had been terrified of leaving them both alone in the battle. I was grateful beyond words that they were both safe and sound, and I wanted a moment with them both before we faced Magnus.

I stepped back and held both of their hands as I stared at them.

"I don't know what's about to happen, or even if I'll survive, but I know one thing without a shadow of a doubt in my mind. I love both of you as much as anyone can love another person, and I'm grateful to have gotten the chance to love you both."

Raven grinned at me, her crimson eyes holding so much love in them. Her hand was warm in my own as she squeezed it.

"I love you too. Always and forever."

Her hand was warm, but it was nothing compared to Eris's scorching embrace. No matter how much my body changed, or how much of my humanity I left behind, her body temperature was as hot as always.

Eris clung to me and buried her head in my chest.

"I love you, Sam, For now, until eternity."

I kissed the both of them once more, and together, we strolled headfirst to the end

Chapter 23 - Like Mother, Like Daughter

Eris

The massive iron gate stood before us, unyielding. The dark stone of the castle dominated my vision except for the latticed gate that denied our entrance to the castle.

Sam walked over and rapped on it with his knuckles. "What are the chances Magnus just lets us in?"

"About as likely as the Alice becoming a nice and decent goddess," Raven said with a snort.

"So not fucking likely," Sam replied.

I sighed. "Probably not." I walked up to it and wrapped my fingers around the cold iron. The sharp scent of metal and rust made me want to sneeze. "We could climb it, or just have Raven fly us over the wall."

Sam chuckled behind me. "Already thought of that. And yeah, those are always options, but we aren't going to surprise Magnus. So if a sneak attack is out of the question, I'd rather make one hell of an entrance."

I stepped back and grinned at him. "Okay. I'm all for it, but what are you thinking?"

He smiled wide and walked to the gate. "Step back."

Sam summoned his four arachnid limbs and stood in the center of the massive iron gate. He gripped the iron bars between his hands and positioned each of his spider legs at the corners. He jerked and grunted as he tried to pry the bars apart.

The gate lurched for a moment, and then the metal squealed in protest, sending a shrill echo through the quiet castle walls. Slowly, he bent the iron back until it couldn't handle it anymore, and it snapped with a low groan.

Sam held the broken pieces of the gate up, and we all stepped into the castle.

As soon as we crossed the threshold, a number of soldiers clad in silver plate mail appeared from out of nowhere and began shouting.

Raven and I rushed in from behind Sam as the guards raised their weapons.

He just laughed as the guards charged us. Sam reared back and launched the fragments of the gate at the oncoming soldiers. The pieces took them in the chest and crushed their armor. After he threw the first volley, he shifted and threw the second from his left.

The heavy iron gate slammed into the guards and stopped them cold. They dropped to the rocky ground and did not rise.

He held his hands up and turned back to us. "What do you think? Good entrance?"

Before we could respond, his smile fell, and all joviality drained from him. His golden eyes seemed haunted, and he tied back his silver hair.

"Well, I tried to keep my spirits up, but that didn't last long."

I understood his apprehension. We were about to face what could very well be our deaths. There was no way we could remain calm and collected with that looming ahead of us.

"Well, it was a damn good entrance, so now let's go kick as much ass as we can," Raven said.

"Couldn't have said it better myself," I said and smiled.

Sam turned to face the stone steps leading to Castle Aliria, and without another word, drew his sword and started up the steps.

The two of us followed behind him as he reached the large wooden door. With a sigh of trepidation, he grabbed the handle and flung it open.

A woman stood in the entryway, waiting for us.

She wore a black and white outfit. A maid outfit, if I was remembering correctly. Her skin was a rich light brown, and her golden-brown eyes were simply stunning. Her long auburn hair was tied back out of her face but shifted and twirled as she bowed to us.

"Welcome back, my lord."

Sam paused. "Magnolia? What are you doing here?"

"Welcoming you," she said and stood from her bow. "Magnus has been waiting for you in the throne room."

"He's—" Sam sighed. "Yeah. Knew the stealth route wouldn't have worked. Lead the way, please. Let's get this over with."

"Right this way." Magnolia turned and began walking through the dark castle halls.

The place was lit by bubbling and flickering green orbs floating in glass lanterns hung along the gray stone walls.

"Mage lights." Sam turned to us. "Don't look at them. They can cause you to lose your mind if you're not careful."

I took his advice and kept my head down as I held onto Raven and we moved through the maze-like hallways that comprised Castle Aliria. I didn't want to admit it, but I was terrified. Not just for Sam, who had to face Magnus, but for myself.

Because I had to face Aliria.

It wasn't something I could ask Raven or Sam to handle for me. I had to do it myself, not only as her daughter, but as the rightful Queen of the Hive. I had to be the one to face her.

Even if I didn't want to.

After a few minutes, which to me seemed at least a hundred years as I wrestled with the decision in my mind, we arrived at the throne room.

Magnolia reached for the door, but Sam stopped her. "You shouldn't go in there with us," he told her. "You know what we're here for, and I don't want you to get caught in the crossfire."

"That's kind of you to say. But my place is by my master's side. I have nothing else to live for now."

With that, she opened the door, and we went inside.

The place hadn't changed since we were last here. The place had a religious atmosphere with the stained-glass windows and columns leading to the raised dais and obsidian throne.

Magnus sat atop it dressed in a pair of black trousers and an emerald green shirt that matched his eyes. His shaggy golden blond hair crested his bright eyes as he smiled at us.

"Sam, glad you could make it. I hope you didn't have too much trouble getting here."

Sam scoffed and held up his hands. "The hell are you going on about?"

Before Magnus could respond, the door on the far wall opened and Aliria stepped out. Instead of the dresses she normally wore, her body was coated in chitin. Like mine, it was smooth, unblemished, and it accented her figure better than any fabric could hope to match.

Her black and golden eyes tracked me as she walked over to the throne, and for the first time in my life, they no longer held motherly concern. They were cold, predatory and dead.

I knew what I'd said to her when she'd shown up as the castle, but it wasn't until that moment that I truly realized that the person standing in front of me wasn't my mother.

Magnus smiled at Aliria before he turned his attention back to Sam and the rest of us. "Well, I can only assume you are here to fulfil our bargain. I gave you two months with your bonded, and while it hasn't been exactly that, now is as good a time as any. Oh, and I'll also need the ring that Eris is wearing. But you can have it back after I get what I need off it."

"What the hell? I'm not here to give you Eris." Sam shifted and gestured to the ring. "And what is so special about that ring?"

Magnus shrugged. "The ring itself is trivial, but it's one of the last artifacts left over from the original programming, and there is a cache of data stored inside it that I need." His humor fell from his face and he sighed. "I know when—when James died, that he granted you ownership of Edna. The data on that ring contains the ownership codes for her, a backup James put in place in case something happened, and Edna transferred to an unworthy master.

"Not that you're unworthy of course, but you don't know how to use her properly. I can transfer her from you to me. No muss, no fuss. It's painless and harmless. Unfortunately, it doesn't change the fact that I still need the codes inside Eris."

Sam levied his sword at Magnus. "You can't have her!"

He frowned and leaned up in his throne. "Are you sure about this course of action, Sam? I'm still willing to have you as a partner. For everything you've gone through, it's the least I can do. You and Raven can live, have a good long life together. I know how much you care for Eris, and if there was another way, I'd take it. But there isn't, and with Jessica and James gone, it's up to me to preserve what I can of this world. I'll do that with your help, or over your corpse. This is your final choice."

Sam stopped and paused. For a long moment, he stared up at Magnus before he turned and looked at me. His gaze was one that I'd never seen directed at me before. It was cold, dispassionate. It was the look of a man that I didn't know.

And as he gazed at me, I understood on some deep institutional level, that Sam was weighing my life in his hands.

My life was his regardless, but I didn't want to die.

I understood that by sacrificing myself, I could save thousands, but there was still hope that Edna could come through for us and figure out a way to save everyone without the need for me to die. If there was even the slightest chance of that, I was going to take it.

But I also understood the choice Sam was weighing in his heart. He loved me, loved me at least as much as I loved him. But was one life worth the lives of thousands?

I knew the answer, but it wasn't one I was willing to accept.

But Sam was a much more practical person than I was. Though I knew he was hating himself at the moment. It wasn't a decision he could make lightly.

He stared at me for a long time before the cold ice in his golden eyes melted, and he smiled at me.

Sam turned to face Magnus and he once more pointed his sword at him.

"She is mine, and I will not let you or anyone else take her from me."

My heart swelled before absolute bone-numbing terror gripped my heart. *This is it. We've officially made enemies with Magnus.*

There's no turning back now.

Magnus sighed and nodded. "Very well. Know that I do not blame you or fault you for your decision, but I also can't allow you to interfere with my plans. My words may not mean much, especially now, but I am truly sorry, to all of you." He stood. "I wish more than anything that there was another way."

As he turned to Aliria, Magnus's eyes hardened.

"Capture Eris alive. If Raven interferes, kill her."

With that, he snapped his fingers, and both he and Sam disappeared.

They were gone, leaving Raven and me alone in the throne room.

"Where the hell did they go?" Raven shouted.

Aliria scowled at her. "Shut your filthy mouth and stay out of the way. If you be a good girl, you'll be back to serving us when this is finished."

Raven snarled at her and shifted, her midnight wings and talons appeared in seconds. "Go fuck yourself, bitch. I always hated you, and like hell if I do another damn thing you say. I'm not your slave any longer."

The chitin around Aliria's head shifted, and it covered her. Twin pools of ethereal green light lit up her face as she willed twin swords into her hands.

"Then die."

She launched herself at Raven.

Even as she pounced, I was moving. I willed my chitin bow into my hands, nocked an arrow in an instant, and released my arrow.

Aliria was so focused on Raven that she wasn't playing attention to me. The arrow took Aliria in the chest and stopped her momentum. She stumbled, and Raven countered.

She raked her talons across Aliria's face and scored five small grooves down her cheek. Though they were only superficial and didn't manage to pierce through the chitin.

As soon as Raven landed her first attack, she flapped her wings and flew backwards as Aliria brought her swords up where Raven had been standing moments before.

I'd already nocked another arrow and loosed it as soon as I had a shot. But this time, Aliria had prepared for it, and she sliced it in half just before it reached her.

"Wait your turn, little fly. I'll be with you in a moment."

"If you think I'm going to sit still and let you hurt the woman I love, you're going to be disappointed!"

I pushed off the ground and raced toward her as I shifted the chitin in my hands, turning my bow into a long dagger. My knife fighting skills weren't as good as my archery, but Sam and Raven had been teaching me.

"Don't worry." Aliria laughed. "You've already disappointed me enough as a daughter."

Fury burned in my chest as I closed the distance.

She turned to me and raised her blades. She swung at me. As her swords arced toward me, I shifted to the side and called my magic to me. I used camouflage as I ducked the strike. Aliria's attack missed me by a hair's breadth as I turned nearly invisible.

My sudden disappearance startled her, and she was slow to react as I slipped around her and slammed my dagger to the hilt in her side.

"Yeah, well I guess that makes us even since you were nothing but a disappointing mother!"

She roared in pain, and the back of her arm connected with me as she flailed about.

I was sent flying back, losing my grip on the chitin knife in the process. I rolled with the strike and came up on my feet.

Aliria whirled on me, and her eyes burned even brighter with rage. She advanced on me, but there was a rush of air.

Raven swooped down from above and tackled Aliria at the waist, and they both went flying. Raven angled herself and slammed Aliria into one of the stone pillars as fast as she could.

She hit the stone, and there was a loud crack when the column broke apart in a cloud of rock dust as they sailed through it.

Raven dropped Aliria and flapped her wings, swooping back up before she hit the ground. She folded her wings and glided back over to me.

The attack had wounded her as well, and she bled from numerous cuts and lacerations. Her leather armor was torn at her ribs, revealing a long, bloody slice across her pale skin.

She winced as she landed. "Bitch managed a good shot when we landed."

"Here." I reached through my chitin and took a potion from the pouch at my waist. "Drink while I hold her off."

As soon as Raven had the potion in hand, I sprinted toward Aliria. As I ran, I formed a new dagger in my hand since my last had been left in Aliria. My footsteps echoed around the eerie throne room, which without Magnus and Sam felt more like a mausoleum.

Aliria stood to her feet, and I found that Raven's aerial attack had done some damage. Her chitin was chipped and cracked in a dozen places.

She shook off the rubble and dust that clung to her and placed a hand to her chest. The chitin armor she wore shifted and molded, dissolving and reforming. She healed the cracks in a second, and her green eyes glowed with superiority.

"Much better," she said. "Thanks for the extra chitin. Now where were we?"

Before I could blink, she launched herself at me. I shifted and rolled as her swords struck where I'd been moments before. I came up behind her and slashed at her exposed back with my dagger. It bit deep, cutting through her exoskeleton and drawing blood.

Aliria cried out as my blade sliced through her flesh, and a splash of ruby red covered my obsidian knife.

She turned and struck with her sword.

I saw it coming at the last second and brought my dagger up to block. Our blades struck, and a rumble filled the room. Her strike had more force behind it, and I couldn't withstand her strike, so I angled my dagger down and stepped back.

Her sword bounced off the gray stone tile, and I rushed in to press my sudden advantage. My knife whistled as it cut through the air toward her face.

A heavy rush of air sounded next to me before an overwhelming force struck my side, and I went sideways.

My head cracked against the floor as I fell, and a sharp pain radiated through me. I tumbled, skidding over the ground until I slowed to a stop. A groan slipped from my lips as I fought down the pain and stood.

Aliria stood a few feet away. Swaying behind her was a large scorpion tail. Its glossy black stinger dripped poison.

"Now look at what you made me do. I don't want to hurt you, Eris. I don't. But you're forcing this upon yourself."

I shook off the ringing in my ears and stood. I raised my dagger at her. "No. You're responsible for this. You could choose to be a good and decent person, but you're just a monster. And I'm appalled that I was blinded enough to ever think you were a good mother. I'm going to stop you, even if I have to kill you to do it."

Though I couldn't see her face, there was a frown in her voice as she spoke. "Guess I'll stop playing around then."

"Took the words right out of my mouth."

I reached into the Hive Mind and pulled on the gifts the mantearians had given me. Their speed and stealth.

My chitin responded to my command, and my feet and arms shifted, molding to my desires. The armor at my feet grew thinner, changing my posture slightly to be more agile, while my hands formed sharp mantis blades. Wickedly sharp obsidian rose off my forearms to turn into my new weapons.

I rushed her, my speed more than doubled. I crossed the few feet between us in an instant and swung my arms at her. She tried to duck, but my sudden speed surprised her, and she couldn't get out of the way in time.

My twin blades carved through her chitin with ease, slicing deep into her body. Blood dripped from the X I'd rendered over her chest. She coughed and sank to her knees.

I knew the wounds I'd dealt her were mostly superficial since her chitin was too strong to really get good penetration, but I had an advantage that she didn't. I was trying to kill her; she was trying to capture me.

Which meant I could go all out.

As she stumbled, I used *Camouflage* and vanished. I slipped to her side and went to sink my mantis blades into her ribs.

Her stinger whipped around, and the tip speared into my stomach. My breath was taken from me as a sharp pain punched me in the gut, and a fierce burning pooled through me.

Aliria turned to me and chuckled. "Did you really think I'd fall for that a second time? So you managed to acquire the mantearians' will. I've lived and fought more than you can imagine, and I know the full extent of the *Camouflage* spell."

I tried to speak but I couldn't get my breath up. My words came out as a raspy cough.

She used her tail to bring me closer to her.

"Now, be a good girl and don't struggle. I'd rather not cause you any more pain than I have to."

The first thing I did was struggle to free myself, but her grip on me was like iron.

"Foolish girl."

She reared back to backhand me, but a rush of air above us caused her to pause and glance up.

Raven had rejoined the fight and floated above us. Even as Aliria looked up, Raven was moving. She brought her wings down, and a dozen of her feathers flung out. They spun end over end until they sunk deep into Aliria's back.

She let out a muffled groan as each of the feathers peppered her. A few must have glanced off her spine because she shuddered, and for a second, her grip on me loosened, and I used all my strength to push off from the stinger.

Fire burned in my stomach as I fell back to the ground.

I was hurt, bleeding, and Raven couldn't repeat the feather attack since she'd used so many. Aliria was wounded, and this was my moment to try the plan I'd had earlier. It was a risk, but so was everything else that had happened in the past few hours.

We were risking everything, and that meant I had to be willing to risk everything too.

Steeling myself, I raced toward Aliria one last time.

The pain in my abdomen made each breath I took ache, but I shoved the pain down as I reached her and tackled her to the ground.

Before she could react, I placed my hand on her chest.

I had no idea if this would work, but I had to try. It was an idea that had been born watching Sam take the chitin from Jasmine, and from me taking the chitin from Kalidan. If we could take the chitin from the dead, why couldn't we take it from the living?

A piece of my chitin was in Aliria, but it had mixed throughout her body, making retrieving it impossible, but I didn't try to pick that one single piece. I tried to pull her entire exoskeleton into myself.

Unlike with the dead, where there was no resistance, when I tried this time, a wall blocked my attempts. There was a pressure that was preventing me from proceeding.

Aliria coughed and laughed. "You're trying to steal my chitin?" She laughed again. "You don't have the strength to break through the will of the Hive Queen."

I bit down my response and focused entirely on trying to push past her resistances.

I smothered my will over hers, trying to find any weakness. It reminded me of what I'd done when I took over Misumena's mind. Our two wills clashed against each other, and in the end, I proved stronger.

I broke through the mind of one of the old gods. I survived the Nymirian Dungeon and proved myself as the rightful ruler of the Hive.

You are nothing but a pretender to the throne. Always have been.

"I am the Hive Queen," I said through clenched teeth. "And you will bow to me!"

I shoved every ounce of my resolve, my iron-clad will against hers, and like her mental state, her will fractured and shattered against my own.

She screamed, a hollow, tortured scream as I shattered her mind. A scream tore from my throat to meld with hers, and our shout rose until I couldn't breathe, and my scream turned to a choked-off sob.

Aliria went limp as her mind broke, and her scream slowly petered out to nothing as she lay there. Her chitin was mine; I could control it as easily as I controlled my own, and I absorbed it into my body.

As the inky pool melted and slithered off her skin, I was faced with the reality of what I'd done. Aliria laid there, her eyes open, her mouth slightly agape. She was alive and breathing, but her mind was gone.

My mother was dead. Her body was just a shell now.

I stared down at her, and I couldn't fight the tears that spilled over my cheeks. I dropped to my knees and cried over her empty body as I let my chitin fade back under my skin.

For a moment, I felt completely lost, until Raven's warm hands wrapped around me and held me close.

"I'm sorry you had to do that," she said, pressing her forehead into my back.

She held me while I cried for my dead mother, for the mother she'd never was but could have been.

I cried for a few minutes until the pain in my stomach forced me to stop. Every time I cried, it just hurt even more, and I couldn't take it anymore. I pulled back from Aliria's body and drank a health potion.

When I was finished, I turned to Raven, whose pure crimson eyes were an inch from mine. Her lips met mine, and the ache in my heart lessened. It would never disappear entirely, but it shouldn't.

I broke the kiss a moment later and stood. I pulled Raven to her feet, and we both turned and stared down at Aliria.

My mother.

"I—I can't leave her like that. But I don't know if I have the strength to do what needs to be done."

She nodded and slipped a hand to her lower back. She pulled out the knife that she kept and pressed it to my hands while still holding onto it.

"I'll be here every step of the way. I will help carry this burden with you."

My voice failed me as Raven led me once more over to the body of my mother.

Her chest rose and fell as her fingers curled slightly over the stone floor. Her body would continue to perform its functions to keep it alive, but her mind was gone, shattered into a thousand pieces, and it wouldn't be coming back.

To leave her like that would be the cruelest thing I could do, but I didn't know if I could be the one who ended her life.

You already ended her life. You destroyed everything that made her who she was. Doing this is a mercy.

I knew that, but my hands trembled as the two of us knelt by her and Raven guided our hands over her heart.

"Are you ready?" she asked.

I couldn't speak as I stared into my mother's face. Her sharp cheekbones and pointed chin. We looked alike, but she had more harsh edges than I did. A fact that wasn't merely skin deep, but I had to believe deep down that she had loved me at one point in her life.

I think she did, but she always cared about herself before anyone else.

I nodded.

Together, we plunged the knife into her chest.

She shuddered as a sigh slipped from her lips when she closed her eyes. Her pale lips moved as a drop of blood ran down the corner of her mouth.

"My little fly," she whispered before she lay still.

My heart stopped as she spoke one last time and fresh tears ran, but I refused to fall to pieces. I wiped my eyes and folded her arms over her chest.

I stood and turned away from her body as one last tear fell down my face. "I hope you can finally find contentment."

Raven's hand found my own, and her lips brushed my cheek.

"Let's go find Sam. I have a feeling he's going to need our help," she said.

I leaned into her as we walked away from the throne room. "Yeah. Let's get out of here.

CHAPTER 24 - ONE LAST FIGHT

Sampson

Inside Magnus's head must have been a cool, dry place. His emerald eyes stared down at me with cool indifference as he spoke. It was clear in his gaze that he would achieve his desired outcome, and he truly didn't care about doing that with or without me.

He would choose whichever option got results with the least amount of harm possible.

And in that moment, I understood a fundamental aspect of who he was that I'd known the entire time on a subconscious level.

Magnus was a bad man, but he wasn't an evil man. He didn't delight in the harm he brought on others, he harmed because in his mind, it was simply the most direct and easiest method to reach his goals.

It was a cold efficiency, but one that I understood.

I, too, wasn't a good man. Though I no longer thought of myself as a monster as I used to, I knew that I still wasn't a good person. I understood and even agreed with Magnus, how he operated, and I even agreed with his plan. It was clear, concise and logical.

If he didn't need Eris, I'd have joined him gladly.

But he did need Eris, and I didn't know if I could let her go.

"I'll do that with your help or over your corpse. This is your final choice," Magnus said. As he finished his speech I was only half listening.

I'd heard the words, and I knew that my time to make a choice was upon me.

My first reaction was to take the sword in my hand and use it to chop off his head, but through the fire of rage in my heart, his cool rationality bled through, and I had to ask myself the question I'd been avoiding for months.

Can I sacrifice the world to save Eris?

Edna was trying her best to find another solution, but even she wasn't certain she *could* find one. Evelyn and Adam had already resigned themselves to fate and left this world behind. I understood why they did it, but it didn't change that they left the entire fate of this world in the hands of Magnus and me.

And we were diametrically opposed to one another.

We could not coexist. One of us had to die.

But even if I won, there wasn't a guarantee that we could save everyone. While Magnus could save some people. He'd shown us that his plan had actual merit and could save at least a few of us. All we had was that Edna might be able to find a solution.

A promise to try. She could try and try, but there was no guarantee that she could succeed. Siding against Magnus might doom the world.

I could help save it. Could help save thousands.

All I had to do was sacrifice Eris.

I let my gaze drop from Magnus and turned around. Eris and Raven stood behind me, conflicting emotions on their faces. I stared at Eris, and her compounded eyes reflected my pale skin and golden eyes a hundred times in her myriad facets.

She was something inhuman. An entomancer. The Hive Queen. And the love of my life.

But she was just one girl.

One life.

Over the lives of thousands.

I couldn't make that choice lightly, so I had to finally consider the choice to give her up. To let her die so that others would live.

It was the selfless decision, and had anyone else been in my position, they might have made the selfless choice.

But I was selfish.

I was angry and bitter when I respawned after Sophia died and Lonny killed me. And I became a man who took that anger out on innocent people who didn't deserve it. I hurt so many people and I never felt sorry for it. Never regretted my actions.

Even when Eris came into my life and made me confront that side of myself, I never felt sorry for what I'd done.

And standing here now, I still didn't feel anything.

I was not a good man. That was an undeniable truth. I was someone who indulged their selfishness at the cost of others far too often.

What's one more act of selfishness in a sea of them?

Even if the world burned because of my actions, I didn't care about that nearly as much as I cared for the woman whose life I held in my hands.

I loved Eris and I wasn't going to let Magnus or anyone else take her away from me.

The look in her eyes told me that she knew what was going through my head and that she would accept whatever my decision was. I loved her even more for that, and it further cemented my resolve.

I would protect Eris and Raven. The rest of the world could go to hell.

My smile matched hers as I looked from her to Raven and then back to Magnus.

I raised my blade once more and pointed it straight at his heart.

"She is mine, and I will not let you or anyone else take her from me."

The light in his eyes withered slightly as he blinked and ever so slightly inclined his head.

The die had been cast; now it was up to us to see how it played out.

"Very well. Know that I do not blame you or fault you for your decision, but I also can't allow you to interfere with my plans. My words may not mean much, especially now, but I am truly sorry, to all of you." He stood. "I wish more than anything that there was another way."

His face looked haggard. He ran his thumb over the ring he wore on his hand.

And then he glanced at me, and all previous traces of who he had been disappeared. He looked at me like I looked at an enemy. I was someone who was now in his way, and he wasn't going to stand for it.

He raised his hand and snapped his fingers.

Suddenly we were no longer in the throne room. I stumbled and fell to my knees as I dropped into a completely different room.

It was massive, comprised of gray stone walls and tiled floors. The iron chandeliers were filled with effervescent mage lights, as were the sconces hanging on the walls. The back half of the room was filled with rows upon rows of weaponry and armor while the front half of the room had been cleared.

Where once a map table had sat was a barren section.

I'd been in here once before. It was Magnus's war room.

"Why are we here?" I asked as I climbed to my feet.

"To give us some privacy, and so the others can't interfere. If you refuse to see reason, then I have no choice but to end you. But you have proven yourself, and for that, I can at least fight you by myself, to make this more fair to you."

"No such thing as a fair fight." I spat. "I'll use any and every trick I have to beat you."

Magnus grinned. "As you should, and I shall not hold back either. But this is a fight between the two of us, as is the fight Eris is having with Aliria. These are the moments that will decide the future of the world. Isn't it exciting?"

"No. I'd rather be anywhere else right now, but you won't stop, and I won't allow you to kill Eris."

Magnus nodded. "A fair point. Then this is it." He held up his hand. "Goodbye, Sam."

As he spoke, I activated *Aura of the Antimage.*

It was the only move I had that could stop him for a second. As Adam told me, his magic had a radius, and he couldn't affect time more than fifteen feet in front of him. We were both in each other's radiuses.

Antimagic billowed invisible on my skin and rolled off in a heavy gust of wind. It swirled in a circle and swept toward Magnus as his spell came toward me.

Magnus could kill me without even moving, but not if I was outside his radius. His spell fizzled out and died as it was consumed by antimagic.

Before my aura could reach him, he disappeared and reappeared just out of range of the aura's effects.

"And there goes your trump card."

I raced forward and raised my blade as I followed the fading antimagic bubble. As long as it was there, I couldn't be affected by his magic. Which let me get in close.

As I was within range of him, I finally unleashed my true trump card.

The ability that Evelyn had given me just before she died. The weapon I needed to even the playing field for Magnus and me.

"*Return to Zero.*"

I held up my hand, and a bright golden glow filled my palm. Light particles danced in my hand as it activated.

A golden wave rose from my hand and shot toward Magnus. He teleported again, but he wasn't faster than light. He held his palms up and stopped the wave with his hands. But it wouldn't be enough.

It was an ability specifically designed to counter his magic. And even if he could manipulate time around him, he couldn't stop it, not entirely, and not for long.

Because *Return to Zero* was pure antimagic. It couldn't be stopped by magic. When it landed, it would rob him of his ability to cast magic and time out the abilities that let him cast magic instantaneously.

It was his counter. The one ability that could steal his power and bring him to my level.

The spells holding the wave back dissolved, and it continued forward until it slammed into Magnus, and he glowed bright golden before the aura faded away.

I stepped toward him, a smile on my face. "*Aura of the Antimage* isn't my trump card. That is. You can consider that a parting gift from Evelyn. And with it, I'm going to kill you. Even dead, she's still helping me to save what's important."

Fury crossed Magnus's eyes before it faded, to be replaced with humor.

"Ah, should've guessed. I underestimated you. But that's fine. I've lived for a thousand years." Magnus stepped back and reached for the sword rack closest to him. "I've learned how to fight without my magic."

He reached to the upper tier of the rack where two swords stood out from the rest. One was black and pulsed with an orange and red light. The hellsword.

While the other was its polar opposite. The silver and golden godsteel sword that made me want to run from it the last time I looked at it.

Magnus grabbed the pitch black hellsword, and as soon as his fingers closed around it, it lit up with wicked intent, like it begged to be used. Flames rose from its edge, and he stepped toward me.

"If Jessica trained you, then you must be a great swordsman. Let's see how you measure up."

He shifted into a familiar sword stance. The same one Evelyn had taught me.

If he was also taught by Evelyn, then this isn't going to be easy.

She was the greatest swordsman on Nexus, and that meant Magnus wasn't going to be a pushover.

I settled into my stance and advanced on him. The pulsating green mage lights danced around us as we slowly approached each other.

As we got within a few feet of each other, the wariness we had dissolved, and Magnus struck first. His blade came down with frightening speed and precision. I parried with the flat of my blade and countered, but Magnus was already out of range.

He was lithe and moved with the grace of a dancer as he stepped back. He grinned and then lunged at me.

I sidestepped and whipped my sword towards his neck. He leaned back as the tip of my steel sailed an inch past his throat. I followed through with my attack and brought the blade back toward him.

Magnus blocked and kicked at my leg. His foot connected with the outside of my knee, and he put a surprising amount of force behind it. My chitin armor absorbed it, but it threw me off balance as Magnus sliced at my arm.

I couldn't recover in time, and a burning slash of pain radiated up my arm.

"First blood to me."

I snarled and willed my chitin shield into my off hand. I rushed Magnus and swung at him. He caught my sword with the flat of his own. I angled the strike downward and slugged him with my shield.

His head snapped back, and he careened back into a row of spears. Before I could press my advantage, he reached for one of the short spears as he rose, and he tossed it at me.

He spoke a quick chant in Script, and a bright green circle appeared in his hand as he threw the spear.

The spear glowed green as it sailed through the air. I brought my shield up just in time and deflected the attack. I batted the spear away, but just as I moved my shield, a sharp pain numbed my arm and I stumbled back.

I looked down to find the same spear I'd blocked, sticking out of my shoulder.

What the hell?

Before I could blink, air whistled, and another spear appeared out of nowhere. I just managed to dodge it as I rolled out of the way.

I crashed into a rack of swords and bashed my head on the pommel of a rather large broadsword.

Magnus stood in the aisle between the racks of weapons, smug superiority alight on his face. He held up his ring on his hand and smiled. "You didn't think I wouldn't have a way to counter *Return to Zero* would you? Just because I can't use my own magic anymore, doesn't mean I can't borrow some stored mana. Oh, and do you like my *Time Loop* spell? It's a nightmare to fight against."

As he spoke, another spear flew toward me from out of nowhere. I brought my shield to block and just managed to stop the spear from taking off my head.

I rose to my feet and tried to close the distance between us so the spell wouldn't end up skewering me.

Magnus was fast, but he didn't have my speed, especially considering I was being boosted by my chitin armor. I closed the distance between us in a matter of seconds just as another spear appeared.

It launched, and I leaned away from it as it sliced past my head. A fierce burn rose from the side of my jaw, but I ignored it as I brought my sword up.

My blade arced toward Magnus, who just managed to block in time. He brought the hellsword around, and it neatly intercepted my strike.

He was good. Nearly as good as Evelyn. Which made him my equal in a sword fight. But his magic gave him an advantage that I didn't have. The only light was that he was running on fumes. He couldn't use his own magic since *Return to Zero* drained him and kept him from replenishing his own mana, but like with Kincaid, he could use outside sources to fuel his spells.

But unlike Kincaid, his ring didn't have half the power of the mana stones. And he couldn't use much more before he ran dry.

I pressed my advantage as we binded, using my superior strength to force Magnus back. Our swords clashed a dozen times in a minute as we both fought for dominance in the small space we found ourselves in.

The racks of weapons constrained us, and we had to be incredibly careful of our foot placement as we fought.

I batted aside a forceful strike of Magnus's and shifted on the balls of my feet, angling the pommel of my sword up as his blade fell off centerline. I bashed him in the nose with the emerald pommel, and his head jerked to the side.

As I struck, I pivoted and swept my leg out. I caught him in the ankle and took him off his feet. His head cracked against the wooden rack as he fell back, and a heavy groan slipped from his mouth. The back of his hand landed awkwardly as he hit the ground, and the hellsword skittered out of his grasp and landed by a rack of hammers.

I stepped toward him, victory a half second away, and I raised my sword to take his head.

His eyes flashed with fear in the dim green light, and I savored his reaction as my blade swept down.

This is the end!

A heavy gust of wind blasted me off my feet, and I flew back into a rack of weapons. I slammed against it, and a world of pain filled my chest, and the snap of bone resounded off the stone. I gasped for air as I toppled over it. The tip of a handful of spears scratched at my armor as I flipped over it and landed on my back.

Even more pain filled me as I cried out. I fought down the pain and dizziness in my head and tried to stand. Everything hurt, but I summoned my strength and stood as blood ran out of my mouth.

I'd lost my sword in the blast and grabbed for the closest weapon I could. It was a half spear, with a thick spearhead and had a good heft to it. I stepped around the rack as Magnus retrieved his hellsword.

"What the hell was that?" I asked.

Magnus grinned at me. "You didn't think I could only do time magic, did you? Even as a chronomancer, I can use more types of magic than that." He held up his hand, and the ring on his finger dissolved. "Alas. That *Windburst* seems to have used the last of the mana stored up."

He swept his arms out and smiled.

"If only I was surrounded by the most powerful artifacts in the world."

I scowled at him. "So that's why you brought us here? Because it gave you an advantage."

"Of course. You didn't really think I had any intention of fighting fair, did you?" He shook his head. "When the fate of the world rests in my hands? I figured you had more tricks up your sleeve than just *Aura of the Antimage*, and I wanted to be able to control the variables as best I could. Now, are you just going to stand there, or are you going to meet your death with some dignity?"

I rushed him with my spear, and it was clumsy in my hands. I hadn't used a spear in years, and it was nothing like wielding a sword.

Magnus easily batted my attacks aside. I just couldn't fight against someone as skilled as him without a sword.

It just wasn't going to happen.

So I backed up, drawing my shield close to me as I tossed the spear at Magnus and leapt back, trying to put as much distance as I could so I could go for a sword.

Magnus ducked the spear throw, and I bolted for the racks of swords.

He laughed as I ran.

"Running away. Fine, go grab yourself a proper weapon while I help myself to all my artifacts."

There was nothing I could do to stop him without a blade in my hands, so I had no choice but to disengage.

I reached the racks of swords and scanned each for the best one to use. My eyes flashed by the godsteel, and as soon as my eyes locked on the sword, the memory of what Magnus had told me came flooding back.

It was a sword not meant for mortals, he'd said. Only those with shards of divinity could wield it. The last time I had gazed upon the sword, I'd been unworthy, but as its silver and golden blade reflected my inhuman face, I understood that this was my sword.

Now it wanted me to wield it.

I reached out and took hold of the silver handle. A rush of warmth filled me as my body relaxed, and the pain I'd been feeling vanished as my body healed on its own. The sweet scent of summertime swept past my nose as I drew the sword from the rack.

Bursts of golden sunlight lit up the edge as I held the most perfect sword in the world. Wielding it was as natural as breathing, and as I retrieved it and walked past the aisles, a new strength invigorated me.

Magnus was on the opposite side of the room, near the bookshelves with scrolls and the glass cases that held artifacts that I had no clues as to what they did.

As I approached, he turned and smiled at me. He now wore several rings and a small golden amulet around his neck.

"So you can wield the godsteel. Part of me is furious that you are holding the sword Jessica forged herself. But another part of me is happy to see it used again. And as her successor, you have more right to wield the blade than I do. I just hope it'll be enough."

With that, Magnus held up his hands, and twin Script circles flared to life, spinning as they formed words I couldn't read, and then dissolved them. He spoke in a rolling tongue as he built his spells. I moved to intercept him before he could complete his spell, but as I moved, he smiled.

"Gotcha." He grinned.

The spells glowed brightly as they finished in an instant, and he fired them off.

A blast of fire magic, *Torrential Inferno,* spun from his hands in a cyclone of blue flames and sped towards me.

I couldn't dodge it in time, and I couldn't block it with my shield. The flames would cook me alive. Something inside me clicked, and I raised my sword. The golden blade glowed brightly as the magical inferno raced toward me. I brought the blade down, and a wave of golden light shot from it.

It met Magnus's spell head on, and my attack absorbed the magic and devoured it.

Antimagic.

The sword was imbued with antimagic.

His spell died, and I rushed him. He fumbled for the sword at his waist, but I managed to reach him before he could draw it.

I slashed diagonally across his chest, scoring a gash from his right shoulder to his ribs. It was deep, and I knew I'd hit at least a rib before he pulled back.

He screamed as his blood rushed out to soak into his emerald tunic. He hissed in pain and danced back as his off left hand clutched at his chest. Crimson ran through his fingers, and he bared his teeth in a grimace as he began casting a spell.

From the golden white glow of the Script circle, it was a healing spell. I couldn't let that spell finish.

I ran toward him and slashed through the Script circle just as he was about to finish casting it.

"I don't think so!"

Magnus stepped back, dancing over the stone tile as my sword passed by his chest, missing his flesh by an inch.

As I brought my blade around again, two voices startled me.

"Sam!"

"We finally found you!"

The voices of Eris and Raven startled me, and I lost focus, allowing Magnus to close the gap and slice a groove on the back of my arm to my tricep.

I hissed in pain as his hellsword bit through my chitin but forced it down and stepped back as I glanced at the girls.

Both of them were worn down, bloody and beaten. But alive. And that was all that mattered.

"What are you two doing here? Go, join the others. I'll come get you when I'm done."

I turned back to Magnus as quite fury settled over his eyes.

"So she's dead then?" he muttered to himself.

He grimaced and pressed his attack on me, fury unhinging his swings.

"Damn you!" he cursed.

I fought against his mad attack; each strike of his blade forced me back as I parried and deflected them. His sword glowed bright red as flames burst along the blade with each swing, and his fury gave unrivaled strength to him.

Footsteps clacked against the stone as Eris and Raven raced over to join me.

"Damn it, why didn't you listen to me?' I asked as Eris slipped under my sword and tried to strike Magnus with her knife.

He disengaged and slipped Eris's thrust.

"Because we're not leaving you, ever!" Raven shouted, sprouting wings. "It's the three of us against the world. I'm not going to let you fight alone."

Magnus batted Eris to the side, slamming his pommel into the back of her head. She tumbled to the ground but rolled with the force and came up back on her feet. She turned and tossed her knife at him.

It sailed end over end toward his back and slammed to the hilt in his shoulder.

Magnus screamed, and Raven and I rushed him.

I put every ounce of weight behind my thrust and aimed for his chest as Raven flew faster than me and raked her claws through the hand holding the sword. Her talons sliced to the bone and severed the tendons that allowed him to hold the blade.

The hellsword dropped to the ground as a heavy drip of blood rushed to meet it.

Magnus was vulnerable.

My aim was true.

The godsteel blade pulsed with a golden light as I shoved it to the hilt in Magnus's chest.

He lurched, stumbling back as the sword pierced through his emerald tunic and into his heart. He glanced down at the blade and smiled as blood trickled out of the corner of his mouth.

Magnus fumbled for a health potion in his inventory, but with only one hand, it made stopping him easy.

I stole the vial from his hand and kicked the sword, sending him to the ground.

He fell back with a clang as the tip of the blade struck stone and laughed as blood pooled beneath him. "A thousand years of effort, to be beaten by a man like you. It'd almost be poetic if it weren't so sad. You've doomed the world, you know."

I shook my head as the three of us stood over him.

"I refuse to believe that," I said as I pulled a knife out of my inventory and knelt.

"Looks like I get to see James and Jessica sooner than I thought," he said and turned his head to me as I placed the blade to the tip of his throat.

As I slit his throat, his gaze turned from mine to Raven. Cold fury remined and he gurgled, raising his hand.

"For taking her from me. May you suffer in a hell of your own making."

Before I could stop him, the necklace around his neck shattered, and a white light filled his palm.

It coalesced into a thick ball and then it shot out in a beam of light and struck Raven in the chest.

The spell caused her to take a step back as she winced in pain.

"Ow," she said as her hand went to her chest. "That hurt."

Then her legs buckled, and she collapsed to the stone floor. Her head cracked as it landed, and her hand fell away from her chest, revealing a hole the size of my fist through her chest, where her heart should be.

"No!"

Magnus lay forgotten as my body moved on its own.

I had the health potion I'd stolen from Magnus in hand as I dropped beside her and pressed it to her lips.

It slipped down her throat and spilled out of the hole in her chest, staining her porcelain skin crimson.

"No, no, no, no. Raven, Raven. You need to drink, love. C'mon. You have to drink."

Her eyes flickered and she opened them briefly. Her hand lifted and then fell back down.

I took it and squeezed.

"Love. Please. Please drink."

Eris dropped to the ground beside me, tears streaming down her obsidian eyes.

"Raven?" she asked.

"I…love—" she choked as her eyes shifted from me to Eris, and the last of the health potion spilled around her lips.

She wasn't drinking. She needed to drink.

Raven relaxed against me and closed her eyes.

"Raven?" Warmth dripped from beneath her to pool in my lap. I hugged her to my chest as blood ran over my hands. "Raven. Wake up. Wake up." I ran my hand over her cheek, smearing her blood over her pale skin. "Please."

But she wouldn't.

Eris shifted beside me and her hand touched my shoulder, but I couldn't meet her eyes, I could do nothing but stare down at Raven.

My eyes burned and hot tears spilled down my cheeks as reality set in and my heart shattered.

Raven wouldn't ever wake up.

She was gone.

And she took half of my heart with her.

Chapter 25 - What Comes After

I cradled her body in my arms as I sobbed. I broke, and everything that I'd been holding back since all this began flooded out of me.

There was nothing I could do to stop it.

I cried for my home that had been taken from me. I cried for Alistair, for Evelyn and Adam. I cried for the lost Gloom Knights who'd been a family to me and who I'd never see again. I cried for Lonny and Sophia.

And most of all, I cried for Raven, who'd been in my life such a short time, but who had irrevocably changed it and who I didn't know if I could live without.

I held her to me and cried as my soul tore in half. It wouldn't ever be whole again.

Eventually, the weight on my legs vanished, and I looked up to find that Raven was gone. Her body had been deleted from the game world.

And that only made me cry even harder.

But as soon as Raven disappeared, a new weight settled into me. Eris wrapped me into a hug, and we cried for our dead lover together.

It could have been hours that we sat there and wept, but the pain was so overwhelming that I couldn't move. We both cried everything we had, and then when there were no more tears to shed, we just sat there and held each other, neither of us saying anything.

There was nothing to say.

Nothing could ever make the world right again.

After a very long time, the two of us curled up together and fell asleep where she died. We slept, and even in my dreams, I couldn't escape my nightmares.

I relived her death again and again. I watched her die over and over, and each time hurt as much as the first.

A rough shake brought me out of the dream, and I awoke to find Gil and Wilson standing over me.

"Sam! Thank the gods. We thought you'd died when you never came out," Gil said, offering me a hand.

It was right in front of me; all I had to do was reach out and grab it. I lifted my hand, only for it to fall back down as I hung my head.

"I…" I lapsed into silence and reached over and brought Eris into my lap.

"Sam?" he asked again. "What's wrong?"

He looked around. "Where's Raven?"

As he spoke, my heart tore all over again. I tried to speak, but my throat was raw, and it hurt too much. I shook my head and then dropped it as fresh tears spilled out. I brushed Eris's hair and tried to keep myself from falling apart all over again.

"Oh, Sam." Gil knelt next to me and his massive arms wrapped around me.

He didn't say anything else. He just hugged me, and I couldn't hold myself together anymore. I cried again.

But this time I wasn't crying alone.

I was surrounded by the last remnants of my family. And I loved them all dearly.

It took a long time to pull myself together, but eventually, I did.

Eris woke up and I stood. My body ached, and I had a massive headache from the potion sickness, but the pain was a good thing. It gave me something to think about.

"Here," Makenna said and handed me a waterskin.

I drank deeply, and though it hurt my throat, the water was wonderous, and I hadn't realized how thirsty I'd been.

When I was finished, I handed the rest to Eris and told her to finish it. She was at least as dehydrated as I was.

After that, I had to get up and do something. I couldn't sit still. I'd fall apart all over again if I didn't keep my mind busy.

Gil once more offered me his hand, and I took it. He helped me stand and I took a look around the war room. It was kind of destroyed. Magnus and I had done a number on the place.

Thinking about Magnus caused me to glance over at his corpse.

He was lying where he died. My sword still stuck in his chest. His body, unlike—unlike Raven's had stayed. Because he was a guardian.

I walked over to him and knelt. Despite everything, he looked at peace in death.

"Give James and Jessica my regards, you son of a bitch." I spat on him and was about to rise when a glint of something stood out on his chest.

It hadn't been there before, but the more I looked at it, the more definite it got. It was a small gray gem, rough cut in the shape of a diamond. The little gem was so strange that I had to pick it up.

The bauble was cold to the touch, and when I picked it up, a notification flashed in front of me.

Mantle of the Chronomancer Guardian

Do you wish to accept?

Yes/No

So this is the true mantle of a guardian.

Despite being her successor, I wasn't the true inheritor of Evelyn's will. Her mantle still lay with her body where Adam had buried it in Machine City.

I hadn't wanted to disturb her body enough to retrieve it, and in the end, I hadn't needed it.

If the mantle could have brought Raven back, I'd have taken it, but it couldn't. And I had no use for it.

I scoffed and selected no. I wanted nothing to do with Magnus. So I turned and walked over to Wilson.

Out of all of us, he would be the best one to make use of the mantle.

I held the gem out to him. "This is the Magnus's mantle. It's what allowed him to control time. Do you want it?"

He raised his eyebrow and stared at the stone like it would catch fire. "You want me to be the next Magnus?"

I shook my head. "No, you're nothing like him. And I know you will use the power responsibly."

He grumbled but took the gem. "Fine. Just because I don't want this falling into the wrong hands." He smiled and tugged at his wiry beard. "What about you, are you going to head to Machine City and retrieve Evelyn's? She did pick you, after all."

I shrugged. "I don't think so."

"Why not?"

I turned and looked at where Raven had died, where Eris sat next to Makenna and Yumiko while she tried to keep from crying again.

There was something inside me that was broken, that wouldn't ever heal. But there was also a part of me that was relieved that it was over. I'd give anything to go back and have Raven back, even if it meant reliving the past few months all over again.

But that wasn't going to happen.

And I was tired.

I turned back to Wilson and smiled at him, clapping him on the shoulder. "Because I think I'm done."

"Done with what?"

"With all of it." I looked over at the golden blade, and I wanted nothing more than to walk away and never touch it again. "I'm done with the guild, with quests and leveling. I'm done fighting. I'm just done."

Wilson nodded and sighed. "Yeah, after everything that's happened, I can't blame you."

After we spoke, I went and picked up Eris. I cradled her to my chest and carried her as we swept back up through the castle and outside.

It had been midafternoon when we arrived, but now, the morning sun peeked over the sands of the Badlands.

The results of the battle had long since faded, leaving only the remnants of the war that scarred the landscape. Our army lounged around at the base of the plateau as the gods stood at the warped and broken gate at the entrance to the castle.

Morgan walked forward with Edna in tow as we descended. She had a wide smile plastered on her face as she strolled toward us.

"So I guess this means that you won?" she asked.

"It's over. Magnus is dead, but we didn't win. Not yet." I turned to Edna who looked up at me with her large cerulean eyes. "I took care of my part and bought us time. It's up to you now to find a solution out of this mess."

She nodded. "Working on it even as we speak. I've tried eight thousand nine hundred and four scenarios without success, but I haven't given up hope."

"Just keep trying. That's all I can ask."

"So what now?" Gil asked stepping forward.

Morgan shrugged. "Things go back to normal. Life goes on. We saved the world today, and we should enjoy that. While we can."

Gil chuckled and crossed his arms. "That's all well and good, we're the godsdamned saviors of humanity and all that." He held his hand out and circled his finger. "But what do *we* do? Our home was destroyed, so was most of our money. We're kinda broke now."

I laughed without actually feeling any humor and turned, holding onto Eris while I thumbed back at Castle Aliria. "I don't think that will be much of a problem, Gil. Magnus had more wealth than we could spend in a dozen lifetimes. I think you'll be just fine."

"And the castle is yours by right of conquest," Morgan said with a shrug.

Gil and the others shook their heads. "Live in the scary castle at the end of the world?" Mika said. "Yeah, no. I'm good."

"Yeah, this place is freaky as hell," Yu replied.

Morgan chuckled and her eyes lit up with humor. "Do with it what you will, I don't care." She turned back to the gods and walked over to them. "Our work here is done. Now we're going back to trying to keep this place from falling apart while Edna finds a way out for all of us. Be seeing you."

With that, the gods and Edna disappeared, leaving us alone. The army slowly began their march back to their kingdoms, and all that was left were the seven of us.

At the edge of the world.

I let go of Eris and set her down before I walked to the start of the incline of the plateau and sat down. I stared out at the rising sun over the sand dunes for a long moment.

We'd done it. Magnus was dead, and so were his plans. Eris was safe. But so were too many of my friends.

And so was Raven.

Was it worth it?

I didn't know. I couldn't answer that question. All I could do was try and rebuild the life that had been shattered.

Or try and build a new one with Eris.

Yeah, I like that idea better.

She came and sat next to me, and together we watched the sun dawn on a new day.

***

The clink of ice jolted me out of my daydream.

I sighed and reached for the crystal tumbler on the stone railing next to me. As I picked it up, the sharp scent of whiskey rolled past my nose and set my mouth watering.

My tanned face reflected in the amber liquid and the glass as I brought it to my lips. Long gone was the pale, corpse-like skin tone, golden eyes, and silver hair. My copper hair fell in my face, and I brushed it back as I drained my glass.

One hell of an adventure.

I raised the empty glass and set it back down as I leaned out over the balcony railing. Below me, the sands of the Badlands ended, and the sea began.

Castle Aliria wasn't Castle Gloom Harbor, not by a long shot, but it was home.

Had been for a long time now.

I ignored the not-so-distant horizon as I had been for years now and went back inside to get another drink.

As I stepped into the extravagant master bedroom, I sighed. No matter what I tried, what manner of furniture or decorations I changed, it was still far too affluent for my tastes. And even after all this time, I hadn't really gotten used to it.

I walked over to the long cherry wood bar with its hundreds of spirits and poured another stiff drink.

Just as I was about to walk back outside, the door to the bedroom opened.

I turned and my eyes widened slightly as Eris walked in.

She wore her riding clothes. A plain set of black cotton pants, and a white tunic with a leather jerkin over it.

"Hey, love," I said as she entered. A bright smile came over my lips as I set my drink down and walked over to her. "Thought you weren't due back until this weekend?"

Eris smiled brightly at me as she met me halfway and pulled me down for a kiss. When we pulled apart, she hugged me.

"I know, but I was missing you, so I decided to come home early."

I grinned down at her. "Won't hear me complain."

"Figured you wouldn't mind." She snagged the whiskey from beside me as she untangled herself from my arms.

She took a sip as she stripped out of her jerkin and unbuttoned the top of her tunic. She kicked off her boots by the door to the balcony and walked out.

I poured myself another drink and followed her back out. I stood next to her and she leaned into me.

"I missed you."

"Missed you too," I said as I leaned over and kissed the top of her head. "How were Gil and Kenna?"

She took another sip of her drink and sighed in content. "They're doing wonderful. The Gray Cask was packed all week. Mika is getting famous for his cooking."

I laughed and took a gulp of whiskey; the fire that burned down my throat was good.

I needed it.

"And with Yu as their bouncer, I bet they have no trouble keeping the peace." I smiled as I thought of them. "I'm glad they're doing well."

Eris turned to me and frowned. "Gil asked about you. He misses you."

I nodded. "I know." I drained my glass and set it back down as I stared down at the waves. "I guess it has been about a year since I last saw him. But the idea of facing him." I shook my head. "He'd try and talk us out of it."

"Yeah," she replied, crestfallen. "And he probably could if we let him."

A gust of wind swept her chaotic blonde hair back. She'd let it grow out a bit, and it stretched past her shoulder blades.

She fiddled with an errant strand and sighed, taking another drink. "I thought about telling him, but I didn't want to upset them before I left, so I didn't say anything."

We both quieted and stared out at the sea.

"Wilson called me," I finally said. "About a week ago. Just to check in."

"Oh, how's he doing?"

"Busy." I shrugged. "But as the leader of the Merchants Guild, I'd expect nothing less."

She snorted into her glass and bumped me with her hip. "What happened to his big retirement speech? After everything he said when we stood in front of the castle that day, I expected him to retire like the others after you all paid off your bounties."

"I've lost count of how many times that man said he'd retire. Dozens. He can't sit still. He's like me that way. Or how I used to be, I guess."

Never thought I'd enjoy not doing anything, but these years have been wonderful, far better than I could have ever asked for.

I sighed as I stared at the empty glass that reflected the horizon in the crystal and with Eris back, I had to face reality. I looked up and out to the sea.

There at the crest of the world, where the sea dipped and curved out of sight, was nothing but pitch blackness.

It stretched as far as the eye could see, a dark, gaping maw that devoured even light. And every day, it inched closer.

The Void had finally come calling.

"Five years." I chuckled as we stared out at the encroaching end. "All we went through. All we lost. And all it bought was five years."

Raven.

I hadn't said or thought her name in so long. It was just too painful. My heart ached like it was tearing apart and I shut my eyes before the tears came.

But I had to say her name, at least one more time.

Eris leaned over and took my hand, shaking me out of the lingering misery in my chest. She gave it a firm squeeze. "Yes, but they've been the best years of my life, and I wouldn't trade them for anything."

"Yeah. Me either."

I forced my gaze away from the darkened horizon and turned around, leaning back against the railing. "Edna?"

There was a rush of air and then the AI was standing next to me. She'd changed her avatar slightly to signify the passing of time. She was taller, and she'd aged slightly, looking now like a woman in her mid-twenties. Her dark hair was a little shorter, but her bright blue-green eyes were the same as always.

"The usual, Master Acre?"

I nodded. "Please."

She sighed and shook her head. "I'm afraid it's the same as when you last asked four months ago. I have tried over one million scenarios, and it's the same each time. I'm afraid there has been no change."

"So the world is still dying?"

"That is correct I'm afraid. At the current rate, the void will reach the shores of Nexus in a month, and full deletion will be complete in under three years."

I ran my hands through my hair and went back inside. I snagged the entire bottle of whiskey off the bar and went back outside, trying to come to terms with the singular fact that had been staring me in the face for five years.

"I doomed the world." I took several large gulps of the whiskey. It didn't help. It never helped and yet I needed it all the same. "And what's worse, I don't regret it. Not for a second."

The hard truth was that Magnus had been right all along.

He was a bastard who was willing to sacrifice everything to save the world, but it had been the right call. I think, deep down, that I knew he was right. It was cold, draconian to the highest degree, and would have cost thousands of lives, but it hadn't been wrong.

Now, instead of thousands dying, everyone was.

Three years and the simulation would end.

Our world would end.

And I didn't care.

Sacrificing the world had given me five years with Eris. Five years without any world-shattering goals or life-altering quests. Five years without swinging a sword or fighting to the death, just five simple—yet wonderful—years.

I turned and looked back out at the encroaching darkness.

"Five years. I doomed humanity for five years of peace, and I don't regret it for a second." I scoffed. "I was right, all those years ago. I am a monster."

Eris shifted closer to me and wound her arm through mine as she leaned her head on my shoulder.

"Maybe you're right. Maybe you are a monster. But then so am I, because besides Raven, I wouldn't change anything if I could go back and do it all over. We'd still be right here, watching the world die together. I think that makes us both bad people."

I nodded and took another swig of whiskey. "I love you. I ended the world for love, and I can live with that…well, I can die, knowing that I could live with that." I pulled away from her and cupped her cheek as I stared down at her. My heart swelled to bursting with love, and I glanced out at the void. "Are you ready?"

She followed my gaze out and shook her head. "No. Not tonight." She took my hand and pulled me away from the railing and towards our bedroom. "I came back early so I could have one more night with you."

Eris grinned.

"Let's make it a good one."

I tore my eyes from the horizon and back to my beautiful wife. I nodded and let my resistance drop as she led me to our bed.

We spent one last night together, and we didn't sleep for a single second. We spent every last moment in each other's arms. And I relished every moment. I burned them into my memory so I would never forget.

Even after.

And in the morning, when the sun crested over the dark void, we got up and got dressed. I wore my nicest set of clothes, black silk with gold trim. It was a set of clothes that Magnus had given me years ago. Eris wore a light forest green tunic and a chocolate skirt. They were the very first clothes she wore when we met, the ones Makenna had given her.

Both outfits felt appropriate.

We left our room, and I didn't spare a single glance back as we marched through the castle. We made only one stop.

I paused and knocked on the door to Magnolia's room.

She came to the door a few moments later, wearing her usual maid outfit that no matter how many times I told her she didn't have to wear it, she did.

"My lord?" she asked before she paused and glanced at our clothes. She frowned. "It's time then?"

I nodded and pulled out a letter and handed it over. "Will you make sure Gil gets this? Your transport has been arranged."

She took the letter with a nod. "Gods know I've tried to talk you out of it enough times, so I won't bother." Magnolia bowed low and curtsied. "It's been a privilege to serve you these years, Master Sam. I hope your journey is everything you're looking for."

"Thank you, Magnolia." I tugged off my shirt to show her my shoulder, where the tattoo of jasmines crawled up my arm. "I kept my promise to remember Jasmine, and I plan on keeping it for you as well. Goodbye."

With that, we left the castle and headed outside. The beating sun and racing sands of the Badlands swirled around us as we stepped out onto the red rock plateau. We turned and began walking around the castle until we reached a small, secluded staircase carved into the rock.

The two of us climbed down the many steps for nearly five minutes. The air progressively got colder, and the humidity beat against my face as water rushed over the rocks as we reached a small, manmade dock carved into the stone.

A large, single mast ship sat nestled in the hidden port underneath Castle Aliria.

We both stared at it before we turned to one another. I stared into Eris's black eyes and sighed. "Are you sure about this? I know we've had this conversation a dozen times, but it's real this time. Are you sure this is what you want?"

Eris didn't respond at first. Instead, she turned and stared at the void, as it swirled and consumed the water and the sky.

After a few minutes, she turned back to me and nodded.

"I am. We've had five years together. Five wonderful years. I couldn't ask for more than that."

"We could have three more. Three more years together is something I want more than anything," I said.

Her eyes softened. "And you think I don't?" She shook her head violently. "I want nothing more than to go back upstairs and crawl back into bed with you, but I know if I do that, if I say, 'Let's wait another day', that one day will turn into another week, another year.

"In another year, the void will have devoured our home. Castle Aliria will be gone, so will Aldrust and Yllsaria. You know that as well as I do."

I nodded, reciting the conversation we'd had a dozen times. "And the dwarves and elves will flee to the west, heading toward the Compass Kingdom and the Pale Everlands, the Sylvanus Darkwoods, anywhere they can go to escape the void. It will be a mass exodus, and refugees will flood in."

"And then it will be nothing but chaos. It will be survival of the fittest as people fight for dwindling resources in a dying world. It will be the apocalypse all over again," she finished. "We could stay. I want that more than anything else in this life. I want to be with you to the last bitter second, but it wouldn't be this. It would be chaos and fear, a constant struggle for survival. And I think we've both had enough of that to last a thousand lifetimes."

Yeah." I nodded. "I know."

It was an argument that we'd had a lot when we'd come up with the plan while drunk one evening. It was a selfish thing for us to do. And while we originally laughed it off, it stuck with us. For a year we debated it, and then we decided to go through with our plan.

Neither of us liked it; neither of us wanted it.

But it was the best option.

"If we stay, our peace comes to an end, and we go back to fighting to survive, killing just for scraps." I shook my head, my resolve strengthening. "The writing is on the wall. And I'd rather die than go through the end of the world again."

"And I'd rather die than watch the world I love fall to chaos."

I smiled and held out my hand. "So we die."

She returned my smile and took my hand. "On our own terms."

I understand, Soph. After all these long years, I understand why you did it.

Death was nothing but an escape from your problems. When the better options have been stolen from you, sometimes it's the only way out.

It was cruel, painful, and left those who loved you behind in a world of pain of their own, but the world was cruel and painful, and sometimes it became too much.

Suicide is cowardly. It's running away from your problems rather than facing them. But even in cowardice, there can be courage.

It takes courage to stand at the edge of the abyss and jump.

Together we stepped onto the ship and cast off.

It was simple to pilot, and while the waves rocked us to and fro, we stayed silent, our decision weighing heavily in our minds.

For an hour we rode in silence as the pitch-black void drew ever closer.

And finally, when we were mere feet from the edge, I slowed the ship to a stop and tossed the anchor overboard.

A giant swirling wall of darkness dominated our world as we stood and made our way to the bow of the ship.

We stood side by side as we stared into the void.

"Sam, I'm scared."

I took her hand and nodded. "I am too." I turned and looked down at her. "Not to die. But what comes after. I've done so many bad things in my life that I don't know which of the nine hells I'm destined for, but I don't want to be there alone."

"I'm sorry I can't go with you," she said.

There it was.

The single thought I'd been avoiding for such a long time.

If I was going to hell, I'd be going alone.

Eris wasn't real. Not in the way it truly mattered.

She was an NPC. An AI. She only existed in this world.

And I'd done my best to forget that.

Eris wasn't real, and neither was Raven. The two most important people in my life were nothing but lines of code in a computer that was currently crumbling to dust in the real world.

When I left this world, I'd do so alone.

Tears brimmed in my eyes, and I turned and wrapped Eris in a hug.

"I changed my mind. Let's go back. I'll fight the whole world if it means I get to spend another three years with you. The end of the world be damned. I'll face demons or gods if it means I can be with you."

Her scorching hot hands wound through my hair as sobs wracked her body. "I'd give anything to stop time and stay in this moment with you forever, but we can't, and I'd rather face the end of my existence than to watch everything I love fall apart."

She stood back from me and wiped her eyes.

"I'm going, Sam. I have to go now or I never will. And I'll go without you if I must."

I shook my head and stood, drying my eyes. Though my heart was in pieces, I knew I couldn't live in this world without Eris.

I was ready.

"We go together."

She smiled, her pale lips and obsidian eyes held so much warmth in them as she held out her hand.

"It's time, Sam."

She was right.

It was time.

So, for one last time, I took her hand and pulled her to me. Our lips met and time stopped. I held her tight and told her with a kiss that she was my life, my love.

My everything.

"I love you, Eris. For now, until eternity."

"As I love you. Until eternity."

Together. Hand in hand, we turned and faced our deaths.

We leapt off the ship and jumped into the void.

After surviving the apocalypse, after losing my family, after a thousand years on Nexus, after finding a reason to live again, and after fighting to hold onto it for as long as I could.

My hourglass ran out.

Eternity beckoned.

And alone, I answered.

Chapter 26 - The End

Death was supposed to be cold. But a soothing warmth enveloped me as the void swallowed me whole.

For a time, whether it be seconds or years, I hung suspended in the never-ending darkness. But unlike the memories I'd shared with Eris from her time in the void, it wasn't cold.

It was warm, and it was like I was drifting through the sea on a hot day; the beating sun and the cool water collided to create the perfect temperature.

And I was content.

My heart refused to hurt, even though I was facing the afterlife alone.

Rather than fight the feeling of peace, I clung to it, because I knew that I likely wouldn't ever get to feel that again whenever the darkness ended, and hell awaited.

So I relaxed and learned to live with the darkness for days, weeks, years. It didn't matter. Time no longer mattered.

Nothing mattered except the blissful warmth that surrounded me.

For all I'd done, the lives I'd ruined for my selfishness, it was far better than I deserved.

And then, one day it was over.

A flash of pain startled me, the first thing I'd felt in the void since I arrived. The pain originated from my hand, and I brought it to my face and gasped as the center of my palm glowed bright orange.

The scar where the *Shard of Divinity* lay buried itched furiously, and it began to glow brighter, burning white-hot all the while.

I tried to scream, but my voice was lost to the silence of the void, and I screamed wordlessly for an eternity before there was a rush and I found myself falling. I spun end over end until the warmth around me faded, and I slammed into something hard.

My head pounded with agony, and my hand ached like it'd been burned off, but when I blinked the tears from my eyes and stared down at my hands as I knelt on my knees, I found it perfectly whole and unblemished.

As my breath came back to me, a cool breeze ruffled my clothes, and I blinked my eyes clear as more tears streamed down my face. When I could see properly, a world of gray stood out underneath my hands.

The gray was gritty, pockmarked and strewn about with smaller chips of gray.

I blinked as the long-forgotten word came back to me.

Concrete? Gravel?

As I stared down at them, I was even more confident in my word choice. I was staring down at roughly paved concrete. Something I hadn't seen in more than thirty years.

Something that didn't exist on Nexus, but certainly existed on Earth.

I knelt there for a moment and came to terms that I wasn't in the void any longer, and I certainly wasn't in any of the nine hells where I belonged.

But that begs the question of where the hell am I?

It took a few moments to find my strength after being weightless for however long I was in the void. But I eventually stumbled to my feet and looked around.

I was in the middle of a street.

But it wasn't the brutal, broken streets that I remembered from the apocalypse; no, the street looked like it had before the Night-Fall.

Clean.

The two and three-story suburban houses that lined both sides of the road were pristine—no broken, burned out buildings. The green lawns were mowed and the cars in the driveways weren't looted and destroyed.

It was Earth, before it ended.

My mind cracked as I tried to understand and come to terms with what I was seeing.

I looked up into the dark orange sky. The sun was low, and dusk stretched over the street. For a good hour, I just stood in the same spot, staring at the sky. The familiar fear of the dark crept back over me. I was waiting for night to come and the ghouls to appear.

I was waiting for the apocalypse to begin again.

But an hour turned into two as I stared up at the orange skyline, but the sun never moved. It stayed in the same spot for hours, casting burning orange light over the world.

Which told me I wasn't on Earth.

That this was a place that just looked like Earth.

With that in mind, I turned around and tried to get a sense of the place. But there was nothing for me to go on. It was just a random street that meant nothing to me.

It was a one lane road, so I picked the direction heading away from the sun and started walking.

I walked for hours, going through residential neighborhoods at random until I eventually found a main road.

It seemed familiar to me. But it had been decades since I'd been back, and it took a moment for me to process.

"I think this is home."

It reminded me of the city I grew up in. And the road that headed into downtown wasn't that far from where I'd lived with my family, all those many years ago.

I had nothing else to go on; no other place called to me as much as home did, so I turned down the next road and began walking.

The upper-class residential houses slowly fell away as I slipped from the nicer neighborhoods to the poorer part of town. I passed a trailer park, crossed the highway, and started down a long gravel road.

It had been more than thirty years since I'd last been down this road. The night that my parents, that Micah died.

The night I failed.

It all came back to me in a rush, but I didn't shed a single tear. Because this time I wasn't running.

I was coming home.

Houses long past their prime stood on either side of me as I walked down the road. The crunch of gravel echoed around the silent street as I neared my house.

Then before I knew it, I stood in front of the single-story house with the fading white paint and cracked window held together by duct tape. Our concrete porch with the wooden swing with mine and Micah's names scratched into the arm rests. The beat-up red pickup truck in the driveway.

It was home.

I stared at the wooden door, and a flash of it broken, bloody, filled my mind before I shook it off and started walking toward it.

As soon as I stepped into the yard, movement from my right caught my eye. A figure stood leaning against the side of the truck. The light of the sun cast their features in shadow and as soon as I took a step, they pushed off and walked toward me.

The sun faded, and I got a look at whoever it was.

My heart nearly stopped beating, and I let out an involuntary gasp.

The man standing in front of me…was me.

But it wasn't me.

His features were gaunt, hollow and emaciated. His skin, pale. Where now I had long, flowing copper hair, his was buzzed, shaved to the scalp. He wore a plain white t-shirt and sweatpants.

It was me, but a me than I had long forgotten.

It was the me that had died, all those long years ago, before I entered the Ouroboros Project.

He smiled at me.

"Hello, Sam. I've been waiting for you for a very long time."

"How?" I asked, stepping closer. "How is this possible?"

He chuckled and shook his head. "That question is so far beyond me that it hurts my head. But I knew." He tilted his head toward our house. "I knew as soon as I tried to open the door and couldn't that I had to wait here. After all, how could I leave purgatory with only half of my soul?"

"Purgatory? This is purgatory?"

Sampson shrugged and held up his hands. "It's one of the many names of this place." He laughed. "Welcome to the Realm Betwixt. The place between places."

I looked around at what looked like Earth. Except for the never-ending sunset, there was no way for me to differentiate this place from home.

It wasn't home, but it was a close enough facsimile that I didn't care.

"The Realm Betwixt." I shook my head. "A stupid name."

Sampson laughed. He snorted and covered his mouth. "I agree, but I didn't fucking name it."

"You didn't?" I looked around at the empty street. There was no one around. In fact, I hadn't seen a single living soul since I'd arrived here. "Then who did?"

"I don't know. A child came by one day, a long time ago. He had long silver hair, and…and suns in his eyes." Sampson shuddered, shaking his head. "Unnerved the hell outta me, but he told me the name of this place, and then confirmed that I had to wait for the other half of my soul. Then he left, and I've been mostly alone."

"Mostly?"

Sampson nodded. "A few souls have come and gone in the innumerable years I've been here. In fact, I have a message for you…us? From two of them. Adam and Evelyn wanted me to tell you that they don't hold it against you. That sometimes even doing the wrong thing can be the right thing."

I burst out laughing. I couldn't help it. That was such a 'them' move that I couldn't help but laugh. I doubled over as some of the ache in my heart eased.

"I'm glad they don't fault me for failing, though I'm kinda pissed they prepared a consolation message in advance when they didn't even know the outcome yet. But in hindsight, it was kinda obvious. They knew I could never give up Eris."

He nodded, not bothering to respond. There wasn't anything he could say.

Speaking Eris's name opened up a pit of absolute misery in my chest. But as quick as it came, I had to push it down before it overwhelmed me. I swallowed my grief for the time being and turned to myself, whose eyes showed that he was feeling the same pain that I was.

We were the same person, after all.

"So what happens now?"

The pained look on his face shifted, and he gave me a small smile as a gust of wind blew past, sending blades of grass scattering around us as the wind ruffled our clothes.

He held out his hand to me, still smiling.

"Now, you take my hand, and we go home. I don't know what lies beyond that door, but my heart tells me it's our family."

I turned and looked at the cheap wooden door that separated us from our house. My heart sped up looking at it. And I too knew, deep down, that he was right.

Our family was just on the other side, waiting for us.

For me to come home.

My heart leapt into my throat at the thought of seeing my parents again. Of seeing Micah again, seeing his shaggy hair, caramel eyes, and crooked smile.

I wanted nothing more in that second than to take my hand and go see my family. To apologize for my failures.

To ask for their forgiveness and set my heart at ease.

I looked at his hand, at its smoothness; the callouses from my decades of a swordsman were nowhere to be seen. I wasn't Durandahl the Blade Master anymore. I wasn't Sam the Hive Knight. I was just Sam.

And I missed my family.

But my family wasn't waiting for me in the house. Not all of them.

I shook my head and sighed, looking up from his hand to his amber eyes. "I'm sorry. I can't take your hand. I know you've been waiting for me for a thousand years, but I've got some waiting of my own to do."

The smile fell from his face and he dropped his hand. His eyes immediately shifted, becoming pained, haunted. Sampson crossed his arms and hung his head, shaking it softy.

"I'm so sorry, Sam, but they're not coming. You know that, don't you? You knew that before you jumped. Eris and Raven are gone. I'm sorry. I'm so sorry."

I nodded, and my heart shattered. Every last bit of grief I'd been holding in flooded out of me, but I didn't have enough energy to cry.

My eyes burned with the strain, but no tears would come. I could do nothing but stand there with my head down, drowning in my grief.

I don't know how long I stood there, but I know it was more than a full day as I struggled to come to terms with my broken self.

But I couldn't. I refused.

To admit that Eris and Raven were gone was something I refused to do. I didn't care that they were artificial, that they weren't real.

Our love had been real.

And if I acknowledged that I'd never see them again, I would be letting go of that love.

I couldn't do that.

And so I stood, wiped my dry eyes, and held out my hand.

"Until eternity wasn't just something we said to each other just because. It was a promise." I smiled at Sampson, my other half. "Gods know we've broken enough promises in our lives. But that's one that I just refuse to break. So take my damn hand. Your waiting is over."

He grinned. "It's good to be home."

Sampson took my hand, and there was a rushing warmth, and a sharp light radiated off him before he vanished before my eyes and an ineffable weight settled in my chest.

I shook it off and smiled. "Yeah, it's good to be home."

As I looked once more to my house, I smiled as the door opened and there, standing in the doorway, was my family.

My mother and father stood arm in arm, smiling at me. My dad's tall, broad-shouldered frame took up most of the space as he ran a hand through his thick red hair while my mother stood beside him, her dress perfect and her golden-brown hair falling down her shoulders.

And then there was Micah.

He smiled widely with his row of lopsided teeth and waved at me. His rich brown eyes told me more than words ever could that he loved me, that it was okay for me to come home.

And finally, the tears came.

They flowed down my face as I got to see my family again. One more time. I got to see the truth in their eyes that they didn't blame me for what happened, and that they loved me and had been waiting for me all this time.

"I love you all," I whispered. "So very, very much. But I can't go with you. I have some waiting of my own to do."

With regret in my heart, I turned away from the welcoming smiles of my family and started down the gravel driveway once more.

"They'd wait for me. So it's the least I can do."

I reached the end of the drive and stood next to the cheap metal mailbox nailed to a wooden post in the ground.

As soon as I stepped off the property, the door to my house shut softly, and I resisted the urge to turn back around and look.

I knelt and sat back against the mailbox.

It was as good as a place as any to sit and wait.

And that's just what I did.

I waited.

I waited for an incredibly long time.

And I kept waiting.

I refused to give up.

And so, I stayed in the place between places and waited.

Time stopped meaning anything a long time ago.

Until, one day, it did once again.

The crunch of gravel snapped me out of my trance, and I turned at the sound.

"There you are," she said, her soft, melodious voice filled with warmth.

My heart nearly stopped at hearing her voice and I looked up, smiling as tears rushed down my face.

Her long, midnight hair fluttered around her pale face in the soft breeze that blew around us. Her crimson eyes sparkled in the dying light of the sun as her blood red lips grinned at me.

"Hey, darling. It's been a long time."

I couldn't stop the tears as my shattered heart repaired itself in an instant and swelled to bursting. I don't remember moving, but suddenly, she was in my arms, and her warm body pressed against me as her heart beat out of her chest as she held me as tight as I held her.

"That it has, love. That it has."

We stood there, in our embrace, for a long time. There was so much to say, and there weren't any words that could express the depth of emotion either of us were feeling.

So we said nothing and just held each other. A simple act that I thought I'd never get to do again.

Through my haze of overflowing emotions, I had to wonder how.

"Words can't express how happy I am to see you, but how are you here, Raven?"

Raven.

Just saying her name after so long was the most incredible feeling in the world. I'd missed it so much.

She smiled and held up her hand, where a scar matching mine stood out next to her pale skin.

"I guess it has something to do with the shard stuck in my skin."

As soon as she spoke, a memory flashed through my head, one that was and wasn't mine. It was a memory of my other half.

Adam stood next to the old truck, him and Evelyn both. They were their human selves, without the glow of their demigod forms. They wore plain shirts and jeans, and it was incredibly strange to see them in normal, modern clothing. They turned to leave when Adam glanced back and smiled.

"Oh, one last thing before I go—you can tell Sam he can thank me when we next meet."

Then they were gone.

Raven stood over me, and she held out her hand.

I smiled as I took her hand and kissed it before pulling her into another long hug.

"I love you, Raven."

She pulled back, and her lips met mine. It was a chaste kiss, but her lips melted against mine, and my heart stopped beating for a moment. I stopped everything and just reveled in her touch. Soon I was breathless, and I had to pull away.

While I figured out how to breathe again, Raven rested her head against mine and kissed my lips once more.

"As I love you. As I have always loved you. As I will always love you." She wiped a few tears from her eyes. "I didn't think I'd ever get to say those words to you ever again, and I'm thankful beyond words that I can. It made the years and years of searching worth it, just to see you again."

She stepped back and twirled, her form-fitting black dress flowing around her ankles, and she turned and smiled at me, all traces of her tears gone, and she gave me the most radiant and heartwarming smile I'd ever seen.

"Now that I've found you, darling, what's say you and I go find our other wayward lover?"

The mere mention of Eris lit a fire in my chest, and for the first time in a long time, hope burned bright in my heart.

I held out my hand and Raven intertwined her fingers through mine. Her hand fit in mine perfectly. Exactly where it belonged.

Now all we were missing was our other half.

I smiled at her and we walked off into the perpetual sunset.

Together.

###

The End

You Are Not Alone

I want to take a moment and address the second to last chapter in the book and the dark themes present in it. The chapter deals with Eris and Sam's decision to commit suicide, and I'd like to talk about that.

I do not condone or advocate suicide.

It is never the answer, and I don't want the takeaway from that chapter to be that you should kill yourself rather than staying to face your problems.

For Sam and Eris, their world was going to end regardless. It was a matter of when, not if. But still it was a cowardly thing to do. They ran away, rather than trying to help solve the issues plaguing Nexus, and it's not something that should be celebrated. It worked out in the end, and Sam got his happy ever after, but this is fiction, not reality.

And I want to specifically bring up the lines I wrote.

"Suicide is cowardly; its running away from your problems rather than facing them, but even in cowardice, there can be courage.

It takes courage to stand at the edge of the abyss and jump."

Now, I do believe this to be true. That it takes courage to commit suicide.

Because I know how the cold steel of a gun barrel gun tastes. My hands shook, and my heartbeat pounded hard enough through my fingers that I could feel the pulse in my mouth. All while the voice in my head told me to pull the trigger.

That moment lasted a lifetime, and a second.

And I hesitated.

Eventually I put down the gun and continued with my life. I lacked the courage to pull the trigger, but that isn't a bad thing.

It's the best thing in the world.

It was the single greatest moment of my life, and I'm grateful every day I lacked the courage to take my life.

And if reading this has made you consider ending yours, I want you to allow your courage to fail you as well. Life is precious, and you deserve to live as much as anyone else.

Maybe more so.

Even if it's to spite the world for daring to exist. Get up in the morning and fight. Fight to stay alive.

Because to do otherwise is unthinkable.

If you're reading this and you think you're alone, I can promise you that you are not alone.

And even if you are, and you have no one around you who you think can understand or is willing to listen and you feel like you're on an island and can't escape:

I'll be there.

I'll be there if you need a friend, or someone to talk to.

If you are reading this and are having suicidal thoughts, I'm willing to listen. To be someone who talks you down from the ledge. Anytime, day or night.

My email is Epsilonundying@gmail.com and my Discord is Toaster-San#7940.

I know what you're going through, and I'm always willing to listen.

You are never alone.

—Grayson Sinclair

Bonus chapter

Swords of Legend: In Remembrance

This story is set many years before the start of Hive Knight, and gives a little insight into Sam and Mika's lives before they were part of the Gloom Knights

Swords of Legend: In Remembrance
An Ouroboros Project Short Story

The clink of mugs resounded through the boisterous tavern. Our ales collided and spilled malty heaven down our hands.

"To the Swords, and another notch in our belts!" Lonny shouted, his steel plate mail clinking as he tipped his mug back, drinking deeply.

Lonny stood out sharply with his armor and rugged good looks. His boyish, chestnut hair and sparkling green eyes were the talk of the tavern, and he already had several of the barmaids swooning over him, and that was before he'd bought everyone in the bar a round.

Following his lead, we all drank our ales with gusto and sat back in our chairs, each with a sigh of contentment. I wiped the foam from my mouth and slammed my mug back down harder than I meant, splashing a few drops of ale over our radiant feast.

Lonny had splurged a bit and gotten a little of everything. The long wooden table was too big for the four of us but housed enough food to feed the entire tavern. *We certainly aren't going to be able to finish it all*, I thought, reaching for my mug only to discover it was empty. *Oh right, I drank it.*

I laughed a bit too loudly and stood up to get another drink.

"Where are you going?" Soph asked, throwing a wry smile my way.

Sophia had a bit of redness in her face. It darkened her golden-brown skin and brought some shine to her bright hazel eyes. She'd tied her walnut hair back into a ponytail during the quest and had yet to undo it. I liked her hair when it was out of her face. She had eyes too pretty to hide them away.

"To get another drink, you guys want any?"

"Sure," she said.

"Yeah," Lonny slurred, at least as deep in his cups as I was. He tossed me a few silvers from his coin purse.

"How about you, Mika?"

"Ugh, sure. My liver could use the exercise," Mika said, brushing his jet-black hair from his thin, angular face as he slumped over, grabbing at his empty mug.

Mika's Asian heritage came out to play as he cursed his mug in Old Japanese, which filtered through the translator in my interface.

Godsdamn, what'd that glass ever do to you? I laughed and pushed myself through the throng of people. The bar was in full swing this evening, and I had to slip and dance around the patrons as they danced to the lute player strumming along while singing loudly.

I moved past a mirror and saw my face reflected in the glass along with half a dozen other strangers. *Ugh, I need to shave again,* I thought to myself as I stared into my amber eyes. My short copper hair needed a trim as well as my nascent beard. *I should ditch the beard, but I might let my hair grow a bit more.*

I stopped staring at myself like a freak and made it to the counter. I ordered another round for everyone, dropping a single silver on the counter for the cute, mousy barmaid nearly spilling out of her top. She'd been eyeing Lonny all night, and I thought I'd help him out.

"Keep the change, it's a tip from him," I said, thumbing back towards Lonny.

The barmaid blushed and nodded, saying she'd be right over with our drinks. Before I went back to the table, the Adventurers Guild quest board caught my eye. I walked over to see that a few new quests had been added since we'd been gone.

Scanning over them, I found one that would be perfect for us. A nest of changelings had taken over a cave and were harassing a town called Wyston near the Northern Mountains. I took the quest flyer from the board, causing the quest to pop up in my interface.

Quest: Extermination (Changelings)
Type: Guild Contract
Difficulty: C
Reward: 2875 Exp!

There was also a reward of three hundred silver coins and a fifty-silver bonus for bringing back the ears, eyes, and teeth. The Mages Guild required the ingredients and were paying well for them. *This quest is right up our alley.* I brought the flyer back, and by the time I maneuvered back to the table, the busty barmaid had already brought our drinks and was flirting heavily with Lonny.

"Thank you for the drinks, but that's all I came here for tonight," Lonny said to the flustered maid.

She walked away with a sour frown and shot me a look. I shrugged an apology and shook my head. *For a guy with his looks, he doesn't get around much. Well, I tried.*

"Hey, guys, look at this," I said, slamming the flyer down on the table in between the suckling pig and cubed boar steak.

Mika looked up from his nap on the table and grabbed for the flyer, but Lonny snatched it before Mika could pick it up.

"I was looking at that, ass," he slurred.

"Wait your turn," Lonny said, laughing. "An extermination quest again, D?"

"They've been working out well for us, why let the streak die?"

Soph looked up, a little pallid at the mention of extermination, which was becoming the norm for her as of late. "Is it NPCs?" she asked.

I shook my head. "Nope, changelings."

"Fuck, I hate those things," Mika said, taking a drink.

I sat back down and grabbed a handful of the cubed boar steak, leaning back and plopping them in my mouth. "Yeah, they're creepy as fuck, but the coin is good, and the experience is better. We can pay rent for the next few months and get a few new pieces of gear."

"I don't know, Duran. We just turned in a quest today, can't we sit back and enjoy our victory?" Sophia asked, her face downcast.

"I thought that's what we were doing right now," I said, trying not to sound desperate, but I needed this quest. "But it's not my decision to make. What say you, oh glorious guild leader?"

Lonny looked around the table at all of us before his eyes settled on Sophia. "If Soph doesn't want to do it, then I say she's right. We just made a good bit of coin; let's rest and recover before we burn out."

It wasn't what I wanted to hear, and I couldn't stop the anger that bubbled in my chest and crept up my cheeks. *Fuck it, if they don't want to do it, that's fine.* I stood up and snatched the quest flyer from Lonny's hand.

"It's all good. I'll do it myself."

I wasn't in the mood for any more celebration, so I left, while the others called at my back.

It was getting colder outside. The wind nipped at my heated face, chilling me. Fall was already edging out summer, and it would be even colder in the Northern Mountains. The streets of the North Kingdom were bare at this time of night, and I wasn't ready to go home. I quickly equipped my long coat. The black cloth settled around me, banishing the chill in the air, and I took off, not caring where I went.

The oil lamps burned in the middle of the street, casting lambent light over the wooden and stone buildings and houses. Many were designed in the half-timbered style, with the wooden support beams exposed next to the whitewashed plaster. I walked until I came to Curran Park. To call it a park was laughable; it was barely more than a patch of grass with a few benches, but it would do as a place to sit and try not to think. To try not to think about everything I'd lost.

I sat back on the bench; the wood creaked as my weight pressed down on it. *I shouldn't have gotten angry at them, but I can't just sit still, not right now. I need something to keep my mind busy.* The others should have understood, but they didn't. They were content. Which was fine any other time, but not this week.

I just leveled up, but I can probably grind another level in the next week or so. Focus all my energy on that for now. I pulled up my *Character Screen* to double-check.

Character Name: Durandal
Level: 53
Exp: 1145/5300
Race: Human
Class: Phantasmagoria
Reputation: Adventurer (Silver Rank)

Stats (-)

Strength: 50

Strength Sub-Stats

Carrying Capacity: 25

Attack Damage: 50

Constitution: 50

Constitution Sub-Stats

Endurance: 50

Endurance Sub-Stats

Battle Fatigue: 50

Battle Fatigue Regen: 50

Agility: 50

Agility Sub-Stats

Movement Speed: 25

Attack Speed: 25

Dodge: 50

Wisdom: 0

Luck: 25

Luck Sub-Stats

Loot Drop: 10

Rare Drop: 10

Charisma: 25

Charisma Sub-Stats

Barter: 10

Footsteps pounded the pavement close by, causing me to shut down my interface and reach for my sword. I stopped from drawing it as a familiar figure came sprinting around the corner. Sophia's hazel eyes met mine, and she bent over, hands on her knees, trying to catch her breath.

"Figured…I'd find you…here," she said breathlessly.

I sat back on the bench. "Well, you found me. Come sit down and catch your breath."

Soph came over and sat beside me, curling her feet under her and leaning on me. She smiled as she looked up. "I can see why you like it here. It's peaceful."

"Yeah."

She laughed, ribbing me with her elbow. "Well, that's enough small talk, you want to tell me what's going on with you? You've been moody and angry lately. Now you're lashing out at us—that's not like you. You usually only get that way around—oh."

I didn't bother responding. I just sat and watched the clouds pass under the moonlight. It was probably a lovely night out, but I couldn't tell.

"When is it?" she asked.

"Tomorrow."

She sighed and scooted closer to me, wrapping her arm around my shoulders. "I'm sorry, D. I know this time of the year is hard for you, but I don't think Micah would want you to keep blaming yourself. I think he'd want you to live and enjoy life."

I opened my inventory and pulled out a flask of whiskey, taking a sip before passing it to her. She took it, took a swig, and gave it back. It went that way for a few minutes, neither of us saying anything. *You're probably right. I know he'd be disappointed in me, but I can't stop. No matter how much I might want to.*

"You know, after the Night-Fall, there wasn't much to be happy about. Every day it was nothing but survival, trying to live in a world of monsters. But then we came here. Micah would've loved this place, even with its darkness and corruption. This world was tailor-made for him, and I don't think it's fair that I get to enjoy it while Micah's bones are rotting in the real world. Because I failed to protect him."

Soph tried to respond, but she couldn't find the words, and she fell silent. There was nothing she could say that would make me feel better, and she knew it. So she did the one thing she could.

She kissed me.

She'd had too much to drink; I could tell by the taste of her lips. She rarely tried to kiss me when she was sober since she knew I always pulled away, but she loved to try when she was drunk. Usually because I was drunk right beside her, and she knew I'd let her.

I wasn't drunk enough, but I was grieving, so it equaled the same thing.

She slipped into my lap and pushed me against the bench, not caring that we were in public, only caring about our lips pressed together.

It was nice, but it always gave her the wrong idea, and she always wanted to push it. A kiss wasn't enough for her when she was like this, and I was never going to sleep with her. It wouldn't be fair to her. She loved me, and I couldn't reciprocate her feelings.

I'm sorry, Soph. I'm not worth your love. I just wish you'd realize that.

I pulled back and put my hands on her shoulders. "Soph…"

"Yeah, I know."

She got off me and took my hands, pulling me to my feet, her smile never wavering despite my rejection.

"Well, if I'm not enough to hold your attention, then how about we go and take care of some changelings?"

"The guild agreed?"

"Yeah, after you ran off, we decided it wouldn't hurt. And the money is perfect, so let's go home and get some sleep. We've got a long day tomorrow."

I shook my head and let out a breath. "Yeah, it always is."

***

At the crack of dawn, we geared up and teleported to Wyston. I'd only been there once before, passing by on another quest near the mountains, gathering rare herbs for an alchemist. I hadn't spent much time in the town itself, but it was quaint.

The air was calm and cold; the frost blowing down off the Northern Mountains brought early snowfall drifting over the sleepy town. A light dusting of white caked around the shingled and thatched rooftops. Smoke curled from the cobblestone chimneys as we walked past a dozen small wooden cottages.

It was early in the morning, but most of the townspeople were already in the caves, harvesting mana crystals by the barrel full. The mountainside boasted the richest vein of mana deposits on Nexus and provided the Mages Guild with the bulk of their supply.

Mana flowed through the veins of this town, and something had clogged an artery.

Having a nest of monsters take refuge in the caves caused a ripple to spread through the small town, throwing a wrench in the works. If people couldn't work, the next best thing was to drink.

The four of us made our way to the local tavern, a place called Crystal's Drip. It was a large stone tavern with thick black slate tiling and a heavy stone chimney. The soft vocals of a singer slipped through the crack in the darkened glass window.

We headed inside, and the place was packed despite how early it was. Nearly every table was filled with disgruntled miners, drinking away their pay and hoping for something to change. Hopeful eyes glanced our way, taking in our weapons and armor as we walked to the bar.

Lonny spoke up first. "We're adventurers sent by the guild to take care of your monster problem. The sooner we start, the sooner everyone can go back to work, so does anyone have any information that would be of use to us?"

An elderly man with wiry cords of muscle spoke up over his beer.

"Couple dozen o' the blighters swarmed the central cave and blocked us off from the crystal deposits."

Couple dozen, that's quite a few. Normal weapons won't stand up to dozens of them. We need to find the alchemy shop.

"Where is the nearest alchemy shop?" I asked.

"Down the road a ways; wooden longhouse, two chimneys, can't miss it."

I tossed the man who'd spoken a silver, and we left the tavern and headed toward the alchemist.

"Balls, it's cold," Mika said, rubbing his arms.

"You're the one wearing thin leather and a few bits of middling light armor," Sophia said, teasing him.

I'd been smart and thrown my coat over my armor. But Mika had too much plate to copy what I'd done. Light armor came in many styles, and I'd chosen reinforced leather over plate and steel. Besides, it was not like we could afford any of the fancier stuff anyway.

"What'd I'd give for some shadowsteel," I mused while we walked.

The others laughed at me. "Yeah, good luck with that. The metal itself costs thousands of gold, not to mention getting the dwarves to forge it for you. It's a pipe dream," Lonny said, thumping his shiny steel plate. "Stick with good solid plate; it's solid and cheap to repair."

Soph twirled in her brown leather armor, her brunette hair spinning as snowflakes fell around her. "I'll stick with armor that doesn't make me a lumbering target for a stray arrow."

Lonny blushed, his face reddening as we neared the alchemist. I ran in, skirted past the cauldrons and hanging herbs, and bought four vials of what we needed, paying four silver to the stocky alchemist staffing the shop. Once I came back out, we started up the mountain to the caves, still bickering back and forth as we walked up the steep incline.

Our jovial tones dropped as we came across the first of the corpses.

Blood ran red from the bodies of half a dozen men, miners who'd been torn to shreds with claws. They were nothing but scraps of flesh and clothing that looked only vaguely human-shaped.

"By the nine kings of hell, look at this massacre," I gasped, kneeling by the first body.

It was a man, but he'd been savaged, and not one part on him had been spared the wrath of the changelings.

"All right, everyone, take some quicksilver," I said, tossing a vial to everyone. "Douse your weapons and let's get in there."

I unstopped my small vial and poured it over my bastard sword. The viscous silver dripped down my blade and hardened quickly with a drying reagent. Quicksilver was especially toxic to any of the fae or anyone cursed by the fae.

It made cutting through them like butter, and I'd take any advantage I could get.

The others did the same, though Lonny grumbled as he did so.

"Dammit, I just bought this sword. It was godsdamned expensive," he said, staring at his silver and gold, ruby inlaid longsword.

"Hey, just because you can wield hero-tier weapons now doesn't mean you had to blow your entire life savings on the damn thing."

"It's nice though, right?" he hedged, waving the blade toward me.

"Yeah, it'll do for killing some changelings," Mika said, applying the quicksilver to his katana. "But it won't matter in the dark. Let's drink some cat's eye and head in."

I pulled the potion from my Inventory and downed it. Sour vinegar and distilled grain alcohol hit my tongue, and I nearly gagged.

"Ugh, tastes like cat piss, pun intended," Soph said, trying not to retch.

My vision blurred as a soft blue light edged into my vision, and suddenly, the early morning light was too much for my eyes.

"Let's go guys."

We marched in, Lonny in the front, then me; Sophia and Mika brought up the rear. The cave was small at the entrance but widened as we got deeper in. The stony, uneven rock walls were lined with torch sconces, hammered into the wall, but they were all doused and would only give away our position if we lit them. We all had cat's eye and could see well enough even though it was pitch black.

From the map one of the miners had given Lonny, there were several small openings in the cave where it widened, and we were about to come across one. I readied myself as we filed into the first sub cave. It expanded to a circle about forty feet around us and housed a ton of makeshift wooden furniture and digging tools. Clusters of mana crystals hung in pockets all around us and gave off a subtle blue-white glow.

In the center of the cavern, cloistered together, were about fifteen changelings.

Some of the ugliest and meanest creatures on Nexus, they were humanoid, with sallow, sagging gray skin and thin, bony features. They all bore the same beady black eyes and wispy tufts of hair on their heads. Each one was only about four feet tall; the males had shriveled, deformed genitalia while the females sported sagging, uneven breasts with coal-black nipples. They all had long arms and legs—and wickedly sharp claws on their fingers.

When they noticed our arrival, they shrieked in high-pitched voices and swarmed us. The cacophony of screeches echoed through the cave as we went to battle.

Lonny unstrapped his heater shield and charged the center while the three of us played backup and made sure they couldn't flank us.

Two of the bastards snuck around Lonny's shield and were poised at his back. I stepped forward and cut one down, slicing through its shoulder and across its chest. Its flesh parted and sizzled like grease in a pan as the silver of my blade burned it away. The other one was too slow to turn. It was a male, and it received a swift kick to its malformed groin, doubling it over. I took its head off while it clutched its broken jewels.

Mika faced down four of them. He brought his sword up and used *Rush Strike*. Wind gathered at his back and propelled him forward in an instant. He appeared on the other side of the changelings, his katana dripping red as the four changelings fell to pieces behind him.

Sophia danced between her targets, her shortsword a painter's brush. She dipped her brush across the throats of three changelings, splattering crimson abstraction across the rocky cave.

I kept a few more of them back while Lonny cut down the ones in front of him. In less than a handful of minutes, we'd cleared the first chamber.

"Not bad, guys," I said, wiping the blood from my blade.

"Yeah, but some of the silver bled away from my sword," Mika replied.

"It'll be fine. There aren't enough changelings to wear all of our silver thin."

We paused, catching our breath and listening. The screams of the changelings had more than likely alerted the others, and while not smart, they were crafty, cunning little fuckers, and we needed to be extra cautious going forward.

The cave branched in three directions, and as bad of an idea as it was, we had to split up. If we didn't, we risked the changelings escaping or ganging up on us.

Lonny and Sophia went straight while Mika and I took the left and right.

We had half an hour until the cat's eye wore down, and the caves were expansive, meaning we had to hurry if we didn't want to risk potion sickness by consuming more than one in a row. The cavern tapered to a tight tunnel as I wormed my way through it.

High pitched yelps and growls resounded off the stone, and I kept my guard up as I slunk over the rock.

The end of the tunnel opened to a small antechamber, roughly carved from the rock. Six changelings crawled over the ground, their gray flesh starkly outlined against the cave floor. When I exited the tunnel, each of them turned toward me and howled in rage, baring their fangs and yellowed claws.

The rancid stench of rotten meat rolled from their breath in waves as they screeched at me.

I stepped to the side as they lunged. Claws and teeth sailed past, and I cut one of them down midair. My sword sliced through it with little resistance, and the first changeling split in half amid a shower of brackish blood.

Before the others could regroup, I kicked one in the chest, sending it crashing back against the rock wall, and I speared through one of the others, a female with long, broken nails who scratched at my face even as my sword split through her heart.

One of her claws gouged a thin line across my cheek, and I growled in pain. The wound wasn't that deep, but the nails of the changelings held a mild poison that stung like the devil. While I dealt with the scratcher, another had slipped around me and clambered up my back.

Its claws found secure purchase in my leather, and it was perched over my shoulder before I could stop it. I didn't have time to stop and deal with it, as I had two more in front of me, and the one that I'd kicked had picked itself off the ground and was ambling over.

Shit. They've cornered me.

Instead of rushing the mass, I backpedaled quickly, slamming against the cavern wall. The one clinging to me squealed as a hundred and eighty pounds crushed its frail body against cold hard stone.

I'd stunned it, and I reached over my shoulder, closing around its neck, and I chunked it as hard as I could. The little bastard went flying towards its friends and barreled into one of them while the others jumped out of the way.

It gave me the opening I needed.

Activating *Flash Step*, I glided past the stunned changelings in half a second and brought my sword in an arc in front of me. I'd sliced through the head of one of them and nicked another. Its blood flowed freely from a gash in its shoulder.

Three were down, and three remained.

With *Flash Step* active, my speed increased by an order of magnitude, and I had two more steps before it wore off. I stepped once more and landed just shy of two of them. One I hadn't touched, but the other was the one I'd thrown. My blade cut down the untouched one and I bashed the other changeling in the temple with my pommel. A sickening crunch echoed around the room as I caved in its thin skull.

Only one left.

I had one more *Flash Step,* and I used it, angling my sword as I flew past the last changeling. My sword dripped red as *Flash Step* ended and the last of the beasts fell over dead.

A waste of Flash Step, *but it was sloppy to let them corner me.*

I didn't like wasting my abilities, especially one of my trump cards. A timer appeared in my interface, counting down from six hours. Six hours until I could use it again. This would all be over long before then.

I quickly looted the six corpses, wiped my blade, and continued on.

I'd worn the silver thin across my blade, but it was still good enough to do the job. It wouldn't matter much even if we hadn't used quicksilver, but it gave us an advantage, and I liked having any I could get.

The antechamber curved, but rather than another tunnel, it opened into a large chamber, even larger than the opening we'd first fought. Inside were over two dozen changelings, clustered together or in smaller groups of three or four.

I'd blundered in as loud as I could, and dozens of beady, dead eyes turned my way.

Oh fuck, I think we were misled on the number of changelings here.

The earsplitting shrieks that rose from their lips were deafening, and they all rushed me.

I could take a good number of them, but not all of them. I would be quickly overwhelmed by a horde of claws.

Cursing, I activated *Blade Shift* and *Dreamstate*. My sword twisted and writhed as if alive before fading translucent and sprouting two copies of the blade, all dancing like a mirage. Only I knew which one was real, and the changelings were mesmerized by the twisting illusion. *Dreamstate* activated a second later, and a thick fog rolled over the rock and stalagmites. Faint whispers hissed and echoed around the room as shadow figures appeared and moved erratically. The dull-minded changelings snapped out of their trance and started to attack the whirling shadows.

A dozen were distracted by my phantasms, but I still had plenty to deal with. I ran forward, cutting a bloody swath as my sword danced between the monsters. Three fell to my blade in seconds, and even if my mirage was keeping them distracted, a few got through and raked at me with their claws. Pain rippled up my spine, and blood dripped down my legs. I lashed out with a kick, catching the creature who had my blood dripping down its claws in the sternum, caving in its chest.

I glanced at my battle fatigue and cursed. It had risen faster than I expected and was over half-filled. If it maxed out, I was dead; I wouldn't be able to stop the monsters from ripping me to shreds.

For each one I killed, there was always another, and my silver ran out after I killed the fifth changeling.

I was contemplating tossing a smoke bomb and retreating when a jarring thud bounded through the cave. A bright yellow glow filled the cavern as Lonny arrived, barreling into the mob with his *Shield Bash*.

He sent seven of them crashing back as he charged into them with his heater shield. As they hit the ground, Soph darted out from behind Lonny and slid her sword home in their chests.

Both of them had cocky grins plastered to their faces along with more than a little monster blood.

"Cavalry's here," Lonny gloated, slicing a leaping changeling in half.

"Took you fucking long enough," I shouted and regrouped with them.

Soph and I backed around Lonny's shield while he fended off the remaining mob. We'd thinned the herd, but we still had over a dozen of them to contend with.

"I've blown through most of my abilities. I've got *Swordfeint* and *Phantom* left."

Lonny laughed, gesturing to the haze that still clung around us. "Yeah, *Dreamstate* saved your ass, that's for damn sure."

"Less talking, more slaying, guys, and where the hell is Mika?"

We didn't have time to ponder as *Dreamstate* stuttered and began to fade. It wouldn't be long before the remaining changelings stopped jumping at shadows and attacked us.

"All right, stand back. I'm going to end this, be ready to play cleanup," Lonny shouted and surged ahead, heedless of our shots of complaint.

As *Dreamstate* vanished, Lonny reached the center, and a rippling force expanded out of him, nearly invisible to our eyes. It lifted the rest of the changelings into the air and sent them flying with the strength of a hurricane.

Lonny's *Scatter Pulse* killed half of them outright and severely wounded the rest. Blood rained from a dozen ruptured organs as the broken changelings landed against the stone. Soph and I rushed in, our blades slicing a bloody swath through the fractured and broken monsters. When it was done, a river of blood ran over the rock, pooling into my boots.

We'd made a right mess of things.

After the last changeling croaked it's dying breath, we looted the corpses and went to find Mika.

We headed through the left tunnel, where Mika should be. We found him a few hundred feet later—he was mid-slice through a particularly monstrous changeling three times the size of normal. His sword glowed a faint blue; sparks of electricity arced and popped off his blade. The metallic tinge of ozone mixed with the foul stench of burnt flesh.

The changeling had knurled, rotting protrusions sprouting in the shape of a crude crown around its head.

Fuck me! A changeling alpha.

It was big, even more grotesque and gangly than its lesser kin and exceedingly dangerous—no wonder it had given him pause.

Mika withdrew his blade and whipped it toward the thing's head, bisecting it neatly just above the nose. Saggy gray brains toppled out as a spray of blood drained from the bottom half of its skull.

Mika stepped back, sheathed his sword, and sagged to the ground. "Fucker was strong. Way above my level. Took godsdamned *Volcanic Thrust* and *Galvanic Slash* to take him."

The presence of an alpha explained the increased number of changelings. Monsters tended to gravitate toward their species alpha when one presented themselves.

"Damn, when's the last time we've even heard of an alpha?" I asked.

"Basilisk alpha, couple years ago in the Badlands. Took four members of the Cardinals to take it down," Lonny said, coming to rest beside me.

"Right, the Cardinals, bunch of sanctimonious pricks. Them and the church."

"They're not that bad. I've even met their leader. Cristina was really cool when we spoke," Lonny said, pride in his voice.

Yeah, rubbing shoulders with one of the strongest players on Nexus, no big deal.

I didn't like the Cardinals, not just because they were the strongest guild, but they were also basically the secret police. The Alliance gave them full autonomy to act how they pleased and damn the consequences.

"Well, regardless, we've got only a few minutes left until our cat's eye wears off, so what say we all get the hell out of the miserable mine?"

The others were only too happy to agree and we were back outside just as our potions wore down. Our armor was torn and bloody, but our spirits were high as we climbed back down the mountainside. Taking down that many changelings and an alpha was praiseworthy indeed. I was beyond exhausted, but not nearly tired enough to forget what today was. I'd kept my despair at bay in the cave, but now that the adrenaline and high of combat wore down, I couldn't stop my thoughts from going there.

I sighed. *Happy birthday, Micah.*

We made it back to the tavern and shared the good news with everyone. A cheer rang through the tavern along with a dozen offers to buy us all a drink. We accepted, though I took my drink outside; I wasn't fit to be good company right now.

As I sat back on a worn oak chair, looking out onto the snowy streets of Wyston, a figure came and sat beside me.

It was a girl, mid-twenties or so, with a cute face and big, blue eyes. Her dark hair twisted in the wind, and she threw her hood over her head in an attempt to combat it.

One glance at her robes, and I knew everything I needed to about her.

"What does the Mages Guild want with me?"

She smiled an innocent smile too perfect to not have been rehearsed. "Well, not just you—your guild. But your guildmates are otherwise indisposed," she said, nodding to the window.

Lonny, Mika, and Sophia were dancing to the music while the tavern cheered them on. It was endearing to see them having so much fun, and a pang of jealousy ran through me that I couldn't let myself have fun like that.

"Well, Ascalon is the guild leader, so I can't make any decisions on behalf of the guild, but I'll at least hear you out."

The mage girl nodded and pulled out a mana crystal. "My team and I were sent up here to collect our shipment of crystals but were obviously delayed when those monsters showed up two weeks ago. We were supposed to be in and out in an hour, but we've been stuck here, and because of the value of our cargo, I fear one of the bandit kings has had time to learn of the shipment."

"You need caravan guards to help ensure the transport makes it back to the North Kingdom."

"Precisely."

I scratched my beard, resisting the urge to pluck the hairs out in annoyance. *Guard work. Slow, boring, but if the Mages Guild is footing the bill, then the pay will have to be pretty good.*

"What's your offer?"

"Twenty-five gold, payable on safe delivery."

I whistled. That was a decent chunk of change. Not the most we'd ever been paid for a gig, but it would pay our bills and any expenses we might need for the next year. We'd have to discuss it as a guild, but we were going that way regardless, and a week's worth of work for that much gold was worth the effort.

"I'll talk to them about it, but I can't make any guarantees."

"That's fine. My name is Holly, and we leave at first light in the morning. We won't wait for you, so be punctual if you plan on accompanying us," she said and stood, before heading back inside.

If this job after job streak keeps up, I'll be happy, but I think the others are probably going to strangle me when I tell them.

The quest popped up in my interface.

Quest: Escort Mission

Type: Random

Difficulty: Unknown

Reward: 1850 Exp!

Below, it listed the monetary reward for the job. It was a good haul for what it actually entailed. *Soph's not going to be happy. She's gotten squeamish lately, but Lonny won't be able to pass up the coin. It's too good, especially since he's basically broke after dropping all his money on that blade of his. We could use the cash.*

"Well, let's go get this over with."

***

The wagon hit a particularly nasty patch of rough road and nearly sent the four of us sprawling to the mud.

"Godsdammit, I hate this job," Mika grumbled, brushing his hair out of his face.

"Don't be so glum," Soph said, clapping him on the shoulder. "Three days of bumpy roads down the mountain is a worthwhile hassle. Besides, we've got one more day, and we're done."

I wasn't as confident. The others were riding high, thinking we'd already passed the most likely spots for an ambush. We'd descended the snowy mountain and were back to the rain-soaked roads that led to the North Kingdom. Lonny and the others thought that the bandits wouldn't dare try to attack us so close to the Compass Kingdom, but I was of a different mind.

We were still over a day's ride from the North Kingdom and any Alliance patrol route. There was still plenty of time for a good ambush or two.

"You still got a bad feeling, D?" Lonny asked, nudging me.

"Yeah. It's foolish to let our guards down. If I were planning to hit the caravan, I'd hit us late tonight or early tomorrow morning, just before shift change."

I grabbed a skin of whiskey from my inventory and took a long pull, just as the wagon hit another bump, spilling amber down my shirt.

"Ah, hell."

The others laughed as I wiped it off, and I held off drinking more because I still couldn't shake the feeling that we were being watched.

It came and went and was quick enough that I couldn't be sure it wasn't just my paranoia playing tricks on me. I kept my eyes peeled, but there was nothing for me to see. I told the others of my suspicions, but they didn't notice anything.

By the time we made camp on the third night, my guild was sick of my complaining. But they also knew I was just trying to keep our heads attached. Even though we were all tired, I volunteered to stay up and keep watch with two of the mages. There were eight of us--four of Adventurers Guild and four of the Mages Guild. I'd barely spoken to any of them besides Holly; they kept to themselves, which was fine by me. I went outside and sat by the crackling fire, giving a nod to the mages on watch.

"Care to share a drink?" Holly asked, sidling up beside me on the log.

I turned my gaze to see Holly, her hood down, with slightly flushed cheeks, wagging a decanter filled with dark amber lit up like a rainbow.

"The hell is that?"

"Mana-infused whiskey. It's the best you'll ever have, I promise."

An offer like that was too tempting to pass up. The Mages Guild was more cult than organization, and they kept tight lips on even the most mundane of things, like enchanted spirits. *It might be my only chance to try it. And I could do with worse company.*

Holly was cute and friendly enough. She was the only one willing to actually have a conversation with us at any rate.

"Sure," I said, smiling. "I'm game."

We passed the bottle back and forth for a while, making idle conversation while the level fell on the decanter. It was delicious. Far more than I had any right to expect and I eagerly awaited my next swig.

The booze hit me strong and didn't let up. After half an hour, my head was spinning something fierce, and I had trouble keeping my head upright. I'd gone way past my limit and I couldn't stand, I toppled over every time I tried.

Holly laughed and smiled at me as she leaned over me.

"Sweet dreams," she said, still smiling down at me.

My head couldn't take anymore, and I slumped to the dirt before passing out.

I awoke to a world on fire.

Screams echoed all around, and half a dozen fires encircled our campsite. Even with the massive hangover, I knew at once what was going on. We were under attack, and it wasn't going well.

I picked my sorry ass up off the ground and drew my sword, glancing around at the chaos for an enemy to fight.

The mages were casting spells as quickly as they could, but they weren't trained for battle magic, and their long Script incantations were woefully inadequate. A younger mage with short blonde hair had his fingers splayed while he built his spell. A bright orange pentagram with swirling letters flashed and then sputtered out as an arrow took the kid in the throat, spraying arterial blood in an arc as he fell back and died.

From the crude shaft of the arrow, I knew our attackers were bandits, but I didn't know how many or where the rest of my guild was. The dead mage kid was the only one around me, so I took off around the wagon to search for my friends.

On the other side of the caravan was where the real battle was taking place.

Two dozen rough-looking men and women surrounded the other mages and the Swords. Lonny stood in the center with his shield and sword, giving the center of the mob hell, but he couldn't cover everyone.

Holly stood behind him, hair lanky with sweat as she held her hands aloft and built a spell. She was much faster than the other kid and snapped off a barrier spell in under ten seconds. A hail of arrows stopped cold as they struck the translucent bubble, and I heaved a sigh of relief.

Holly has some skill. Building a spell that quick should have cut some corners, but that barrier is holding well.

I ran over to join them but didn't get there in time, and Sophia screamed.

A few of the bandits broke through the barrier and swarmed the side where Sophia was, the weak point of the formation. They stepped through the barrier like it wasn't even there, and I realized that Holly had absolutely cut a few corners. The barrier couldn't stop slow-moving objects, which let the bandits waltz right in.

A tall, shaggy-haired male with deeply tanned skin grabbed Sophia and pulled her toward him with a lustful glint in his eye. Soph turned on reflex and brought her short sword up to his neck, lightning-fast. The brute should have had his disgusting head shorn from his body, but Soph's blade stopped an inch from his neck.

Soph went pale and hesitated. The brute slugged her across the nose and took her sword from her.

Shit!

Lonny and Mika were busy holding the brunt of the force back and couldn't rescue her even if they wanted to. It was up to me.

Fuck the consequences, they're not laying one more finger on her!

I activated *Flash Step* and was on the brute in a second. I grabbed Soph and flung her back before I rammed the tip of my sword through Brute's chest. His shoddy leather armor parted like cloth as I split his heart in two. He clutched at my sword lodged in his chest, cutting deep slices into his hands as he desperately tried to remove it.

I pulled it free and kicked his spurting body to the earth.

Killing the brute had been satisfying, but I was now in the heart of the bandits, and six of them converged on me. I had known I was going to be cut off when I rescued Soph, and now I had to face the consequences.

Three of them slashed at me in unison, two men and a woman, all with rusted swords and axes. I angled my sword, and *Flash Stepped* behind them. My blade met resistance as I cut through the woman's neck. She was the center target, and as I came out of my second *Flash,* I brought my sword down on my third target, biting deep into his right shoulder. I brought the strike toward his collarbone and hewed through it.

Blood and marrow ran in rivers from his torn sinew and bone, but he wasn't dead. I took his sword arm out of the equation and it allowed me to focus on the remaining bandits in front of me. I had four to deal with, and only one *Flash Step* left.

I sidestepped a thrust from the bandit closest to me and whipped my sword across his neck when he left himself open.

Pain sliced deep into my arm as one of the three remaining bandits cut me. A long flap of skin peeled away from my bicep as blood slithered down my arm.

"Fuck me!" I seethed.

The pain was distracting, and the slick blood made holding onto my sword a nightmare.

Well, let's see how you handle your own nightmares.

I activated *Dreamstate,* and as the ethereal fog rolled through, the trio started jumping at the shadows that weren't really there. Holly screamed when *Dreamstate* reached her, but I couldn't stop and explain that it wasn't real. *Dreamstate* only worked on NPCs. If I told her it wasn't real, the bandits would see through it too.

I cut down the trio, who were too busy attacking things that didn't exist to worry about me. My sword spilled their blood freely, and then I went to join my guild. The others were just as capable at handling bandits and had carved through the rest like straw dummies. Less than a handful remained by the time I'd killed my group. Soph had regrouped behind Lonny, and he'd taken their leader hostage. The remaining bandits laid down their weapons and got down on their knees.

The fight was over.

Holly dropped the barrier and we all checked ourselves over. Besides the flayed chunk of skin missing from my arm, I was fine. Soph had a broken nose, but a scream of pain later and I'd set it back in place.

Lonny had a few nicks, but both he and Mika were otherwise unharmed. The mages took the most losses. Two of the four were dead.

"Dammit, this wasn't supposed to happen," Holly cursed under her breath while moving her dead comrades.

Yeah, tell me about it. This was a clusterfuck of epic proportions.

I gathered up the weapons and loot from the dead bandits. Nothing amazing, but it would earn at least a decent bit of coin. Lonny and Mika played wardens to the five remaining bandits. We had two choices, either we could bind them and haul them back to the Alliance, or we could kill them here and now. Their fate would be the same regardless, and it would be less work for us to just kill them now.

"What do you guys want to do?" I asked, walking over to them.

"I say we kill them; save us the trouble," Mika said.

"Seconded."

Lonny was quiet for a moment, but our conversation didn't go unnoticed by the bandits, and they all started speaking up when we mentioned killing them. They hurled a torrent of bribes and death threats our way, but the leader stayed quiet. He just looked at us with a curious expression played across his face.

"Got something you want to say?" I asked.

"Hey, we're just hired thugs. Killing us gains you little, but what if I give you our employer? That's got to be worth our freedom, right?"

Lonny and Mika shot the leader a confused look.

"Who the hell hired you?!" they both shouted.

The bandit leader just smiled, knowing he'd hooked them, but I relished the look of surprise that dawned on his face when I walked over and slit his throat.

Blood drenched the front of his armor as he toppled over and gasped as his lifeblood ran dry. The others looked at me like I'd sprouted horns, both clearly asking if I'd lost my mind. They shouted wordlessly at me, which drew the outcry of the others.

Holly and the other mage, as well as Soph, rushed over when Lonny and Mika started sputtering nonsense.

"Explain yourself, D," Lonny said, his eyes pinched close together.

"The leader was trying to barter for useless information. It wasn't worth letting him live."

"I'd say knowing who tried to kill us is incredibly important info!"

"Not when I already know who it was," I said, smiling grimly. "Isn't that right, Holly?"

Holly paled and immediately threw her hands up in defense. The light of the fire behind her cast a sinister glow around her. "I don't know what you're talking about," she said, her voice breaking.

"Sure you do. You hired the bandits to rob and murder us, probably were going to let them have half the cargo, while you took the other half. High-quality mana crystals sell for a fortune, after all."

"Why the hell would I hire you if I was going to rob my own caravan?"

It was a fair question, but one I had already guessed at. I drew my sword and ambled towards Holly. "You needed bodies on the ground to sell the ambush. Hard to survive an attack with just a couple mages. We were convenient, yet I surprised you when I stayed up on watch instead of going to sleep like the rest of my friends—that's why you got me drunk."

Holly had a poor poker face, and she'd just confirmed that I was right on the money. She growled at me and ran back towards the caravan. "I won't let all this work be undone by you four!"

"Too late for that. You're either coming peacefully or in pieces. Your choice."

Holly splayed her fingers and started rattling off a spell in Script. Her hands glowed blue as the Script circle appeared in her palm. As the spell finished, another dome flared to life around her, and I slammed face-first into it when I ran at her.

I fell back with a groan and angrily picked myself off the ground.

Ow! Godsdammit, that hurt.

The spell was a stronger version of the one she'd used when we fought the bandits, and she'd erected it just as fast, so that was just another nail in her coffin. She made her first barrier weak on purpose.

"Can't cut through that with that shit sword, Durandal. Best just give up and go home," Holly shouted, prying open one of the chests of crystals. "I can keep this up indefinitely with these crystals, so just try me, assholes!"

"Dammit." *She's right, my sword isn't high enough tier to cut through her magic. I'd need a hero-tier—*

"Lonny, hold up your sword!" I shouted, turning to him.

He acquiesced and drew his bright and shiny new sword, holding it aloft to me. I dropped my sword and activated *Phantom*. An exact replica of Lonny's sword appeared in my hands; it glowed an ethereal translucent purple, but it held the same exact properties of the real thing.

I swung towards the barrier with all my might and after a few well-placed strikes, the translucent glass cracked under my onslaught and shattered.

Holly scrambled for a handful of crystals, but I pinned my ghost blade through her shoulder and slugged her across the face. She dropped unconscious, and I picked her up and hauled her off the wagon.

I brought her to the others and unceremoniously dropped her to the dirt next to the other bandits.

The four of us surrounded them, and the others began talking about what to do with them. Sophia wanted to take them back alive and have them arrested, and like usual, Lonny agreed with whatever Soph suggested. Mika was on my wavelength. They would all be executed regardless, so why not just get it over with?

"Why don't we just kill them and take the crystals for ourselves?" I asked.

The others wore concerned expressions plastered on their faces.

"What? They're worth a fortune."

Lonny shook his head. "We're not thieves, D."

"Hey, it's not stealing. It's spoils of war."

But Lonny and the others weren't having it. They vetoed that idea quick, which left us with a couple hundred thousand mana crystals to return and five prisoners to deal with. We may have decided to not keep the crystals, but we still had to deal with the people.

"I still say kill them," I said.

"Agreed."

"We don't have to kill them," Soph said, running over to me. "We can turn them over to the Compass Kingdom, let the Alliance sort them out."

"It equals the same thing, Soph, we both know it. We don't have enough members to guard the prisoners and protect the wagons. No, easier to just kill them," I said and drew my sword.

Soph protested loudly at my back, but no one stopped me. Holly was the only one who could use magic and even tied up, I didn't want to leave her alive to cause trouble. Her neck was on the chopping block first.

She was still unconscious and didn't even feel it when I stood her on her knees and hacked off her head.

Holly died a painless death, which was the best she could have hoped for.

The other bandits were less fortunate, and they screamed bloody murder as they died. In a handful of minutes, the thugs were dead, and it was one less thing I had to worry about.

I cleaned my blade of the blood and walked back to the group gathered around the fire. The last remaining mage hadn't been a part of Holly's plan, and so we left him alone. He'd had a rough day and turned in to get some sleep.

We decided to camp out until morning and then haul the chests back to the Mages Guild. But that left us with a lot of time to kill. Soph turned in too, despite my protests for her to stay up.

"Sorry, D. I'm just not feeling too good right now," she said with a parting wave before climbing onboard one of the wagons.

"You guys noticed anything off about Soph lately?" I asked softly.

Mika shrugged and pulled out a bottle of mana-infused whiskey. "Not a clue," he said and took a swig.

"Maybe it's all the jobs we've been taking," Lonny said with a shrug.

"No, I don't think so. I'm talking about things like tonight. She hesitated when she had a bandit dead to rights, should've taken the fuckers head off, but she stopped cold."

"I dunno, man. Might just be standard fatigue setting in, we've all been pushing ourselves lately. How about we take a couple weeks off after this? We've earned a vacation."

I sighed and ran my hands through my hair. "Yeah, you're probably right."

We had been running a lot lately, and it was entirely my fault. I wanted to run from my failures and keep myself busy, but Micah's birthday had passed, and it was time to let the others rest. I would never forget my little brother, but his death would fade for a time like it always did, and I could pretend to be happy for a while.

It wasn't healthy, but it was what I had to work with.

"Hey, Mika, pass the bottle."

###

The End

Author's Note

Thank you for reading my book!

Thank you to everyone who is reading this. It's been a journey two years in the making, but we finally got to the end. To be honest with everyone, I had the ending planned out before I ever wrote a word of Hive Knight. I wrote a post-apocalyptic story(which is a prequel to the entire Trinity of the Hive books) that may or may not ever see the light of day. I wanted to write a story where the hero ultimately failed, where everything was riding on his shoulders, and he chose to let it fall. Many stories have heroes making noble sacrifices to save the world, but reality is often much more complicated than simple right and wrong. Sam choosing to save Eris over the world was a very human choice, in my opinion, and one that I myself would struggle with choosing was I in his shoes.

And though he got his happy ending, this may not be the last you see of Sam, Eris, and Raven. They still have one last part to play before all is said and done.

Until then, thank you for sticking with my story to the bitter end.

—Grayson Sinclair

About the Author

Grayson Sinclair loves books, has loved them since he was a child. Reading has always been a passion of his, even when he really should have been focused on other things, like school. The worlds in books were always more magical and exciting than anything real life could offer, and he hopes a few of you will get lost in his worlds for a short time.

His website is Graysinclair.com, or you can find him on:

- Facebook (https://www.facebook.com/GraySinAuthor)
- Twitter (https://twitter.com/EpsilonUndying)
- Reddit (https://www.reddit.com/user/EpsilonUndying/).

While you wait for the next book in the Trinity of the Hive series, why don't you check out the short story by Grayson set in the same universe? **Swords of Legend: In Remembrance.**

https://bookhip.com/NAWGLX

ABOUT THE PUBLISHER

Starlit Publishing is wholly owned and operated by Tao Wong. It is a science fiction and fantasy publisher focused on the LitRPG & cultivation genres. Their focus is on promoting new, upcoming authors in the genre whose writing challenges the existing stereotypes while giving a rip-roaring good read.

For more information on Starlit Publishing, visit their website:
https://www.starlitpublishing.com/

You can also join Starlit Publishing's mailing list to learn of new, exciting authors and book releases, including **Grayson Sinclair's next book!**
https://starlitpublishing.com/newsletter-signup/

For more great information about LitRPG series, check out the Facebook groups:
- GameLit Society
https://www.facebook.com/groups/LitRPGsociety/
- LitRPG Books
https://www.facebook.com/groups/LitRPG.books/

THE LITRPG GUILDMASTERS

Who we are: The LitRPG Guildmasters is a group of dedicated LitRPG and Gamelit authors trying to spread the word of our favorite genres. By working together and introducing new people to amazing books we hope to expand the genres that we love. Sign up to our Newsletter to get a **free book:**

https://www.subscribepage.com/lagnewsletter). Follow us on Facebook to keep up to date on our latest work (https://www.facebook.com/LitRPGGuildmasters/).

If you love LitRPG check out:

- The LitRPG Guild Website: https://www.litrpgguild.com/
- Our Discord server: https://discord.com/invite/9BWStZf
- The LitRPG Adventurers Guild Facebook Group: https://www.facebook.com/groups/LitRPGAdventurers

LitRPG Guildmasters Titles:

Altered Realms: Ascension by B.F. Rockriver
Brightblade by Jez Cajiao
Ethria: The Pioneer by Aaron Holloway
Grim Beginnings: The Ashen Plane by Maxwell Farmer
Primeverse by R.K. Billiau
Shattered Sword by TJ Reynolds
Tower of Gates: Hack by Paul Bellow
Cipher's Quest by Tim Kaiver
Watcher's Test by Sean Oswald
Star Divers by Stephen Landry
Fragment of Divinity by Jamey Sultan
Hive Knight by Grayson Sinclair
Condition Evolution by Kevin Sinclair

To learn more about LitRPG, talk to authors including myself, and just have an awesome time, please join the LitRPG Group!
https://www.facebook.com/groups/LitRPGGroup/